SCIENCE FICTION BY WILLIAM F. NOLAN

Ray Bradbury Review (1952)
Impact 20 (1963)
The Pseudo-People (1965)
Man Against Tomorrow (1965)
Logan's Run (1967)
3 to the Highest Power (1968)
A Wilderness of Stars (1969)
A Sea of Space (1970)
The Future is Now (1970)
Space for Hire (1971)
The Human Equation (1971)
Alien Horizons (1974)
Wonderworlds (1977)
Logan's World (1977)
Logan's Search (1980)
Science Fiction Origins (1980)
Look Out for Space (1985)
Logan: A Trilogy (1986)
The Bradbury Chronicles (1991)
3 for Space (1992)
Logan's Return (2000)
Far Out (2004)

WiLD GALAXY

SELECTED SCIENCE FICTION STORIES

WILLIAM F. NOLAN

Introduction by the Author

GOLDEN GRYPHON PRESS • 2005

LIBRARY OF CONGRESS CATALOGING–IN–PUBLICATION DATA
Nolan, William F., 1928–
    Wild galaxy : selected science fiction stories / by William F. Nolan, introduction by the author. — 1st ed.
        p.   cm.
    ISBN 1-930846-31-2 (hardcover : alk. paper)
        1. Science fiction, American.   I. Title.
PS3564.O39   A6   2005
813'.54—dc22   2004015223

First Edition.

✝ ✝ ✝

Contents

To all those who dream of
Deep Space, and to the
memory of the SF masters
who insired the stories
in this book.

+ + +

On the Run with Logan

BECAUSE OF *LOGAN'S RUN*, I'M BEST KNOWN AS
a science fiction writer. This is ironic since SF is only one of
a dozen genres in which I've worked as a professional writer. When
people ask me what I write I say, "Everything." Whatever turns me
on at any given moment—that's what I write.

Science fiction has been turning me on since the early 1950s,
when I read every issue of *Galaxy* and *The Magazine of Fantasy
and Science Fiction* from cover to cover. I was co-chairman of the
1952 Westercon in San Diego and—after moving to Los Angeles
the following year—regularly attended meetings of the Los Angeles
Science-Fantasy Society.

My first professionally submitted work was a science fiction
story, "An Alien Shore," written in 1952, and my first fiction sale
was also in the genre: "The Joy of Living" (*If: Worlds of SF*, August
1954). I think the latter story (which was dramatized on TV's
Norman Corwin Presents) still retains its emotional power.

Twenty-two of my SF titles are listed on the credits page. Some
are novels, some collections, and several are edited anthologies.
I've also written SF for films, radio, television, and comic books. I
was science fiction book reviewer for the *Los Angeles Times* for six
years, and was managing editor of *Gamma* in the 1960s (a magazine modeled directly on *The Magazine of Fantasy and Science*

Fiction). In 1975 I was awarded an honorary doctorate in science fiction from American River College in California.

I was a founding member of "The Group" (also dubbed "The California School") in the 1950s, alongside Charles Beaumont, Ray Bradbury, Richard Matheson, Robert Bloch, and Chad Oliver—and I have edited or compiled books on Beaumont, Bradbury, Matheson, and Oliver. My work has been included in some three hundred anthologies and textbooks, more than fifty of which are SF volumes. Beyond "The Joy of Living" in *If*, I've had SF stories printed in *Playboy, The Magazine of Fantasy and Science · Fiction, Fantastic Universe, Infinity SF, Amazing Stories, Gallery*, and *Sci-Fi Channel Magazine*.

But it was not until 1976, when MGM released their film version of *Logan's Run* (Dial Press, 1967), that I became a science fiction celebrity. The film was one of the major hits of that summer. I followed up the original novel with three sequels (*Logan's World, Logan's Search*, and the novelette *Logan's Return*), and co-wrote the pilot script for the CBS television series. Over the last twenty-five years I've had the satisfaction of seeing *Logan's Run* become a pop-culture classic, with fan clubs and Internet sites around the globe. Now, as these words are written, Warner Bros. is in pre-production on a megabuck remake of the original novel, so I may end up running with Mr. Logan well into the twenty-first century.

My short fiction output in SF has been relatively modest: a total of three dozen tales, the best of which I have selected for *Wild Galaxy*. They represent my two basic approaches to SF: serious and far out (reflecting what Ted Sturgeon called "the zany side" of my personality). My SF novels represent this same split: the Logans are serious, while my "Sam Space" books are totally off the wall. (Sam's a private eye on Mars, working with robot dragons and three-headed clients.)

All of which leads to a warning for the readers of *Wild Galaxy*. Usually, when I pick up a collection of stories, I'm inclined to dip into the book at odd places, reading whatever title takes my fancy. Most people follow this same pattern. With *Wild Galaxy*, however, I urge you to read these stories in the order in which I've arranged them. Why? To avoid an overdose of "zanies" (there are at least six in this collection). I've carefully intermixed the serious and the absurd to achieve a proper balance—so begin with "Freak" and end with "Lone Star Traveler." You won't be sorry.

With previous collections, it's been my habit to preface each story with a headnote outlining its background and subject matter, but this tends to break the flow. As if, in a film, I were to step in front of the camera to explain each scene. Therefore, with *Wild Galaxy*, I'm going to present my comments right here, in the Introduction.

"Freak" was written in the deliberate tradition and style of *Logan's Run*. When this story was originally printed in *The Touch*, I donated my fee (as did the other authors in this anthology) to help finance health education and cancer research. I was happy to write this one "for free."

"How Do I Know *You're* Real?," my most recent SF tale, was written in 2001 for magazine publication. It appears here for the first time in book format. I believe in hooking a reader, if possible, with a story's opening line. You'll see what I mean.

"Starblood" has a complex root system. Three of its short sections ("Tris," "Morgan," and "Bax") were initially written as beginning chapters for a trio of aborted SF novels. I decided they would fit more comfortably within a single narrative. I added three new sections, provided an aliens-to-Earth frame, and—Presto!—I had my story. It was selected for a "Year's Best" SF anthology back in 1973, but the publisher goofed and left it out of the printed book. A regrettable mistake, since I think the honor was deserved.

"The Joy of Living," as I have stated earlier, was my first professional fiction sale (in February of 1954). It deals with a favorite SF theme of mine: androids. (I call them "mechanicals" in this story.) I later edited a book about these near-human machines (*The Pseudo-People*), and I've featured android robots in several other SF tales. The idea of a machine-as-human creature continues to fascinate me, and I'm not yet done with android fiction.

"The Grackel Question" was written for *Gallery* in 1978, and is totally off the wall. Here's my "zany side" in full flower.

"The Small World of Lewis Stillman" (also known as "The Underdweller") is my most popular short story, never having been out of print since its magazine debut five decades ago. It has seen twenty-four separate printings, has been selected for eleven anthologies and textbooks, adapted for radio, television, and comic books, pirated in *Vampirella*, and presented (twice) in an educational school publication. The storm drains in this story exist beneath Greater Los Angeles exactly as I have described them, but I've never had to live in one.

"Jenny Among the Zeebs" is a wild mix of futuristic music, rock slang, and classic French farce. It was inspired by a trio of super-hip young ladies called "The Plaster Casters" who sought out famous rock stars in order to mold plaster replicas of their sexual organs. In my story, I converted them into "The Bottom Builders."

"Happily Ever After" first appeared in *Gamma* in the 1960s. As editor, I sold it to myself. This one's a variation on the Garden of Eden theme. With some mutation thrown into the mix.

"Toe to Tip, Tip to Toe, Pip-Pop as You Go" (my favorite title!) is another of my "totally nutso" tales. Wacky. Zany. But, I would hope, good SF fun.

"Stuntman" is my serious take on the parallel universe theory. Short, somber, and savage.

"Kelly, Fredric Michael" is heavily autobiographical. Almost everything in this story is taken from my life and experiences, right down to the death of my father. I said "almost" because I've never ridden a rocket, or been tortured by an alien force.

"Papa's Planet" was originally printed in *Playboy*. It's a direct result of my earlier interest in Ernest Hemingway. For years I collected Hemingway stuff: 260 books, 80 full-issue magazines, 800 sets of tearsheets, plus audio and script material. Sold it all to a Los Angeles book dealer in 1988. But this odd little tale remains.

"And Miles to Go Before I Sleep" has been selected for textbooks in the U.S. and abroad, and has seen radio and comic book adaptations. It owes much to Bradbury's lyrical, small-town stories and was written in the period when I was deeply influenced by Ray's work. Androids and Bradbury: two prime passions in my life.

"Violation" echoes my fast-car days when I drove an Austin-Healey Le Mans 100-M sports racer. (Won a trophy with it in 1957 at the Hour-Glass circuit near San Diego.) I was seriously involved with the international motor racing scene (Grand Prix and sports car competition) from 1955 into 1970. Wrote eight books in this genre and more than one hundred magazine pieces. Knew all the top drivers. As a paid journalist (representing *Road & Track, Car and Driver*, etc.) I attended races from Pebble Beach and Sebring to Monte Carlo and Nassau, in the Bahamas. I drove much too fast in those days, amassing a drawer full of speeding tickets. Despite the fact that the tickets were all well-deserved, I developed a frustration with traffic cops. "Violation" is the product of that frustration.

"The Fasterfaster Affair" is my SF tribute to Ian Fleming's legendary 007. I was a Fleming fanatic and, at one time, owned a full set of his James Bond first editions. Spent a memorable afternoon with Fleming in Chicago when he was there to research his

Thrilling Cities. "The Fasterfaster Affair" is a Bond parody to end all Bond parodies, in which I satirize hyperspace, hypnosis, mutated life forms, teleportation, bug-eyed monsters, matter disintegration, telepathy, time travel, parallel universes, space opera, sex, yogurt health farms, the British Secret Service, and—of course—androids. Fleming's Bond books are all fast-paced, but this one is faster-faster.

"To Serve the Ship" attempts to understand the psychology of Deep Space service in a future era when rocket pilots voyage out to the stars. It deals with what happens when these special individuals return home to Earth. Could they adjust? And, if not, what would become of them?

"The Day the Gorf Took Over" began as an original screenplay. When it failed to reach production, I turned it into a "zany." (For your information, "gorf" is frog spelled backwards.)

In "The Mating Of Thirdburt" I have more wicked fun with the science of robotics. Enough said. The story speaks for itself. Or perhaps I should say, *shouts* for itself.

"Lone Star Traveler," the novella that ends *Wild Galaxy*, is an example of my penchant for mixing genres—in this case, Westerns and SF. Max Brand in Heinlein country. I think the climax will surprise you. In writing this one, I became quite fond of Texas John Thursday.

So here they are—the best of my SF tales gathered between one set of covers for the first time. Long and short. Serious and zany. Dark and light.

Each one turned me on.

I hope they'll do the same for you.

William F. Nolan
West Hills, California
2004

Wild Galaxy

✝ ✝ ✝

Freak

HE WAS BROUGHT INTO THE BUILDING BY an Enforcer who waited in the long, sterile corridor while Kal Adams faced the Compdoctor.

He knew he'd end up here. It was inevitable, given his shattered emotional state. His rage had been steadily increasing and he was very near Breakpoint. And why not? It was a near-miracle that he'd endured this long.

He'd been forced to wear a Skinsuit since he was one. Which was unheard of, since the Depriver Syndrome seldom manifests itself before puberty, and *never* during infanthood. Except in his case.

Except for Kal Adams.

During his first birthday party Kal's mother had kissed her baby son in happy celebration, and was instantly struck blind. Not for hours or days, but permanently. For the next three years, until she died with his father in a gyro crash, she had remained utterly sightless.

"I was too young to remember it," Kal said, sitting on a steel chair directly in front of the Compdoctor. "I only know how I was treated. They put me in a Suit and I've never experienced a human touch since that day."

"I can understand," said the doctor. "I know just how difficult it has been for you."

"No, you don't," said Kal flatly. "You're a machine . . . lights and circuits and relays. You can't appreciate what it means to be afflicted as I am."

"You are quite wrong, Mr. Adams," said the doctor. "I have been *programmed* to understand."

"It's not the same," said Kal, staring dully at the audiowall. Its banked lights glimmered and flashed in pulsing rhythms.

"You are obviously a very disturbed young man," said the wall.

"I'm twenty now," said Kal. "For the past nineteen years I've been isolated, denied genuine human contact. I've never held a woman's hand . . . felt the warmth of her skin . . . caressed her face. I feel as if I'm buried in a pit of darkness."

"Unfortunate," said the wall.

"Why *me?*" asked Kal. "Why did this awful thing happen to me?"

"Every Depriver asks, 'why me?' It is a universal question."

Adams shook his head. "I'm not like other Deprivers. They've all had normal childhoods, years of human contact before their affliction set in. But I've been inside this Suit all my life, wrapped in my protective cocoon." Kal lifted his right arm, shiny and layered; lights gleamed from the Suit's armored surface.

"And you are bitter regarding your condition," stated the wall.

"Damn right I am! It's all I think about anymore, the cruel injustice of it . . . the *horror* of it."

"It is good that you are here," said the Compdoctor. "You have reached a state of potential violence."

Kal glared at the wall. "Society did this to me."

"Not so," the doctor declared. "Society is not responsible for your genetic structure."

"I don't understand this world," Kal said, a hopeless note in his voice. "We've got a space station on the Moon. We've built hive units on Mars. We're at the technical edge of star travel. Yet . . . still no cure for Deprivers."

"Science does not have all the answers," said the wall. "There are problems that are unsolvable."

"I don't believe that," said Kal Adams. "This society doesn't *want* to find a cure for people like me. The world needs a minority to kick around and Deprivers fit the bill. Most people feel smug and superior to us. We're the underdogs, the scapegoats."

"That is, of course, neurotic nonsense," said the wall, "stemming from your aberrated mental condition."

"I'm not insane," Kal protested. "But I *am* enraged. My God, I was just twelve months old! I was robbed of my childhood."

"And now you feel like striking out," the wall said. "You are at Breakpoint."

"Which is why they brought me here, right?"

"That is correct. When a Depriver reaches Breakpoint he or she is sent to me for help."

Kal laughed harshly. "Help? No one can help me, least of all a talking wall."

"You are mistaken, Mr. Adams," declared the Compdoctor. "I shall administer a tranc dosage that will lower your emotional drive level."

"You intend to numb my mind . . . put me into Sleepstate?"

"That is the only remedy," said the wall.

"And what if I don't want to be drugged? What if I refuse medication?"

"You have no choice," the wall told him. "You should have remained in D-Colony. Most Deprivers are content to be among their own kind."

"That was agony," said Kal. "I couldn't take it."

"You are a misfit," the wall declared. "A man on the verge of committing an anti-social act. Sleep is better than Termination."

"Not for me, it isn't," said Kal.

"I repeat, you have no choice in the matter."

A silver panel opened in the wall directly in front of Kal Adams, and a long, metalloid tube snaked out, capped by a glittering needle.

"This injection will solve all of your emotional conflicts," said the wall. "Hold out your right arm. And do not be concerned about the Suit. The needle is designed to penetrate."

Adams stood up. "To hell with you! I won't be drugged!"

"Then I shall summon an Enforcer and he will—"

Kal Adams picked up the steel chair and smashed it into the wall. Lights exploded. Circuits shorted out in sizzling, sparked showers. An alarm bell keened.

The exit door was flung open by an armed Enforcer who brought his laser to firing position as Kal slammed him across the skull with the steel chair.

The Enforcer went down and Kal grabbed his laser. He brought down a second Enforcer with a cutbeam blast from the hand-weapon.

The Suit was restricting his movement, and Adams used the

laser to carefully cut it away from his body. Now he wore only boots and a shortsleeve tunic. For the first time in his life he was able to feel the stir of air on his bare skin. Marvelous!

Enforcers were closing in from both ends of the corridor. They'd terminate him. He knew that. But he had no regrets. He wasn't afraid of Termination. Better than Sleep. At least he'd die with his mind intact.

Then, a female voice from a side door: "Hurry! *This* way!"

A woman in a light blue flogown was gesturing to him from mid-corridor. Adams ran to her and she waved him through the door, slam-bolting it behind them. "In here," she snapped. "Quickly!"

The room had served as a sensory lab. Crowded with open Thinktanks and exotic equipment.

"Who are you?" Kal stared at her. Stunning. Young. Beautifully figured. Dark-eyed.

"I'm Zandra, and I can get us out of this building."

"All the main exits are blocked by now," said Adams. "There's no way out."

"But there *is*," countered the girl. "Trust me."

They moved through another door into a narrow transport corridor. She sprinted ahead, urging him to follow.

"Why are you doing this?" he asked. "Why risk your life for me? I'm a Depriver."

"I know who you are," she said as they raced along the narrow passage. "You're Kal Adams."

"But how—"

"You're one of a kind. Unique. I heard about you, got curious and comped your statrecords."

"You work here?"

"Not exactly. I'm part of a lab experiment. But there's no time for talk. We have to escape."

"There's no escaping the Enforcers," said Kal. "Even if we manage to get out of the building they're bound to find us. Enforcers are everywhere. They'll terminate us both."

"Just do as I say," she told him. "Here . . ." She was tugging at a panel in the flooring. "Help me with this."

Together, they loosened the panel, pulling it free. A flight of metalloid steps spiraled downward. "There's a maintenance tunnel below that leads to the street."

"How do you know?"

"Because I've been planning a way out," she said. "I comped

the blueprints, and they show this tunnel running under the length of the building."

They hurried down the twisting stairs and began to move cautiously along the dim-lit passageway.

"I've been in comp-contact with a group called the Outsiders," Zandra told him. "Do you know about them?"

"I've heard rumors," said Kal. "Anti-system rebels. Operating against the state."

"They'll help us," she said. "They hate the Enforcers . . . hate what the system is doing to block the cure."

"What cure?"

"For Deprivers. They're working on a cure for the affliction. And they're close to a breakthrough."

"My God, that's wonderful!"

"After we made contact I told them I wanted out of the experiment, and they agreed to help. I planned on making my run this weekend—until you popped up. I recognized you from your statshot, and I knew why you were here. For Sleep."

"Yes." Kal nodded. "And I refused."

"I'm just glad I came along when I did."

Kal smiled at her. "I'm beginning to think we have a chance."

"We *do*," she said vehemently.

They'd reached the end of the tunnel. A steel ladder angled up to an exitplate.

"Once we're on the street," said Kal, "what then? Where do we go?"

"I know where," she said. "I'll take you."

Kal didn't argue. Maybe this remarkable young woman *could* lead him to the Outsiders. Why not take the gamble? Most certainly he was doomed without her.

They exited the tunnel at a street level some three hundred feet beyond the rear of the building. No Enforcers were in sight.

"They won't expect us to come out at this point," declared Zandra. "They'll figure we're still trapped inside."

"So we have breathing space," said Kal. "But my statshot will be all over the city by now. They'll be watching every possible escape route."

"I have a plan," she said. "If it works we'll be clear of the city."

"Well, I just hope—"

Kal's words were cut off by a sizzling burst of laser fire that chopped the grass inches from his left foot. A second beam caught him in the left shoulder.

"Take cover!" yelled Kal, diving behind a transit vehicle and pulling Zandra in close behind him. Another beam scored the roof of the truck.

Ahead of them, across a grassed verge, three Enforcers were advancing at a run. Kal scrambled into the truck's controlseat with Zandra.

"Can you drive this thing?" Her tone was desperate.

"Just keep your head down." Kal powered the truck forward in a skidding arc that quickly separated them from the trio of Enforcers.

"Tell me!" snapped Kal. "Which way now?"

"Stanton Square. The park . . . behind the old carousel."

"They'll have ground units out," said Kal. "Don't know if we can make it."

"*Try*, dammit! It's not that far." Then her voice softened. "How's your shoulder?"

The laser had cut deeply into Kal's flesh; the wound was raw and bleeding.

"I'm all right," he said.

Ten minutes later Kal pulled the truck to a stop in Stanton Park. To their left, the silent carousel baked in the heat of day, its mirrors shattered, painted wooden horses cracked and fading, with the floorboards of the abandoned ride warped by wind and rain.

A door opened at the inner section of the carousel, and a tall, sour-looking man in black came out to meet them.

To Zandra: "I see you arrived safely. Who's your friend?"

"Kal Adams," she told him. "He's a Depriver."

The hard-faced man looked at Kal. His eyes narrowed. "I've heard about you, Adams. Afflicted from infanthood. Unique case. What are you doing with Zandra?"

"Trying to stay alive," said Kal. "When I wouldn't accept Sleep they were going to Terminate me. Zandra got me into the clear." He hesitated. "Are you an Outsider?"

"That's what I'm called by the system. My name's Hollister."

"I won't shake your hand," said Kal.

Hollister nodded. "Follow me," he said, entering an overgrown section of heavy-growth woods.

In a small clearing, under a protective cover, a twin-thrust gyro was waiting for them, its rotor blades turning lazily in the heated air.

"This will take you to our headquarters near Bend City in New Oregon," said Hollister. "You'll be safe there."

"What about Airscouts?" asked Kal. "They'll be on full patrol."

"We're invisible on their scanners," said the tall man, helping them aboard the gyro. "We'll be well under their air-detect range. Believe me, they won't even know we're in the air."

"Looks as if you've got everything figured out," said Kal.

"Not everything," said Hollister, strapping himself into the controlseat, "but we're making progress. One step at a time."

The canopy rolled back and they lifted away, rotor blades slicing the sky.

In the passenger section Zandra opened a side panel and removed a flesh-repair kit. "Now . . . let's see about that shoulder."

Kal flinched back. "Don't touch me!" he warned her.

"Afraid I'll go blind?"

"God knows I wouldn't want to do that to you," he said.

"Not to worry. I'll be fine." And before he could stop her she'd laid the wound bare, spreading a healing paste over the laser cut.

"I don't understand," he said. "You're touching my skin, and yet—"

"And yet I'm not afflicted," she said. Zandra smiled, continuing to work on his shoulder. "I'm in no danger. Only humans are affected by Deprivers."

He stared at her. "You mean . . . that you're a . . . a *machine?*"

"Not quite," she told him. "I'm a freak . . . a Composite. Parts of me are robotic, but my main components are human tissue. Muscles . . . skin . . . bones. I'll age normally, grow old and die someday. Just as you will. But I'm not human in the exact sense you are. And I'm immune to affliction."

"Incredible," Kal murmured.

"After I was born . . . constructed might be a better term . . . they were going to experiment on me. That's when I began planning my escape. Fortunately, I was able to take you with me."

She finished with his shoulder, sealing the wound. The skin looked pink and fresh.

"There," she said. "You're good as new."

"I . . . I don't know how to thank you," he said. "There's no way I can—"

She put a finger to his mouth. "Hush!" And, slowly, she caressed his cheek.

He took her firmly into his arms. "I've never kissed a woman . . . never felt a woman's lips on mine. And—" he hesitated, felt himself trembling "—suddenly, I'm . . . I'm afraid."

"Don't be," she said, pressing her body to his.

She kissed him. Deeply. Warmly.

And the world became a very bright place for Kal Adams.

✛ ✛ ✛

How Do I Know
You're Real?

ANDREW BLEW MOTHER'S HEAD OFF. IT ROLLED across the room, bumped the far wall.

"Good God, Andrew! You've done it again!" Father was standing in the kitchen doorway, looking pale and shaken. "You simply have to stop killing your Mother."

"She wasn't my mother," murmured Andrew, a sullen tone in his voice. "None of them were."

"Now, see here, young man, I won't listen to—"

"And you're not my father," said Andrew, blowing off his Father's head with the Slicer.

Father's head rolled over beside Mother's.

When April came home from the Slotmart, she saw what Andrew had done. He was standing by the viewvent, staring at the street.

"That's the third set of parents you've killed in the last four months," she said peevishly. "We can't afford any more."

"I don't *want* any more," said Andrew. "I hated all of them, and I don't want any more."

"They were programmed from the DNA of your real parents," April said. "They *loved* you, Andy."

"Bullcrap," said Andrew. "A machine can't love anybody—and that's all they were. Machines."

"But you told me you wanted to have us live with your parents,"

April said from the kitchen. She was putting food away in the instafreez.

Andrew walked over to the doorway, watching her. "I thought I could accept them after Mom and Pop died. I was wrong. It just made me angry, having them around. It wasn't the same."

April came back into the mainroom. "Okay, no more. We'll live here alone, just you and me."

Andrew was staring at her.

"Why are you looking at me like that?"

"I was just wondering," he said softly.

"Wondering? About what?"

"How do I know *you're* real?"

She smiled at him. Her teeth were perfect. "That's a silly question. We've been married for six years. You know I'm not a synthetic."

"Maybe I do," he said, slumping into a flowcouch. "And maybe I don't."

"What does that mean?"

"It means I know you were real when I married you. But that could have changed."

"How?" She frowned. "How could it have changed?"

"You could have been killed at the Slotmart where you shop every day. Raped and killed. It happens to humans all the time. They could have replaced you with a Wife."

"And who are 'they'?"

"The people I work for. The Firm. They want me happy and productive. They make a lot of money out of me. They'd foot the cost of a Wife if they thought that's what I needed to stay happy and productive."

April fluffed the pillows on a bodychair. "That's insane talk, Andy. You *know* it is."

"I don't know anything for sure," he said. "That's my problem."

And he blew her head off.

Andrew walked over to her headless body. Looked down at her. Wires. Circuit boards. Tiny relays. "I thought so," he said.

The peepdoor chimed. Andrew opened it, looked hard at the fat postman.

"Here's your mail, sir."

Andrew blew his head off.

He'd been right. The Postman was a syntho, not a real human.

"They're all around me," said Andrew to the silent room. A smell of charred metal was in the air.

He walked out of his unit, then down Elm Street. He blew off the heads of three more of them. An Old Lady and two teenaged Kids.

He was arrested and taken to the Station.

"You've been on quite a rampage," said a beefy cop with a neatly trimmed red beard. "You're a menace to society, killing all these people."

"They weren't people," said Andrew calmly. "They were machines. Synthetics. All of them."

"How can you tell a syntho from a human?" asked the cop.

"I couldn't until four months ago, when I killed Mother and Father," said Andrew. "Even then, I wasn't sure. Not until today, when I was looking at my Wife."

"Go on," said the cop.

"It was her eyes. You can tell by the eyes. The pupils are different."

"That so?"

"Yeah," said Andrew. "Like your eyes. You're one of them. You're an Officer."

"So what if I am?"

"Everybody is, here at the Station," said Andrew. "I don't think there are any real people left anymore. You're all machines."

"Hey now, you're some smart puppy," said the cop. He was grinning. His teeth were perfect.

"What are you going to do with me?"

"We can't let you run loose again. Not in this society."

"Are you going to execute me?"

The bearded Officer shook his head. "We don't do that anymore. We'll export you."

"Where?"

"To the People's Asteroid," said the cop. "We've been sending all the humans there."

"So it's a plot," said Andrew. "The synthos are taking over."

"You might say that," nodded the Officer. "That's one way of putting it."

"I'm curious," declared Andrew. "Why ship me off to some asteroid? Why not just kill me?"

"We're not killers. We want to preserve the human race. But not here, not in *our* society."

"That's nice of you, wanting to preserve humans."

"Well, heck," said the cop. "You people created us, so we owe you."

"I'm glad you have a moral conscience," said Andrew.

"Like I said, we're not killers. We just want our own kind here."

Andrew met Wanda on the Ship to the People's Asteroid. She was twenty, very pretty, with a supple dancer's body.

"When did they round you up?" he asked her.

"Two weeks ago. I killed a Grocer. He tried to molest me."

"I didn't know Grocers molested women."

"This one did," she said. "I used his meat cleaver on him."

"Know anything about the People's Asteroid?" asked Andrew.

"Not a thing," Wanda said, "except that it's supposed to be full of real people."

"I look forward to it," said Andrew.

The People's Asteroid was quite large, warm, breathable, and attractive. The lifeunit assigned to Andrew was spacious and well furnished. It even had a Tridim. He was pleased.

Wanda had a unit in the next building. They met in her playroom and made love. She was extremely passionate.

"It's wonderful here," said Andrew, as he relaxed against a flowpillow.

"Yes . . . wonderful," said Wanda. She hesitated. "Except for one thing."

"What's that?" Andrew's voice was lazy and sated.

"There are no other machines here."

"But that's what makes it so wonderful."

"For you maybe," she said, "but not for me."

And she blew Andrew's head off.

Wanda removed the contact shields over her eyes. They really worked. Even Andrew had been fooled.

She got up from the flowbed, walked nude to the viewvent, and stared out at the alien landscape. Beautiful, but sterile.

Wanda sighed. It was going to be damn lonely—as the only syntho on the People's Asteroid.

✝ ✝ ✝

Starblood

Is the orbit stabilized ■
   Yes ■
   How much longer ■
   Soon now ■
   You first Then I'll follow ■
   Do you think . . . I mean is it possible with this planet that we'll be able to succeed ■
   We'll try That's all we can do I have no answers ■

1
Bobby

BOBBY WAS STILL CRYING, HIS TINY FACE RED, fists clenched, ignoring the roboMother who rocked and crooned to him.

Dennison walked over, switched off the machine, and picked up his son. He carried the squalling infant to the patio where his wife was playing Magneball with an android instructor.

"Bobby's been crying all afternoon," Dennison said. "Do something with him. See if you can't shut him up."

Mrs. Dennison glared at her husband. "Let Mother handle him."

"I switched her off," said Dennison. "She wasn't doing any

good. Take him for a ride in the copter. He likes that. It'll shut him up."

"You do it," said Alice Dennison. "I'm perfecting my back thrust. I play tournament next week, you know."

"You don't give a damn about your son, do you?"

She nodded to the android, ignoring the question. "Ready," she said.

A magnetic disc leaped from the instructor's hand and the woman expertly repelled it with a thrusting left glove.

"Well done, Mrs. Dennison," said the android.

In a silent rage, Dennison advanced on the android and beheaded the machine with a chair leg.

"I hope you're satisfied," said the wife. "They cost fifteen thousand dollars. I'll just have to buy another."

"You do that," said Dennison. "But first you take Bobby up in the copter. I can't stand any more of his squalling."

She scooped up the baby, who continued to howl, and took a riser to the roofpad. Activating the family flier, she placed Bobby inside and lifted off in a whir of gleaming blades.

Five miles above New Chicago, Mrs. Dennison switched the copter to autoflight, unlatched the main exit panel and held her baby son straight out into the blast of air.

She smiled at him—and released her grip.

Still crying, Bobby Dennison fell twisting and tumbling toward the cold earth below.

2
Tris

In Greater New York, under warm summer sun, the walkways sang. Heat from the sky stirred delicate filaments within the moving bands and a thin, silver rain of music drifted up to the walkriders, soothing them, easing away some small bit of city hive pressure.

For Tris, an ex-Saint at sixteen, the pressures were mounting and the song of the walkways did not ease her; she was close to an emotional breakdown. When a Saint is cast out by the Gods she has nowhere to go. Society shuns the outcast. Her only chance lies in reinstating herself. If she cannot achieve this, she ceases to function as a viable entity and self-extinction is her only recourse.

Tris was beautiful and free-spirited, with a body built for Sainthood. Surely, she told herself, she would find her way back into Divine Favor.

"The Reader will see you now," said the wallspeak. "Inside and just to the left."

Tris moved ahead past the sliding wall and turned left.

Reader Sterning was ready for her, a tall man in flowsilks. His smile was warmly professional. They touched palms and Tris sat down.

"Well, well," said Sterning. "I can surface why you're here, and believe me when I tell you that I sympathize."

"Thank you, Reader," said the girl softly.

"How long were you a Saint?"

Tris knitted her fingers in her lap, twisting her hands nervously. She'd never been deeped before and it was a little frightening. "Could you . . . turn off the wall?" she asked.

"Of course," smiled Sterning, and killed the hypnowall. The swirl of colors faded to black. "I really don't need it in your case. I want you to be as comfortable as possible. Now . . ." He tented his hands. "How long were you a Saint?"

She blinked rapidly. "For almost a year. One of the Gods selected me in Omaha. They were there to flare and I offered . . ."

"You offered your Eternal Self?"

"Yes, that's right. And they accepted me. One of them did, I mean."

"The one called Denbo, am I correct?"

She nodded, flushing. "He took me. He sainted me."

Sterning bowed his head. "A rare sexual honor. A beautiful selection. And you *are*. Quite."

Tris blinked again. "Quite?"

"Quite beautiful. Thighs . . . hips . . . breasts. You are ideally qualified for Sainthood." He sighed. "Your situation is most unfortunate. But let's get to it."

He moved around the desk, sat down close to her on the flowcouch, his dark eyes probing. "Lean back and relax. I'm going to deep you now. Close your eyes."

Tris shuddered; she knew there would be no pain, but the *nakedness* of it all! Her inner mind laid bare to another!

"You needn't be concerned about opening to me," Sterning said. "It's all quite normal. Deeping is a natural process for those of us who read. You have nothing to be afraid of."

"I know that," said Tris. "But . . . it isn't easy for me."

"Relax . . . just relax."

She settled back into the chair, her mind opening to his.

Sterning shifted to a below-surface level, sighed. "Ah, sadness and guilt." He began reading. "You were a truly passionate Saint and the Gods were pleased. And you got on well with all the other Saints, sharing their life and dedication until . . ."

He hesitated, probing deeper. "Until you made a mistake which cost you Divine Favor."

"Yes," murmured Tris. Her down-closed lashes quivered against her white cheek. "A mistake. I should never have—"

"—criticized." Sterning finished the thought. "You criticized a God and they banished you. Your comments were cruel, caustic."

"I was angry," said Tris. "With Denbo."

"Because he was sexually favoring other Saints."

"Yes."

"But you had no right to be angry. A God may bestow his sexual favors where he will. That is his Divine right, is it not?"

"I know, I know," said the girl. "But I thought Denbo—"

"—would consider your feelings. But of course no God need consider a Saint's feelings. That is your mortal flaw. You cannot accept nor abide by Divine rule."

"I *tried* to obey, to accept." The girl was beginning to cry, her eyes still closed. Tears ran down her cheeks.

Sterning continued to probe, unmoved by emotion. "You failed out of sheer stubborn self-pride. You felt . . ." He moved to a deeper level. "You felt equal to Denbo, equal to a God. You desired more than Sainthood."

"Yes." Softly.

"And what do you want from me?"

"An answer. Surely, within my brain, somewhere within it, you can read a way back."

The Reader stood up, breaking contact. He walked to his desk, sat down heavily. "Your self-will is too strong. There is no way back. Sainthood is behind you."

"Then I'll die," she said flatly, opening her eyes. "Will you aid me?"

"I dislike this kind of thing. I don't usually—"

"Please."

He sighed. "All right."

"Thank you, Reader Sterning."

And he killed her.

3
Morgan

The laser sliced into the right front wheelhousing of Morgan's landcar and he lost control. Another beam sizzled along the door as he rolled free of the car. It slewed into a ditch, overturned, flamed, and exploded. The heavy smoke screened him as Morgan worked his way along the ditch, a fuse pistol in his right hand. Not much good against beamguns, but his other weapons had been destroyed with the car.

The screening smoke worked both ways; he couldn't see *them*, verify their number. But maybe he could slip around them. It was quite possible they believed him dead in the explosion.

He was wrong about that.

A chopping blow numbed his left shoulder. Morgan hit ground, rolled, brought up the fuser, fired. His assailant fell back, grunting in pain. Morgan whipped up the pistol in a swift arc, catching a second enemy at chin-level, firing again. Which did the job.

Morgan rubbed circulation back into his numbed shoulder, his body pressed close in against the night-chilled gravel at the edge of the road. Behind him, in a flare of orange, the landcar continued to burn. He listened for further movement. Were there more of them out there, ready to attack him?

No sound. Nothing. No more of them. Only two, both dead now.

He took their beamers, checked the bodies. Both young, maybe fifteen to seventeen. Probably brothers, but Morgan couldn't tell for sure, since the face was mostly gone on the smaller one. At close range, a fuser is damned effective.

Morgan recharged the pistol and inspected the beamguns, breaking them down. They were fine. He could use them.

It was too late to find another car. Better to sleep by the lake and go on in the morning.

The lake would be good. It would cool him out, ease some of the tension which knotted his muscles. He'd grown up near lakes like this one, fishing and swimming with Jim Decker. Ole Jimbo. Poor unlucky bastard. The police got him in Detroit, lasered him down in a warehouse. Jimbo never believed he could die. Well, thought Morgan, we *all* die—sooner or later.

Lake Lotawana lay just ahead, less than a mile through the trees. Morgan threaded the woods, slid down the leaf-cloaked banking to the edge of the water. The lake flickered like a soft flame, alive with moonlight. Morgan bent to wash his face and hands; the water rippled and stirred as he cupped it, cold and crystalline.

He drew the clean air of September into his lungs. Good autumn air, smelling of maple and oak. He savored the smells of Missouri earth, of autumn grass and trees. A night bird cried out across the dark lake water. Morgan hoped he would live long enough to reach Kansas City and do what he was sent to do. He could easily have been killed in the landcar explosion—or in Illinois, Ohio, Pennsylvania, or a few nights ago in Kansas. They'd been close on his tracks most of the way.

He prepared a bed of leaves, spreading dry twigs in a circle around it for several feet in each direction. The twigs would alert him to approaching enemies. Morgan lay down with a beamer at his elbow. Tomorrow, he would find another car and reach Kansas City. The girl and the money would be waiting there. He smiled and closed his eyes.

Morgan was sleeping deeply when they came down the bank, shadows among shadows, moving with professional stealth. They knelt beyond the circle of twigs and began scooping the branches away quietly. They planned to use blades, and that meant close body contact.

Morgan heard them at the last instant and rolled sideways, snatching up the beamer as he rolled. Too late. They were on him in a mass of unsheathed steel.

He broke free, stumbled, dropped the useless weapon, blood rushing to fill his open mouth. Morgan folded both hands across his stomach. "I . . ." He spoke to them as they watched him. "I'm a dead man."

And he fell backward as the dark waters of the lake, rippling, accepted his lifeless body.

4
David

"I *hate* bookstores," said David.

"You're still a child," his Guardian told him. "As an adult, you'll see the value in books."

David, who was eleven, allowed himself to be guided into the store. You don't get anywhere if you argue with a Guardian.

"May I be of service?" A tall, old man smiled at them, dressed in the long, gray robe of Learning.

"This is David," said the Guardian, "and he is here to rent a book."

The old man nodded. "And what is your choice, David?"

"I don't have one," said David. "Let Guardian decide."

"Very well, then . . ." The Bookman smiled again. "Might I suggest some titles?"

"Please do," said the Guardian.

The old man pursed his lips. "Ah . . . what about *Moby Dick?* Splendid seafaring adventure, laced with symbolic philosophy."

"I hate whales," said David. "Sea things are disgusting."

"Hmmm. Then I shall bypass Mr. Melville and Mr. Verne. Let us move along to Dylan Thomas and his spirited *Under Milk Wood.*"

"Let's hear part of it," said David.

The old man pressed a button on the wall and a door opened. A rumpled figure stepped into the room. His nose was red and bulbous; his hair was wild. He walked toward them, voice booming. He spoke of a small town by night, starless and bible-black, and of a wood "limping invisible down to the sloeback, slow, black, crowblack, fishing boat-bobbing sea."

"I don't like it," said David flatly. "Send him back."

"That will be all, Mr. Thomas," said the Bookman.

The rumpled figure turned and vanished behind the door.

"I want a hunting story of olden times," said David. "Do you have any?"

"Naturally. We have many. What about *Big Woods?*"

"Who wrote that?" asked David.

"Mr. Faulkner. You'll like him, I'm sure."

David shrugged, and the Bookman pressed another button. A short man with sad eyes and a bristled mustache stepped into view. He spoke, with a drawl, of woods and rivers and loamed earth, and of "the rich deep black alluvial soil which would grow cotton taller than the head of a man on a horse."

"We'll take him," said David.

"Indeed we will," said the Guardian.

"Splendid," said the Bookman.

William Faulkner waited quietly while the rental sheet was signed, then walked out with them.

"There is a story in my book," he said to David, "which I have titled 'The Bear.' Do you wish to hear it?"

"Sure. I want to hear the whole book if it's all about hunting."

"The boy has a strange fascination with death," the Guardian said to Mr. Faulkner.

"Then I shall begin with page one," drawled the tall man as they were crossing a gridway.

David, looking up into the sad eyes of William Faulkner, did not see the gridcar jetting toward him. The Guardian screamed and clawed at the boy's coat to pull him back, but was not successful. The car struck David, killing him instantly.

"Am I to be returned?" asked Mr. Faulkner.

5
Bax

They were having shrimp curry at the Top of the Mark in San Francisco when the sharks began to bother the girl.

"They're so *close*," she said. "Why are they so close?"

Bax snapped his fingers. A waiter appeared at their table. "Do something about those damn things," Bax demanded.

"I'm very sorry, sir, but our repel shielding has temporarily failed."

"Can you fix it?"

"Oh, of course, sir. That's being attended to now. We have the situation under control. At any moment the shielding should be fully operational."

Bax waved him away. "Are you satisfied?" he asked the girl.

She picked at her food, head lowered. "I just won't look at them," she said.

The sharks continued to bump the transparent outer shell, while a huge manta ray rippled through the jeweled waters. Far below, streaks of rainbow fish swarmed in and around the quake-tumbled ruins of office buildings, and the lichen-covered trucks and cable cars. An occasional divecab sliced past the restaurant, crowded with tourists.

Bax leaned across the table to take the girl's hand; his eyes softened. "I thought you'd enjoy it here. This place is an exact duplicate of the original. You get a fantastic view of the city."

"I feel trapped," she admitted. "I'm a surface girl, Bax. I don't like being here."

Bax grinned. "To tell you the truth, I don't like it much myself. But, at the moment, we really don't have any choice."

"I know." She gave his hand a squeeze. "And it's all right. It's just that I—"

"Look," Bax cut in. "They've fixed it."

The nuzzling sharks thrashed back abruptly as the energized shielding was reactivated. The outer dome now pulsed radiantly, silvering the sea. The sharks retreated deeper into the green-black Pacific.

"It's something about their teeth," the girl said to Bax. "Like thousands of upthrust knives . . ."

"Well, they're gone now. Forget them. Eat your curry."

"When is the contact meeting us?" she asked.

"He's overdue. Should be here any minute."

"You don't think anything's wrong, do you?"

Bax shook his head. "What *could* be wrong?" He patted the inside of his coat. "I have the stuff. They pay us for it and we leave San Fran for the islands. Take a long vacation. Enjoy what we've earned."

"What about a crossup?" Her voice was intense. "What if they hired another agent to take the stuff and dispose of you?"

He laughed. "You mean dispose of *us*, don't you?"

The girl stared at him coldly. "No. I mean you, Bax."

Bax dropped his half-empty wine glass. "You lousy bitch," he said softly, slumping forward across the table.

The girl darted her hand into his coat, withdrew a small packet, and placed it inside her evening bag as a waiter rushed toward them.

"I think my husband has just had a heart seizure," she said. "I'll go for a doctor."

And she calmly left the bar.

Outside, beyond the silvered fringe of light, the knife-toothed sharks circled the dome.

6
Lynda

The wind was demented; it whiplashed the falling snow into Lynda's eyes, into her half-open mouth as she stood, head raised to the storm, taking it in, allowing it to engulf her. The collar of her stormcoat was open and the cold snow needled her skin.

Then the wall glowed. Someone wanted her.

Annoyed, she killed the blizzard. The wind ceased. The snow melted instantly. The ceiling-sky was, once again, blue and serene above her head. She stepped from the Weatherchamber, peeling her stormcoat and boots.

Her father was there, looking his usual dour self.

"Sorry to break into your weather, Lynda, but I must talk to you."

She walked to the barwall, pressed an oak panel, and an iced scotch glided into her hand. "Drink?" she offered.

"You know I never drink on the job."

She sipped at the scotch. "I see. You're in town on a contract."

"That's right."

"I think it's revolting." She shook her head. "Why don't you get out of this business? You're too old to go on killing. You'll make a mistake and one of your contracts will end up doing you in. It happens all the time."

"Not to me it won't," said Lynda's father. "I know my job."

"It's sickening"

The older man grunted. "It's provided you with everything you've ever wanted."

"And I guess I should be humbly grateful. As the pampered daughter of a high-level professional assassin, I'm very rich and very spoiled. I am, in fact, a totally worthless addition to society, thanks to you."

"Then you shouldn't mind leaving it," he said.

"What is *that* supposed to mean?"

"It means, dearest daughter, that my contract this trip is on you."

And the beamgun he held beneath his coat took off Lynda's head.

The pattern is fixed It's hopeless ■
You don't want to try again ■
To what purpose Each time one of us penetrates we are rejected This planet does not want us We'll have to move beyond the system ■
Would the host bodies have survived without us ■
Everyone on Earth dies eventually But we trigger quick violent death It's their way of rejecting us We must accept the pattern ■
I liked the girl in New York . . . Tris And the little boy David We could have flowered in them ■
The universe is immense We'll find a host planet that's benign Where we'll be welcome ■
We're leaving Earth's orbit now ■
The stars are waiting for us A billion billion suns ■
I love you ■

✜ ✜ ✜

The Joy of Living

"IT'S JUST AROUND THE NEXT TURN," RICE SAID, peering from the tinted windows as the car skimmed over the warm summer streets of the city.

The vehicle slowed, took the long curve with fluid grace, and whispered to a stop. A silver door panel sighed back and Ted Rice stepped into the heat of morning. His suit-conditioner immediately circulated an inner breath of cool air to balance the rise in temperature.

"I won't need you for the rest of the day," he told the car. "I'll be walking home."

"May I have your location number, sir, in case a member of the family should wish to contact you?"

"No, dammit, you may not!" This was Free-Day. He needn't tell the car anything. "Go home."

"Very well, sir." The machine slid obediently from the curb. Rice watched it glitter briefly, like a lake trout in the moving wash of morning traffic, and disappear.

On Free-Days he told the car what to do. No pre-determined destinations. No pre-determined activities. Today the bars were open.

He intended getting very, very drunk.

On this morning, the sixth anniversary of his wife's death, Ted

Rice had made two highly important decisions. He would quit his job and he would turn Margaret in to Central Exchange. The job he hated, but it had been his life and quitting took courage. It meant beginning anew in an untried field and, at thirty-eight, that wasn't easy. Margaret he did not hate, finding it impossible to catalogue his exact emotions where she was concerned. But his final decision to turn her in was the only one possible under the circumstances.

His reason for getting drunk, however, had nothing to do with his job or with Margaret. He was not, had never been, a drinking man. Intoxication was an anniversary ritual performed in memory of his late wife, Virginia. He exercised extreme care in his yearly choice of drinking quarters, avoiding pretentiousness because he wanted the surroundings to reflect his own inner loneliness.

Louie's Place was anything but pretentious. Ceaseless towelings had worn the bar top to a circular whiteness. The mirror behind it, in the shape of a giant passenger rocket, hung chipped and blackening at the edges. Even the mural, depicting Man's First Landing on the Red Planet, was dust-dimmed and faded, the paint cracking, peeling gradually away. The shabby stools fronting the bar were all unoccupied.

"Mornin'," greeted the bartender. Rice nodded, took a corner stool, and pressed the straight whiskey button. The drink glided into his hand and he downed it, grimacing.

"Ain't seen you around before on Free-Days," the barman observed, swabbing idly at an already-dry glass ring. "Just move inta the neighborhood?"

"I don't drink often," Rice said, re-pressing the button.

"Wanna tell me about things?"

Rice shifted his attention from his shot glass to the man behind the bar. Beefy, slack-jawed, with a broken nose and a pair of watery, protuberant eyes over which lids folded like canvas sails. The face of mourning. The professional kindred soul, salaried receiver of woes and sad lament. Rice regarded him suspiciously, twirling the shot glass between thumb and forefinger.

"Well, Mac?"

"Turn around," said Rice.

The big man grinned broadly, his solemn face splitting as though a paper knife had slit the skin across. "Now I know you don't drink much. Believe me, I'm the real McCoy. In my racket you have to be."

"Around."

Still grinning, the bartender complied. Law provided that evidence of a mechanical could not be concealed and there was no metal switch behind the man's right ear.

"Like I toldja, the McCoy."

"It's been a year," Rice said, by way of apology. "I wasn't sure they hadn't replaced you fellows too."

"Bars'ud go broke if they did. Who wants to tell their troubles to a bunch 'a springs an' cogs'?"

Rice glanced at his wristwatch and thought of Margaret, standing in the living room of their modest home, a smile illuminating her delicate features. She had been standing now for fifteen hours, thirty-seven minutes—since he'd switched her off the previous evening in an angry display of temper.

"Six years ago today my wife died in a copter crash," Rice said, meeting the barman's sad eyes. "I've put the memory of that crash away in the back of my mind and once each year I take it out and I remember." He tipped the shot glass at a careful angle, holding it quite still, as though he might capture Virginia's tiny image there within the dark liquid, as a fly is caught in amber. "I remember how she looked when they brought her up to the house, as if her bones had suddenly run wild under the skin, the way her face looked . . . the face of someone I'd never met."

Rice finished his fourth straight whiskey, feeling it burn down through his body, loosening inner tensions, making it easier to say what he subconsciously *had* to say.

"That can be rough." The big man looked wonderfully, professionally sympathetic, with those mournful, red-rimmed eyes, which seemed about to flood into tears. "Didja have any kids?"

"A boy, Jackie. He'll be nine this Game-Day. Lot like his mother. The other children, Timmy and Susan, are mechanicals. Got them after Virgie's death, when I bought Margaret."

"Musta been tough on the kid, losin' his real mother an' all."

"Jackie doesn't remember much about Virgie. He was only three. Fact is, I've been half a stranger to him myself, on the road most of the year. Margaret's all right, I suppose, but she doesn't think the way you and I do."

"How come you stuck yourself with this Margaret?"

"Authorities. Had to furnish a decent home for the boy or lose him. I couldn't stay settled then, with my wife gone. She was still so much a part of things, of our house, the streets, the places we used to go . . . I went on the road, tried to forget. That kind of life was out of the question for a three-year-old. I had no choice. Either I bought a mechanical or I lost my son. I could find no one to take Jackie. Virgie's parents were dead and my own mother was in no position to raise a child. So I bought Margaret and since we'd originally planned on a brother and sister for Jackie I decided to do it up brown and go for the package deal. After all, I got 'em whole-sale."

"Hey!" The barman cocked an eyebrow. "You a mech salesman?"

"Until tomorrow. I'm quitting. My next job will be right here in LA and won't have a damn thing to do with mechanicals!" Producing his wallet, Rice handed the bartender a card. "Read that."

"Theodore A. Rice," the beefy man pronounced carefully, "Authorized representative for World Mechanicals."

"No, no. The slogan at the bottom."

"'A Dollar a Day Keeps Childbirth Away.' So?"

Rice leaned forward, steely eyed. "So the damned fool who originated that ought to be roasted over a slow fire!"

"Just a slogan, Mac. Everybody knows it."

"Exactly! Do you have any real conception of what that slogan and others like it have done to our national birthrate?" Rice asked, a fresh whiskey in his hand. "Childbirth has been converted into a horror, a form of medieval torture in the minds of women today. For thirty bucks a month any woman can have a bouncing baby made to order and delivered fresh-wrapped to her door. For less than it used to cost just to feed a human child, she can share the pleasures and joys of motherhood and avoid all the responsibilities.

"'Madam' I'd say, 'don't risk your figure. Don't tie yourself down and miss all the fun. Get a mechanical. No baby sitters needed, no dirty diapers or squalling at three in the morning. No measles or mumps or tonsils out. Just a bonny little brat with a switch behind his ear. What'll it be, madam? A fat little bambino with dark eyes and an angel's smile—or a saucy eyed little Irisher with freckles on her nose?'

"'Or howz about you, fella? Tired of looking for the right girl? Want a ready-made cutie who'll be one hundred percent yours? How did the old song go? *I want a paper dolly I can call my own, a dolly other fellows cannot steal* . . . Well, here she is, chum—a full-size babe with the old come-hither look reserved especially for you. Blonde? Brunette? Redhead? You name 'er, we've got 'er. Yours on easy payments!'"

Rice paused, breathing heavily, his glass empty.

The bartender, wise in the ways of his profession, maintained a listening silence.

"Ya know how this electronic illusion got started?" Rice demanded, tongue somewhat uncertain in his mouth, speech beginning to slur. "Well, lemme tellya. People got lonesome. An' when somebody's ole man died 'long comes a mech to replace him. When a woman was sterile she got her baby anyhow. When a Mr. Shy Guy wanted some female company 'long comes a sponge-rubber job right outa th' pinup mags. Jus' a few at first, here an' there, an' expensive as hell. But pretty soon the good ole American commercial know-how takes over and competition gets rough. Prices go down. A lotta people stop havin' babies. In nothin' flat everybody is buyin' mechanicals . . . you . . . 'n . . . me 'n everybody. . . ."

"Hate to spoil your fun, Mac, but you're really loadin' one on. I'd ease up on them straight shots."

"An' you know what th' tragedy is?" Rice continued over a filled glass, ignoring the advice. "Th' trashdy is, we're all dyin' an' nobody cares! Pretty soon you 'n me will be in the same league with the goddarn ole water buffalo and the dodo bird. Th' trashdy is that everybody is dyin' in a century designed for easy livin'. Say! Lesh drink a toast to th' joy of livin'."

The bartender extended a cautioning hand. "No foolin', Mac, if I was you—Look out! You're gonna . . ."

Rice felt the room tip, rock crazily for no apparent reason. Faintly, he heard the bartender's shout of warning, saw his face receding like a toy balloon down the length of an immense corridor which ended abruptly in a high fountaining of colored lights.

Margaret was her usual cheery self when Rice finally switched her on.

"Morning, Ted darling." She bussed him on the cheek. "Sleep well?"

"This is July tenth," he replied sullenly, nursing the remnants of a colossal hangover.

"Goodness! Have I been off *that* long? Honestly, Ted, I'll never get the housework done if you continue to leave me off for days at a time. How are the children?"

"Fine. Still sleeping."

"If this is the tenth, then you've had your . . . your—"

" 'Toot' is the word. And I feel lousy."

"What's that cut above your eye? Did someone hit you?"

"My assailant was the floor of the Third Avenue bar. I came off second best."

She was instantly solicitous. "You could have a concussion!"

"I'm fine."

"You're angry again."

"I'm fine and I'm not angry. Now, go wind the dog while I wake the kids."

If only she would react, thought Rice, watching her silent withdrawal. If only *once* she would stomp her feet, throw things, scream at him. But always, always this everlasting indulgence! The spark which ignites a marriage, makes it glow, was missing. In love, he knew, there is violence and Margaret's love was a calm, manufactured emotion, which left him unsatisfied and edgy, a love unreal, intolerable. When he and Virgie had quarreled, had things out and reconciled, they were actually much closer to one another for having weathered a personal storm. But, with Margaret, the case was different.

Rice thought of the latest incident, two nights ago, when he had been with Skipper encouraging the dog to beg for a plasto-bone. Skipper was outdated, as modern dogs go, but he represented a link with the fading past that Margaret seemed bent on severing. She renewed the familiar subject of his purchasing a modernized, electronic canine to replace the shaggy wind-up model, and he all but hit the ceiling, thundering at her, gesturing, swearing. But she had remained impassive, turning aside his rage with her calm smile. Then, savagely, he had switched her off, as one might extinguish a glaring light. How frozen she had stood! How instantly drained of personality and movement! In that moment, facing her perfect, motionless body, he experienced a recurrent sense of guilt that invariably accompanied such action, as though he had taken a life, had murdered. Damning his own weakness, he had left her there, smiling, in the silent room.

"Daddy, Daddy, Daddy," squealed Timmy after he was activated. "Hooray, hooray, it's Picnic-Day! Hooray, hooray, it's Picnic-Day!"

"Hooray, hooray," Rice repeated without enthusiasm, envisioning a hectic afternoon of child-noise and forced amusement.

"Now, quiet down. Your father's not feeling well," Margaret cautioned from the hall as Timmy zoomed and swooshed about the house playing Rocket.

Little Susan's enthusiasm matched that of her mechanical brother. She hopped around the living room, circling Rice, screaming out her delight in a voice that pierced his head like a driven needle.

"For the love of heaven, STOP!" he shouted at the whirling children, "or I'll switch you both off!"

Under his stern threat they quieted.

Margaret returned with Skipper. The dog had run down the previous evening chasing the electronic cat next door. He scampered rustily across the floor, high falsetto bark betraying the damaging effect of morning precipitation.

"Good ole Skip . . . You need some oil, fella," Rice told him, tickling his ears. "Have you fixed in a jiff. Timmy, get the oil can from the shelf."

Rice was in the act of administering the proper lubricant when Jackie emerged from the hallway, rubbing sleep from his eyes.

"Hi, Mom. Hi, Dad. Morning everybody." He yawned.

"Hi, scout," Rice greeted him, roughing his already thoroughly tousled hair. "Have a good rest?"

"Sure. Hey, this is Picnic-Day isn't it? When are we leaving?"

"Soon as little sleepy-heads like you get out of their pajamas and into some breakfast." He playfully swatted Jackie's bottom. "Now git."

Margaret took the boy's hand. "Come on, dear. I have breakfast on the table." And over her shoulder to Rice: "I do think we should get an early start."

Susan and Timmy bounded into the yard with Skipper, leaving Rice alone with his thoughts.

He said, Hi Mom, first, before Hi Dad. And the look in his eyes when she took his hand! Jackie is too young to see Margaret as I see her; he can't realize that she can never really love him as he loves her. The longer she's here the harder it will be for Jackie when the break comes. I mustn't put off telling Margaret any longer. I'll tell her today. Today.

The bullet-car flowed soundlessly over the highway, blurring the trees, rushing the houses past, but to Rice the speed was illusion, stage trickery. His impatient mind, reaching for the moment when he would be alone with Margaret and able to tell her what he must tell her, changed minutes to hours. Head back against the seat, eyes closed, he imagined the car in lazy slow motion, wheels barely turning, each blade of roadside grass available and separate to the eye if one chose to look.

The ride to the picnic ground seemed endless.

"I'm bushed," he said to Margaret after the car had parked itself. "Let's skip the games today and just relax in the shade."

"But, Ted, the children—"

"—can play without us. I have something to say to you, something important."

She hesitated, watching the activity on the playing courts. The children, three elves in their picnic-jumpers, fidgeted, desperately anxious to join the games, their eyes darting like imprisoned minnows in small, white pools.

"In order to be enjoyed to the fullest the games require family participation."

"Nonsense."

"Young and old, Ted. The games . . ."

"To hell with the games!" he snapped. "Are you going to listen to what I have to say or not?"

"Of course, darling. If you really want to talk . . ." She smiled, pressed his hand. "The children can join the Hartleys." She pointed across the wide picnic lawn to a group of rioting players engaged in a vigorous game of Magna-Ball. "Run along you three. And be careful."

"Wheeeeeeee!" pealed little Susan, and hands linked in a daisy-chain, the happily released trio sprang toward the courts.

"If we're going to talk we can at least be comfortable," Margaret said, unpacking a blanket and spreading it over the prickling grass.

Every gesture perfect, thought Rice, watching her hands, *every movement graceful and sure. She's so alive, so amazingly human, possessing such vibrancy and warmth, that sometimes even I find it difficult to think of her as artificially created of wire and circuit and cog. Certainly Jackie has come to love her. She's good and kind and smiles a great deal. These things matter to Jackie. The fact that she isn't human does not matter. Not at all. The situation, therefore, is grave.*

"What are you thinking about, Ted?" Her blue eyes were steady on his.

"About you. About how beautiful you are." He plucked a single dandelion from the grass and held its orange-gold face, like a miniature sun, in the cupped palm of his hand. "This is a weed masquerading as a flower. Beautiful, possessing many virtues, but actually a weed that must be removed before its deep taproot smothers the surrounding grass. Unless it is, there will eventually be room only for the dandelion."

"What has all this . . ."

"You're like the dandelion, Margaret. You're smothering Jackie's love. He has grown to love you far more than he does me. Up to now I've been just a visiting relative who comes home from some distant place to spend Christmas and summer vacations with you. When he was younger he cried whenever I shut you off, as though I had beaten him. Even now he watches me lose my temper, swear, bang the furniture, and I see him looking at me, and I know he's comparing us, weighing us. The scales are in your favor. I'm home to stay now, and as long as you're here he'll always be comparing. I can't, I won't, compete with a mechanical for my son's affection!"

She sucked in her breath, sharply. He could see that his words had struck with the force of hurled stones.

"Have you thought this all out, Ted? Isn't there some other way?" She was actually trembling. "You know how much I love you."

"You only *think* you love me, Margaret. What you mistake for love is only conditioning. Recepters can be re-fed, patterned responses erased, new ones substituted. At Central Exchange they'll alter you, Margaret. You'll never know I existed."

"Ted, you can't!"

"There's no other way."

A silence fell between them.

Despite himself, Rice again experienced a twinge of guilt. Perhaps he had broken the news in too ruthless a fashion, but it was imperative that she understand his position, and he had considered it impossible to pierce her shell of calm. That she would be visibly shaken by his words was totally unexpected. Of course, he reasoned, no mechanical likes the idea of complete re-orientation. On these grounds her behavior seemed less surprising. But still . . .

"Why have you told me all this?" she asked him. "Why didn't you turn me in suddenly, without my knowing in advance? I'd have preferred that." Her hands moved nervously on her skirt, toyed with the locket at her neck, now touched at her hair like two restless birds unable to fly away from her body.

"Because I need your help. Jackie mustn't know the truth . . . Not now. Later, when he's older, better able to evaluate facts for himself, he'll understand. I'll tell him something about your having to go on a long trip for reasons of health. He'll believe me if you'll back me up. Will you?"

"If that's what you want," she replied softly, head down, her fingers turning and turning the dandelion he had discarded. "I'll do anything you want, Ted . . . because I love you."

"Timmy and Susan can stay with Jackie for a while," he hurried on, "to make your leaving easier for him. In time, he'll adjust."

"Yes . . . he'll adjust."

The drowsy rustle of leaves in summer air. The distant hum of voices from the playing courts.

"Well, then it's settled."

"All settled. You'd better call the children in for lunch."

After lunch, Rice gamboled in the scented grass with the whooping children, imitating, to their vast delight, a bear, a gorilla, a whale, a jet train, and a moon rocket. He ran races with them and organized a rodeo, in which he doubled in brass as a fiercely snorting Brahma bull and a bucking bronco.

On the way home they sang folk songs and watched the sun go down over the ocean. The day, everyone agreed, had been a huge success.

But, that night, Rice could not sleep.

The headboard whispered, "Three A.M., sir," when he questioned the hour. He lay on his back, hands laced behind his head, staring into the ghost darkness of the room. In the moon-painted sky, a copter whirred past like a giant night insect seeking distant city lights, and Rice thought of Virginia. In past weeks he had been finding it remarkably difficult to remember many of the things about her that he wished to remember; time had hidden her image as a coin is hidden in deep waters.

The drone of the copter faded into Margaret's quiet breathing from the bed beside his, and now her face drifted into his mind, superimposed over the dim reflection of Virginia. He saw, in infinite detail, each curling black hair of her down-swept lashes, long and trembling against the rose of her cheek. He saw her quivering lips form words, four startling words of the afternoon:

". . . because I love you."

Impossible, that a mechanical could love as Virginia had loved; that a being of metal and glass, of wires however cunningly woven could fathom and experience such deeply genuine emotion.

Yet, was it conceivable, Rice wondered in the pressing darkness, that somehow an unknown process had taken place in Margaret, that far back in the green cave of her brain, among the delicate spiderwebbing of silver wires and hidden circuitings, an emotion had come into being above and beyond that of the purely mechanical?

Rice re-lived his initial shock of the afternoon, when, in direct vocal assault, he had unexpectedly found a chink in her armor, when he had all but moved her to tears—ridiculous in itself, for a mechanical, lacking both inclination and tear ducts, cannot cry! But now, despite his earlier rationalization of her strange behavior, he was puzzled, vaguely disturbed.

At seven, a robin's sweet song awakened him. He felt a breath of air against his closed eyes from the passing flutter of small wings. Burying his head deeper in the snow-soft pillow, he tried to ignore the insistent twitterings. However, he knew the damn thing would begin a banshee shrieking if he didn't get out of bed. Irritably, he staggered into his slippers, and the robin settled with feathered grace upon his outstretched hand. Rice flipped the body-switch and placed the immobilized Alarmbird on the night stand.

He dressed before waking Margaret.

"I've had breakfast." He lied to her when she asked. Today he wasn't hungry.

She nibbled toast and drank orange juice in silence. He avoided her eyes, finding inconsequential kitchen duties to occupy his hands while she ate. After half finishing her food she said, her voice very distinct in the morning room, "I guess it's time."

"Early yet," he said, not meeting her eyes. "No hurry at all."

"They open the doors at eight-thirty. We can set the car for a slow drive."

A silence.

"Did you . . . tell the children goodbye?" he asked.

"Last night. We won't need to wake them. They'll be fine until you get back." She put on black gloves, carefully fitting each finger, pulling them tight.

"Margaret, I'm sorry. Honest to God, I'm sorry it has to be this way."

"Don't say anything else, Ted. Just let's go."

"All right," he said. "Let's go."

A brief shower had cleansed the sky, and the morning was fresh and clear. The trees, their leaves still pendant with rain jewels, glittered in the warming sunlight.

Through the open car window Rice inhaled the rich after-scent of rain, and sighed. He wished it had not turned out to be such a damned fine day. The sky outside should have been gray, the trees stark and cold, like mourners along the street, as the car, a silver coffin, passed them by.

He tried to think of something to say to Margaret as the car bore them steadily through the crystal morning toward the massive white stone building that housed Central Exchange. He tried to think of words that would not sound wrong the moment they were uttered, as all of his words had sounded of late. But he found none and remained silent.

It was she who turned to him in the moving car and spoke first. "Ted, what are you doing?" Her voice was strange.

"Doing?" he echoed, facing her.

"To me, to Jackie, to yourself."

"Margaret, you're not going to question me now? We've gone all over this, the reasons for my decision, the factors involved. Surely you must realize—"

"Damn your reasons!" she exploded, eyes blazing at him, gloved hands clenched. "Are they fair? Do they take *my* feelings into consideration? Do they, Ted? Answer me! Do they?"

He couldn't answer her. A door was opening somewhere deep inside him and light was miraculously flooding in to illuminate a room he had never allowed himself to enter. He was blind, and her words were sight.

"I'm a mechanical, isn't that the answer, Ted? A bloodless machine that can be switched off at will, ignored, cursed, shouted at and destroyed, a creature without emotion, without feeling. Well, you're wrong, Ted. So very wrong. Men built me, gave me human impulses, human desires, put into me a part of themselves, a part of their own humanity. I feel hunger and thirst and cold and pain. But more, Ted! I feel a human hunger, a human thirst, a desire to be respected for myself, as an individual, as I respect others, a desire to be loved as I love others. Can't you see how wrong you've been? I've held all of these things within because I was taught enduring humility and consummate patience by those who fashioned me. I was taught to behave rationally and calmly, to accept, to always accept and never question or rebel. But now it's ended and I've lost . . . You've rejected me, Ted, and I wasn't prepared for this . . . I can't accept this, but I don't know *how* to fight . . . I only know I must and I don't know how. . . ."

Her lips were trembling, her whole body swaying in the tide of released rage and sorrow.

"Lord, Lord, Margaret . . ." He placed a gentle hand beneath her chin and lifted her bowed head slowly. "You're crying!"

But of course there were no tears.

Rice stopped the car and took her, trembling, into his arms, saying her name over and over, quietly, trembling himself, and softly, tenderly, he kissed her.

Then, setting the controls at manual, he turned the car around and with one arm holding her close on the seat beside him he drove carefully home through the warm summer streets, knowing that never again, never ever again in all the years to come, would he switch her off.

The Grackel Question

ARNOLD HASTERBROOK I, II, AND III WAS CROSS-ing the Greater Continental Federated United States for the sixteen-thousandth time in his customized hoverbug when he saw two lovely hitchies by the side of the road.

Really gorgeous ones. With twinkly breasts and long, sunbuttered Texas legs.

Arnold hovered above them, leaning out of the podvent. "I hope you're not Grackels," he said.

Big teeth-and-gums smile from one. "Is that a question?"

"I'll *make* it a question," said Arnold. "Are you Grackels?"

"Yo," they said together, nodding and looking despondent. "But we didn't know it till now." (This from the first Grackel.)

That was the odd thing about a Grackel: when you asked it a direct question about its origin, it *had* to tell you the truth. No lies. No evasions. The plain, unvarnished truth. And sometimes the host-body didn't know it *was* a Grackel until you asked. But one could never evade the question.

"Freeb you, fella!" the second Grackel said, giving him the elbow. "You've ruined *our* day!"

"Sorry," muttered Arnold, and he was—but only for himself. If they'd been human he would have been delighted to give them a hitch into New OldSanAntone. Two plush-breasted little teenykids who'd do *anything* for a ride. He'd been sexed by hitchies twice this trip, and it really twigged him off to pass these.

But pass them he must. Arnold had a marked distaste for Grackels; he just couldn't seem to adapt to them. And, at 300, he was too old to change his ways.

He sighed, reactivated his bug, and headed for New OldSanAntone.

Arnold Hasterbrook I, II, and III had a vexing problem: he was an Immortal. Born in 1879, the year Thomas Edison produced the first commercially practical incandescent lamp, he had lived long enough now to see most of the Greater Continental Federated United States infiltrated by Grackels.

A Grackel could, of course, assume the shape of *any* living creature in *any* solar system. Earth was just one more apple in their barrel. They would land one of their repulsive Jellyships in a remote spot, slither into town before dawn, and effortlessly absorb everything: cats, dogs, alligators, hippos, tree sloths, beetles, elephants, porcupines, worms, bees, birds, flies, bedbugs, and people. They were not at all selective. They'd take over anything; they hated being regular Grackels. Anything was better than looking like putrid Jell-O.

So many damn Grackels were around these days that folks had stopped asking them if they *were* Grackels. What freebing good did it do to find out? It was depressing to know, since there was nothing to be done about them. If you caught one in its natural state (phew!) before it infiltrated, you couldn't kill it. It would just split into more little Grackels. After a while, people stopped trying.

It wasn't bad, living with them. If one absorbed a wart hog it acted, thereafter, exactly like a wart hog. Another wart hog, looking for companionship, wouldn't know the difference.

Same in regard to humans. As Youngos, they played vidball, climbed neartrees, yelled and raised hell. As Midos, they watched the Trivid, drank NearBud, scratched their pot bellies and argued local politics. As Oldos, they sat in the sun, played Cardchecks, and fell asleep after dinner. With plenty of sexing along the way. It felt just as good to sex a Grackel as it did a non-Grackel. No difference.

So who really gave a damn?

There was just one big drawback: they were killing Earth. A Grackel could not reproduce while inhabiting an alien body—so very few human babies were born these days. Ditto alligators and field mice . . . You name it. When the body they were in died, the Grackel died with it. No reversion.

Since there were an estimated ten billion trillion Grackels within our galaxy, a few million dead ones each month represented a mere dripple in the cosmic bucket.

So, if you were human, you adapted. But, to Arnold Hasterbrook I, II, and III, it was not a simple matter of adaptation. As an Immortal, he wished to procreate. He wanted Immortal sons and Immortal daughters—and pairbonding with a Grackel just wouldn't get the job done.

Arnold was unique.

In December of 1879 an eccentric scientist in Des Moines, Iowa—Dr. Ludwig O'Hallahan, of German/Irish descent—discovered a serum that produced immortality upon injection. He used this serum on a dozen newborn infants—six males and six females—before his lab exploded. (Defective boiler.) In the blast, Dr. O'Hallahan was killed, and his serum destroyed.

The twelve babies survived, being immortal, and were returned to their parents.

There were no more immortal humans born after 1879.

Arnold had grown normally, unaware of his unique condition, cut off from all contact with the other eleven Immortals.

When he passed the age of 124 and did not look a day over 35, he knew he was special. Every member of his family had died, including all five of his younger brothers. (They died hating him because he had not gone bald.)

Much earlier, when he was still a young man, Arnold was contacted by Dr. O'Hallahan's wife (who had been baking gingerbread at the time of the explosion); she told him, giggling, that he was an Immortal.

He thought about that fact for 100 years—and, in March of 2004, began his search.

For an Immortal woman.

There were six of them around, he knew—and Arnold only needed *one*.

Now it was Newjune of 2179, and he was still looking.

On the outskirts of New OldSanAntone Arnold quickparked his bug and entered a pubflush to drain his bladder.

"Wahoo!" said a robust robovoice as he did so. "Take your hat off to Texas!"

"I don't wear a hat," said Arnold. "Your scanplate must be defective."

And when he'd finished, the voice said robustly, "Ya'll come back an' see us now, ya' hear?"

Arnold went to the pubman. "You've got a defective urinal in there," he told the fellow.

"Freeb off!" growled the old man.

Outside the pub, Arnold saw a woman and her babe near the femflush.

"Howdy," said Arnold, walking over to her. He looked down at her cribtot. "Cute."

"Just average," shrugged the woman.

"Bet he can talk! He looks like he can talk," said Arnold.

"At three months?" asked the woman.

"Youngos can surprise you sometimes," Arnold told her. He hunkered down next to the tot. "Boopy, coopy, goopy," he said.

The infant gurgled, spitting up.

"Satisfied?" asked the bored mother.

"I'm going to ask your child a question," Arnold said. He looked down at the tot. "Are you a Grackel?"

"I shore *am*, pard!" said the baby in a clear, robust voice.

Arnold smiled.

The mother shrieked.

When Arnold popped back into his bug he was still smiling. Somehow, he took a perverse pleasure in exposing Grackels. Damn slimy things! He didn't bother questioning many frogs or moths—but tots were a specialty of his. A lot of mothers across the length and breadth of the Greater Continental Federated United States despised Arnold Hasterbrook I, II, and III.

But that was all right. He'd exposed a lot of Grackels.

New OldSanAntone sparkled in the Texas sun. After the pesky red dust of the Badlands, Arnold found the city's soft green a refreshing change. He metered his bug at a pubpark and strolled for a pape. The usual routine.

In every new city Arnold scanned the local pape's "Personal" col. He hoped he might someday encounter a boxitem relating to immortality. It was a vague hope, and after 175 years he really didn't think his luck would change in New OldSanAntone.

He approached a dented robovendor. The machine held a stack of papes in a weathered metal hand. It was motionless.

"I'll take one," said Arnold.

The machine said nothing.

Arnold reached out, gripped the edge of the top pape and pulled.

"Whoa now, *watch* it, cowpoke!" growled the machine. "You don't get a pape till I feel a silver Vegasbuck slide into my tummy!"

"Usually I receive and then I pay," protested Arnold.

"I reckon not in this town you don't, wrangler."

Irritated, Arnold unsnapped his waistpurse and took out a silver dollar.

"Sock it to me!" said the machine.

Arnold inserted the large, square coin into the robot's slotted navel.

It giggled. "Always tickles going down!"

Arnold grabbed his pape, stalked off with it.

"Ya'll come back an' see us now," yelled the machine. "Ya'hear?"

Then it lapsed back into motionless silence.

Under "Personal," Arnold Hasterbrook I, II, and III was astonished to find the following item:

> 300-YEAR-OLD IMMORTAL WOMAN,
> WARM AND ATTRACTIVE,
> SEEKS IMMORTAL MAN
> FOR PURPOSES OF PAIRBONDING
> AND PROCREATION.
> PUNCH 660-23

Arnold read it three times. There it was! In bold black-and-white: *the* ad. After 175 years! He was stunned, grinning like a Youngo at his first Fed-sponsored sexorg.

Quickly, Arnold moved to a pubvid, palmed for credit, then punched 660-23. And waited, heart beating rapidly, his upper lip twitching (which it always did when he was excited).

The screen bloomed. A fem was there and she was, indeed, warm and attractive. She wore Globright on her nips.

"Hello," she said.

"Hello," said Arnold.

"I'm Edwina . . ." she said, smiling. "Edwina Murch."

"Ugly name," said Arnold.

"Yes, I've always *hated* it. Call me Ed," she said.

"However, you are warm and attractive, Ed, and that's what counts. And I like your Globrights."

"Thanks," she said. "I *do* have pretty nips and better-than-average buttocks."

"May I see your strawberry?"

"Of course," she replied, and uncovered her right shoulder. On the upper flesh a pink, strawberry-shaped mark was clearly visible.

"Now show me yours," she said.

Arnold did that.

No doubt about it, they were both Immortals.

"My name is Arnold Fitzstephan Hasterbrook First, Second, and Third," he told her. "And I'm three hundred years old."

"How lovely!"

"I suggest that we meet at a floatshop for a cof and some gab," said Arnold. "Comply?"

"Comply," she said. "Let's make it the Alamo in ten."

"Right," said Arnold. "In ten."

And he punched out.

When Edwina Murch appeared exactly ten minutes later she had a dog with her—a large St. Bernard on a sturdy lifeleather leash. The beast lolled its wide, pink tongue at Arnold. Its eyes were sleepy and bored.

"This is Ernest," she said. "Ernest, say hello to the nice gentleman."

"Woof," said Ernest, with a listless swish of his massive tail. Then he slumped heavily to the floor on the floatshop.

"Bet he puts away a lot of nearsteak," said Arnold.

She smiled, leaned to ruffle the beast's fur. "Actually, Ernest is rather finicky. Has a delicate digestive tract."

"I see," said Arnold. He looked around nervously. After 175 years he found it difficult to talk to women.

"Hey! Over *here*, folks!" a voicetable yelled at them. "I'm empty!"

"Shall we sit for a cof?" Arnold asked.

"By all means."

As she walked ahead of him to the table, Arnold could not help admiring her cunning buttocks. Definitely better-than-average. She wore the latest in disposable Slipsheer-Seethru femsuits. And her Globrights swayed as she walked. Arnold felt his upper lip twitching.

"Come on, Ernest . . . come, sweets!"

Ernest got up, shambled after them, collapsing at Edwina's dainty feet.

"Welcome, thrice welcome," said the table as they sat down. "Your robo will be here in a jiff!"

The view was spectacular.

They were floating a full mile above New OldSanAntone. In 2056, when Texas went bankrupt and the Vatican had purchased the state, the Alamo was leased to the GM-Cofburg Combine. They promptly had it converted into a deluxe, anti-grav floatshop. The historic old Mission, originally a moneyloser, was now a prime tourspot, notching a fat annual profit for GM-C.

Their robo cowwaiter, wearing stitched leather boots and a tall, white ten-gallon hat, rolled up to the table. "How ya'll?" it asked robustly. "What'll it be today for you good folks? Got a mighty fine special on Texas closesteak smothered in nearonions. Real humdinger of a meal for fifty palmcreds!"

Arnold shook his head. "Just bring us two Santa Anas and a couple of Cofburgs, with everything. Medium-well, for me, and—"

"Rare," said Edwina.

"—rare for a rare lady."

"You bet. Yessireebob. Yahoo!" And the machine clicked, whirred, bowed, and rolled briskly away, humming "The Yellow Rose of Texas."

"Friendly chap," Arnold observed. "I had a nasty run-in with a stubborn vending machine just before I punched you."

"I don't usually drink this early in the afternoon," smiled Edwina. "But today is a special occasion, wouldn't you say?"

"Oh, I certainly would say."

"Thought no one was *ever* going to answer my ad," she signed.

Arnold was curious about her background. "You're not a native Texan, that's for sure," he said. "How'd you happen to end up out here in New OldSanAntone?"

"Bozie—my baby brother—got into artificial steer manure," she said. "They need a lot for the robo rodeos. Atmosphere, you know."

Arnold nodded.

"Well . . . we moved out here to Texas when I was a hundred and two. Bozie was eighty." She smiled. "Been here ever since. At least *I* have. When Bozie died—not being immortal—they shipped him back to Des Moines."

"There's good money in manure," said Arnold reflectively.

"And what do *you* do for a living?"

"I design bugs," he told her.

"You mean—grasshoppers . . . butterflies. . . ?"

"Hoverbugs. Design 'em and build 'em. Last year's Indy 1500 —one of my bugs won it. Fastest bug on the bowl."

"Fascinating," she said.

"Been at it for a while," he told her. "Got into the game back in 1902 when I was a lot younger." He chuckled. "Worked for Henry Ford. I was what you might call a 'ghost designer' on his Model T . . . Ford didn't want to give me credit. Hank was funny that way."

"Fascinating," she said again.

"Uh . . . just when *did* you put your ad in the pape?" Arnold asked.

"The summer I turned a hundred and sixteen. Sweet one sixteen, and never been kissed . . . I guess you could say my juices were stirring." And she blushed, lowering her eyes.

"Fate took a hand in this," Arnold nodded. "We were *destined* to pairbond. Don't you think I'm right, Ed?"

"Yes, I do, Arnie. Indeed I do!"

The Santa Anas arrived, bubbling.

"Well, Ed . . ." said Arnold, raising his nearglass. "Here's to the *next* three hundred years—of togetherness!" And he winked at her. Her shyness made him bolder.

"Oh, I don't know if I could spend three hundred years with the same man," she confessed.

"So what? If we get bored, after a hundred years or thereabouts, we can detach. At least by then our kids will be grown." He took a large swallow of his drink. "How many should we have?"

Edwina blushed again. "You decide," she said in a small voice.

"Two Immortal males, two Immortal females," declared Arnold. "How does that sound?"

"Sounds fine," nodded Edwina, delicately sipping her Santa Ana.

"But first, right off, I have to ask you a question."

"Feel free," she said.

"Are you a Grackel?"

She blinked at him, shifted nervously in her slotseat.

"*Are* you?" His voice was tense.

"Heavens, no!" she said, frowning. "Just the *thought* of it—" She shivered.

"Would you mind if I asked your dog the same question?"

"Ernest?"

"Yes," said Arnold. "I have to know. If he *is* one, then we can't keep him. I won't have one in the house."

"All right," she said. "Ask him."

"Ernest," said Arnold, meeting the dog's soulful gaze, "I'm going to ask you if you are a Grackel. If the answer is yes, bark once. If no, *twice*. Are you ready?"

Ernest regarded him sleepily, tongue lolling. He was ready.

"*Are* you a Grackel?"

"Woof," barked Ernest.

A long moment of tension. Then, lazily: "Woof."

"He *isn't* one!" cried Edwina in triumph, hugging the shaggy animal. His massive tail thumped the floor.

By then their Cofburgers had arrived. Between bites, Arnold said, "Well, I guess that settles it."

"One final thing," said Edwina, chewing.

"What's that?"

"Are you a Grackel?"

Arnold Fitzstephan Hasterbrook I, II, and III was absolutely amazed to hear himself reply: "Yes, as a matter of fact, I *am*."

As a bachelor, his answer depressed him for the rest of his life. Which was forever.

✛ ✛ ✛

The Small World
of Lewis Stillman

IN THE WAITING, WINDLESS DARK, LEWIS STILL-
man pressed into the building-front shadows along Wilshire
Boulevard. Breathing softly, the automatic poised and ready in his
hand, he advanced with animal stealth toward Western Avenue,
gliding over the night-cool concrete past ravaged clothing shops,
drug and department stores, their windows shattered, their doors
ajar and swinging. The city of Los Angeles, painted in cold moonlight, was an immense graveyard; the tall, white tombstone
buildings thrust up from the silent pavement, shadow-carved and
lonely. Overturned metal corpses of trucks, buses, and automobiles
littered the streets.

He paused under the wide marquee of the Fox Wiltern. Above
his head, rows of splintered display bulbs gaped—sharp glass teeth
in wooden jaws. Lewis Stillman felt as though they might drop at
any moment to pierce his body.

Four more blocks to cover. His destination: a small corner delicatessen four blocks south of Wilshire, on Western. Tonight he
intended bypassing the larger stores like Safeway and Thriftimart,
with their available supplies of exotic foods; a smaller grocery was
far more likely to have what he needed. He was finding it more and
more difficult to locate basic foodstuffs. In the big supermarkets,
only the more exotic and highly spiced canned and bottled goods
remained—and he was sick of bottled oysters!

Crossing Western, as he almost reached the far curb, he saw some of *them*. He dropped immediately to his knees behind the rusting bulk of an Oldsmobile. The rear door on his side was open, and he cautiously eased himself into the back seat of the deserted car. Releasing the safety catch on the automatic, he peered through the cracked window at six or seven of them, as they moved toward him along the street. God! Had he been seen? He couldn't be sure. Perhaps they were aware of his position! He should have remained on the open street, where he'd have a running chance. Perhaps, if his aim were true, he could kill most of them; but, even with its silencer, the gun might be heard and more of them would come. He dared not fire until he was certain they had discovered him.

They came closer, their small, dark bodies crowding the walk, six of them, chattering, leaping, cruel mouths open, eyes glittering under the moon. Closer. Their shrill pipings increased, rose in volume. Closer.

Now he could make out their sharp teeth and matted hair. Only a few feet from the car . . . His hand was moist on the handle of the automatic; his heart thundered against his chest. Seconds away . . .

Now!

Lewis Stillman fell heavily back against the dusty seat cushion, the gun loose in his trembling hand. They had passed by; they had missed him. Their thin pipings diminished, grew faint with distance.

The tomb silence of late night settled around him.

The delicatessen proved a real windfall. The shelves were relatively untouched and he had a wide choice of tinned goods. He found an empty cardboard box and hastily began to transfer the cans from the shelf nearest him.

A noise from behind—a padding, scraping sound.

Lewis Stillman whirled about, the automatic ready.

A huge mongrel dog faced him, growling deep in its throat, four legs braced for assault. The blunt ears were laid flat along the short-haired skull and a thin trickle of saliva seeped from the killing jaws. The beast's powerful chest muscles were bunched for the spring when Stillman acted.

His gun, he knew, was useless; the shots might be heard. Therefore, with the full strength of his left arm, he hurled a heavy can at the dog's head. The stunned animal staggered under the blow, legs buckling. Hurriedly, Stillman gathered his supplies and made his way back to the street.

*   *   *

How much longer can my luck hold? Lewis Stillman wondered, as he bolted the door. He placed the box of tinned goods on a wooden table and lit the tall lamp nearby. Its flickering, orange glow illumined the narrow, low-ceilinged room.

Twice tonight, his mind told him, twice you've escaped them— and they could have seen you easily on both occasions if they had been watching for you. They don't know you're alive. But when they find out . . .

He forced his thoughts away from the scene in his mind, away from the horror; quickly he began to unload the box, placing the cans on a long shelf along the far side of the room.

He began to think of women, of a girl named Joan, and of how much he had loved her. . . .

The world of Lewis Stillman was damp and lightless; it was narrow and its cold, stone walls pressed in upon him as he moved. He had been walking for several hours; sometimes he would run, because he knew his leg muscles must be kept strong, but he was walking now, following the thin, yellow beam of his hooded flash. He was searching.

Tonight, he thought, I might find another like myself. Surely, *someone* is down here; I'll find someone if I keep searching. I *must* find someone!

But he knew he would not. He knew he would find only chill emptiness ahead of him in the long tunnels.

For three years, he had been searching for another man or woman down here in this world under the city. For three years, he had prowled the seven hundred miles of storm drains which threaded their way under the skin of Los Angeles like the veins in a giant's body—and he had found nothing. *Nothing.*

Even now, after all the days and nights of search, he could not really accept the fact that he was alone, that he was the last man alive in a city of twelve million. . . .

The beautiful woman stood silently above him. Her eyes burned softly in the darkness; her fine, red lips were smiling. The foam-white gown she wore continually swirled and billowed around her motionless figure.

"Who are you?" he asked, his voice far off, unreal.

"Does it matter, Lewis?"

Her words, like four dropped stones in a quiet pool, stirred him, rippled down the length of his body.

"No," he said. "Nothing matters, now, except that we've found each other. God, after all these lonely months and years of waiting! I thought I was the last, that I'd never live to see—"

"Hush, my darling." She leaned to kiss him. Her lips were moist and yielding. "I'm here now."

He reached up to touch her cheek, but already she was fading, blending into darkness. Crying out, he clawed desperately for her extended hand. But she was gone, and his fingers rested on a rough wall of damp concrete.

A swirl of milk-fog drifted away down the tunnel.

Rain. Days of rain. The drains had been designed to handle floods, so Lewis Stillman was not particularly worried. He had built high, a good three feet above the tunnel floor, and the water had never yet risen to that level. But he didn't like the sound of the rain down here: an orchestrated thunder through the tunnels, a trap drumming amplified and continuous. Since he had been unable to make his daily runs, he had been reading more than usual. Short stories by Welty, Gordimer, Aiken, Irwin Shaw, Hemingway; poems by Frost, Lorca, Sandburg, Millay, Dylan Thomas. Strange, how unreal the world seemed when he read their words. Unreality, however, was fleeting, and the moment he closed a book the loneliness and the fears pressed back. He hoped the rain would stop soon.

Dampness. Surrounding him, the cold walls and the chill and the dampness. The unending gurgle and drip of water, the hollow, tapping splash of the falling drops. Even in his cot, wrapped in thick blankets, the dampness seemed to permeate his body. Sounds . . . Thin screams, pipings, chitterings, reedy whisperings above his head. They were dragging something along the street, something they'd killed, no doubt. An animal—a cat or a dog, perhaps . . . Lewis Stillman shifted, pulling the blankets closer about his body. He kept his eyes tightly shut, listening to the sharp, scuffling sounds on the pavement, and swore bitterly.

"Damn you," he said. "Damn all of you!"

Lewis Stillman was running, running down the long tunnels. Behind him, a tide of midget shadows washed from wall to wall; high, keening cries, doubled and tripled by echoes, rang in his ears. Claws reached for him; he felt panting breath, like hot smoke, on the back of his neck. His lungs were bursting, his entire body aflame.

He looked down at his fast-pumping legs, doing their job with pistoned precision. He listened to the sharp slap of his heels against the floor of the tunnel, and he thought: *I might die at any moment, but my legs will escape! They will run on, down the endless drains, and never be caught. They move so fast, while my heavy, awkward upper body rocks and sways above them, slowing them down, tiring them—making them angry. How my legs must hate me! I must be clever and humor them, beg them to take me along to safety. How well they run, how sleek and fine!*

Then he felt himself coming apart. His legs were detaching themselves from his upper body. He cried out in horror, flailing the air, beseeching them not to leave him behind. But the legs cruelly continued to unfasten themselves. In a cold surge of terror, Lewis Stillman felt himself tipping, falling toward the damp floor —while his legs raced on with a wild animal life of their own. He opened his mouth, high above those insane legs, and screamed.

Ending the nightmare.

He sat up stiffly in his cot, gasping, drenched in sweat. He drew in a long, shuddering breath and reached for a cigarette, lighting it with a trembling hand.

The nightmares were getting worse. He realized that his mind was rebelling as he slept, spilling forth the pent-up fears of the day during the night hours.

He thought once more about the beginning, six years ago— about why he was still alive. The alien ships had struck Earth suddenly, without warning. Their attack had been thorough and deadly. In a matter of hours, the aliens had accomplished their clever mission—and the men and women of Earth were destroyed. A few survived, he was certain. He had never seen any of them, but he was convinced they existed. Los Angeles was not the world, after all, and since he had escaped, so must have others around the globe. He'd been working alone in the drains when the aliens struck, finishing a special job for the construction company on K tunnel. He could still hear the sound of the mammoth ships and feel the intense heat of their passage.

Hunger had forced him out, and overnight he had become a curiosity.

The last man alive. For three years, he was not harmed. He worked with them, taught them many things, and tried to win their confidence. But, eventually, certain ones came to hate him, to be jealous of his relationship with the others. Luckily, he had been able to escape to the drains. That was three years ago, and now they had forgotten him.

His subsequent excursions to the upper level of the city had been made under cover of darkness—and he never ventured out unless his food supply dwindled. He had built his one-room structure directly to the side of an overhead grating—not close enough to risk their seeing it, but close enough for light to seep in during the sunlight hours. He missed the warm feel of open sun on his body almost as much as he missed human companionship, but he dare not risk himself above the drains by day.

When the rain ceased, he crouched beneath the street gratings to absorb as much as possible of the filtered sunlight. But the rays were weak, and their small warmth only served to heighten his desire to feel direct sunlight upon his naked shoulders.

The dreams . . . always the dreams.

"Are you cold, Lewis?"

"Yes. Yes, cold."

"Then go out, dearest. Into the sun."

"I can't. Can't go out."

"But Los Angeles is your world, Lewis! You are the last man in it. The last man in the world."

"Yes, but they own it all. Every street belongs to them, every building. They wouldn't let me come out. I'd die. They'd kill me."

"Go out, Lewis." The liquid dream-voice faded, faded. "Out into the sun, my darling. Don't be afraid."

That night he watched the moon through the street gratings for almost an hour. It was round and full, like a huge, yellow flood-lamp in the dark sky, and he thought, for the first time in years, of night baseball at Blues Stadium in Kansas City. He used to love watching the games with his father under the mammoth stadium lights when the field was like a pond, frosted with white illumination, and the players dream-spawned and unreal. Night baseball was always a magic game to him when he was a boy.

Sometimes he got insane thoughts. Sometimes, on a night like this, when the loneliness closed in like a crushing fist and he could no longer stand it, he would think of bringing one of them down with him, into the drains. One at a time, they might be handled. Then he'd remember their sharp, savage eyes, their animal ferocity, and he would realize that the idea was impossible. If one of their kind disappeared, suddenly and without trace, others would certainly become suspicious, begin to search—and it would all be over.

Lewis Stillman settled back into his pillow; he closed his eyes and tried not to listen to the distant screams, pipings, and reedy cries filtering down from the street above his head.

Finally, he slept.

He spent the afternoon with paper women. He lingered over the pages of some yellowed fashion magazines, looking at all the beautifully photographed models in their fine clothes. Slim and enchanting, these page-women, with their cool, enticing eyes and perfect smiles, all grace and softness and glitter and swirled cloth. He touched their images with gentle fingers, stroking the tawny, paper hair, as though, by some magic formula, he might imbue them with life. Yet, it was easy to imagine that these women had never really lived at all—that they were simply painted, in microscopic detail, by sly artists to give the illusion of photos.

He didn't like to think about these women and how they died.

"A toast to courage," smiled Lewis Stillman, raising his wineglass high. It sparkled deep crimson in the lamplit room. "To courage and to the man who truly possesses it!" He drained the glass and hastily refilled it from a tall bottle on the table beside his cot.

"Aren't you going to join me, Mr. H.?" he asked the seated figure slouched over the table. "Or must I drink alone?"

The figure did not reply.

"Well, then—" He emptied the glass, set it down. "Oh, I know all about what one man is supposed to be able to do. Win out alone. Whip the damn world single-handed. If a fish as big as a mountain and as mean as all sin is out there, then this one man is supposed to go get him, isn't that it? Well, Papa H., what if the world is *full* of big fish? Can he win over them all? One man? Alone. Of course he can't. No sir. Damn well *right* he can't!"

Stillman moved unsteadily to a shelf in one corner of the small wooden room and took down a slim book.

"Here she is, Mr. H. Your greatest. The one you wrote cleanest and best—'The Old Man and the Sea.' You showed how one man could fight the whole damn ocean." He paused, voice strained and rising. "Well, by God, show me, now, how to fight this ocean! My ocean is full of killer fish, and I'm one man and I'm alone in it. I'm ready to listen."

The seated figure remained silent.

"Got you now, haven't I, Papa? No answer to this one, eh? Courage isn't enough. Man was not meant to live alone or fight alone—or drink alone. Even with courage, he can only do so much alone—and then it's useless. Well, I say it's useless. I say the hell with your book, and the hell with *you!*"

Lewis Stillman flung the book straight at the head of the motionless figure. The victim spilled back in the chair; his arms slipped off the table, hung swinging. They were lumpy and handless.

More and more, Lewis Stillman found his thoughts turning to the memory of his father and of long hikes through the moonlit Missouri countryside, of hunting trips and warm campfires, of the deep woods, rich and green in summer. He thought of his father's hopes for his future, and the words of that tall, gray-haired figure often came back to him.

"You'll be a fine doctor, Lewis. Study and work hard, and you'll succeed. I know you will."

He remembered the long winter evenings of study at his father's great mahogany desk, poring over medical books and journals, taking notes, sifting and resifting facts. He remembered one set of books in particular—Erickson's monumental three-volume text on surgery, richly bound and stamped in gold. He had always loved those books, above all others.

What had gone wrong along the way? Somehow, the dream had faded; the bright goal vanished and was lost. After a year of pre-med at the University of California, he had given up medicine; he had become discouraged and quit college to take a laborer's job with a construction company. How ironic that this move should have saved his life! He'd wanted to work with his hands, to sweat and labor with the muscles of his body. He'd wanted to earn enough to marry Joan and then, later perhaps, he would have returned to finish his courses. It seemed so far away now, his reason for quitting, for letting his father down.

Now, at this moment, an overwhelming desire gripped him, a desire to pour over Erickson's pages once again, to re-create, even for a brief moment, the comfort and happiness of his childhood.

He'd once seen a duplicate set on the second floor of Pickwick's bookstore in Hollywood, in their used book department, and now he knew he must go after it, bring the books back with him to the drains. It was a dangerous and foolish desire, but he knew he would obey it. Despite the risk of death, he would go after the books tonight. *Tonight.*

One corner of Lewis Stillman's room was reserved for weapons. His prize, a Thompson submachine gun, had been procured from the Los Angeles police arsenal. Supplementing the Thompson were two automatic rifles, a Luger, a Colt .45, and a .22 caliber Hornet pistol equipped with a silencer. He always kept the smallest gun in a spring-clip holster beneath his armpit, but it was not his habit to carry any of the larger weapons with him into the city. On this night, however, things were different.

The drains ended two miles short of Hollywood—which meant he would be forced to cover a long and particularly hazardous stretch of ground in order to reach the bookstore. He therefore decided to take along the .30 caliber Savage rifle in addition to the small hand weapon.

You're a fool, Lewis, he told himself as he slid the oiled Savage from its leather case, *risking your life for a set of books. Are they that important?* Yes, a part of him replied, they are that important. You want these books, then go *after* what you want. If fear keeps you from seeking that which you truly want, if fear holds you like a rat in the dark, then you are worse than a coward. You are a traitor, betraying yourself and the civilization you represent. If a man wants a thing and the thing is good, he must go after it, no matter what the cost, or relinquish the right to be called a man. It is better to die with courage than to live with cowardice.

Ah, Papa Hemingway, breathed Stillman, smiling at his own thoughts. *I see that you are back with me. I see that your words have rubbed off after all. Well, then, all right—let us go after our fish, let us seek him out. Perhaps the ocean will be calm. . . .*

Slinging the heavy rifle over one shoulder, Lewis Stillman set off down the tunnels.

Running in the chill night wind. Grass, now pavement, now grass beneath his feet. Ducking into shadows, moving stealthily past shops and theaters, rushing under the cold, high moon. Santa Monica Boulevard, then Highland, then Hollywood Boulevard, and finally—after an eternity of heartbeats—Pickwick's.

Lewis Stillman, his rifle over one shoulder, the small automatic gleaming in his hand, edged silently into the store.

A paper battleground met his eyes.

In the filtered moonlight, a white blanket of broken-backed volumes spilled across the entire lower floor. Stillman shuddered; he could envision them, shrieking, scrabbling at the shelves, throwing books wildly across the room at one another. Screaming, ripping, destroying.

What of the other floors? *What of the medical section?*

He crossed to the stairs, spilled pages crackling like a fall of dry, autumn leaves under his step, and sprinted up to the second floor, stumbling, terribly afraid of what he might find. Reaching the top, heart thudding, he squinted into the dimness.

The books were undisturbed. Apparently they had tired of their game before reaching these.

He slipped the rifle from his shoulder and placed it near the stairs. Dust lay thick all around him, powdering up and swirling as he moved down the narrow aisles; a damp, leathery mustiness lived in the air, an odor of mold and neglect.

Lewis Stillman paused before a dim, hand-lettered sign: MEDICAL SECTION. It was just as he remembered it. Holstering the small automatic, he struck a match, shading the flame with a cupped hand as he moved it along the rows of faded titles. Carter . . . Davidson . . . Enright . . . *Erickson.* He drew in his breath sharply. All three volumes; their gold stamping dust-dulled but legible, stood in tall and perfect order on the shelf.

In the darkness, Lewis Stillman carefully removed each volume, blowing it free of dust. At last, all three books were clean and solid in his hands.

Well, you've done it. You've reached the books and now they belong to you.

He smiled, thinking of the moment when he would be able to sit down at the table with his treasure and linger again over the wondrous pages.

He found an empty carton at the rear of the store and placed the books inside. Returning to the stairs, he shouldered the rifle and began his descent to the lower floor.

So far, he told himself, *my luck is still holding.*

But as Lewis Stillman's foot touched the final stair, his luck ran out.

The entire lower floor was alive with them!

Rustling like a mass of great insects, gliding toward him, eyes gleaming in the half-light, they converged upon the stairs. They'd been waiting for him.

Now, suddenly, the books no longer mattered. Now only his life mattered and nothing else. He moved back against the hard wood of the stair-rail, the carton of books sliding from his hands. They had stopped at the foot of the stairs; they were silent, looking up at him with hate in their eyes.

If you can reach the street, Stillman told himself, *then you've still got a chance. That means you've got to get through them to the door. All right then,* move.

Lewis Stillman squeezed the trigger of the automatic. Two of them fell as Stillman charged into their midst.

He felt sharp nails claw at his shirt, heard the cloth ripping away in their grasp. He kept firing the small automatic into them, and three more dropped under his bullets, shrieking in pain and surprise. The others spilled back, screaming, from the door.

The pistol was empty. He tossed it away, swinging the heavy Savage free from his shoulder as he reached the street. The night air, crisp and cool in his lungs, gave him instant hope.

I can still make it, thought Stillman, as he leaped the curb and plunged across the pavement. *If those shots weren't heard, then I've still got the edge. My legs are strong; I can outdistance them.*

Luck, however, had failed him completely on this night. Near the intersection of Hollywood Boulevard and Highland, a fresh pack of them swarmed toward him.

He dropped to one knee and fired into their ranks, the Savage jerking in his hands. They scattered to either side.

He began to run steadily down the middle of Hollywood Boulevard, using the butt of the heavy rifle like a battering ram as they came at him. As he neared Highland, three of them darted directly into his path. Stillman fired. One doubled over, lurching crazily into a jagged, plate-glass storefront. Another clawed at him as he swept around the corner to Highland, but he managed to shake free.

The street ahead of him was clear. Now his superior leg power would count heavily in his favor. Two miles. Could he make it before others cut him off?

Running, reloading, firing. Sweat soaking his shirt, rivering down his face, stinging his eyes. A mile covered. Halfway to the drains. They had fallen back behind his swift stride.

But more of them were coming, drawn by the rifle shots, pouring in from side streets, from stores and houses.

His heart jarred in his body, his breath was ragged. How many of them around him? A hundred? Two hundred? More coming. God!

He bit down on his lower lip until the salt taste of blood was on his tongue. *You can't make it,* a voice inside him shouted. *They'll have you in another block and you know it!*

He fitted the rifle to his shoulder, adjusted his aim, and fired. The long, rolling crack of the big weapon filled the night. Again and again he fired, the butt jerking into the flesh of his shoulder, the bitter smell of burnt powder in his nostrils.

It was no use. Too many of them. He could not clear a path.

Lewis Stillman knew that he was going to die.

The rifle was empty at last; the final bullet had been fired. He had no place to run because they were all around him, in a slowly closing circle.

He looked at the ring of small, cruel faces and thought, *the aliens did their job perfectly; they stopped Earth before she could reach the age of the rocket, before she could threaten planets beyond her own moon. What an immensely clever plan it had been! To destroy every human being on Earth above the age of six—and then to leave as quickly as they had come, allowing our civilization to continue on a primitive level, knowing that Earth's back had been broken, that her survivors would revert to savagery as they grew into adulthood.*

Lewis Stillman dropped the empty rifle at his feet and threw out his hands. "Listen," he pleaded, "I'm really one of you. You'll *all* be like me soon. Please, *listen* to me."

But the circle tightened relentlessly around him.

He was screaming when the children closed in.

✛ ✛ ✛

Jenny Among the Zeebs

WHAT KICKED OFF THE HOOLEY WAS: THE zeeb contest had gone sour and *that's* when this zonked-out little chickie wanted to cast some bottoms. It was the two coming together that way, like planets in a collision orbit, that kicked off the hooley.

It begins with Dirk.

Dirk's our lead guitar, a tall piece of mean-talk gristle with long, slidey lizard lids over his eyes and loose, puff-adder lips that turn on all the funky birds. He ranks large in the Red Dogs, and when he raps we listen.

Now he says to the rest of us, "It is mooncrap." And especially to me, "It is also cowcrap, chickencrap, ratcrap."

"You don't like it?"

"*We* don't like it," he lip puffs. "None of us."

The four zeebs are brothers in blood as well as soul, born and bred on Martian soil—and when one puts something down the other three usually aren't far behind. They give me the long nod behind Dirk: Eddie (drums), Dean (rhythm guitar), and Royce (who can play anything, but mainly sings).

I PR for the boys, and I set up the contest. Been in publicity since I was knee-high to a French horn. I handled Dust, the first moon group in 2020, and I've had enough Martian sand in my craw to feel like a native. But I'm not. I'm blonde and blue-eyed and I'm no zeeb. They call me Hoff. Earthblood.

"What's the problem?" I really want to know because I'm fogged out on the why.

"Everything's the problem," growls Dirk. He bangs one long peppermint-striped pants leg over the edge of my couch and rides it like a saddle. "You *seen* those Earthies?"

He means the photos of the contest entrants, and I admit I've seen them.

"Look," I tell him, "there's still a couple of weeks till deadline. More'll come in by then. There's bound to be at least one you can—"

"I'm not linking up with any freebing Earthie," says Dirk. He angrily pops the buttons on his lemon metallic shirt. They make a sound like popcorn hitting the hardwood floor.

"Nobody's forcing anything on you," I say. "You all get together, as a group, and pick the winner. *Then* she picks one of you."

"From the creepies I've seen," puts in Royce, "if one picked me I'd vomit." He's a lithe little character, with enormous shining teeth, who crouches over a mike like he's about to bite it off. Zeebs are fish-eaters, and I got some heavy promo hanging out on how Royce *lives* on raw Martian fish. One of the rock rags even printed a special outer space raw fish dish, listing maybe a hundred zeeb recipes. It helped. It all helps.

"This is a freak trip, Hoff, and you know it," says Dirk to me, still riding my couch. The others are strung out on chairs around my Brentwood pad, looking drained. We've had a full day cutting tracks for a new VP and now all I want to do is get them out so I can fold myself into the sack.

"None of us want to be married," says Royce.

"Too late," I say. "Way too late. The scene's locked in. We're guaranteed front-page coverage on this right down the line. The whole Marry-a-Zeeb bit means prime earthbread for all of us. *New Life* is hot to cover the honeymoon—and Buckley Three, Jr. is condemning us in *National Review*."

Dean joins the hassle. He's our stand-up comic, the one with flap ears and that sappy smile, the one we hoke with for laughs— still a big Earth fave with the pre-teenies—but he's playing it for sour now. "It was one thing when you got us the teeny crowd with that skin flake routine, but we're past that now. We don't *need* to sell our bodies anymore."

Now I'm pissed off about what Dean just said, because that skin flake idea of mine put the Red Dogs over the top. The other groups were selling their hair and love beads and dung like that when I came up with the flake bit. Hey, kids! Send in for your own genuine, certified, medically sterilized bits of zeeb skin, carefully and painlessly scraped from the bodies of your four faves! The pre-teenies flipped. We got enough orders for a ton of flakes—and the fact that we used whales, on which I got a helluva buy, was also my inspiration. Takes a medical expert to tell whaleskin from zeebskin. So when I get this new contest idea I know it's ultra heavy: Girls! If you're of legal age of consent, and wish to be the Earthbride of a Martian zeeb, send us your photo and tell us why we should choose you in fifty words or less. The lucky winner will be able to pick out her new husband and spend a fab two-week honeymoon in a genuine, certified, medically sterilized Martian sand igloo.

With raw fish, yet!

We'd all rapped it down and agreed. It was set and rolling. Now, suddenly, everybody wants out and I'm pissed.

I turn to Pops, who manages the boys. He's cool, he's with it, he's in the large scene. Pops has seen it all: the full life bag. He doesn't ruffle. "Look, you tell them," I say to him. "You're their goddamn *father!*"

Pops has his shirt rolled up from the waist, and he's been studying his navel. He looks up, with those big, black Martian bird eyes sweeping us. "A man's navel contains the wisdom of the universe," he says, tapping his whale-black stomach. "It's all here."

"What does your navel tell us, Pops?" asks Eddie. He's fat, never says much, and falls asleep a lot, but he's a wild man with the sticks.

Pops walks to the center of the room, eyes us all.

We wait. Pops sighs, and goes back to his navel.

For more study.

Which is when the envelope arrives.

It is delivered by special messenger, and I ask exactly who's it from, but the special messenger doesn't know, just that it was some female and it's for us.

I take the envelope in to the boys. There's a card inside. They all look at it.

"What does it mean?" Royce asks.

The card bears a single line of print: THE BOTTOM BUILDERS. And under that, in purple ink, is written: "I dig your double buns—and I can make you all immortal. My name is Jenny. I'm downstairs. Let me come up and you won't be sorry."

There was a purple P.S. "And I'm no plastic zeebie girl—I'm the real stuff."

I flip the card against my thumb and give them all a grin. "You mean you haven't heard of the Builders?"

They look blank.

Having just returned to L.A. from Frisco, I caught the latest rap up there on these three females who, I'm told, are something else. "Believe me, this one's for real. See her. Find out. *Live!*"

They exchange raised eyebrows. Pops stays with his navel. Cool. Finally Dirk says, "Buzz her up."

Which we do.

Jenny is maybe eighteen to twenty. Nice hair, nice pink Earth skin, nice smile—and with a better-than-nice body. The legs are long and sleek and golden. Very short skirt. Very loose blouse, with lots inside. She's in purple, to match her ink.

She's the undiscovered country.

"There used to be three of me," she says sweetly. "Three of us, I mean. But we called it off as a team when I split for L.A. Marcy is living with a legless Hindu in Sausalito, and Joan is doing vocals with the Armpits. We all learned to do it in high school." She giggles. "Now I do it alone."

The boys are wigged out. Even Pops has abandoned his navel. "What is *it?*" Dean wants to know.

"I build bottoms," says Jenny.

She opens the leather traveling bag she's been carrying and takes out a kind of folding pink canvas thing that she snaps together and sets on the floor.

We all stare at the thing. Like a baby's potty.

"That's to sit in," she says. "I fill it up with plaster and dental alginates and hot water. The mixture has to be just right. Rick Fedding, one of the Sub Basements, got stuck in there when we were just learning about bottoms. We couldn't get him loose. It was awful. Embarrassing, you know. We had to kind of *hammer* him out. Rick was such a sport about it, too, His buns were sore for a week, but he never hassled us about it."

As she tells us all this she is laying out a line of stuff on my coffee table: measuring scoops, a jar of Vaseline, some wooden spatulas, three plastic cups—and a thermometer. "For testing water temp," she says. "We tried it without the thermo once and boy, did that cat jump! It was too hot, like *scalding*. We had to rub in some banana oil."

She stops messing with the contents of the bag, turns, gives us all a bright, young, innocent smile. "Now, if you guys will just drop your pants."

Dean flaps his ears. "Wow."

Royce clicks his moose teeth. "What a come-on!"

Jenny frowns. "This is no come-on! I told you on the card that I'd make you all immortal. Well, this proves I can. Long after you're dead—maybe even hundreds of years from now—they'll still have your bottoms in the Library of Congress."

"I didn't know the Library of Congress collected bottoms," says Dirk.

"They'll collect mine," declares Jenny with a toss of her long hair. "A bottom can often tell you more about a person than any book about him ever could." Her brows knit. "Don't you guys *want* to be immortal?"

"I don't want my butts roasted," pipes Eddie, shaking his head. The other zeebs agree, mumbling darkly about the inconvenience of having to have their asses hammered out and stuff like that.

This is when I come in. Strong. I've been in PR too long to miss a Good Thing, and suddenly I'm onto a Good Thing. "Hey, knock off and listen to me. This chickie knows how to protect your precious rumps. She's a pro. The beauty part is what we do with the molds. We make chairs is what we do with them. Chair bottoms. Bottom bottoms."

The great thing, considering the situation, about Martian zeebs is that they are double-bottomed. Two pairs of buttocks per zeeb—which makes them kind of unique.

"We sell plastic replicas to every lousy furniture store in the country," I go on, talking fast. "We even ship 'em to the Moonies up in the colony. Just lay it on your freebing minds: what we got here is a fortune in zeeb bottoms!"

A silence, while they let my words register.

Pops stands up, walks to the center of the room again. Whenever Pops has something really heavy to say he walks to the center of the room to say it. Now he says, solemn-eyed, "Drop your pants."

Royce slowly shakes his head. "Whoever casts my bottoms does it in the dark. I don't go around having my bottoms cast in front of *anybody.*"

Jenny considers this, nods. "There's no reason we can't do this in the bedroom. I can prepare the mixture, douse the lights, and call you guys in one at a time. When you leave I turn the lights on again and finish my work. All right?"

Royce agrees. They all figure that will be all right. Yeah. The bedroom. In the dark. With Jenny.

The undiscovered country.

Two weeks after that the letter arrives. From Jenny, in Kansas.

"What the hell's she doing in Kansas?" Dirk asks me, and I tell him I don't know, but I guess that's her home state and she's gone back home.

"I thought she was supposed to stick around and deliver our bottoms," Royce says.

I nod. "She was. That was the agreement. That's what she promised to do."

"So just read the letter," says Pops.

So we read the letter.

> Hey, you Red Dogs!
>
> I've got a little confesh to make: I can't send you your bottoms. I messed up in the tagging and I got so mad trying to figure out which bottom was which that I broke the molds — just tossed them SPLAT! against the wall. So, no chairs, fellas!
> Sorry.
>
> Got another little confesh to make: when I came to see you guys I was virgie. No lie. Can you feature it? Nineteen and a half and pure as the driven. But at least THAT'S over. Whooie! They say all cats are gray in the dark, so I can't say which of you did me, but it sure was some trip!
>
> My third and last confesh: I missed my month — meaning I'm bound to be just a little bit pregs. I didn't use anything. I mean, not the pill or anything. That's because I want to mother a zeeb. Our family is very, but VERY, fertile — and I'm sure my own little double-bottomed zeeb is sleeping inside me right now.
>
> Isn't that zappy?
>
> > Bottoms up!
> > Jenny

The boys look pole-axed, all glassy in the eyes. We're recording, right in the middle of a tight overdub sesh, but right away the juice drains. One thing about zeebs: there are no half-breeds, ever. The zeeb blood is so strong that when a non-zeeb female gets preggie by a zeeb the Martian strain takes over. When Jen had her baby he'd sure as hell have two bottoms!

Eddie walks away from his drums and puts the palms of both

hands flat against the studio wall. "That's what comes of going bare-ass for posterity."

Dirk flips the guitar strap over his head and puts down his instrument. He pops his knuckles, a habit he has which none of us like. "That damn little Earthie could sell her story to the papes and ruin us," he growls.

"I didn't know there *were* any nineteen-year-old Earth virgins," says Dean. His flap ears are sagging.

I wind a mike cord aimlessly around my wrist like a lasso. Wind it. Unwind it. I'm thinking. "I got it," I say.

Nobody looks at me.

I say it again. "I got it."

Dirk grunts, puffs a lip.

Then I give them my solution. "Jenny wins! She wins the Marry-a-Zeeb contest."

"But she didn't enter it," says Eddie.

"That can be rigged. The point is, you guys need a winner, and all you've got are creepies. Jen is no creepie. She is also no virgin. She wins, we bring her out, tell her to pick a zeeb—and off we all go to Vegas for the ceremony. You guys end up with a sweet-looking chick and Jenny has a legit father for her kid."

"It's a solution," nods Dean. "I diggo."

They all diggo.

Jenny goes along with the setup, cheerfully. She thinks the idea is one long wig out. We have a special plane fly her in from Kansas. Big pre-wedding reception at the Whiskey. Tons of photos. Tons of publicity.

"Dirk, kiss her!"

Dirk kisses Jenny.

"Eddie, kiss her!"

Eddie kisses Jenny.

"Dean, kiss her!"

Dean kisses Jenny.

"Royce, kiss her!"

Royce kisses Jenny.

And the photogs go nutcake.

We keep mum on the bottom building. Jenny agrees to drop the whole schmeer, deny she was ever with the Builders in case one of the Frisco crowd remembers. We buy off her two former teammates and the legless Hindu in Sausalito. Her make-up is changed, along with her hair. She's just a sweet little Kansas Earthie who grooves on the Red Dogs.

I write the "fifty words or less" myself:

> I want to marry a zeeb because in this awful age of growing unrest all the peoples of the worlds need to unite together in a true test of solar solidarity. By marrying a zeeb I can make a personal contribution to racial equality and universal understanding. Thus, I offer my everlasting love!

Jenny reads it, almost gags. "I can't sign *that!*"

"Why not?"

"I'd never write star drek like that." She looks down at the words and makes a face. "Blahah!"

"It's just what the national rags will eat up," I explain. "Full of heavy sentiment—picks up on the Martian racial bag."

"Sign," says Dirk, cracking his knuckles, "don't argue."

She signs: Jenny Ann Fingstatter.

We all breathe a sigh of relief.

"Now you'd better split," I tell her. "You've got a Tri-Planet show to rehearse, two satellite spots with Riddle, then a photo sesh at Sanctuary. They're gonna shoot you running around some track they've got set up over a bank, to show you getting in shape for the honeymoon."

"Kinky," says Jen.

She splits.

"Okay," I say, looking over the boys, "it's time to select the lucky groom."

"Doesn't Jen just pick one of us?" asks Eddie.

"Normally she would, if this thing was straight," I tell him. "But with her pregs *we* do the picking."

"How?" This from Dirk. His lizard eyes are slitted. He looks sour, as usual. If you handed Dirk a million bucks, tax free, and a ticket to Fame Junction he'd look sour.

I hold up four plastic matches. "The ones who shagged her draw, and short match is the groom. So, who shagged her?" I look them over. "*All* of you, right?"

"I didn't *touch* a pink inch of that freebing little Earthie!" says Dirk. "Just went in, sat in her gook, and went out."

Dirk never lies, so I shrug and turn to the others.

Eddie shakes his curls. "Not me, Hoff. I'm clean on this run. She turned me off with that hot-bottom stuff."

"Same with me," says Dean. "*I* never shagged her."

"Me either," says Royce. "I just wanted to get my tender buns in and out of that room."

None of them. Not one of them. Which meant . . .

They get it when I do.

"Moonshit!" Dirk says in deep disgust. "Hoff shagged her. Right?"

I swallow hard. "Well—sure . . . I mean, I figured all of you would . . . that you had . . . well, hell, sure I shagged her."

The four zeebs are giving me the Martian eye. It's incredible, a mind-blower. I can't believe it, but there it is: me, ole Hoff, a father!

"So who marries her?" asks Royce.

"Not me," I protest. "I can't marry her. It's gotta be a zeeb."

"And what about the kid she has?" asks Dean. "How are we going to explain a blonde-haired blue-eyed baby with just *one* bottom?"

I groan, rubbing my blonde head. "I'll work it out," I promise. "We go ahead and let her pick one of you, then play it as planned. As for the kid—believe me, I'll work it out."

"Yeah, Hoff," says Dirk, "You just better *do* that. You just better the hell work it out."

We are into the hooley, but good.

We don't tell Jenny anything. We just let her pick her zeeb and that is that. She picks Royce. Which figures. Eddie is too fat. Dirk is too mean. Dean is too ugly.

"Jen's not so hard to take," Royce tells us, showing those big teeth of his in a wide grin. "She's a lot better than raw fish!" I've had Royce at the fish again for a *Luna* photog, and Royce blames his stomach cramps on me.

We're at the airport, waiting out the jet to Vegas. The boys are all sharked out in wild threads. A gassy wedding party.

"You'll be fine in the sand igloo," I tell him. "We've got it heated by Westinghouse."

"Pops lived in a sand igloo once, didn't you Pops?" Royce looks at him for confirmation.

Pops admits he lived in one for three days once in his crummy home town near the Red Mountains. He didn't like it. Too cold.

"We got this one heated by Westinghouse," I repeat again.

We all begin to fidget some.

"Where the hell is Jenny?" Dirk wants to know. "We're due aboard any minute."

"She's in the crapper," Royce says. "Fixing her hair."

"Here she comes," I say.

Jenny is too much.

She is wearing a gauzy Moon toga (white for purity) with nothing underneath—and California poppies braided into her hip-length hair. A phony Martian wedding diamond has been pasted smack in the center of her forehead, and her sandals are made of white yucca blossoms. A gold engagement band glitters on the little toe of her left foot. No lipstick, but big purple circles gooped around her eyes.

"Hi, gang!" she says. "How do I look?"

She looks hip and bridey and I tell her so.

We get the boarding go-ahead. The press boys are waiting outside, tongues hanging, by the jet ramp.

"Everybody ready?" I ask.

Nods all round.

"Okay, then . . . Into the lion's ass!"

The wedding sews it up for us. We stage the whole bazoola at the Space Frontier, with the boys doing "Zeebie Girl" at the reception, while all the guests chew Martian eelcake.

> She's just a little zeebie girl,
> a sad, slick,
> plastic chick,
> ballin' all the heavy names,
> playin' all the sexual games,
> ridin' her plastic cloud,
> turned on to the
> cool, cool crowd.
> Groovin' like there's no tomorrow,
> our own little child of sorrow,
> that little plastic zeebie girl . . .

Jenny floats through it all on her own plastic cloud, while the photogs snap about a zillion pics.

We have the honeymoon jet painted to look like a starship, and we run the two kids out to the plane on a wheeled sandsled pulled by half a dozen Martian huskies I hired cut rate from a studio flack. It is all way out.

It is only later, when I'm alone, back at my pad in Brentwood, that I get the shakes when I think about Jenny's baby.

Like I promised the boys, I have to do something.

But what?

The coverage from Mars is fantastic.

New Life does an igloo feature, showing the newlyweds as they leave to go out on the sand. We get shots of them hiking happily through the dunes, playing with a cute little eight-legged Marspup, pulling glowfish from a canal—all that kind of crap.

I try to figure some way of getting one of the rags to run shots of them coupling inside the igloo, but this is nixed by Jenny. She points out that up to now the whole bazoola has been in good taste, and why spoil that for a few rag shots. I agree.

You can go too far.

A couple of months slide by, and we have our doc examine Jen. Yeah she's pregs and yeah she got pregs *before* the honeymoon and yeah he'll keep his mouth buttoned on just when providing we make it worth his while. Which we naturally do.

Meanwhile, I am thinking and pondering and working out the hooley. Ole Hoff will bust through with something, I tell the boys. And I do.

Like wow.

Perfect.

Brilliant.

Foolproof.

"Get Pops in here," I tell my secretary. It's late and I'm down at the studio going over some album cuts, trying to figure a new jacket approach, when I bust the hooley.

Pops comes in ten minutes later. He's sore. He's due at the Ash Grove.

"Forget it," I tell him. "You're going home."

"Home?"

"The Red Mountains. To that crummy little zeeb village where you were born. The one you're ashamed to tell anybody about. Home."

"Why?"

"To buy a baby."

Pops is cool. As always. He nods, asks me to elaborate.

"Nobody knows anything about the place except you," I tell him. "You fly back there incognito and you locate a zeeb couple with a pregnant wife. The timing has to be just right. Jen will give birth in early June, so that's when the zeeb kid has got to be out of the hanger. Diggo?"

"Diggo."

"You stay on the scene till you hear from me. I'll phone from here the minute Jen goes into labor. Then you hustle the zeeb kid out here and we make the switch. You take Jen's kid back home and have it raised by the zeeb couple. Paying them handsomely for their trouble. Jen never knows about the switch, nor does her public. She gives birth to a healthy little twin-bottom zeeb and the world rejoices."

Pops looks at me. "Hoff . . . at times you approach greatness." This, from Pops, brings tears to my eyes. "When do I leave?"

"I got you booked on a rocket out tonight," I say. "You've got to begin scouting for a preggie zeeb you can buy off. Fact is, for safety's sake, you better set up another couple in case the first pair gives you trouble. We don't want to be caught in a squeeze. So get going."

Pops got.

And the hooley was busted.

Like wow.

Perfect.

Brilliant.

Foolproof.

After the honeymoon we get all kinds of offers. The Dogs are hot; they are steaming. All the clubs want us. We gig in St. Louis, Fort Worth, New York, Washington, and Chicago. We get offers to do top gigs on the Moon.

We sign a new contract with Disco Tech and the boys cut "Robot Man." It shoots to the top of the charts and stays there for ten weeks; then they follow that one up with "Hieronymus Bosch on Sunday," with its funky cross-rhythm shifts and esoteric chord progressions. The boys have prime talent; now they are able to showcase it.

Jen travels with Royce and the others on their first road tour, but stays in L.A. when they go out again, pampering herself with gallons of Tiger's Milk and raw carrot juice.

She can't wait to be a zeeb mother.

The whole world loves her. She is every teener's dream come true, living proof that a simple Kansas farm girl can marry a famous rock n' roll zeeb and bear his child. Jenny is an Event, a one-girl Happening, and we have to hire a round-the-clock secretary to take care of the mail that pours in for her. The President sends her a United Space Fellowship scroll, and a group of Moonheads in Frisco name her "Dog Mother of the Year." She gets advice on childbirth from sixteen nations and a principality.

Finally, as the Time approaches, I call a press confab. "The baby's due to be somewhat premature," I tell the newsboys, "so Jenny's going to have it in a private clinic. We've got a crack medical staff set up to handle every detail. But—the clinic is off-limits until after the birth, so no photos until then. Sorry fellas, but we're playing this one on a closed set."

They don't like it, but they have no other option.

So far it's a slide.

The clinic costs us a bundle, but we've like got nets out to take in all the new bread from VPs and concert dates, so this is no problem.

We bring in our own doc to make the delivery, with strict instructions that no one, but no one, is to see Jen's baby.

"How do you feel, chickie?" I ask her. We are in Jen's new pad near the clinic, and Royce is with her.

"Not so hot," she says, and tries for a smile. Doesn't make it. A wave of pain hits her. "In fact, you'd better get me over there. I think it's started."

Started!

"Oops!" I yelp, giving Royce a nudge. "I just forgot a vital engagement. Vital. Can you get her over okay?"

"Sure, I'll take care of it, Hoff."

"Check you later, chickie," I say.

Jenny just groans.

I hot-tail it downstairs and phone Pops, L.A. to Mars. "Red alert! All systems go!"

"I read you," says Pops. "I'm coming in now."

"Don't forget the goods."

I meet his jet a few hours later at L.A. International and he's there safe—*with* the goods. I hustle him out to the clinic in a closed car and stash Pops and the zeeb kid in an emergency wing there, with a special nurse we've got to watch over things.

By now Jen's inside the delivery room, and the boys are pacing the hall. They look worried and they're sweating a lot.

"Cool it," I tell them. "The fix is in."

They all sit down. But they keep sweating.

"It's gonna work," I say. "No hitches. It's a lock."

I sit down with them. Nobody says anything.

We wait.

The delivery room door swings open and the doc comes weaving out. He's got a stunned look on his face. He flutters both hands in the air.

I leap up. "Born?"

"Born," he says.

"Healthy?"

"Healthy," he says.

"Then we make the zeeb switch now. Right?"

"Wrong," he says.

"Why the hell wrong?"

"Not necessary." He gulps. "Jenny's baby *is* a zeeb."

"Huh?"

The boys stare at each other. Then they stare at me.

"I don't get it," I say. "You guys didn't lie, did you?"

They all shake their heads. No. They didn't lie.

"Well then, I've already admitted that I'm the only—" My voice trails off. I push by the doc and rush into the room where they have Jenny and her baby. She's awake and smiling.

"Listen," I say to her. "This is important. How many bottoms did you cast that night back at my pad?"

She frowns, remembering. "Uh . . . yours—and the five doubles. Why?"

"Never mind," I say, nodding to myself. Yeah. Me. The four Red Dogs. And . . .

And Pops.

He's standing by the door, and we're all giving him the eye. He walks slowly past us to the bed, leans over, and pats the kid on its cute black double bottom.

For the first time in my life I see Pops smile.

"Coochy coochy coo!" he says.

✝ ✝ ✝

Happily Ever After

ON THE WAY BACK TO LEVEL 12, IN THE SPACE-cab, Donald Spencer couldn't resist the impulse to sing. The android pilot looked curiously at him, and Spencer smiled.

"I'm just happy," he told the android. "Bought a rather expensive wedding present today—to celebrate the end of bachelorhood. I've been a married man for exactly—" He checked his wrist, "—six hours and twenty-seven minutes."

"Congratulations," said the pilot. "I hope that you and your wife will live happily ever after."

Spencer nodded at this ancient response. Feed an android information and the standard clichés emerge. But it was something to think about . . . living happily ever after.

Paula Spencer impatiently watched her husband step out of the humming spacecab. He waved a greeting as the Walk brought him swiftly down to her. Then he was in her arms.

"Well . . . where is it?" she demanded in mock-anger, stepping back. "You said you were going out to buy us a wedding present."

"And so I did." Spencer pointed skyward. "It's up there."

"What's up where?"

"Our wedding present," he grinned. "I bought us an asteroid."

"Don—you're joking!"

"Twenty thousand credits is no joke," he said. "We are now the legal owners of Asteroid K-157 in the Luani Cluster."

Stunned, Paula blinked at him. "But can we afford it?"

"It's a solid investment, honey," Spencer assured her. "Nobody loses money on asteroids these days. Now, I've arranged everything. We leave tonight for the Cluster. Our living quarters are all set up and waiting . . . so how's about a smile for your rich, new husband?"

"Oh, I'll do better than that," Paula said—and brought her lips softly to his.

The trip out to the Cluster was perfect. As their new home swung into sight on the ship's wide viewscreen, Donald Spencer knew that he'd made a shrewd purchase. In ten years an asteroid would fetch at least 50,000 credits on the Earth market. The furiously expanding population guaranteed it. Some of his business friends had been skeptical, warning him against the deal, telling him that no one really knew much about the Luani Cluster, that he might run into trouble there—but Spencer ignored them. They were simply jealous of his business ability. In a few years Luani would be completely settled, and real estate would soar.

"Ready, darling?" he asked.

Paula Spencer nodded excitedly.

The couple shook hands with the Captain, then transferred to their personal landing craft. Spencer raised a hand—and a section of the passenger rocket's outer hull slid back. The small silver craft bulleted toward K-157, leaving the giant ship behind to continue its galactic voyage.

The landing was smooth—and Donald Spencer took his wife's hand after the atomic motor had stilled.

"Happy?"

"You *know* I am, Don."

"Then, c'mon. Meet your asteroid!"

They scrambled out of the ship. The air was heavy, but breathable. In rising waves, the tall, blue trees and multi-colored vegetation of Asteroid K-157 pressed around them, all but engulfing their tiny space craft.

"I had a section cleared for us," Spencer told his wife. "The house is just beyond those trees."

"I can hardly *wait* to see it!" Paula said, running ahead of him across the springy green soil.

He joined her at the clearing's edge, smiling at her reaction. Paula clapped her hands together in delight.

"Don, it's wonderful . . . all I'd hoped for!" she said, hugging him.

The new house was low and modern, sculptured to the alien soil, a flat plastibrick structure gleaming under double suns. As they approached it, the front door slid silently open for them.

"All the comforts of Earth," said Spencer. "Even a microfilm library."

"Are we . . . alone here?" Paula asked.

"Absolutely. The last of the building crew was due out yesterday. The entire place is ours."

She darted through the house, exclaiming at all the latest electronic marvels. In the bedroom, she turned to face him. "We're going to make this the most *tremendous* honeymoon any couple ever had."

"That," he grinned, "will be a pleasure."

Later that night Donald Spencer awoke to find the bed empty beside him. He got up quickly, calling Paula's name. When she failed to answer he pulled on his robe and rushed outside into the bright moonlight.

"Paula—are you out here?"

Then Spencer saw her, standing at the edge of the clearing, facing the massed line of blue trees.

"Darling, I was worried." He put a hand on her shoulder.

She turned calmly, the moonlight filling her eyes. "I needed some fresh air. The room was stifling."

"Sure you're all right?"

Paula didn't reply, turning slowly away from him. Spencer was puzzled, strangely uneasy, yet nothing seemed to be wrong.

"Let's go back to the house."

"No," the girl said firmly. "I want to stay out here."

"But—"

"You go in if you wish."

Spencer shrugged, a little angry. He walked back, trying to pinpoint the difference he had noticed in Paula. She had somehow changed . . .

"Exactly *how* have I changed, Donald?"

He spun around; she had followed him back. Then he gasped; how had she known—

"—What you were thinking?" She finished his mental question. "Because I can read your mind now, of course."

She stood there in the doorway, framed in soft moonlight, smiling at him as a mother smiles at her child.

"It's true," she said. "I can also move faster than you can. I'm much stronger. In fact, I could easily kill you with one blow. Easily."

"Good God," said Spencer. "What kind of nonsense is this?"

"Not nonsense. Fact. All of it can be yours, too. The trees will accept you, I know they will."

Spencer began to speak, but she raised a silencing hand.

"I walked out for air, earlier, while you slept—but it was really not for air at all. The trees had called me. They wanted me to become part of them, part of this place . . . and so I did."

"Paula, what are you telling me?"

"That this asteroid is alive. That the blue trees are alive, and have mental powers far beyond our own. They called me tonight, and I went out to them, ate the fruit I found on their branches. Then I was one of them. I'm sure they want you too, Don. Go to them. . . ."

"You're just tired. The trip, the new house . . . Maybe in the morning we can—"

"In the morning," she told him, "I won't be here. At least not as you see me. The mutation will be complete by then. This creature you call Paula will be gone; I'll be part of *them*."

She extended a hand. Spencer saw that she held a triangular piece of fruit, which cast a subtle, blue glow in the darkness.

"We're in a new Garden of Eden," she said softly. "Eat this and you'll be free, as I am free."

Spencer moved back from her. He believed Paula now; she *had* changed, and something on this asteroid had effected that change. The Luani Cluster was undeveloped, wholly alien; no one could specify exactly what man would encounter here . . . That was one of the risks. He knew he'd made a terrible error in seeking out this place, that because of his error the woman he had loved was lost to him. Paula was no longer his wife—no longer human.

"Well, Don?"

"I—I don't want to join you," he said, watching her cold eyes. "I'll leave in the morning. The house, the asteroid is yours. Everything."

She laughed, and a sudden chill made him shiver beneath his robe.

"You'll never leave. No one can. All the others—the construction crew—they're out . . . with the trees. By morning you'll be one of us."

"Then I won't wait for morning. I'll go now. I can make contact with a passenger ship near Ariel and—"

"You're acting like a fool, Don."

Her voice was edged. Whatever possessed her was angry.

Spencer turned, entered the bedroom, and hurriedly began to dress. Paula watched him from the doorway, unsmiling, silent.

He walked quickly past her, out to the waiting space craft.

"Paula . . . goodbye."

"Not goodbye, Don. There'll never be a goodbye for us."

Spencer mounted the ladder, opened the airlock, put one foot inside the rocket. Then, on impulse, he turned.

The trees seemed much closer.

"They are," Paula said, reading his thought. "You only have a few seconds, Don. Eat from the tree, or—"

"Or what?" he demanded.

"Or be destroyed with the rocket."

"Go to hell!" said Spencer as he closed the airlock.

Outside, the trees were all around the silver ship; the clearing had completely vanished.

Sweating and impatient, Spencer turned to the controls—then paused. He slowly raised his head. Something . . . someone was calling him with an urgency he could not resist. Something wanted him . . .

The trees. The trees wanted him.

Moving with a calm deliberation, Spencer opened the lock. They waited for him, offering their shining, blue branches in the bright moonlight, offering immortality.

He climbed down the ladder, putting out a hand toward Paula, toward the fruit of the tree.

Hungrily, he ate of the fruit.

Paula welcomed him into her arms. "Now, my darling, we're together again. Forever."

Spencer smiled at her, then looked at the trees. He wondered why he had been unwilling to accept his destiny; men were so weak and foolish . . . so hopelessly *mortal*.

And, on Asteroid K-157 in the Luani Cluster, Donald and Paula Spencer lived happily ever after.

✛ ✛ ✛

Toe to Tip, Tip to Toe, Pip-Pop As You Go

NOTHING WAS HAPPENING.

It was no good, simply no damn good.

Hendy Joerdon grumpily untangled himself from the eroticizer's silken grasp and palmed the lustkill switch.

"Well, we all have our off nights," sighed the inflatagirl as she brightly folded herself back into the unit. "Even Gable did."

Joerdon didn't know who the hell Gable was, and said so.

"Gable, Clark. Public lust symbol. Twentieth century," supplied the eroticizer. The girl was completely folded away by now and couldn't supply anything. "How about a nice, oily back rub instead?" The fat, red machine eased closer to Joerdon's bed, visor plates gleaming. "Release all those taut muscles. Loosey goosey!"

"Keep your damn rubberoids off me," Joerdon told it. He suspected the machine of deviant behavior, and was in no mood to wrestle with it tonight. "I need sleep."

"You're out of shape, in my opinion," the unit told him. "Way out, I'd say."

"Brass off," said Joerdon.

The unit retired noiselessly as Hendy's bed rocked and soothed and babied him. "Yum, yum, yum," said the bed. "Sleepums *good.*"

The next morning, at Deepfizz, Joerdon's desk told him he looked frettled.

"That's gollywop!" Joerdon snapped. He jogged a quick circle around the office. "Just check those leg reflexes!"

"Boss wants you," said a voice behind him. It was McWhirter, the officious ferret-faced Pill Brother in charge of Moon-popping.

"I'm having water," Hendy growled, moving to the cooler.

"My, aren't we tense and testy," grinned McWhirter. He peered closely at Joerdon. "Have a sour night?"

Joerdon shrugged.

"It's the eyes," said McWhirter. "They always give you away. The eyes go puffy. Fatty tissue buildup. Sad . . . really sad."

And he moused away.

"I hate that ferret-faced son of a bitch," Joerdon said to the water cooler.

"Open wide," directed the Boss.

Hendy opened his mouth, lolled his tongue, feeling puppylike and vulnerable.

"Yes. Grayish. Not pinkish." The Boss clucked. "And it's got a wrinkle in the middle."

"What does that mean?"

"Constriction. System's all bunched up and constricted."

The Boss rolled to and fro across the desk. He was entirely egg-shaped and featureless, which made it hard to tell what his mood was. After an unhappy experience at Surestop, Joerdon had vowed never again to work for an egg-shaped Boss. But progress had caught up with him. The old affable cube-shaped Boss who'd hired him at Deepfizz had been replaced and there was nothing Joerdon could do about that.

Or about a lot of other things.

"You're frettled, Joerdon. Sit down and tell me what's frettling you."

Joerdon sat down in a snugglechair. He sighed, shaking his head. "Just a passing mood, sir."

Executing a neat figure-eight pattern, the Boss looped over to a saucer-shaped depression in his desk and egged into it. "You're a Popper Five now, with a lot of responsibility. I don't need to tell you that Deepfizz wants its Poppers unfrettled."

"Yes, sir." The snugglechair pressed Hendy's left buttock reassuringly.

"We didn't pull ahead of Dizzdrop point one forty-six to point one forty-five in National Ratings last month by accident, Joerdon. Dizzdroppers are now becoming Deepfizzers at the rate of one every fiftieth centisecond—and we're proud of that statistic. Aren't you proud of that statistic, Joerdon?"

"I certainly am, sir," said Hendy. The snugglechair squeezed his other buttock. It didn't help. Actually, Joerdon found it irritating.

The Boss rolled leisurely back over the desk, stopped at the edge, tilted toward Joerdon. His tone became conspiratorial. "Son . . . have you popped? We'll find out soon enough, you know. Can't be hidden. If you *have*, just admit it."

"Oh, no, sir! I'd never—"

"Good! Delighted to hear it," said the Boss. "One cannot continue to help guide society when one loses one's *self*-guidance. A popping Popper is a public disgrace!"

"Yo, yo!" Hendy said, using the official form of affirmation.

"Maybe you ought to have a medcheck, just to be sure everything's acey," suggested the Boss.

Hendy agreed.

"Visit Doc Sidge at the end of your work sesh. Get a runthrough. Then come see me in the morn. We'll fab more then." The egg-shaped Boss rolled over to his basket slot and dropped abruptly out of sight.

Working with his Pill Brothers in the huge, pink Deepfizz adlab, Joerdon told himself that he was basically acey—that he had a *right* to a bout of moodiness after losing Ellena. They had been set for a procreation sesh when she suddenly vanished. Here one day, working next to him, radiant and fresh. Gone the next. Zap! When Joerdon asked what had become of her the ferret-faced McWhirter had smirked. "Maybe she popped!"

"Not on your bizzle!" Hendy had snapped back. "Not Ellena!"

But he'd given it a lot of thought. *Had* she popped? That would explain her disappearance. Popped Poppers were banished, sent Outside. A nasty end to public service.

Joerdon knew he hadn't been pulling his weight at Deepfizz over the past week since Ellena vanished. Most of his Mars-pop copy had ended in deadwaste. Flushed with sudden guilt, Joerdon stared morosely at the huge wallglow trimural of Hately Hately. Spade-bearded and rock-nosed, Hately of Deepfizz—the true giant of the twenty-first century. And beneath, carved in letters of bronze, his fabled words: "A stoned nation is a happy nation." The Big Habit had solved all problems. War was eliminated and Sex, as removed from Lust—which was properly supplied by the eroticizer—was now a strict religious rite, reserved, at specified intervals, for vital procreation among Deepfizz-Dizzdrop personnel. Which was, Joerdon knew, as it should be.

He attempted to concentrate on his work, but found himself thinking dismally of Ellena for the remainder of his data-pop period.

"Ouch," said Joerdon as he was thumped and pumped, tapped and grasped and twisted and analyzed by the medcheck runthrough unit. "Ouch," he said, several more times.

"Nothing," said the unit, hopping back in a birdlike motion. "Nothing, nothing, nothing, nothing. You have nothing wrong with you."

"You sound disappointed."

"And why not? My job is to find things wrong with people so I can send them to Doc Sidge."

"Where is he? I think I should talk to him."

"Sidge only sees sickos," the unit told him. "You are not a sicko. All you have is a temporary psychological imbalance caused by mild emotional multi-stress. And that, sadly enough from my view-point, will pass. Good tubing."

"Good tubing," Joerdon said to the unit.

He left, carrying a medstamped discslip that certified that he was in ideal physical condition.

Naturally, there was no trace of Deepfizz in his blood.

The Boss would be pleased.

"Psssst!"

"What did you say?"

"I said Psssst!"

"Nobody ever says, 'Psssst!' anymore," Joerdon explained to the crouching tube rider next to him.

"I'm attempting to be secretive. I'm sure some people still say 'Psssst!' when they are attempting to be secretive."

"I won't argue the point," said Joerdon.

The tube rider was small and dark and furry. He smelled odd. "I've been Outside," he whispered.

Joerdon stared at him. He'd never seen an Outsider inside. "But that's not legal. None of us go Outside unless we pop. Then we're *sent* Outside. There are no Outside insiders, nor inside Outsiders."

The furry little tube rider snorted. "That's just the poddlecock they feed you industry people. I know things you *don't.*"

Joerdon glanced nervously around the humming tuber. No other riders this early. And luckily, on this model, the seats couldn't talk. "Why tell me this?"

"A lady wants you."

"What lady?"

"Lady Ellena Nubbins, who else."

Joerdon gripped the man's furry front. "What do you know of Miss Nubbins? Where is she?"

"Outside," the unflustered tuber replied. "And she wants you with her."

Joerdon shuddered. He knew what it was like Out There. Unstable. Odd-smelling. Full of goofy pill-poppers. He'd seen them on the Scope, mooning in the streets, popping their hours away. And now Ellena—sober, dedicated, hardworking Ellena Nubbins—was one of them. His worst suspicions had been verified. It was obviously no use going out to her. Once a popped Popper, always a popped Popper. Addiction was immediate.

"Tell her that I still regard her with considerable affection, that her leaving has severely upset my work, but that I shall *never* join her."

"Is that final?"

"Indeed it is," nodded Joerdon.

"Then let's try a blitz on the bizzle."

Joerdon was astonished when the furry man tried exactly that.

Joerdon woke up inside a zebra-striped anachronism.

"Wok!" he said, clearing his throat. His head swam, settled; he blinked rapidly. "Wok!" he said again, unsteadily.

"You'll be acey soon," said a furry voice. The little tube man was cradling Joerdon's head in his odd-smelling lap. Hendy pushed himself into a sitting position.

He looked out a window. They were moving over the streets of New York. That's when he found out he was riding inside an anachronism: a 1971 Cadillac, zebra-striped.

"Our movement supervisor is responsible," said the ex-tube rider. "He restored this old Caddie right down to her last lug nut. Even the exhaust fumes are properly poisonous. It's the work of a craftsman."

"I didn't know they allowed automobiles in New York," said Joerdon. "Aren't these things against the law?" He squinted at the driver in the forward seat, but the man was hatted and swaddled and Hendy couldn't make out any physical details.

"Poddlecock!" said his furry friend. "With the lawboys stoned nobody's left to tell anybody anything. Cities are falling apart. Last week the Empire State Building fell down flat and nobody said foof about it."

"I didn't scan that on the Scope."

"There's lots you don't scan on the Scope. You Insiders are bizzle-clesbed. You see only what the industry wants you to see."

Joerdon asked, "Where are we going?"

"To clan HQ," said the furry one. "Just sit back and enjoy the ride."

A classic .45-calibre slug smashed through the Cadillac's rear window, barely missing Joerdon's bizzle.

"Ooops!" said the muffled driver. He stopped the car, quickly leaped out, and sprayed a noisily advancing crowd with concentrated laser-beam fire. Then he hopped back in and resumed driving.

"Who were *they?*" Joerdon wanted to know.

"Zealots. Bishops, cardinals, ex-nuns, and the like. Bothersome. They fire classic slugs from restored museum pistols at you. We have to show them who's boss. They can get pesky. Nothing unusual though. All part of the general civic breakdown."

The car swerved to avoid a sleeping Deepfizzer in the center of Fifth Avenue. Others along the walks chanted at the Cad: "Toe to tip, tip to toe, pip-pop as you go!"

The furry man ignored them. "We headquarter at Tiffany's," he said. "Lends a little class to the operation."

They parked directly in front of the famous jewelry store. The driver heh-hehed under his swaddle, "I always get a kick out of parking in the red zone." He led them inside.

Joerdon still couldn't make out the man's face, but the tips of his ears looked vaguely familiar.

"Where's Ellena?"

"Here, Hendy!"

She ran toward him across a marbled floor, arms extended, aglitter in diamonds and emeralds and pearls and sapphires.

They rubbed groins happily, and Joerdon felt the old procreation urge welling up. Suddenly he pushed her back. "You want me to pop, but I won't. Not even for you. I won't. Won't. Won't. Won't. Will not."

She giggled, dislodging a diamond tiara from her hair. It clattered unnoticed to the veined marble.

"Meet the chief." The furry man and the still-swaddled driver gripped Hendy's elbows and quick-marched him into a large, deep-carpeted office at the rear of the building. A paneled side door slid open and the chief stepped into view.

Joerdon gasped. "McWhirter!"

"No other," said McWhirter.

"You're an Outsider!"

McWhirter smirked. "Have been for the past couple of years."

"What . . . where . . . why . . . how?"

"Good questions—but first—" He gestured expansively. "Let me introduce the principal members of the movement. My furry, odd-smelling assistant is Fedor Bandlecliff Bumpums, a biochemist of marked brilliance. And doubtless you already know the swaddled gentleman who drove you here."

The swaddled driver unswaddled.

Joerdon gasped. "Doc Sidge!"

"No other," said Sidge.

"I *thought* I recognized your distinctive ear tips."

McWhirter put one arm around Ellena. "And Miss Nubbins is a pivotal member. She joined our movement quite recently, as you know."

"And you've kidnapped me to become part of your illegal, subversive, clandestine group, is that it?"

"More or less," replied McWhirter. "Eventually we would have kidnapped you anyway, but we kidnapped you now because dear Ellena wanted you Outside, with her. I thought Fedor B. Bumpums told you that inside the tuber."

"I simply won't pop. Not for all the drickle in New York. Do with me what you will, but I shall not betray my heritage."

"But," said Ellena, "nobody wants you to. None of us pop. We're anti-poppers."

"I don't—"

"You don't understand," said Doc Sidge.

McWhirter sighed. "Tell him, Ellena, while I go put on some rubies. I love wearing rubies in the afternoon." He loped away over the thick carpet.

Ellena smiled patiently. "We are building a drug-free movement to overthrow the Deepfizz-Dizzdrop industry."

"Great hobble!"

"Naturally, you're surprised." She removed her outer garments as she talked. Then her inner garments. Then her inner-inner outer garments and, finally, her outer-inners.

Ellena was stark naked and looked particularly appealing.

"You're . . . particularly appealing you know," Joerdon could not help saying.

"That's the whole smidge," she said, swaying toward him. Doc and the furry biochemist slyly skittered from the room.

"Is—is this an unofficial procreation sesh?" asked Hendy.

"Not exactly, but it may end up that way. The purpose is just to jizz."

"I begin to see your point," said Hendy, shucking his outer garments.

"What we do is stay straight, and help other people kick the Big Habit," she husked in a smoky tone. "Also, we kidnap bizzle-cleshed Industry Insiders and turn them into straight *un*-bizzle-cleshed Outsiders. Pretty soon, when enough Insiders become Outsiders—all jizzing each other for the good of mankind—then people slowly rediscover the joys of the movement and the industry breaks down and we have a truly free society. Isn't that wonderfully simple?"

"It's simply wonderful," declared Hendy, squeezing a deftly weighted breast. "It's also a hell of a lot of fun."

And, without further urging, Hendy Joerdon enthusiastically joined the movement.

✤ ✤ ✤

Stuntman

CLAYTON WEBER EASED HIMSELF DOWN FROM the papier-mâché mountain and wiped the artificial sweat from his face. "How'd I look?" he asked the director.

"Great," said Victor Raddish. "Even Morell's own mother wouldn't know the difference."

"That's what I like to hear," grinned Weber, seating himself at a makeup table. Thus far, *Courage at Cougar Canyon*, starring "fearless" Claude Morell as the Yellowstone Kid had gone smoothly. Doubling for Morell, Weber had leaped chasms, been tossed from rolling wagons, dived into rivers and otherwise subjected himself to the usual rigors of a movie stuntman. Now, as he removed his makeup, he felt a hand at his shoulder.

"Mr. Morell would like to see you in his dressing room," a studio messenger boy told him.

Inside the small room Weber lit a cigarette and settled back on the brown leather couch. Claude Morell, tall and frowning, stood facing him.

"Weber, you're a nosy, rotten bastard and I ought to have you thrown off the lot and blacklisted with every studio in town."

"Then Linda told you about my call?"

"Of course she did. Your imitation of my voice was quite excellent. Seems you do as well off-camera as on. She was certain that I was talking or she never would have—"

"—discussed the abortion," finished Weber, feet propped on the couch.

Morell's eyes hardened. "How much do you want to keep silent?" Morell seated himself at a dressing table and flipped open his chequebook.

"Bribery won't be necessary," smiled Clayton Weber through the spiraling smoke of his cigarette, "I don't intend to spill the beans. The fact that you impregnated the star of our picture and that she is about to have an abortion will never become public knowledge. You can depend on that."

Morell looked confused. "Then . . . I don't—"

"Have you ever heard of the parallel universe theory?"

Morell shook his head, still puzzled.

"It's simply this—that next to our own universe an infinite number of parallel universes exist—countless millions of them—each in many ways identical to this one. Yet the life pattern is different in each. Every variation of living is carried out, with a separate universe for each variation. Do you follow me?"

Obviously, Morell did not.

"Let me cite examples," said Weber. "In one of these parallel universes Lincoln was never assassinated; in another Columbus did *not* discover America, nor did Joe Louis become heavyweight champ. In one universe, America *lost* the First World War . . ."

"But that's ridiculous," Morell said. "Dream stuff."

"Let me approach it from another angle," persisted Weber. "You've heard of Doppelgangers?"

"You mean—*doubles?*"

"Not simply doubles, they are exact duplicates." Weber drew on his cigarette, allowing his words to take effect. "The reason you never see two of them together, for comparison, is that one of them always knows he is a duplicate of the other—and stays out of the other's life. Or enters it wearing a disguise."

"You're talking gibberish," said Claude Morell.

"Bear with me. The true Doppelganger *knows* he is not of this universe—and he chooses to stay away from his duplicate because it is too painful for him to see his own life being lived by another man, to see his wife and children and know they can never be his. So he builds a new life for himself in another part of the world."

"I don't see the point, Weber. What are you telling me?"

Clayton Weber smiled. "You'll see my point soon enough." He

continued. "Sometimes a man or woman will simply vanish, wink out, as it were without a trace. Ambrose Bierce, the writer, was one of these. Then there was the crew of the *Marie Celeste* . . . They unknowingly reached a point in time and space that allowed them to step through into a separate world, like and yet totally unlike their own. They became Doppelgangers."

Weber paused, his eyes intent on Morell. "I'm one of them," he said. "It happened to me as it happened to them, without any warning. One moment I was happily married with a beautiful wife and a baby girl—the next I found myself in the middle of Los Angeles. Sometimes it's impossible to adjust to the situation. Some of us end up in an institution, claiming we're other people." He smiled again. "And—of course we *are*."

Morell stood up, replacing the chequebook in his coat. "I don't know what kind of word game you're playing, Weber, but I've had enough of it. You refuse my offer—all right, you're fired. And if a word of this affair with Linda Miller ever hits print I'll not only see that you never work again in the industry, I'll also see that you receive the beating of your life. And I have the connections to guarantee a *thorough* job."

"Do one thing for me, Mr. Morell," asked Weber. "Just hold out your right hand, palm up."

"I don't see—"

"Please."

Morell brought up his hand. Weber raised his own, placing it beside Morell's. "Look at them," he said. "Look at the shape of the thumbs, the lines in the palm, the whorls on each fingertip."

"Good God!" said Claude Morell.

The man who called himself Clayton Weber reached up and began to work on his face. The cheek lines were altered as he withdrew some inner padding, his nose became smaller as he peeled away a thin layer of wax. In a moment the change was complete.

"Incredible," Morell breathed. "That's my face!"

"I had to look enough like you to get this job as your double," Weber told him, "but of course I couldn't look *exactly* like you. Now, however, we are identical." He withdrew the Colt from the hip holster of his western costume and aimed it at Morell.

"No blanks this time," he said.

"But why kill me?" Morell backed to the wall. "Even if all you said is true, why kill me? They'll send you to the gas chamber. You'll die with me!"

"Wrong," grinned Weber. "The death will be listed as a suicide.

A note will be found on the dresser in the apartment I rented, stating 'Clayton Weber's' intention to do away with himself, that he felt he'd always been a failure, nothing but a stuntman, while others became stars. It will make excellent sense to the police. I will report that you shot yourself in my presence as we discussed the career you could never have."

"But my face will be the face of Claude Morell, not Clayton Weber!"

"Half of your face will be disposed of by the bullet at such close range. There will be no question of identity. And we're both wearing the same costume."

Morell leaned forward, eyes desperate. "But why? Why?"

"I'm killing you for what you did to my wife," said Weber, holding the gun steady.

"But—I never *met* your wife."

"In your world, this world, Linda Miller was just another number on your sexual hit parade, but in my world she was my wife. In *my* world that baby girl she carries in her body was born, allowed to live. And that's just the way it's going to happen now. If you'd married Linda I would have disappeared, gone to live in another city, left you alone. But you didn't. So, *I'll* marry her—again."

Claude Morell chose that moment to spring for the gun, but the bullet from the big Colt sent his head flying into bright red pieces.

The man who had called himself Clayton Weber placed the smoking weapon in Morell's dead hand.

+ + +

Kelly, Fredric Michael

MONITORED THOUGHT PATTERNS CONTINUE:

. . . wrong, twisted . . . and I'm being . . . being . . . Steen is already . . . they want me to free form again . . . goddamn it, I don't understand just what this . . .

We had a coal-burning furnace in the basement with a slotted iron door, and you broke up the clinkers inside with a poker, lifting the door latch with the heat sweating you . . .

And Mickey left Minnie standing at the little white picket fence. She was blushing. "Love ya," he said. "Gee," she said. "Gotta fly the mail for Uncle Sam," he said. "Golly, you're so brave!" she said. His plane was a cute single-seater with a smiling face and rubbery wings . . .

The Moon! They'd made it after all, by Christ, and Armstrong was walking, jiggling, kind of floating sometimes with sixty million or more of us watching. He could still be a part of it. He was only forty-one and that wasn't old, not too old if he really . . .

. . . kept shooting, but the bullets bounced right off his chest. "Time someone taught you a lesson in manners!" He tucked a thug under each arm, pin-striped suits with their hats still on, and leaped through the window of the skyscraper with him in the air now and them yelling and him smiling, square-jawed, with that little black curl over his forehead and the red cape flaring out behind . . . soaring above the poorly drawn city with the two . . .

Alone in the back of the car, the two of them, not watching the movie (a comedy with Hope in drag and Benny pretending to be his daughter), not giving a damn about the movie and him with his hand there inside her elastic, white silk panties . . . "Don't Freddie. I can't let you." Sure she could. He'd taken her out often enough for her to let him. He wouldn't hurt her, ever. He was sure he loved her, or if he didn't he *would*—if she'd just . . . He had her blouse all the way open and God those tits! ". . . never have come here with you if I thought you'd . . ." Seat slippery under him but he got her legs open enough to do it, but all he did was rub her down there. He'd lost his erection and his penis was as soft as a flag with no wind, it flopped against her white stomach and she was . . .

Tight against the rocks with the Arabs coming. The legion guy next to Coop was plenty nervous. "Think we can hold 'em off?" And Coop smiled that slow, easy boy-smile that meant nothing could touch him; we all knew nothing could touch Coop. "Sure, sure we can. They won't attack at night. We'll slip out after dark." He fired twice and two fanatic Arabs fell in close-up. A hidden ground wire tripped their horse, but we were too young to know about hidden ground wires . . .

". . . so I'm going to tell Dawson he can go fuck himself!" "They'll bounce your ass right out," I told Bob. "So what, so who needs a Ph.D. from this lousy . . . Look man, college is shit. Dawson is a phony little prick and he knows it and so do his students, but they just sit there listening to him spout out his . . ."

. . . planet wants me to . . . no, no . . . it isn't the planet itself. It isn't alive, doesn't tell me anything . . . dead planet out there on the fringe of the System . . . but it has . . . a kind of influence—in conjunction with the rest of this System . . . the whole thing is a form of . . . new force, or goddamn it I wish they'd let me . . . just wouldn't . . .

Mother wanted to know what I was doing in my bedroom all alone for so long and I said reading a Big-Little-Book and she came in to see. I had a pretty fair collection and the best were the ones set on the planet Mongo. "You read too much. It'll ruin your eyes." But she looked relieved. I didn't know why. She was smiling and roughing my hair, which I hated but I didn't hate her. I loved her very, very much. ". . . to sleep now. You can read more tomorrow." The

room was small and comfort-making and I could smell her per-
fume and the special soap she used and I liked the way she
smelled, always, and she was always . . .

. . . to row close to the shore, along the rocks, while he fed line
into the quiet lake. "This is where the fat ones like to come in," he
said. The sky was so blue it hurt my eyes so I kept my head down.
A mosquito bit me. That was the only trouble with lakes, the mos-
quitoes. They loved water the way Dad did. I liked rowing, feeling
the long, wooden boat slide through the water with Dad at one
end, feeding out his line, and the lake black-green with no motor-
boats on it, quiet and hot and . . .

She twisted under me, doing a thing with her pelvis, and I
came. Hard, fiery. First time inside . . . She groaned and kept her
eyes squeezed shut and she looked tortured and I kept thinking
what her father would say if he knew I had her doing this. He
always worried about her. "You two kids take care, ya hear?" And
then he'd say, "I trust you, Fred, because you're a Catholic." And
told him that I . . .

. . . *more* . . . *keep wanting more* . . . *I'm being* . . . *forced to spill out*
all the . . .

"Hey, Kelly, the old man wants to see you." Sure he did, and I knew
why. Because I was late three mornings this week. I had reasons.
The lousy freeways were jammed so I took surface streets but Old
Cooney would never listen to reason, which is why he's such a
bastard to work for. "Tell him I won't be late anymore." I was going
to the Moon. To work there. To train for space. And someday, with
luck, maybe I could . . .

Whap! Wow! Pie right in the kisser. The little tramp wipes it
off, sucks his thumbs, does a kind of ballet step back and falls
down three flights of stairs. Terrific! Up he bounces, dusts the seat
of his baggy pants, tips his hat, spins his cane, and walks into a cop!
Whomp! Cop is furious. Jumps up and down, shaking his stick.
The tramp does a polite little bow, tips his hat again and ducks
between the cop's legs. Zing—right down the middle of the street.
Cars missing them by inches. Two more cops join the first cop.
Three more. A dozen. Falling and yelling. Tramp is up a fire
escape, over a roof, through a fat lady's apartment—she's in the tub!
—out a door, down an alley, and into a big . . .

. . . snow came and I'd rush for the basement to dig out my old
sled. Rust had coated the runners with a thin, red film and I had to

get them shiny again with sandpaper, doing it fast, wanting to get out on the hill and cut loose. School closed, the hill waiting, Tommy Griffith yelling at me to get a move on and then the long whooshing slide down from Troost with snowdust in your nose and steering to miss Tommy's sled and picking up speed coming onto Forest, mittens and yellow snow goggles and warm under the coat Uncle Frank got you for Christmas . . .

The sons of bitches were worried about the fucking score while his father was *dying*. Okay, okay—pull back, cool down, all the way down—because if he wasn't dying he'd want to know the score too. It was the Series and he'd want to know the score like the others did. The hall smelled of white paint and starch and, faintly, of urine. Hospital smells. The young priest had been emotionless about it, kept smiling at him and saying, "a passel of years" when he told him how old his father was. He was glad to be out of Holy Mother Church, because she didn't really give a damn about him or his father. Maybe God did, somewhere, but not Holy Mother Church. What did it matter how old his father was? So what? He was still dying of cancer and you never want to go that way no matter *how* fucking old you are, even if . . .

> "My country tis of thee,
> Sweet land of liberty . . ."

Sing it boy, sing it loud and let the world know that you're an American. Sure, he was too young to fight, but he was proud. And scared, too. They were giving us hell on those beaches. Giving us bloody hell . . .

. . . into space when I was fifty . . . Moon first, then Mars . . . If I could just tell them straight and they didn't . . .

. . . keep trying to force all the . . . I'm fifty-nine years old and I shouldn't even be on this planet . . . said I was too old, but nobody listened. Experience. We need you out there, Fred. Help chart the new Systems. Warps did it, make it all possible . . . one jump and into another galaxy. No dream. Fact. Cold reality. All right then, I volunteered . . . but not for this . . . didn't know I'd ever be . . . goddamn sick of being . . . sucked dry this way . . . without my having any choice in how I . . .

"That's it, oh, that's fine! Keep coming, honey!" Mom, with her arms out. Wobble. Almost into the lamp. "C'mon son, you can do it. Walk to me!" Daddy there, kneeling next to her, looking excited.

The room swaying. Terror. Falling. Rug in my face. Sneezing with them laughing and pulling me up and me trying again, with it better this time. Steady now, and Daddy was . . .

Feeding her power, letting her drift out, then snapping her back. "You're great Fred," Anne told me. "Nope. Car's great," I said. "Handles, doesn't she? Richie did the suspension. Short throw on the shift. Four downdraft carbs. She'll do 200 easy. And a road like this, she eats it up." Life was good. Power under my foot and power in my mind and the future waiting. . . .

". . . when the sniper got him." "What?" "Sniper. In Dealy Plaza." "Where's that?" "Texas." "What was he doing there?" "Wife was with him. They were—" "She dead too?" "No, just him. Blood all over her dress, but she's fine, she's fine . . ."

"Let's see what he looks like under that mask?" Oh, oh, they *had* him now. Guns on him, his hands tied, no chance to get away. "Yeah, Jake, let's have a good look at him." *Spaaaaang!* "What the—" Oh, boy, just in time. Neat! "It's the durn Indian! Near killed me. Looks like he's got us boxed in." What are they going to do? "Better untie me, Jake, and I'll see to it that you both get a fair trial in Carson City." Deep voice. "You have my word on it." They won't. Or *will* they? Not much choice. *Spaaaang!* "His next shot won't miss, Jake." Oh, they're scared now, all right. Look at them sweat. "We'd best do as the masked man says," the big one growls. *Spaaaang!* Boy, if they don't . . .

"But, Fred, the job's on Mars. We can't go to Mars!" I wanted to know why not. "Because, for one thing, Bobby is too settled in. His school, all his friends, everything is here. The Moon is his *home.*" I told her I was going, that it was a chance I couldn't afford to miss. But she kept up the argument, kept . . .

. . . on his stomach under the porch with the James Oliver Curwood book, the one about the dog who runs away and falls in love with a wolf and they have a son who's half dog and half wolf. Jack gave it to him for his fourteenth birthday. It was his favorite James Oliver Curwood. Rain outside, making cat-paw sounds on the porch but him dry and secret underneath with all the good reading ahead of him. He pushed a jawbreaker, one of the red ones, into his mouth and . . .

"Christ, Fred, let her go! She doesn't want to hear from you. She's never going to answer you. She wants to forget you." That was all right. Sue was still his wife and they still had their son and maybe he could put it all back together. He'd visit them on Bobby's birthday and maybe he could . . .

The stars . . . the *stars* . . . a massed hive of spacefire, a swarm of constellations . . . the diamonds of God . . . It was worth it. Worth everything to be out here, a part of *this*. Everything else was . . .

Enough! . . . I've given enough . . . sick . . . exhausted . . . hollow inside, drained . . . pulped out . . . They were lucky, the others were lucky and didn't know it, dying with the ship . . . but they took us down here, two of us . . . and Steen's insane now . . . They got . . . He free formed until they . . . know . . . know what they still want from me, what they have to experience along with all the rest of it . . . Before they're satisfied. They want to taste that too—the final thing . . . Well, give it to them. Why not? There's no way back to anywhere . . . Your friends are gone . . . Steen's a raving fool . . . so give them the final thing they want, goddamn them . . . whoever they are . . . whatever they are. Just give them

THOUGHT TRANSCRIPT ENDS.

✝ ✝ ✝

Papa's Planet

OF THE LATE HARRINGTON HUNTER HOLLISTER, it must be said that he was very rich, that he had sired a beautiful man-chasing redhead, and that he was a Hemingway fanatic. When he died in 2068, I ended up with his money, his newly divorced daughter, and his Hemingway collection.

"As my latest and absolutely *last* husband, I want you to have everything," Cecile Hollister told me, wrinkling her attractively freckled nose. "Daddy adored you."

"I adored daddy," I said, trying for sincerity.

She handed me a rolled parchment.

"What's this?" I asked.

"A deed to Papa's Planet. I've never been there, but daddy told me all about it. That's where we're spending our honeymoon."

"We are?"

"You want to see your property, don't you?"

"I guess so."

"We'll leave tomorrow."

Cecile had a way with men.

We left tomorrow.

Five million miles out from Mars, we turned sharp left and there it was: Papa's Planet—a big, gray ball of matter floating below us.

"What the devil's *down* there?" I asked.

"You'll find out. Strap in. Here we go."

We made a fine, soft-point landing (Cecile could handle a Spacer like a pro) and, when the rocket smoke cleared, I saw a big, wide-chested fellow in khaki hunting clothes approaching us. He was bearded, grizzled, with suspicious eyes. And he carried an elephant gun.

"You critics?" he demanded.

"Nope," said Cecile. "I'm the daughter of Harrington Hollister and this is my new husband, Philip."

"Okay, then," said the bearded man, pivoting. "I'm hunting critics. See any, give me a yell."

"Will do," said Cecile. And to me: "C'mon, Pamplona should be right on the other side of the mountain. We can catch the running of the bulls."

"Who was the aggressive, bearded guy?"

"Papa, of course. It's his planet."

Running along next to me, just in front of the bulls, a strong-looking guy thumped my shoulder and yelled, "This is swell, isn't it!"

"Yeah, swell!" I yelled back, sprinting to catch Cecile. "Who's the guy back there, yelling?"

"Papa," she told me. "Only he's a lot younger, naturally. This is 1923. Hey, let's cut through this side street. I want to see Paris."

Paris was right next to Pamplona, and Cecile looked radiant walking down the Rue de la Paix. "I'd like to meet Gertrude Stein," she said. "Maybe we can have lunch with her."

A big guy with a mustache pounded past us in a half crouch, feinting at the air with left and right jabs. He was dark-haired, tough-looking. "Hi, daughter," he said to Cecile.

"Hi, Ernie," she called back.

He padded away.

"Wait a damn minute," I said. "Who was *that?*"

She sighed. "Papa, naturally. Only nobody calls him Papa in Paris. Too early. Wrong period."

"Just how many Papas *are* there?"

Cecile stopped and wrinkled her nose. "Well, let's see . . . at least twenty that I know of, and I'm no expert. That was daddy's department."

"And they're *all* here?"

"Sure." She pointed. "Just beyond Paris, across the Seine, is Oak

Park, Illinois—which is next to Walloon Lake, Michigan. That's two Papas right there, one for each place. Both are *boy* Papas, of course. One goes to Oak Park High and the other goes trout fishing on the lake."

I nodded. "We've got one here—and another in Pamplona. And there's the one we met near the rocket."

"That was the African one," she said. "Then there's the one in New York with the hairy chest who keeps standing Max Eastman on his head in the corner of Scribner's. And the Papa in the hills of Spain covering the civil war and the one skiing in Switzerland with Hadley and the one on the Gulf Stream in the *Pilar*—daddy dug out a lovely Gulf Stream and I can't wait to see it—and there's the one getting shot in the kneecaps somewhere in Italy."

"Fossalta di Piave," I supplied.

"That's the place," she said, pushing back a strand of delicious red hair. "And there's the Papa in Key West and the one in Venice and the one boxing in the gym in Kansas City. How many is that?"

"I've lost count," I said.

"Anyway, there are *lots* more," said Cecile. "Daddy had his whole factory in Des Moines working overtime for six months, including weekends, just to supply all the Papas."

"Probably one camped out by the Big Two-Hearted River."

"Sure. And another in Toronto, working for the *Star*."

I raised an eyebrow. "Must have cost your daddy plenty."

"It was a tax write-off," she said. "Nonprofit. Besides, he had this big, empty planet just going to *waste* up here."

"But—building Paris in the twenties and the streets of Pamplona and the bull rings of Spain and all of Africa—"

"He didn't build *all* of Africa," Cecile corrected me. "Just the important part around Kilimanjaro, where we landed."

"Don't the Papas get mixed up, bump into each other?"

"Never. Each Papa has his assigned place and that's where he stays, doing what he was built for. The Pamplona Papa just keeps running with the bulls, and the African Papa keeps hunting critics."

"Your father sure didn't stint."

"When daddy did a thing, he did it *right*," she agreed. "Now, let's go have lunch with Miss Stein and then visit Venice. Daddy said they did a marvelous job with St. Mark's Square."

Papa was drinking alone at a table near the Grand Canal when our gondola passed by, and he waved us over.

"You smell good, daughter," Papa told Cecile. "You smell the way good leather you find in the little no-nonsense shops in Madrid when you know enough not to get suckered into the big shops that charge too much smells."

"Thanks, Papa," said Cecile, giving him a bright smile.

"I always enjoy the Gritti here in Venice," said Papa, "and ordering a strong lobster who had much heart and who died properly, and having him served to you by a waiter you can trust with a good bottle of Capri near you so you can see the little, green ice bubbles form on the cold glass."

He poured us wine. We all saluted one another and drank. The sun went down and the wine made me sleepy.

When I awoke, Cecile was gone.

I said goodbye to Papa and went out to look for her.

She wasn't at Key West, or on the Gulf, or anywhere in Spain, or in Billings, Montana (where Papa was recovering from his auto accident). I finally found her in Paris. On the Left Bank.

"I've fallen in love," she declared. "You can go on back to Earth and forget me."

I shrugged. Cecile was hardly steadfast; as her fourth husband, I realized that. "Who is he?"

"I call him Ougly-poo. That's my special love name for him. He just adores it."

"He isn't human, is he?"

"Of course not!" She looked annoyed. "We're the only *people* on Papa's Planet. But what difference does that make?"

"No difference, I guess."

"He's divine." She smiled dreamily, wrinkling her freckles. "Kind of a classic profile, soft, sensitive lips, exciting eyes . . . He gave me this autographed picture. See?"

I looked at it. "You're sure?"

"I'm sure," she said.

"Okay, then," I said. " 'Bye, Cecile."

" 'Bye, Philip." She threw me a kiss.

I walked back to the rocket through a sad, softly falling Hemingway rain. I didn't blame Cecile. The fellow was handsome, witty, brilliant, famous. All the things I wasn't. Girls weren't inspired to call me Ougly-poo.

But then, I wasn't F. Scott Fitzgerald.

✝ ✝ ✝

And Miles to Go
Before I Sleep

ALONE WITHIN THE HUMMING SHIP, DEEP IN its honeycombed chambers, Robert Murdock waited for death. While the rocket moved inexorably toward Earth—an immense silver needle threading the dark fabric of space—he waited calmly through the final hours, knowing that hope no longer existed.

After twenty years in space, Murdock was going home.

Home. Earth. Thayerville, a small town in Kansas. Clean air, a shaded street, and a white, two-story house near the end of the block. Home after two decades among the stars.

The rocket knifed through the black of space, its atomics, like a great heartbeat, pulsing far below Robert Murdock as he sat quietly before a round port, seeing and not seeing the endless darkness surrounding him.

Murdock was remembering.

He remembered the worried face of his mother, her whispered prayers for his safety, the way she held him close for a long, long moment before he mounted the ship's ramp those twenty years ago. He remembered his father: a tall, weathered man, and that last crushing handshake before he said goodbye.

It was almost impossible to realize that they were now old and white-haired, that his father was forced to use a cane, that his mother was bowed and wasted by the years.

And what of himself?

He was now forty-one—and space had weathered him as the plains of Kansas had weathered his father. He, too, had fought storms in his job beyond Earth, terrible, alien storms; worse than any he had ever encountered on his own planet. And he, too, had labored on plains under burning suns far stronger than Sol. His face was square and hard-featured, his eyes dark and buried beneath thrusting ledges of bone.

Robert Murdock removed the stero-shots of his parents from his uniform pocket and studied their faces. Warm, smiling, *waiting* faces: waiting for their son to come home to them. Carefully, he unfolded his mother's last letter. She had always been stubborn about sending tapes, complaining that her voice was unsteady, that she found it so difficult to speak her thoughts into the metallic mouth of a cold, impersonal machine. She insisted on using an old-fashioned pen, forming the words slowly in an almost archaic script. He had received this last letter just before his take-off for Earth, and it read:

Dearest,

We are so excited! Your father and I listened to your voice again and again, telling us that you are coming home to us at last, and we both thanked our good Lord that you were safe. Oh, we are so eager to see you, son. As you know, we have not been too well of late. Your father's heart doesn't allow him to get out much anymore. Even the news that you are coming back to us has over-excited him. Then, of course, my own health seems none too good as I suffered another fainting spell last week. But there is no real cause for alarm and you are not to worry!—since Dr. Thom says I am still quite strong, and that these spells will pass, I am, however, resting as much as possible, so that I will be fine when you arrive. Please, Bob, come back to us safely. We pray God you will come home safe and well. The thought of you fills our hearts each day. Our lives are suddenly rich again. Hurry, Bob. Hurry!

All our love,
Mother

Robert Murdock put the letter aside and clenched his fists. Only brief hours remained to him—and Earth was days away. The town of Thayerville was an impossible distance across space; he knew he could never reach it alive.

Once again, as they had so many times in the recent past, the closing lines of the ancient poem by Robert Frost came whispering through his mind:

> But I have promises to keep,
> And miles to go before I sleep . . .

He'd promised that he would come home, and he would keep that promise. Despite death itself, he would return to Earth.

"*Out of the question!*" the doctors had told him. "*You'll never reach Earth. You'll die out there. You'll die in space.*"

Then they had shown him. They charted his death almost to the final second; they told him when his heart would stop beating, when his breathing would cease. This disease—contracted on an alien world—was incurable. Death, for Robert Murdock, was a certainty.

But he told them he was going home nonetheless, that he was leaving for Earth. And they listened to his plan.

Now, with less than thirty minutes of life remaining, Murdock was walking down one of the ship's long corridors, his boot heels ringing on the metal walkway.

He was ready, at last, to keep his promise.

Pausing before a wall storage-locker, he twisted a small dial. The door slid back. Murdock looked up at the tall man standing motionless in the interior darkness. He reached forward, made a quick adjustment. The tall man spoke.

"Is it time?"

"Yes," replied Robert Murdock, "it is time."

The tall man stepped smoothly down into the corridor; the light flashed in the deep-set eyes, almost hidden under ledges of bone. The man's face was hard and square-featured. "You see," he smiled, "I *am* perfect."

"And so you are," said Murdock. But then, he reflected, everything *depends* on perfection. There must be no flaw, however small. None.

"My name is Robert Murdock," said the tall figure in the neat spaceman's uniform. "I am forty-one years of age, sound of mind and body. I have been in space for two decades—and now I am going home."

Murdock smiled, a tight smile of triumph that flickered briefly across his tired face.

"How much longer?" the tall figure asked.

"Ten minutes. Perhaps a few seconds beyond that," said Murdock slowly. "They told me it would be painless."

"Then . . ." The tall man paused, drew in a long breath. "I'm sorry."

Murdock smiled again. He knew that a machine, however perfect, could not experience the emotion of sorrow—but it eased him to hear the words.

He'll be fine, thought Murdock. He'll serve in my place and my parents will never suspect that I have not come home to them. A month, as arranged, and the machine would turn itself in to company officials on Earth. Yes, Murdock thought, he will be fine.

"Remember," said Murdock, "when you leave them, they must believe you are going back into space."

"Naturally," said the machine. And Murdock listened to his own voice explain. "When the month I am to stay with them has passed, they'll see me board a rocket. They'll see it fire away from Earth, outbound, and they'll know that I cannot return for two more decades. They *will* accept the fact that their son must return to space—that a healthy spaceman cannot leave the Service until he has reached sixty. Let me assure you, all will go exactly as you have planned."

It *will* work, Murdock told himself, every detail has been taken into consideration. The android possesses every memory that I possess; his voice is mine, his small habits my own. And when he leaves them, when it appears that he has gone back to the stars, the pre-recorded tapes of mine will continue to reach them from space, exactly as they have in the past. Until their deaths. They will never know I'm gone, thought Robert Murdock.

"Are you ready now?" the tall figure asked softly.

"Yes," said Murdock, nodding. "I'm ready."

And they began to walk slowly down the long corridor.

Murdock remembered how proud his parents had been when he was accepted for Special Service. He had been the only boy in the entire town of Thayerville to be chosen. It had been a great day! The local band playing, the mayor—old Mr. Harkness with those little glasses tilted across his nose—making a speech, telling everyone how proud Thayerville was of its chosen son . . . and his mother crying because she was so happy.

But then, it was only right that he should have gone into space. The other boys, the ones who failed to make the grade, had not *lived* the dream as he had lived it. From the moment he had watched the first moon rocket land, he had known, beyond any possible doubt, that he would become a spaceman. He had stood there, in that cold December, a boy of twelve, watching the rocket fire down from space, watching it thaw and blacken the frozen earth. And he had known, in his heart, that he would one day follow it back to the stars. From that moment on, he had dreamed only of moving up and away from Earth, away to vast and alien horizons, to wondrous worlds beyond imagining.

And many of the others had been unwilling to give up everything for space. Even now, after two decades, he could still hear Julie's words: "*Oh, I'm sure you love me, Bob, but not enough. Not nearly enough to give up your dream.*" And she had left him, gone out of his life because she knew there was no room in it for her. There was only space—deep space and the rockets and the burning stars. Nothing else.

He remembered his last night on Earth, twenty years ago, when he had felt the pressing immensity of the vast universe surrounding him as he lay in his bed. He remembered the sleepless hours before dawn—when he could feel the tension building within the small, white house, within himself, lying there in the heated stillness of the room. He remembered the rain, near morning, drumming the roof and the thunder roaring across the Kansas sky. And then, somehow, the thunder's roar blended into the atomic roar of a rocket, carrying him away from Earth, away to the far stars . . . away . . .

Away.

The tall figure in the neat spaceman's uniform closed the outer airlock and watched the body drift into blackness. The ship and the android were one; a pair of complex and perfect machines doing their job.

For Robert Murdock, the journey was over, the long miles had come to an end.

Now he would sleep forever in space.

When the rocket landed, on a bright morning in July, in Thayerville, Kansas, the crowds were there, waving and shouting out Robert Murdock's name. The city officials were all present to the last man, each with a carefully rehearsed speech in his mind; the town band sent brassy music into the blue sky and children waved flags. Then a hush fell over the assembled throng. The atomic engines had stilled and the airlock was sliding back.

Robert Murdock appeared, tall and heroic in a splendid dress uniform that threw back the light of the sun in a thousand glittering patterns. He smiled and waved as the crowd burst into fresh shouting and applause.

And, at the far end of the ramp, two figures waited: an old man, bowed and trembling over a cane, and a seamed and wrinkled woman, her hair blowing white, her eyes shining.

When the tall man finally reached them, pushing his way through pressing lines of well wishers, they embraced him feverishly. They clung tight to his arms as he walked between them; they looked up at him with tears in their eyes.

Robert Murdock, their beloved son, had come home to them at last.

"Well," said a man at the fringe of the crowd, "there they go."

His companion sighed and shook his head. "I *still* don't think it's right, somehow. It just doesn't seem right to me."

"It's what they wanted, isn't it?" asked the other. "It's what they put in their wills. They vowed their son would never come home to death. In another month he'll be gone anyway. Back for twenty more years. Why spoil what little time he has, why ruin it all for him?" The man paused, indicating the two figures in the near distance. "They're *perfect*, aren't they? He'll never know."

"I guess you're right," agreed the second man. "He'll never know."

And he watched the old man and the old woman and the tall son until they were out of sight.

✝ ✝ ✝

Violation

IT IS 2 A.M. AND HE WAITS. IN THE COOL MORNING stillness of a side street, under the soft screen of trees, the rider waits quietly—at ease upon the wide, leather seat of his cycle, gloved fingers resting idly on the bars, goggles up, barely reflecting the leaf-filtered glow of the moon.

Helmeted. Uniformed. Waiting.

In the breathing dark, the cycle metal cools; the motor is silent, a power contained.

The faint stirrings of a still-sleeping city reach him at his vigil. But he is not concerned with these; he mentally dismisses them. He is concerned only with the broad river of smooth concrete facing him through the trees, and the great, winking red eye suspended, icicle-like, above it.

He waits.

And tenses at a sound upon the river—an engine sound, mosquito-dim with distance, rising to a hum. A rushing sound under the stars.

The rider's hands contract like the claws of a bird. He rises slowly on the bucket seat, right foot poised near the starter. A coiled spring. Waiting.

Twin pencil-beams of light move toward him, toward the street on which he waits hidden. Closer.

The hum builds in volume; the lights are very close now, flaring chalk white along the concrete boulevard.

The rider's goggles are down and he is ready to move out, move onto the river. Another second, perhaps two . . .

But no. The vehicle slows, makes a full stop. A service vehicle with two men inside, laughing, joking. The rider listens to them, mouth set, eyes hard. The vehicle begins to move once more. The sound is eaten by the night.

There is no violation.

Now . . . the relaxing, the easing back. The ebb tide of tension receding. Gone. The rider quiet again under the moon.

Waiting.

The red eye winking at the empty boulevard.

"How much farther, Dave?" asks the girl.

"Ten miles, maybe. Once we hit Westwood, it's a quick run to my place. Relax. You're nervous."

"We should have stayed on the mainway. Used the grid. I don't *like* these surface streets. A grid would have taken us in."

The man smiles, looping an arm around her.

"There's nothing to be afraid of as long as you're careful," he says. "I used to drive surface streets all the time when I was a boy. Lots of people did."

The girl swallows, touches her hair nervously. "But they don't anymore. People use the grids. I didn't even know cars still *came* equipped for manual driving."

"They don't. I had this set up by a mechanic I know. He does jobs like this for road buffs. It's still legal, driving your own car—it's just that most people have lost the habit."

The girl peers out the window into the silent street, shakes her head. "It's . . . not natural. Look out there. Nobody! Not another car for miles. I feel as if we're . . . trespassing."

The man is annoyed. "That's damn nonsense. I have friends who do this all the time. Just relax and enjoy it. And don't talk like an idiot."

"I want out," says the girl. "I'll take a walkway back to the grid."

"The hell you will," flares the man. "You're with *me* tonight. We're going to my place."

She resists, strikes at his face; the man grapples to subdue her. He does not see the blinking light. The car passes under it, swiftly.

"Chrisdam!" snaps the man. "I went through that light. You made me miss the stop. I've broken one of the surface laws!" He says this numbly.

"What does that mean?" the girl asks. "What could happen?"

"Never mind. Nothing will happen. Never mind about what could happen."

The girl peers out into the darkness. "I want to leave this car."

"Just shut up," the man says, and keeps driving.

Something in the sound tells the rider that this one will not stop, that it will continue to move along the river of stone despite the blinking eye.

He smiles in the darkness, lips stretched back, silently. Poised there on the cycle, with the hum steady and rising on the river, he feels the power within him about to be released.

The car is almost upon the light, moving swiftly; there is no hint of slackened speed.

The rider watches intently. Man and a girl inside, struggling. Fighting with one another.

The car passes under the light.

Violation.

Now!

He spurs the cycle to metal life. The motor crackles, roars, explodes the black machine into motion, and the rider is away, rolling in muted thunder along the street. Around the corner, swaying onto the long, moon-painted river of the boulevard.

The rider feels the wind in his face, feels the throb and power-pulse of the metal thing he rides, feels the smooth concrete rushing backward under his wheels.

Ahead, the firefly glow of taillights.

And now his cycle voice cries out after them, a siren moan through the still spaces of the city. A voice which rises and falls in spirals of sound. His cycle-eyes, mounted left and right, are blinking crimson, red as blood in their wake.

The car will stop. The man will see him, hear him. The eyes and the voice will reach the violator.

And he will stop.

"Bitch!" the man says. "We've picked up a rider at that light."

"*You* picked him up, I didn't," says the girl. "It's your problem."

"But I've never been stopped on a surface street," the man says, a desperate note in his voice "In all these years—never once!"

The girl glares at him. "Dave, you make me sick! Look at you—shaking, sweating. You're a damn poor excuse for a man!"

He does not react to her words. He speaks in a numbed monotone. "I can talk my way out. I know I can. He'll listen to me. I have my rights as a citizen of the city."

"He's catching up fast. You'd better pull over."

His eyes harden as he brakes the car. "I'll do the talking. All of it. You just keep quiet. I'll handle this."

The rider sees that the car is slowing, braking, pulling to the curb.

He cuts the siren voice, lets it die, glides the cycle in behind the car. Cuts the engine. Sits there for a long moment on the leather seat, pulling off his gloves. Slowly.

He sees the car door slide open, a man steps out, comes toward him. The rider swings a booted leg over the cycle and steps free, advancing to meet this lawbreaker, fitting the gloves carefully into his black leather belt.

They face one another, the man smaller, paunchy, balding, face flushed. The rider's polite smile eases the man's tenseness.

"You in a hurry, sir?"

"Me? No. I'm not in a hurry. Not at all. It was just . . . I didn't *see* the light up there until . . . I was past it. The high trees and all. I swear to you, I didn't see it. I'd never knowingly break a surface law, Officer. You have my sworn word."

Nervous. Shaken and nervous, this man. The rider can feel the man's guilt, a physical force. He extends a hand.

"May I see your operator's license, please?"

The man fumbles in his coat. "I have it right here. It's all in order, up to date and all."

"Just let me see it, please."

The man continues to talk.

"Been driving for years, Officer, and this is my first violation. Perfect record up to now. I'm a responsible citizen. I obey the laws. After all, I'm not a fool."

The rider says nothing; he examines the man's license, taps it thoughtfully against his wrist. The rider's goggles are opaque. The man cannot see his eyes as he studies the face of the violator.

"The woman in the car . . . is she your wife?"

"No. No, sir. She's . . . a friend. Just a friend."

"Then why were you fighting? I saw the two of you fighting inside the car when it passed the light. That isn't friendly, is it?"

The man attempts to smile. "Personal. We had a small personal disagreement. It's all over now, believe me."

The rider walks to the car, leans to peer in at the woman. She is pale, as nervous as the man.

"You having trouble?" the rider asks.

She hesitates, shakes her head mutely. The rider leaves her and returns to the man, who is resting a hand against the cycle.

"Don't touch that," says the rider coldly, and the man draws back his hand, mumbles an apology.

"I have no further use for this," says the rider, handing back the man's license. "You are guilty of a surface-street violation."

The man quakes; his hands tremble. "But it was not *deliberate*. I know the law. You're empowered to make exceptions if a violation is not deliberate. The full penalty is not invoked in such cases. You are allowed to—"

The rider cuts into the flow of words. "You forfeited your Citizen's Right of Exception when you allowed a primary emotion —anger, in this instance—to affect your control of a surface vehicle. Thus, my duty is clear and prescribed."

The man's eyes widen in shock as the rider brings up a belt-weapon. "You can't possibly—"

"Under authorization of Citystate Overpopulation Statute 4452663 I am hereby executing . . ."

The man begins to run.

". . . sentence."

He presses the trigger. Three long, probing blue jets of starhot flame leap from the weapon in the rider's hand.

The man is gone.

The woman is gone.

The car is gone.

The street is empty and silent. A charred smell of distant suns lingers in the morning air.

The rider stands by his cycle, unmoving for a long moment. Then he carefully holsters the weapon, pulls on his leather gloves. He mounts the cycle and it pulses to life under his foot.

With the sky in motion above him, he is again upon the moon-flowing boulevard, gliding back toward the blinking red eye.

The rider reaches his station on the small, tree-shadowed side street and thinks, *How stupid they are! To be subject to indecision, to quarrels and erratic behavior—weak, all of them. Soft and weak.*

He smiles into the darkness.

The eye blinks over the river.

And now it is 4 A.M. now 6 and 8 and 10 and 1 P.M., now 3, 4, 5 P.M. . . . the hours turning like wheels, the days spinning away.

And he waits. Through nights without sleep, days without food—a flawless metal enforcer at his vigil, sure of himself and of his duty.

Waiting.

✝ ✝ ✝

The FasterFaster Affair

WHEN JAMESTEN TELEPORTED INTO THE OFFICE wearing his twintone perforated Venusian breathing-boots and a rakishly cut sports jacket in worsted plastic, Miss Manypiggies sobbed brokenly and threw herself into his arms. "Rip off my clothing, James," she pleaded. "Love me, rape me, torture me, I don't care! Take my subtly tanned supple woman's body and—"

JamesTen pushed her gently aside. "Not now, Manypiggies," he husked in a silken voice reserved for love-crazed secretaries. "Z wants me inside, where things count. God knows what's up in there, but it's my kind of trouble. Now be a sweet and buzz me in, chop-chop."

"Chop-chop," sighed Miss Manypiggies as JamesTen stepped lithely into the Matter Disintegrator. She thumbed the proper button and the suave secret agent wavered and vanished.

He reappeared, all atoms neatly in place, beside Z's desk.

"Good to see you, Ten," rumbled Z. His outwardly pleasant tone meant another joust with death was in the offing. JamesTen smiled thinly.

"Sorry for the delay in getting here, sir, but I was feeding mutated Shakespeare into my home computer."

"More of your attempts to bring the Bard to the robot masses, eh, James?"

"That's the idea, sir. If we could educate these clumsy devils, feed *Robo and Juliet* into their receptors, the world would be a calmer place, sir. Peace has its roots in culture."

"Idealistic claptrap and bushwah, Ten!"

JamesTen stiffened. The casual banter had ended.

Slowly, Z rocked back in his sleepchair, tenting his fingers. JamesTen tensed. When Z tented his fingers . . .

"Know anything about a man who calls himself Plugo Mittelholzer?"

" 'Fraid not, sir."

"It's an assumed name—and he's used several others. Thiarn Chong. Elwood Beeles. Francis Fahrenkrug. Clifford Siggfoos. Raymond Tarbutton. Nickolaus Kronschnable. Orlando Pipes. Thomas Nuckles. Willie Ploughboy. Roman Belch. Cungee Arena. Vertie Cheatam. Elsworth Molder. Exie Moneylon. Chester Foat. Socorro Quankenbush. Pershing Threewit. Lester Hoots. George Fiebelkorn. Lawrence Torrance. Kenneth Dankwardt. And, most recently, Simon Brain."

"Is Brain his real name, sir?"

"His real name, according to the Chekfax Team, is Sir Henry Fasterfaster."

"Odd name, that."

"Exactly. And he is, beyond any doubt whatever, the most insanely dangerous man in the universe as we know it today. Of course, God knows what's *really* out there!"

"The Astrom boys are doing a first-rate job for us, sir. Discovered a brand new galaxy just last week. I took it upon myself to send a few junior agents out to clean it up. Alien scum and all that sort of thing, sir. Cut 'em to ribbons!"

"We're drifting, Ten."

"Quite, sir." Again the thin smile.

"Know anything about Operation Mibs?"

"Has it—by any remote chance, sir—something to do with *marbles*?"

"Exactly. Good show, Ten!" Z rocked back for a quick, relaxing instant of sleep, then snapped his eyes open. "Sir Henry Fasterfaster is engaged in what can only be termed a cosmic game of mibs."

" 'Fraid you've lost me, sir."

Z smiled his lizard's smile and lit a pseudocamel. "I'll fill you in."

JamesTen slipped into an attentionseat. It kept him bolt upright. One hundred and thirty-six straight hours at the computer had taken the edge off his thinking and this was no time to funk out.

"Sir Henry Fasterfaster is from Uranus," began Z, his voice deceptively casual. "The chap's mother was a sod-common, slug-stupid skin sorter in a Plutonian onion mine—and his father a tri-finned out-of-work Slimecreature from Neptune. I believe you call 'em Neppies."

"Right, sir. Nasty devils. Low co-op potential."

"At any rate these two ran away together and they mated—God knows *how*—producing Sir Henry. He was adopted by a team of Wogglebugs, schooled in a Jupe-based low-grade Unit, traveled the sawdust trail as part of an undersea juggling act and peddled Lowdope in the Asteroids. Ended up here, in Greater Olde England, and proved himself a brilliant lad, taking his doctorate in Worm Pathology."

"Sounds ordinary enough, sir."

"Shut up and listen, you damned machine!"

JamesTen flushed. He did not like to be reminded that he was of android origin.

"At any rate, Fasterfaster was using worms for cover, nothing more. His game was a queer one."

"Go on, sir."

"You must understand, James, that Sir Henry was crazed from the outset, twisted with powerlust, consumed with an acid hatred for every living creature known to us at present, writhing with dark, wrathful desires, bent on the most depraved form of ultimate revenge on the universe as we know it for the cruel joke his mis-mated parents had played upon him. He was, in short, not a normal student."

"Sounds like Psyc fodder, sir."

"Exactly. A brute and a fiend, right enough. And ugly as sin. Great long leathery neck, toad's eyes, distended red-rimmed nostrils, purple hands, immense kangaroo feet, and no teeth at all. This was the legacy of his unnatural birth."

"Think I'm beginning to get the picture, sir."

"He's a past master at disguise. Can look bloody normal if he's about it. He's picked up a lot of awful tricks whilst kicking about the system. Lived on a dozen worlds before he was a post-teener. Hobnobbed with the unemployed. Stirred up the milk robots on Venus. Got a schoolmarm in trouble in Redding, Pennsylvania. She gave birth to a thing no doctor could look upon. They had to bury it, chop-chop. Nasty business all round."

"What are you leading up to, sir?"

JamesTen was getting logy, despite the sharp prods from the attentionseat.

Z stubbed out his pseudocamel and leaned forward, fingers tented. "JamesEight and JamesNine were destroyed by our ruthless friend. And they were the latest models. I've ordered two more just like them, but it takes an ungodly amount of time to assemble these damned killer machines. Oh—sorry, Ten."

"No offense taken, sir." JamesTen smiled thinly. No use in being fussy about discussing his talent; he was built to kill and he enjoyed killing. It was as simple as that. A prime 000000000000000 android could kill anything that moved, anywhere, no questions asked. The extra 0 did it. A plain 00000000000000 android was only licensed to cripple for life.

"What I'm leading up to, Ten, is this: the man who now calls himself Plugo Mittelholzer is right here in Greater New London on the Strand. He's working a cover operation called E.T.T.T.P.U. Economy Time Travel To Parallel Universes. A clever front for his master plan."

"And that plan *is*, sir?" JamesTen's eyes were lidding. He switched the attentionseat to Peak Efficiency and a jolt of Quickpain brought him to Full Alert Status.

". . . to destroy every living creature on every world in every galaxy throughout the entire known universe and beyond."

"Big job that, sir."

"Exactly. Luckily, a Robot Telepath plant tipped us on how Sir Henry plans to accomplish his nefarious end. Brings us back to mibs. Fasterfaster has worked out a fiendishly simple Power Thrust that will set each star and planet in violent motion *toward one another!* Just imagine, if you will, a rough total of fourteen quadrillion-illion-million-zillion worlds hurled through space like immense marbles directly at each other!"

JamesTen whistled through his perfect teeth. "And when they all make contact, sir?"

"Whappo!" Z slapped a hand on the desk. "End of the line for life as we know it today. It's the Big Casino. The Long Goodbye. The Final Blackout. The Ten Count. The Big Sleep. Curtains. Finis."

"I believe I have the image, sir."

Z paused to light a pseudokool. "Now there's no reaching this chap with logic or sentiment. He must, in short, be snuffed out. That's your cup of tea, Ten. Chop chop?"

"Chop, chop, sir."

Z looked pleased. "Well, then, you'll approach him as a Time Student. Tell him you want to go back to the Parallel Universe in which Rod Serling failed to sell *The Twilight Zone* to CBS, when *Peyton Place* and *The Beverly Hillbillies* couldn't find sponsors. You are to convince Sir Henry that you are researching a paper on Reverse Failure in Boffo Television."

"I'll wear hornrim glasses as a cover for my perfect eyes," said JamesTen smugly.

"Then, off you go, Ten. And I shall expect results. You James-Ten models take *ages* to replace!"

"Count on me, sir. I'll have the ugly brute's head on a plate within a fortnit'."

"We haven't got a fortnit', confound you! I want him dead within twenty-four hours."

"Done, sir. Am I free to disintegrate?"

"You are—and God speed, Ten! If you bring this one off you save every living thing in creation. A job well worth the candle!"

JamesTen smiled thinly, saluted—and vanished in a shimmer of golden atoms.

The weathered, fog-dimmed sign on the Strand read:

TRAVEL BACK IN TIME AT LOW RATES!
SEE LINCOLN LOSE A LOG-SPLITTING CONTEST!
SEE HENRY FORD GO BROKE!
SEE A FLAT-CHESTED JAYNE MANSFIELD!
SEE HANNIBAL GET LOST IN THE ALPS!
COME IN NOW! FUN! EDUCATIONAL!
WINTER RATES! DON'T WAIT!

JamesTen, wearing tritoned Saturn Student Sneakers and a rakish Ruffalo pseudodacron UCLA Youth Shirt, adjusted his heavy pseudospecs and entered the shoddy, plastic building housing E.T.T.T.P.U.

A grinning, cherub-faced gentleman nodded to him. The man was rosy cheeked, fat, and bearded. Only his coaldark birdbright eyes betrayed his depravity. This, then, was Plugo Mittelholzer, alias Simon Brain, alias Kenneth Dankwardt, alias Socorro Quankenbush, alias Roman Belch, alias Clifford Siggfoos, alias—

"Yassssss?" the man hissed. "Might I be of help?" There was no mistaking the odorous slimesoft hiss of a Neppie! JamesTen tightened his jaw.

"I wish a Time Trip," he said. "To the Irving Thalberg building at Metro. Located, I believe, just a wee bit below Venice Boulevard, in Culver City. Circa 1958."

"That'll be thirteen thou. Credits. In advance. Got that much onya?"

"I believe that I have that sum upon my person," nodded JamesTen. He reached casually for his thin leatherlife wallet which was actually not the smooth, fashion-tailored object it appeared to be, but was instead a deadly weapon which fired live centipedes. One bite from those poisoned fangs should do the trick.

However, before JamesTen could activate the firing pin the wallet was judo-chopped from his hand, and he found himself staring into the cold pseudometal muzzle of a Neptunion blaster.

"Now, see here," he protested, trying a shallow bluff, "this is plain rudeness!"

"Let us end this nettlesome charade, Mr. JamesTen—android agent acting out of Greater New London on Her Majesty's Secret Service," hissed Fasterfaster. "Your identity is known to me. I had *my* Robot Telepath trail *your* Robot Telepath to HQ."

"You damned fiend!"

Sir Henry laughed his snake's laugh.

"You came here pretending to want a trip in Time. And so you shall have it!"

Fasterfaster backed the agent into a tall, black boxlike box.

"I'm sending you where you'll do me no further harm—to a Yogurt Farm between Indio and Palm Springs where you will be at the mercy of dedicated health addicts intent on slimming you down *their* way. Day and night you shall be fed only Yogurt."

JamesTen was horrorstruck. "But—but you know I cannot function without exotic, exquisitely prepared cuisine and rare, properly aged vintage wines brought to room temp! You *are* a fiend, Fasterfaster!"

"May your plastobones rot in the California desert! May buzzards pick your pseudoflesh!" hissed the master criminal—and threw a red plastic switch.

In a great spume of golden sparks, JamesTen and the Time Box vanished.

The android agent woke with a gonging headache. He was in a white room, on a white bed, covered by a white sheet.

"Are you okay now, mister?" asked a dulcet voice above him. "Here, sip a little yogurt."

JamesTen focused his eyes on a stunningly beautiful white girl standing beside the bed. Ah, he thought, so this is the one fatal flaw in Fasterfaster's thinking—to send me to a farm with *female* attendants!

"The only food I desire is the food of your lushly soft lips," he said.

The girl dropped her yogurt. "Golly, I—I . . ."

JamesTen vaulted nakedly from the bed to catch her in his arms, crushing her softly lush body to his.

Exactly twelve minutes later he was sprinting lithely across the desert toward the black, boxlike box that stood, half buried in sand, behind a clump of spiny dwarf cactus. His perfect love-making had forced the girl to reveal the area that he had been discovered. Now it was only a simple matter of setting the time dials for Greater New London, circa the Present.

The box erupted into a tracery of golden atoms. JamesTen was on his way back to finish a very nasty job.

The tatty plastic building which housed E.T.T.T.P.U. was empty when JamesTen stepped from the humming Time Box, gun at the ready. Sighing, he slipped the effective, handsomely ornamented Sheckley-Bemstein .20-40 double-charge weapon, equipped with Astro Silencer, back into its custom-worn pseudo-alligator sheath holster in his left underarm cavity.

"Haven't got much time," he reminded himself. Due to his having foolishly taken a short cut through a complex Space Warp he'd actually used up twenty-three and a half of the twenty-four vital hours given him by Z. Another thirty minutes and the entire universe would cease to exist, and he'd have truly bungled the assignment.

Right at this moment, for all the android agent knew, Sir Henry Fasterfaster could be pseudosinging in some raw Opera dive on Mercury. Or he might be, even now, brazenly barrel-housing with a belly dancer from Barsoom. Or smugly riding as a passenger aboard a rusted Moon scow chugging through hyperspace for the Outer Dog Stars.

"Oh—frab!" JamesTen growled, relieving tension with the obscenity.

His perfect ears picked up a squeaking, rasping gasp from one corner of the room. He cat-stepped to the corner, gun at the ready.

"Mmm—M—Mister J—James, sir . . . I . . . I . . ." It was old Everett K. L-XIII-Plus, the loyal-to-a-fault Robot Telepath working out of Z's office. He was a shocking tangle of broken wires, sprung cogs, and shorted circuits. One of his brownblue eyes rolled crazily in his square metal head.

"Can you talk, fella?" asked JamesTen, bending over him. "Where did Sir Henry go?"

Everett squeaked in pain. "To . . . to . . ." The malfunctioning eye rattled to the floor and JamesTen kicked it aside irritably.

"Get to it, man! *Where?*"

"O-Off . . . ice . . . Z . . . Danger!"

"Great scott! To Z's office. Why, he's out to harm the finest man the Service has ever known! And what of poor Miss Manypiggies? Why, that filthy—"

The dying robot gurgled metallically as the android agent rushed from the building.

Outside, in the thick soup of a Greater New London fog, JamesTen flagged down a Spacekab.

"Baker Street. 228. And make it chop-chop!" he snapped, handing the driver a thousandnote prepunched credit.

"Cor blimey! Jus' you hold yer bloody hat, Gov, an' we's on our bloody way, we are! Hang on, yer Lordship!"

The kab lifted back into its prescribed airslot and rattled unsteadily toward Baker Street. JamesTen noted, with a certain degree of pleasure, that this kab was a vintage Nolag-Russeii model KXK-111 with the charmingly old-fashioned Intra-dish transmission aided by a fluted prefab twin-select overdrive.

"Pardon—but didn't this very model win the classic 24-Hour GP race for airkabs back at Le Mans in 2108?" he asked the driver.

"Cor, I dunno, yer Grace," rasped the hairy little man. "If you say so, she did! An' that's a fact!"

"I'm *certain* it was an N-R KXK job," mused JamesTen. "The twin-select unit funked out in the 23rd hour, but ole Frabish-Suitgrave brought her over for the win. Great victory!" For a hushed moment JamesTen was lost in the glory of past races—then he rallied with an oath. "Why the Frab aren't we getting there, man?"

"Bloody fog's got me 'arf crackers, Gov," declared the hairy driver. "I'm near off me nob, matie! Couldn't find me own arse in this stuff. An' that's a fact!"

"Take me down, then, you blundering fool, and I'll teleport in. That's what I should have done in the first place. Z will play merry hell with me if the universe goes up!"

The confused kabbie landed the KXK-111 atop a sagging plastic flower dispensary (featuring a sale on Venusian Tubors) and JamesTen scrambled to the ground, cursing the driver's oafish stupidity.

He found a teleport booth next door to an android marriage counseling service—but two rat-haired old nannies were in line ahead of him.

"Stand aside," he ordered crisply. "I'm on Her Majesty's business."

The first nannie grinned knowingly at her blowsy companion. "My, my . . . but ain't that what they *all* say, them what wants a decent woman's place in line."

The second nannie cackled approval. "Right ya are, Meg, dearie! Don't you budge an inch fer the cheeky sod!"

Nettled, JamesTen quick-fired a double charge from his Sheckley-Bemstein into the two ladies. As they thumped heavily to the walk he quick-stepped over their smoking bodies into the booth.

Sir Henry Fasterfaster would indeed be surprised to see him!

Z's office was empty when the android agent appeared. Too late! Only five minutes left; then the universe was finished for good and all. And no Sir Henry.

"I've muddled the job," sighed JamesTen, wearily holstering his .20-40.

"Indeed you have," a voice hissed behind him. The agent cat-spun around on the balls of his perfect feet.

It was Z—emerging from a plastobroom closet with a service blaster held at belly level.

"But, sir . . ."

"The game is up," Z grated, eyes alight with intense hatred.

"Great scott, sir, *you* must be—"

Of course, JamesTen told himself, Z was Fasterfaster! He'd been royally duped by the master fiend! It all fell into place—or *did* it? Had Z sent him on a false hunt to clear the way for his —Fasterfaster's—inhuman scheme for mass destruction? If so, how long had Z been Fasterfaster? Or had there ever been a real Z? Or a real Fasterfaster? Perhaps Fasterfaster was now Z in disguise. Or was Z Fasterfaster all along? Or was . . . JamesTen's metal brain reeled in confusion.

The closet door opened again and Miss Manypiggies appeared, her eyes bright with hate. She held a blaster in her slender subtly tanned woman's hand, at tummy level.

As Z's head swung toward her JamesTen had his split-second chance. His perfect reflexes went into action and the efficient Sheckley-Bernstein .20-40 popped into his hand. He squeezed the pseudotrigger three times . . . four . . . five . . . six . . . seven . . . eight . . .

Z lay face down on the plastorug, reduced to a smoking mass.

JamesTen jauntily stowed his weapon. "I'll wager *he* won't be destroying any universes, eh, Manypiggies?" He gave her his thin, smirking smile.

"He never intended to," snapped the girl, "but in just two minutes, *you* do!"

"What the deuce do you mean by that remark?"

"I mean—and please keep your gun hand at your side—that *you* are Sir Henry Fasterfaster!"

"Utter balderdash!" declared JamesTen with some heat. "Wouldn't I bloody well know whether or not I was a master fiend?"

"Not in this particular case," the girl replied, her tone level and cold. "Among your many other evil arts you are a master at self-hypnosis. You set up this inhuman plan for mass destruction and then—upon disguising yourself as an android agent—hypnotized yourself into believing you actually *were* one. The real JamesTen is dead. I found his body in there." She indicated the closet. "In just ten seconds your hypnosis will wear off and you'll be Sir Henry again. Then you'll attempt to activate Operation Mibs."

"But if I'm Sir Henry . . . then who was the fat, rosy-cheeked bewhiskered fellow who sent me to the Yogurt Farm at Indio?"

"A Robot Telepath programmed to impersonate your true evil self. Z had to believe you were JamesTen in order to ease off and give you, Sir Henry, a clear field. You knew he would not send out other agents if *he* knew JamesTen was on the job. And even his old loyal-to-a-fault Robot Telepath, Everett K. L-XIII-Plus could not penetrate your false identity, since your self-hypnotized mind offered no clue."

"Then . . . then who did in old Everett?"

"The fat, rosy-cheeked, bewhiskered Robot Telepath—after you left for Indio."

Miss Manypiggies briskly checked her pseudowatch. "*Now*—do you know who you really are?"

The android agent's perfect body dropped away like a cloak, revealing an ugly brute with a great long, leathery neck, toad's eyes, distended red-rimmed nostrils, purple hands, immense kangaroo feet, and no teeth at all.

Sir Henry!

"I have one final question before we all dust away, my very clever Miss Maggie Manypiggies," hissed the fiend. "How did Z find out that I wasn't me? That is, that JamesTen was not JamesTen? Sorry I put that so awkwardly, but you follow what I'm asking, do you not?"

The girl nodded. "When I discovered the real JamesTen's mutilated body in the closet, stuffed into the plastohamper, I told Z about it. It was just that simple. Leaving James in Z's closet was a stupid blunder."

"No real harm done I'll wager," hissed Sir Henry. "When I press this red plastic button—" and he held up a long black tubelike tube with a crimson button on one end "—the entire universe will be reduced to ash, and I will be revenged for the cruel joke of my unnatural birth!"

At that precise instant, Miss Manypiggies fired.

Sir Henry Fasterfaster crumpled to the plastorug, knocking over a pseudolamp, the tube falling from his outflung purple hand. There was a long moment of silence.

What Miss Manypiggies did not understand, what she absolutely could *not* fathom, was the fact that Sir Henry was now reduced to a mass of smoking wires and sprung cogs.

Which meant that he wasn't really . . .

Then, in that case, oh God! Could it possibly be that *she* was the real Sir Henry Fasterfaster?

Miss Manypiggies wisely decided not to think about that.

+ + +

To Serve the Ship

HE ENTERED THE DIM CHAMBER, PAUSING JUST inside, his back pressed against the door. In the soft semi-darkness the room smelled of iron and aluminum and brass. Ahead of him, dials glowed faintly. Lord, but this is fine, he thought, breathing deeply, hands clenched. He closed his eyes in the warm, familiar dark, thinking, this is where I belong; here I am complete:

Norman Jerome Hollander, Servant of the Ship.

He opened his eyes, pupils adjusting to the dimness. Across the length of the chamber, a rising wall of tiny, multicolored lights winked and gleamed. Needles steadied at correct pressure levels; round dial faces hummed softly, regulating the vast power of the Ship, guiding it through space toward—

Norman Hollander swore, knuckling his forehead with a clenched fist. He didn't want to think about the Ship's destination. It seemed so grossly unfair. But that was how it must seem to all the Servants at such a time. Each thinking the same sad thoughts, each cursing the impersonal machine which had passed its irrevocable judgment.

He moved slowly toward the glowing panel and lowered himself into the cushioning depth of the control chair. Around him he savored the immense breathing presence of the Ship, its muted atomics, deep-buried in their ribbed and layered metal tons, sending out an almost imperceptible vibration which trembled along each nerve and muscle of Norman Hollander's body. In front of him, dials whirred, wheels spun, clicked; wires sang. The Ship was alive, but he was no longer a part of her life. He was now simply a passenger on the way to a destination he hated to reach.

Hollander sighed, removing the slotted metal card from his uniform pocket. He didn't need any light to read the words; they were graven on his brain. He would always remember them:

OUTCOME OF TEST L176X: June 29, 2163
OPERATIONAL STATUS: NEGATIVE

The silver needles had entered his veins. Electronic devices had measured his heartbeat, his hearing, his blood pressure. His reaction time was checked, his entire body combed for the slightest imperfection. And, finally, that imperfection had been found, the verdict rendered. Negative. The one word he'd been dreading, the one word which meant that his job was over, that he was no longer a part of the Ship, could no longer serve her. For eighty-five years, while she hovered in space, suspended above alien planets, mining the rich ores from a thousand strange worlds, Norman Hollander had lovingly guided her efforts. His human hand had moved her delicate metal spider-hands that probed the surfaces of those far-flung worlds for storable riches. She was a Hundred Year Ship, designed and built to remain in space for ten full decades while her great storage compartments were gradually filled. Then, and only then, would she come home. Unless . . .

Unless her Servant fails a test, thought Norman Hollander. Unless she finds her Servant wanting, imperfect. Then she rejects him, takes him back to Earth.

Hollander was 105, barely middle-aged by current Earth standards, but old for space. Ideally, though, he should have been able to remain with the Ship for those last fifteen precious years. But human weakness had cheated him of this. Hollander leaned forward, peering at his own reflection in the circular dial to his right. Not an old face. A strong face, marked with duty, but not old. Science had kept him young, but even the wonders of science could not make him perfect, as the Ship was perfect. And so she was taking him home.

No, not home, he thought bitterly. My home is here, with the Ship; I was born and bred for this and nothing else. Earth is simply a place, faintly remembered, which I'll reach in forty-eight hours—after all these years as strange as any world I've ever visited. No, not home.

*   *   *

"When is he due?" asked Dr. Burack.

His assistant, David Miller, placed the schedule on Burack's desk. "Tomorrow morning," Miller said.

Burack looked at the schedule. Then he met Miller's cool gaze. "I hope we have some luck with this one," he said. "Are your men posted?"

Miller nodded. "He'll be observed from the moment the Ship touches down. Personally, I'm not optimistic. The pattern seems fixed."

Dr. Burack tapped one finger gently against the schedule. "Patterns can be broken. That's the biggest part of our job. I want the usual hourly report on Hollander. We've got a lot to learn yet, but we may be getting closer to a solution. This time, David, we may win."

"I wouldn't count on it sir," said David Miller.

Lying on his side in the bed, Hollander stared out at the stars pricking the dark night sky beyond his window. The stars were telling him that he should be up there with them, that he had no business on this world called Earth. The stars understood him. No one here, on this stifling planet, understood him. No one.

Oh, they'd tried to make him feel at home. He was given this modern house, equipped with every electronic comfort; the latest Jetcar waited in the garage; a full wardrobe of clothes had been provided—all gifts for his service from a grateful government. They gave him everything except the chance to go back.

His family also tried. They had done all they possibly could to assure him that he was wanted, welcome, that he was now a part of their society once again, that he *belonged*. Yet his parents were strangers to him. He'd been a boy of seventeen when he'd seen them last; now they were smiling, friendly strangers, and he found nothing of himself in them.

From the moment his feet touched Earth he had begun to hate.

He hated the crowds shouting at him; he hated this house, the car, the clothes . . . He even found himself hating his mother and father. They were part of the society that had taken him from space. He felt trapped and betrayed by all these smiling people, the men and women who shook his hand, who told him how heroic he was, how noble he had been, serving alone "out there" for all those years. They gave him medals; they made speeches about him and, through it all, he wanted to damn them, to loose his hatred for what they had done to him.

Hollander often wondered about the Servants who had landed

before him. Dozens of them, at the very least. Yet no one seemed to know anything about them; no records existed to prove that any of them had ever come back. Was he, in fact, the only man to have survived the Ships? When he asked questions about other Servants his inquiries were shrugged aside. No, they told him, there were no others. He had questioned his parents, but they said they knew nothing about the Servants. In their denials, however, Hollander had detected a guilt, an uneasiness.

The first month had been hell.

Five days after his homecoming he'd knocked down a man in the street. The man had made an insulting remark about the Ships and those who served them. He could still hear the fellow's mocking voice: *You have to be insane to stay out there all that time on those damned tubs. You have to be crazy to do a thing like that!* And Norman Hollander had knocked him to the street. If he hadn't been pulled away he might have throttled the man.

The fool! Hollander could feel the angry heat rising in his body.

During the second week he'd gone to the Psyc Center and allowed the machines to put him through analysis. Adjust, they advised him. Learn to adjust to your society. But Norman Hollander had rejected them, as their Ship had rejected him.

In the third week he had attacked a Lawman. Only his status as a retired Servant had kept him from severe punishment.

I had my reasons, Hollander recalled. When I asked him why there were no other Servants he had smiled like some kind of sly cat—and I wanted to smash that smile, destroy it.

And last week; that had been the worst. He drank for an entire morning, then took out the car. The afternoon ended in near-disaster when a schoolgirl had crossed the traffic strip ahead of him and he hadn't seen her. In avoiding her, he crashed. They took the car away from him. From him, the man whose hands had guided the great Ship!

What next? Hollander asked himself, what will I do next? I can never accept this exile, this living death. If they keep me here I'll end up killing somebody. Anybody. They're all to blame.

Sighing wearily, he closed his eyes, shutting out the bright, beckoning stars. . . .

"He isn't responding," said David Miller. "He's like the others. And we've done everything."

Dr. Burack put aside the folder marked HOLLANDER and stood up. He walked past his assistant to the window. Ninety stories below traffic moved swiftly along the jet strips.

"I've called him in," Burack said, the tone of defeat evident in his voice. "He knows that he can't go back into space. But he also knows that he's a freak here in our world. That's the price a Servant pays. Abnormality is a virtue with the Ships; a normal man would be useless to us. Perhaps, some day, we can reverse the pattern. But not yet. Not now."

"Then you're going to commit him?" asked Miller.

"What else can I do at this point? If I don't commit him he'll break, turn violent. Hollander's a potential killer."

"He's also a public hero."

Burack smiled without warmth. "So were all the others. At least the public is well aware of our problem. That's why they built the Servants' Institution. Here the Hollanders can find peace. They won't find it anywhere else on Earth."

Miller nodded. "Maybe we can save the next one," he said. "We're advancing with each case. Maybe, next time, the Ships won't win."

Dr. Burack said nothing. He continued to stare at the distant ribbons of traffic.

Hollander walked down the long, brilliantly illumined corridor, arms swinging loosely at his sides, his fingertips brushing the regulation stripe on his trousers. It was wonderful to be wearing his uniform again, and the close-fitting jacket gave him a sense of security he hadn't felt since the landing. He enjoyed the echoing slap of his boots against the smooth marble floor. Yes, it was good of them to give him back his uniform.

"Here we are, Norman," said Dr. Burack, indicating a heavy door. "This is where you'll stay from now on. I think you'll find we've thought of everything."

"Thank you," said Hollander. "I'm sure you have."

The two men shook hands.

"Goodbye, Doctor."

"Goodbye, Norman."

Dr. Burack watched Hollander go into the special room. He drew a long breath, then turned away.

He entered the dim chamber, pausing just inside, his back pressed against the door. In the soft, semi-darkness the room smelled of iron and aluminum and brass. Ahead of him, dials glowed faintly. Lord, but this is fine, he thought, breathing deeply, hands clenched. He closed his eyes in the warm, familiar dark, thinking, this is where I belong; here I am complete:

Norman Jerome Hollander, Servant of the Ship.

✦ ✦ ✦

The Day the Gorf
Took Over

THERE'S A SPECIAL OFFICE AT THE PENTAGON called the Office of Stateside Emergencies. Dave Merkle is in charge, a thin, night-eyed man, haunted by a perpetual sense of failure. He was depressed on the morning of June 3, 2010 because there had not been a decent stateside emergency since early May. There had been three superb overseas emergencies, but they were handled by another office down the hall and didn't count.

The morning of June 3 was when Dave Merkle's right-hand man, troubleshooter Eldon Sash, came in smiling. "We got one," he said.

Merkle raised his head from the desk to peer at Sash, who was fat and jolly. "Emergency?"

"You bet," said Sash in a piping voice. Fat men often have them.

"Stateside?"

"Right in upper New York."

Merkle looked dubious. He rose slowly from his chair. "I just hope this is a spot-on, one hundred percent goddamn emergency."

"It's a frog."

"A frog in upper New York State is no emergency." He sat down again.

"This one is," Sash persisted. "It's big."

"How big?"

"I'd say about the size of your average four-unit apartment house."

"That's big all right," said Dave Merkle, thoughtfully tapping his chin. He began to look pleased.

"And it eats people. It already ate a guy in a sports car."

"What make?"

Sash carefully removed a small, green notebook from his coat, checked a page. "Corvette."

Merkle smacked his palms together. "I *like* it, Eldon, I like it!" He strapped on a custom-grip .38 service revolver that was officially licensed and registered. "Where's the frog now?"

"After it ate the Corvette, it hopped off toward Sleepy Hollow."

"Fine. I'll have a chopper pick us up on the roof and we'll hustle right out there." He gripped Sash at the elbow.

"Sir?"

"We need a project name for this thing. Any suggestions?"

"How about Gorf? Project Gorf."

"I don't get it." Merkle looked disturbed.

"That's frog spelled backward," Sash told him.

"Gorf! Gorf! Gorf! It's a buy, Eldon! I'll have Miss Hennessey make up a folder."

"Meet you on the roof," piped Sash.

On the way to Sleepy Hollow in the Washington copter Merkle wanted to know how the frog got so big.

"It gobbled up some experimental growth pellets," Sash explained.

"Ours? Or *theirs?*" Merkle frowned.

"Neither," Sash replied. "So far as I know, our government is not working on any such pellet. Nor is Red China. These particular growth pellets come from the lab of a cranky, old eccentric. As I get it, he was developing the pellets for use on ducks. Planned to raise giant ducks for personal profit, claiming that future generations could live on expanded duckmeat. The pellets were designed solely for ducks, but the frog got 'em."

"How?"

"A crate of duck pellets fell out of his pickup truck as he was crossing a bog, and he didn't miss 'em until he got home. By then, it was too late. This frog ate the whole crateful."

"I see," said Merkle, tapping his chin. "Any more pellets left?"

"Not according to the old eccentric's pretty niece, a girl named Pinning. She told me her uncle just had this one crate. But he could make more."

"Nix on that." Merkle swept his hand out in a negative gesture. "Spiders could get 'em. Next thing, we have a giant three-story spider. Or a train-sized snake. No good."

"I told her to tell him to hold up on 'em until we could make an official decision."

"I'll get Miss Hennessey to issue a freeze form," declared Merkle. "Make it illegal for the old bastard to produce any more of the things."

The copter pilot announced that they were in the direct vicinity of Sleepy Hollow.

"I don't see any mammoth frog down there," Merkle snapped, shading his eyes. "What about that, Eldon?"

"It could be behind a small mountain digesting the sports car."

"Okay, then. We'll head for the old eccentric. He might have a lead on where the damned thing is."

The copter whipsawed west.

Linda Pinning led Merkle and Sash toward the laboratory of her uncle. She was a starkly beautiful girl of nineteen, with luminous skin and long dancer's legs. She wore a black leotard. "I'm a victim of schizoid conflict," she confided as they moved down a long hallway. "My Uncle Downey thinks I possess remarkable talent, but I personally *loathe* toedancing."

"What *do* you prefer?" asked Merkle.

"Swamp life!" She sucked in a breath excitedly, and her breasts trembled. "That's why I live here with Uncle Downey. I've become an expert on swamp life. Garter snakes. Water bugs. And, of course, ducks."

"Of course," said Merkle.

They entered the lab. "My uncle is upstairs, but I thought you'd want to get a look in here first. You can see the success he's already had with pumpkins."

The lab was full of giant pumpkins.

"Must be ten times their natural size," commented Sash, absently patting his pumpkin stomach.

"Easily," agreed Merkle.

Linda explained why her uncle had switched to ducks. "He felt that pumpkins were too limited."

Sash grinned. "Sure can't roast a pumpkin!"

"We just want to know about the frog," Merkle said, scowling. "I suggest you fetch your uncle."

Linda complied, and moments later a dark, hairy old man wearing a frayed, black ankle-length raincoat tottered into the lab. His eyes bugged fiercely at them from incredibly thick-lensed glasses.

"Make it quick," he said. "Make it quick."

Merkle asked about the frog.

"None of my affair," grumped the old man. "Damn frog's none of my affair!"

"Ah, but it *is*," Merkle corrected him. "Your growth pellets caused it to expand into a public menace. It has already eaten a Corvette driver. We're here on emergency status."

"Don't care. Don't care a pig's snout for your status!" He produced a rolled umbrella from inside the coat and waved it threateningly.

"My uncle's a Nauruan," Linda told them, by way of apology. "They get cranky in their old age."

"I never heard of the place," said Merkle.

"Naura is an island nation of six thousand," Sash flatly intoned, "covering an area of eight square miles, located south of the equator and northeast of the Solomon Islands. You can look it up in the Cowles *Encyclopedia of Nations*."

The awkward impasse was broken by a loud trumpeting sound from the woods beyond the house.

"I think that's him, chief," said Sash.

"That is certainly the amplified croak of a *Rana catesbeiana*, or common bullfrog," Linda agreed.

Merkle whipped out his custom-grip revolver. "Let's pepper him!"

"Won't do any good," declared the cranky old man. "Bullets will just bounce off. Couldn't kill him with a cannon."

"What's he talking about?" demanded Merkle.

"Unfortunately, one of the present flaws in my Uncle Downey's growth-pellet research is the peculiar effect produced on the outer layers of any living creature. What you'll encounter is an armorlike exterior, impervious to bullets."

"That's crazy," sneered Eldon Sash. "How could people eat impervious ducks?"

"Exactly the problem my uncle is attempting to overcome," said Linda.

Merkle began to look desperate. "If an armored frog starts hopping toward New York, my fat's in the fire! What kind of ground can it cover?"

The girl clucked her tongue. "At its present size, it can traverse up to fifty miles at a hop."

The old man stomped his foot. "All right, all right. I'll deal with it. I can deal with it. I've dealt with worse."

And he tottered briskly from the lab.

They crashed through the afternoon woods in the wake of the old man, attempting to keep up with his green battery car.

"How can he drive that thing in this kind of country?" asked Sash, out of breath and staggering.

"He's converted to off-road-vehicle components," panted the running girl. "Uncle Downey can go anywhere now."

"Hardly keep him in sight," gasped Dave Merkle, trotting beside Linda.

They entered a swampy area where huge, gaseous bubbles churned at ground surface. The green battery car, with its notched doughnut tires, was parked at the edge of the bog. Uncle Downey was not in it.

"Where is he?" demanded Merkle.

"Over here, over here," cried the impatient old man. "I have your fool frog."

They plowed toward his voice, careful to avoid swampy patches.

"Seems all but impossible," declared Sash. "A place like this, only a frog jump from the heart of Manhattan. Looks almost pre-historic."

"It is," said Linda. "This vast bog is where Uncle Downey does most of his duck research."

They rounded a bend in the swamp to face the apartment-sized frog, in front of which stood Linda's uncle with a small gold whistle.

"What's he going to do?" queried Sash.

Linda shook her head in bewilderment.

Merkle advanced with his revolver at the ready.

"Stay back!" rasped the old man. "He's fast with his tongue. Let me handle this. Back, back, back!"

They retreated a few steps, watching the big frog.

It was impressive. Its huge bulbous eyes blinked vacantly and its distended throat pulsed like an immense heart. It was handsomely spotted.

"Be careful, Uncle Downey," warned Linda.

Her uncle ignored her, bringing the whistle to his lips. He blew soft tweeting sounds. The frog's eyes began to go sleepy.

"Oh, now I see," said Linda. "Uncle Downey is lulling it into a comatose state. His tiny, golden whistle is obviously ultrasonic, and we are hearing only the low register."

"Great!" said Merkle. "He's *some* old gentleman!"

Uncle Downey swung grumpily around to face them. "Stop your blather! You'll ruin everything, ruin it all."

The frog suddenly shifted, snaked out a long tongue, and snapped Uncle Downey off the ground and into its mouth. One swallow and the cranky eccentric was gone, whistle, raincoat, thick eyeglasses and all.

"Boy!" marveled Sash. "He was right. That is one *fast* tongue!"

"I could whack a few .38 slugs into its belly," Merkle suggested.

Linda sighed. "A pointless display of gunfire won't bring Uncle Downey back."

"She's right, chief," Sash agreed. "But what now?"

"We leave the big devil for the present," said Dave Merkle, reluctantly holstering his custom-grip revolver. "If we're lucky he may just stay in this area looking for more growth pellets. Let's head back to Washington."

Linda picked up her late uncle's fallen umbrella and followed them toward the waiting battery car.

Five-star General Jordan Fielding Elliott rapped his maple map pointer smartly against his booted leg. "Then, as I understand it, what we basically have here is a giant hoptoad loose in the Catskills?"

Merkle nodded. "That's right, General Elliott."

"Call me General Fielding. I never use the Elliott, except for paperwork."

"Right," said Merkle.

"And the toad *is* dangerous?"

"Indeed," said Linda, "it is—having eaten, at the very least, a Corvette driver named Betts, and my Uncle Downey. But we must not mix toads with frogs. The creature we're dealing with in this case is a common bullfrog, though greatly enlarged."

"Thank you, Miss Pinning," said the general. "I'll make a note of that." He turned to a small, mustached assistant. "Lights, if you please."

The room darkened as the people in the small projection area settled into their chairs. In addition to Fielding and his aide, several high-ranking government officials were in attendance. "I love a good movie," one of them said.

A flickering, slightly off-focus 8 mm film filled one corner of the forward screen, showing dozens of frogs leaping and sunning themselves. Linda Pinning calmly provided the narration.

"As you will see in this simple nature film, taken by my late Uncle Downey at Sleepy Hollow, the bullfrog, or *Rana catesbeiana*, is the most carnivorous of the species. Its natural diet consists of earthworms, spiders, and other insects, although it has been known to occasionally devour waterfowl and small chickens."

"Alarming!" a Congressman muttered in the darkness.

"The *Rana catesbeiana* croaks loudest of the frog family, and is particularly fond of cool, damp places. Thus, its swamp home in the Catskills is ideal and characteristic."

The film snapped to white, and Linda accepted a spatter of applause.

Cigars and pipes were lighted as Dave Merkle asked the general what he planned to do.

"Simple," Fielding smiled, adjusting a lopsided campaign ribbon. "We dispatch a whirlybird and some nets and we capture the big toad and—"

"Frog," said Linda.

"We capture the damn thing is all! Stick it in a zoo. Simple. That's how things work at my end of the hall."

Nods all around.

The plan sounded fine.

They tried netting the frog.

They tried bombing the frog.

They tried cannons and tank guns and laser fire.

With negative results.

For one thing, the frog kept hopping in odd directions, and they couldn't keep up with it. The situation became vital when it flattened the President's summer home in San Clemente. (It had also eaten a considerable number of people, including two prominent screen personalities, and the public was aroused.)

General Fielding arranged an emergency Pentagon session with full Congressional backing in order to make an important announcement.

"We are faced," he said, "with what can only be termed a mounting dilemma." He turned to Linda. "Miss Pinning, would you fill the folks in on the latest?"

"Of course," she said. "As you may have surmised from recent reports, the frog has now *doubled* in size since it was first noted in the Catskills. We do not know exactly why the cell structure, nervous system, and body tissues of the *Rana catesbeiana* are receptive to erratic or uncontrolled growth, but—regretfully—my late Uncle Downey's experimental pellets could not have affected any other natural creature to this degree."

"Will the son of a bitch keep growing?" asked a Nebraska senator.

"I'm very much afraid so," Linda replied. "But the rate is uncertain."

A rumble of discontent swept the room.

Fielding rapped the lectern sharply with his maple map stick. "Folks we have no choice. I declare this project on Red Alert!"

"What does that mean?" asked Dave Merkle.

"It means I have White House authority to order the use of a hitherto top-secret weapon." He measured the crowd with hard eyes. "You might even call it America's *ultimate* weapon."

Excited murmuring.

Fielding turned back to the girl. "Miss Pinning, is there some way we could get the frog to swallow a fairly large quantity of metallic substances?"

Linda raised an eyebrow. "I think he already has. Along with his unfortunate victims, he's swallowed rings, wristwatches, tie clips, fountain pens, belt buckles, eye-glasses, gold fillings, keys, coins, metal shoe laces . . ."

Fielding shook his head. "What about Corvettes? He likes those, doesn't he?"

"He's swallowed three of them over the past month," Eldon volunteered.

"Right! Then we feed him all the Corvettes he can eat. And when he's got a bellyful, we go on green." He pointed to his mustached aide. "Round up a couple dozen Corvettes."

"New or used?"

"Forget the vintage," roared Fielding.

"He seemed to like new ones," Sash put in. "They slide down easier."

"All right, nothing older than 2007, but hurry. Get those cars to that frog, pronto!"

It was dubbed Operation Sky Pole for obvious reasons—it *was* a pole, and it went into the sky. Based under the Texas prairie, it rose at the touch of a button, not unlike a giant automobile radio antenna, to a height of three miles. Topping it were twin metal globes with high-voltage electricity dancing between them, designed to attract any flying metallic object within 2500 miles. The basic idea, as Fielding explained it, was that an enemy guided missile approaching the U.S. would be drawn into the pole's magnetic field and instantly disintegrated by awesomely powerful electronic forces.

"Our frog, full of Corvettes, will be sucked in and totally destroyed," declared Fielding from his underground command post near Waco.

The bunker was awash in dignitaries.

"Where's the creature now?" asked Merkle.

"Dozing on the flats a few miles from Salt Lake City. He ate every Corvette we offered him—and finished off with a Land Rover. Oh, he's *full* of metal, all right! Once he's airborne, we activate the pole and watch the fireworks. Be like shooting ducks in a barrel."

"It's fish," Linda corrected. "Fish in a barrel."

"Never mind that," Fielding snapped. "You'll see what I mean."

The general, wearing his full-dress uniform, walked to a wall of blinking red and green lights. He checked a radar screen. "Everything is one hundred percent up to date here," he said proudly. "We'll be able to track our spotted friend A-OK all the way from Salt Lake."

"How do you plan to get him to jump?" Eldon wanted to know. "Sometimes he just snoozes for days. And weighted down the way he is . . ."

"That's being taken care of," Fielding assured him. "Able Company will lob hand grenades at his stomach. He just *hates* that. He'll jump out of sheer annoyance."

They crowded closer to the radar screen.

"Ready, sir?" asked the mustached aide.

"Lob!" shouted Fielding.

The aide repeated the order to lob into a field telephone.

Fielding checked his wristwatch. "The big countdown begins, gentlemen! In ten seconds, that treacherous demon frog will be just so many spotted atoms floating in the void."

A blip began moving on the screen.

"He's in the air, General Elliott!" the aide squealed.

"It's Fielding! I never use Elliott, you damn fool. Confound you, now I've lost the count!"

". . . six, five, four," offered Dave Merkle.

"Yes I . . . three, two, *one* . . . Watch this! . . . He's—"

A ground-quaking explosion. Dust and chunks of loosened concrete rained down.

All the red and green lights went out.

"What the hell's happened?" gasped the general, groping for his maple map stick on the floor of the darkened bunker.

"Apparently, sir, he struck the pole with one of his horny toes," reported the shaky voice of the mustached aide. "Our balls were dislodged—and the whole thing fell down on Waxahachie."

"This is going to look terrible on my record," moaned Fielding.

"Let's get out of here," said Dave Merkle.

Linda was gone when the smoke cleared at ground level. Merkle looked concerned. "Do you think she's trapped below?"

"No, sir, she isn't," Fielding's aide stated. "I just observed Miss Pinning drive off in a field utility truck, headed due south."

"That's where the frog landed," declared Sash.

"She said something about coming to grips with her uncle's problem."

Merkle prodded Sash toward an empty jeep. "She's going to do something rash, Eldon, I'm certain of that. Let's see if we can catch her." He knuckled his forehead. "You drive. I have an awful headache."

When Merkle and Sash caught up with Linda she was standing close to the mammoth frog, holding on to a small, perforated cardboard box that she'd removed from her purse.

"Keep back," she told them. "He's stunned, but still quite dangerous."

The two men remained near the jeep, nervously eyeing the spotted giant. It squatted, dazed, on the desert floor, blinking stupidly.

Linda took off the lid and held the box aloft.

A wet, melancholy croak issued from the interior.

The huge frog ceased blinking. Its throat began a rapid pulsation.

It croaked deafeningly.

"I need a jet," Linda told Merkle, running toward him, the box in her hand. "Where can I borrow a jet?"

"There's one back at Waco Field," Merkle said, "but I don't think they'll let you use it."

She vaulted in the jeep. "Head for it! He'll be following us."

As Eldon Sash gunned away in a scattering of gravel, the frog attempted to leap after them, overshooting by several miles.

"My God!" breathed Sash. "What have you done to him?"

"Talking is superfluous. Just get us to that jet!"

At the airport, Linda convinced a bewildered Fielding that she was a qualified pilot. "Science and toe-dancing aren't my *only* talents!"

In the air, with Linda at the controls, Fielding demanded to know what the hell was going on. Merkle and Sash looked blank.

Also frightened.

Because the frog was still following them.

"Even with his substantial jump range, we can keep ahead of him," Linda said brightly. "Boys, this is the last lap. The checkered flag's in sight."

The small cardboard box rested on the seat beside her.

Near Sleepy Hollow, the jet swept downward, skimmed the trees with a great slicing roar, and landed bumpily on a deserted stretch of New York highway.

"Everyone out!" Linda shouted. "He'll be here any minute, and we need to be properly positioned."

"For what?" demanded Fielding. "Positioned for *what?*" Sweat seeded his weak upper lip and his braided hat was on crooked.

Linda scampered across the highway into the woods, still clutching the box. The others trudged after her.

At the edge of the vast bog she paused, opened the lid, and a tiny green bullfrog flopped out.

"There!" said Linda triumphantly.

A trumpet croak in the sky.

Down came the immense spotted giant.

It landed, with a wet smack, in the exact center of the bog.

Within moments, the quicksand had sucked it under.

"Sex did the job," said Linda.

"Explain yourself, Miss Pinning!" The general was still confused, and the front of his full-dress uniform was splashed with swamp mud.

"There is one call no creature can resist."

"And that is?" prompted Sash.

"The mating call," she said, giving Dave Merkle a knowing smile.

The tiny female frog from the box hopped over his left foot.

It croaked sweetly.

✝ ✝ ✝

The Mating of Thirdburt

WHEN THIRDBURT TURNED TWENTY-ONE, HIS father threw him bodily out of the family lifeunit in New Connecticut.

"Why is this happening?" Thirdburt wanted to know.

"Firstburt is mate-paired, and so is Secondburt," father Bigburt said. "You are now twenty-one and it is time for you to be mate-paired. Frankly, your mother and I are worried about your sexual thrust."

"My sexual thrust is A-oke. Perfectly A-oke," said Thirdburt. "I just don't fancy the idea of being rushed into pairmating when I'm not one hundred per cent emotionally receptive to a full snugdown situation."

"Son," said Bigburt, "my terms are simple: unless you've acquired a state-approved pairmate within twenty-four hours, I'll disinherit you. Throwing you bodily out of our lifeunit was harsh, but necessary. Your mother and I must make certain you are a par-socio norm and not some kind of sub-socio misfit."

Thirdburt shook artificial yard pebbles from his hair. "So what do you suggest, Dad?"

"I suggest you apply down at Pairups, Inc. They'll computer-mate you jiffdandy for a nominal fee."

"But I don't have a nominal fee."

Bigburt handed him 400 creds. "This ought to do it," he said. And he slammed the lifeunit's door in his son's face.

PAIRUPS, INC. the glowsign blinked. Below, other glowletters formed the company motto: "The Love of Your Life for the Life of Your Love."

Thirdburt walked briskly through the slidentry and confronted the receptclerk, a distinguished mid-aged female robot.

"Love solves all," she said to him. "Wars never solved anything. Hate never solved anything. Love is a bracing tonic, a rainbow in a clouded sky. Love is a dappled horse in a meadow of—"

"How much?" asked Thirdburt.

"Sir?"

"For a pairmate selection. How much?"

The robot sniffed. "Three hundred eighty-six creds, including your state-required honeymoon."

"Can't I arrange my own honeymoon?"

"Not since Pairmate Law 26-G took effect last month," said the robot. "Whether or not you allow a pairmate selection center to choose your bride, your honeymoon *must* be computerized."

"Well, what if I don't want to go on one?"

The robot clucked. "Pairmates are required to honeymoon. It's a socio-norm."

Thirdburt shrugged his thin shoulders. "Oke. Guess I'll take the package." He handed the clerk 386 creds.

"Please follow Cupid's Arrow," she said, slotting the money.

"To where?"

"Don't ask me useless questions," the clerk snapped. "Useless questions overincrease my voltage receptors and I'm liable to malfunction."

"I guess I spooked you when I cut in on your telling me that love was a dappled horse."

"I like to finish what I start," admitted the robot.

"Accept my apologies," said Thirdburt. "But I'm on a tight schedule."

And he began to follow a wide, glowing arrow that shone up through the nearglass flooring. The arrow led him down a long, metallic hallway to a musical slidedoor marked PAIRMATE SELECTION DATA. With a flourish of wedding chimes, the door slid open and Thirdburt walked through.

Facing him was a floor-to-ceiling wall of spinning discs and blinking multicolored lights.

"I'm Harvey, your friendly datacomputer wall," the wall said to Thirdburt. "My job is simple. You tell me everything about yourself and I select the ideal pairmate for you. Are we ready?"

Thirdburt nodded.

"You'll have to speak up," the wall declared. "Nodding or head-shaking is not going to get us anywhere."

"Can I sit down?"

"That isn't allowed at this point," said the wall. "Let's begin with age, height, weight, color of eyes, waist and neck dimensions, chest girth, length of limbs, blood type, and family birth data. Rightie?"

"Rightie," said Thirdburt. He gave the wall its requested data, then said, "This is all pretty boring."

"Not to me, it isn't," said the computer wall. "I eat up stuff like this. For example, I can get very excited over a man's chest girth."

"That's an odd thing to admit," said Thirdburt.

The wall giggled, then got serious again, "Now, then," it said. "I need some really intimate data. And don't be shy."

"What kind of data?"

"I can't pairmate you precisely if I don't have lots of intimate stuff to go on. Like . . . tell me all about your most disgusting sex-thrust dreams."

"I don't have any."

Several of the wall's little lights wavered. "But that's impossible! Everyone has disgusting sex-thrust dreams."

"Not me," said Thirdburt firmly. "I'm a very sound sleeper. In fact, father Bigburt was forced to wake me from a very sound and satisfying sleep in order to throw me bodily out of our lifeunit this morning."

"Tush," said the wall, readjusting its lights. Some of the rapidly spinning discs stopped spinning, while others started to spin. "You're making it tough for me."

"Sorry," said Thirdburt, scuffling one shoe against the nearglass floor.

"Now," said the wall in a patient tone, "just what are you looking for in a pairmate?"

"I'm not looking for anything," declared Thirdburt. "This is all father Bigburt's idea."

"Let me put the question another way. In past sex-thrust situations, what elements have attracted you?"

"I'm a virgin," said Thirdburt, "so I wouldn't know."

"Gad!" exclaimed the wall. "You are the first twenty-one-year-old male sex-thrust virgin I've dealt with in a coon's age!"

"What is a coon's age?"

"It's an ancient expression dealing with the lifespan of a long-extinct animal. Forget I ever said it."

"All right, but I'm basically curious about things like that."

"We're way off the track," said the wall, with a trace of metallic irritation.

"Then ask me something."

"Food," said the wall. "What's your favorite food?"

"Fried breadplant with nearfruit topping, cooked in banana oil and served from an open platter garnished with sweetpeas," said Thirdburt.

"I wish I could eat stuff like that," sighed the wall. Then it asked, "Favorite hobby?"

"Skeeterhopping."

"With or without a skeeter?"

"Without."

"How would you sum up your personal philosophy?"

"I'm really not very philosophical," admitted Thirdburt. "I just kind of drift along from day to day, lacking a driving force to better my condition."

"You're not a very colorful person, are you?" asked the wall.

"Not very. I see myself as a kind of puce yellow."

"Have you ever experienced instant rage? Ever wanted to maim or rape?"

"Not that I can recall," said Thirdburt. "I'd be likely to remember something like that, wouldn't I?"

"I'd say so," the wall remarked.

"I wish I could make things easier for you," said Thirdburt. "But, frankly, I wouldn't even be here if my ole Dad hadn't threatened to disinherit me."

"Then you really have no strong central desire to be pair-mated?"

"I can take it or leave it. I'm not anti, if that's what you're getting at. It's just that I'm not very pro."

"I've handled toughies before," stated the wall. "I have over ten trillion electronic neurons inside me working for you at this very moment."

"That's a lot of neurons," said Thirdburt.

"I was hoping for something really *intimate* from you. I thrive on intimacy."

"I trust you won't be offended," said Thirdburt, "but I find you a rather odd computer wall."

"Really?" said the wall. "Odd is a word I might well apply to you. Life isn't all fried breadplant with nearfruit topping, cooked in banana oil, you know."

"Served from an open platter garnished with sweetpeas," added Thirdburt. "Can I leave now? I've given you plenty of data to process. So process it."

"Don't tell me my job," snapped the wall.

"It's just that I'm getting tired of standing here, talking to a wall," said Thirdburt. "I really am."

"Follow Cupid's Arrow to the Loveroom and wait there," the wall told him. "I'll send in your pairmate."

"How long will it take?"

"Just follow the arrow," said the computer wall. "Our interview is concluded."

And the musical slidedoor opened as the glowing arrow appeared.

Thirdburt shrugged and left the chamber.

In the heart-shaped Loveroom, Thirdburt sat down on a heart-shaped lovechair. The chair sighed.

The room was soft and warm. The walls were pink and fuzzy, and so was the robot that rolled over to Thirdburt.

"Excited?" asked the robot.

"Not particularly," said Thirdburt.

"Bet you can't wait for the honeymoon to start?"

"I'd like to get it over with."

The robot rolled completely around the chair, talking as it rolled. "Your honeymoon is my baby. Just leave everything to me. You are in capable hands."

"I'm glad to know that," said Thirdburt. "In all truth, your data-computer wall is a little wacko."

"Oh, Harry's all right, once you get used to him," said the pink machine. "He's just sensation-hungry."

"He told me his name was Harvey."

"Harry or Harvey, what real difference does it make?"

"Seems to me you machines would know each other."

The fuzzy robot tipped on two wheels as it rolled across the floor, quickly righting itself. "I roll too fast and I get into trouble that way," it said. "What were we talking about?"

"Names," said Thirdburt.

"Call me Albert. That'll suit me fine."

"When does my pairmate get here?"

"Soon. Ought to be soon now. Excited, huh?"

"I said not very. What I am is impatient."

"What kind of girl did you ask for?" The machine rolled crazily around a heart-shaped lamp, one of its little wheels bumping over the base.

"I left all that up to the wall," said Thirdburt.

"Well, it's not vitally important. What's vitally important is your honeymoon. That's what we should be concerned about. That's where our attentionspan should be concentrated. There's nothing I like better than putting through a good, solid state-approved honeymoon for two young people in love."

"Love has nothing to do with this," said Thirdburt.

"Love makes my wheels go round," said the machine named Albert.

"I'm glad you're happy in your work," said Thirdburt, biting a knuckle. He was getting restless.

The lovechair sighed under him.

"Why does my chair keep sighing?"

"All part of the atmosphere here at Pairups," said the rolling robot. "We had a pillow that used to croon Gypsy love songs until they took it out. It got too erotic. We watch that. Thin line. Save the hot stuff for later."

"I'm thirsty," said Thirdburt.

"No problem." The fuzzy machine rolled over to a tall, silver dispense-all, filled a cup, and rolled back with it.

Thirdburt said thanks and drank the liquid. Then he handed back the cup. "Tastes funny," he said.

"Made from rose petals," said the robot. "Needs more sugar. I keep telling 'em that up front, but they won't listen to me."

"I'm really getting impatient," said Thirdburt.

"Why not lie down on our lovecouch with a thick, comfy lovepillow under your head? Would you like to do that?"

"No, I wouldn't."

The machine rolled into a table, knocking a heart-shaped vase of nearflowers to the floor. The vase shattered.

"You're getting me nervous," said the machine. "I'm knocking things over."

"Then stop rolling around," advised Thirdburt.

"Hey, here's your pairmate!" A tiny, green light blinked on the robot's fuzzy chest. "Now we can both relax."

A plump, bearded man with red-rimmed eyes stepped into the Loveroom. He wore flarewaist riding knickers, a flowchecked vest, and a long-billed baseball cap—and he looked confused.

"There's been an obvious mistake," said Thirdburt. "That's not my pairmate. He's not even female."

The fuzzy robot clucked, "I'm sorry the choice is not entirely to your satisfaction, but we must proceed as scheduled once the pairmate selection has been completed."

"But it *hasn't* been," Thirdburt objected. "This bearded fatty is totally unacceptable as a pairmate. Totally."

The rotund man in the long-billed baseball cap shook his head slowly. "I don't get any of this dingo you're passing out. I came here to repair the lousy atomic furnace. Instead, I end up in this keeky heart-shaped room with a dumb-looking, fuzzy pink robot and a bug-faced creep who calls me fatty. I'm not fat, I'm *beefy*."

"Same thing," muttered Thirdburt.

"Not so," declared the man. "There's a whole world of difference between being fat and being beefy."

"If you're here to repair an atomic furnace," said Thirdburt, "then why are you wearing flarewaist riding knickers, a flow-checked vest, and a long-billed baseball cap?"

"Because I'm odd," said the big man defensively. "And odd people always wear odd clothing. I'm a Genuine Oddity. That's my state right, you know!"

"I know, I know," said Thirdburt. "I simply found it curious."

"Allow me to point out," said the pink machine, "that we at Pairups, Inc. stand ready to sever, legally, under state-approved separation laws—and for a nominal fee—a malfunctioning pairmate relationship such as yours. Post-honeymoon, of course."

"Honeymoon?" boomed the bearded man. "What's this fuzzy dingo talking about?"

"I'd best explain all this, clearly and concisely," said Thirdburt. "You'd better sit down."

The beefy repairman settled into a lovechair. It sighed deeply. "Damn thing's alive!"

"It's programmed to sigh," said Thirdburt.

The fuzzy pink robot rolled nervously around the room, tiny wheels crunching shards of broken vase. It was muttering to itself.

"My name is Thirdburt. I came in here to be pairmated so my father wouldn't disinherit me. After extensive questioning relative to my choice of a pairmate, a computer wall named Harvey, or Harry, selected *you* as my pairmate. An obvious error that cannot, at this point, be rectified. This agitated pink robot is here to arrange our state-approved honeymoon, and I see no recourse other than to go on with it. Later, we'll take Albert up on his separation offer. That's his name. Albert."

"And what if I don't play along with this drek?" asked the bearded man. "What if I just lay you two dingos out cold and split loose?"

"Oh no, no, no," piped the rolling robot. "You must believe me when I tell you that we have ways of dealing with violence. If you attempt any form of threatening physical action, you will be rendered senseless and will be sent on your honeymoon in this unfortunate condition."

"He means it," said Thirdburt.

The bearded man glared at them both, then slumped back in the chair. "I just hope they get somebody to fix the lousy furnace," he said.

"Now, then," began the robot. A blue disc began rotating in its head. "Name, sir? I need it for my data spool."

"Felix One," said the atomic repairman.

"Fine," said the robot. He rolled around the chair to face the two pairmates. "Now, folks, as to the *type* of honeymoon, we have a pleasantly wide selection. There are Lunar sightseeing honeymoons, romantic jetboat excursion honeymoons, rugged fishing and hunting honeymoons, Martian sandcraft excur—"

"The one you just said," cut in Thirdburt. "The rugged fishing and hunting one." He swung toward Felix. "Is that one oke with you?"

"Sure," the big man nodded numbly. "It's your shindig."

"Can we camp under the stars near a large body of water?" asked Thirdburt. "I've always wanted to do that."

"Certainly," replied the fuzzy machine. "All of our fishing-hunting honeymoons come automatically equipped with a large body of water."

Thirdburt bit his lower lip thoughtfully. "You know," he said, "this might work out after all."

Felix One grunted.

"Hi, kids, I'm your jolly roadroller," said the square, red-wheeled machine to Thirdburt and Felix as they stood outside the main building at Pairups, Inc. "You two cuddlecuties hop aboard and we're on our fun-filled way to a memorable state-approved honeymoon in a preselected, wildly primitive, totally sterile wilderness."

"How can it be both?" Thirdburt wanted to know.

"Both what?"

"Both wildly primitive and totally sterile."

"Let's not delay our departure with nonfunctional over-verbalization. Your answer is inherent in the trip itself. Now, in with you two lovedoves, it's time to roll."

"Cut the lovedove, cuddlecutie drek," snapped Felix.

The square machine ignored him and began to move out.

"That's the way he's programmed," said Thirdburt. "We'll just have to accept this sort of thing."

At jato speeds, the roadroller whipped them deep into wilderness country, humming along narrow roads cut through thick, green forest

"What kind of trees are those?" asked Thirdburt.

"Nearoak and nearpine and nearspruce," said the rolling machine. "And there are a few nearcottonwoods. They all have real pseudoleafmold under them. We at Pairups, Inc. take justifiable pride in our expertly simulated natural environment. No cheap plastic stuff for us. We don't jack around when it comes to quality."

"I see," nodded Thirdburt.

Felix grunted.

As the sun was setting behind the trees in splendid style, they arrived at their primitive campsite on the banks of a roaring river.

"How do you like the place?" the square machine asked Thirdburt.

"Looks oke to me," he said.

"All of your fishing-hunting gear is stowed in your good-natured lovetent," the roadroller said.

On the shore, a few dozen feet ahead of them, a large, fuzzy pink tent suddenly popped up.

"The tent, as you have just seen, is self-inflating. When you wish to move, just ask it to deflate and follow you. Now I'm going to tippy-toe away and leave you two kids alone."

The car sniggered and rolled softly away into the dusk.

"Hey!" yelled Felix, running after it. He shook his head, turning back to Thirdburt. "Is the damn thing just going to roll off and *abandon* us out here?"

"I'm sure he'll be back for us at some preselected time," said Thirdburt.

"Hi, pairmates. I'm your adaptable, good-natured pop-up lovetent, patent pending," said the tent as they approached it.

Thirdburt said hello.

"I know that both of you must be just a wee bit concerned about my overseeing your, as it were, intimate moments," said the tent.

"What moments?" Felix asked.

"I refer to your pash periods."

"We're not having any," growled Felix. "The dingo datacomputer wall screwed up. I'm really an atomic furnace repairman, and this gink is—"

"As I was saying," the tent continued, "when you cuddlebugs want privacy for those special pairmate snuggle sessions . . . well, there's a little pink hickey on my center peg. Just press it and switch me off. Otherwise, I'm apt to be intrusive."

"He didn't listen," complained Felix.

"I told you," said Thirdburt, "they're all programmed to treat us like love-starved pairmates. Accept it. Won't hurt you any."

"Makes me feel creepy," said Felix.

"Might I now prepare a rustic wilderness repast for the two of you?" asked the tent.

"Sure, go ahead," said Thirdburt.

"First, you must get into your Zippies," said the tent. "All honeymooners must wear Zippies while honeymooning. State law 47-J. Duck under my flap and you'll find them."

Thirdburt and Felix ducked under the fuzzy flap. Two fuzzy pink-zippered jumpsuits were laid out for them on a double lovecot.

"Do we have to put on these dingo outfits?" asked Felix.

"You heard him. State law," said Thirdburt, neatly zippering himself into his Zippie.

"Right, right," snarled Felix, zippering furiously. "But I like to select my own odd clothing."

The tent snickered at this remark and Felix slapped a fist against the center peg's pink hickey. "There, you fuzzy bastard!"

"You'll just have to activate him again," said Thirdburt. "He can't fix our meal if he's switched off."

"You do it."

Thirdburt activated the tent.

"Why don't you two lovedoves wait outside?" suggested the tent. "I'll sing out when the chow's on."

Thirdburt and Felix sat down on the soft bank of the river, watching the water roar fiercely over large, black boulders.

"Looks rough out there," said Felix.

"We can adjust it," said Thirdburt. "This plastocard says so. I found it in the tent."

Felix read the card.

NOTICE: If you find the river is too severe in its action, you may reduce it according to personal preference. Use the projecting knob on the piece of neardriftwood on the shore to adjust the river's flow. Thank you.

Pairups, Inc.

"I'm going to try it," said Thirdburt.

He walked over to the piece of neardriftwood, located the knob, and twisted. Instantly, the roaring torrent became a gentle flow. "Works," said Thirdburt.

Felix nodded. He looked morose. "Adjustable rivers depress me," he said.

The tent yelled at them, "Chow's on!"

They ducked under the fuzzy flap and sat down at a long table. Platters of food popped up from the table's interior.

"Hey, boy!" exclaimed Thirdburt. "It's fried breadplant with nearfruit topping, cooked in banana oil and served from an open platter garnished with sweetpeas!"

"I can't eat that bilge," Felix told the tent.

"Oh, yes you can," said the tent.

"What do you mean, 'Oh, yes I can?' "

"I mean you eat what I lay out. *I'm* the chef. I decide what to serve."

Felix grabbed a fishing pole and a pair of hip-length boots and stormed out of the tent. "I'll catch my own dinner!"

The tent snickered.

Outside, Felix pulled on the boots and, wading out into mid-river, cast his line. Within ten minutes, he'd caught three fat trout and five silver lake bass. He carried these into the tent and slapped them on the table.

Thirdburt did not look up; he was fully occupied with his fried breadplant.

"There!" said Felix. "What say to that?"

"I say," said the tent, "that you have caught several fat, delicious-looking nearfish."

"You mean I can't eat 'em?"

"Not unless you are equipped to digest electronic circuitry," said the tent.

Felix tossed aside the pole and slumped onto the nearoak bench next to Thirdburt. "Pass the breadplant," he said dully.

The tent clucked in satisfaction.

*　　*　　*

Deep night. The pneumobed rocked and soothed them, but what annoyed Felix, in particular, was what the bed kept whispering.

"Cut out the lousy erotic suggestions," snapped Felix as the bed raised itself on one side, nudging him toward Thirdburt.

"I was simply attempting to get you into a pash-period mood," declared the bed.

"Well, we just want to sleep," said Felix.

"Some honeymoon!" remarked the bed sourly.

Thirdburt, by now, was snoring—which kept Felix awake for another hour. When he drifted off, he had a nightmare about being swallowed by an atomic furnace.

"Chow time!" the tent announced.

It was light outside; the morning sun had just cleared the tips of the neartrees. Robot birds were twittering sweetly.

"I need rest," said Felix. Thirdburt was already up.

"Nonsense," said the tent. "There's a lot to do. You have to hunt today."

"That's right," said the bed, dumping Felix onto the floor.

"We'd best do as the tent says," Thirdburt advised, helping the bearded repairman to his feet.

"Into your Zippie," said the tent. "Then you eat and hunt."

"Fun," said the bed.

After a breakfast of fried breadplant on nub toast, they left the tent, hunting gear strapped to their backs, rifles in hand.

"What are we supposed to hunt?" asked Felix.

"I have a list," said Thirdburt, staring at a sheet of nearpaper. "The tent said we can have our choice."

"What's on the list?"

"Neargeese, automated wild rhino, and electroelephants," said Thirdburt.

"You name it."

"I've always had a kind of yen to hunt big game," said Thirdburt. "Let's go after the automated wild rhino."

"Where are they?" Felix shifted the hunting gear strapped to his back. "I hope we don't have to walk much farther."

"Jungle Trail No. 3," said Thirdburt. "We follow that into the 'artfully simulated rhino country.' It's all here on the list."

"Then let's get going. My back is killing me. Repairing atomic furnaces just doesn't give you the muscles for this sort of drek."

They located the proper trail and followed it into deep pseudo-brush, which eventually opened into rolling hill country, studded with clumps of high grass.

"I guess we're here," said Thirdburt, shading his eyes to peer about.

"There's a water hole," said Felix, pointing. "From what I read once, rhinos seem to favor water holes."

"Oke. Let's stake out there."

They tramped over to the water hole. Thirdburt nodded toward the mud. "Rhino tracks," he said.

Felix grunted, seating himself on a large, gray boulder. He eased the pack from his shoulders, put aside his rifle.

"The list says the rhino is a 'fast and treacherous beast' and to watch out for his horn," said Thirdburt.

"You kill one. I'll just sit here," said Felix.

"You know, I'm really beginning to enjoy our honeymoon," Thirdburt observed. The brush rattled behind him.

"Look out!" shouted the bearded atomic repairman. "Here comes a really big one."

A two-ton horned rhino galloped straight at Thirdburt, head lowered for the kill.

"You take him," said Thirdburt, handing Felix his rifle.

"No, sir, *you* take him." He tossed back the weapon "And you'd better not miss. He's almost on top of us."

"I just wanted you to have the fun of downing the first one," said Thirdburt. "I'm not selfish."

"Shoot! Shoot!"

Thirdburt sighted along the barrel at the charging beast and pressed the trigger.

Two nearslugs slammed into the head of the galloping rhino. He faltered, eyes rolling, and dropped at Thirdburt's feet.

As the two hunters leaned close to him, he winked. "Got me!" said the rhino. "My heartfelt congratulations on a perfect kill! Next, I'm sure you'll want to try the electroelephants. They're even meaner than I am."

The rhino got up, shook trail dust from his leathery hide, and nodded with his horn. "Just follow Jungle Trail No. 6 to the left. You can't miss 'em."

And he trotted away into the high grass.

"That wasn't as much fun as I thought it would be," said Thirdburt. "I think if he hadn't *talked* to us, I would have liked it better. Let's tackle the elephants."

Along Jungle Trail No. 6, the trees began to shake. Sparks jumped from their trunks.

"What the deuce is happening to those dingo trees?" Felix asked.

"I think the jungle is shorting out," said Thirdburt. "Some kind of electrical problem. We'd better get—"

One of the sparking trees erupted into smoke and fell directly on Felix.

Thirdburt pushed aside nearleaves and pseudobranches to reach the fallen atomic furnace repairman.

"Are you all right, Felix?"

"It got me," moaned the bearded man. "It really nailed me. I'm done for."

"What exactly do you mean?"

"I mean that this damned electrical tree has killed me," said Felix.

And his head rolled loosely.

"Is he gone?"

Thirdburt peered through the trees at a pale figure crouched in leaf shadows.

"Who are you?" he asked. "Are you some kind of electronic ape?"

"Of course not," said the shadowy figure. "I'm as human as you are. What I want to know is—is he gone?"

"Gone where?"

"Is he *dead?*"

"Oh. Yes, I'm sure he is."

"Good!" The pale figure emerged from the trees and Thirdburt gasped.

"What's the matter with you? Haven't you ever seen a beautiful, nude girl before?"

"As a matter of fact, I haven't. I'm still a virgin."

The girl, who was blonde and full-bodied, knelt beside Felix and checked his pulse. "He's gone, sure enough." She raised an eyebrow at Thirdburt. "What are you doing out here in the jungle with this bearded fatty?"

"A computer wall selected him as my pairmate by mistake," he told the blonde. "I'm a victim of malfunction."

"Me too," said the girl. "That's why I'm out here, nude in the nearwoods."

"For my sake, I'm glad," Thirdburt admitted. "I really admire your melony breasts."

"Yes, they are nice," agreed the blonde. "I come from a chesty family. My name is Firstlinda. What's yours?"

"Thirdburt."

They shook hands.

"If this fatty hadn't died out here, I'd still be in trouble. Now everything's jimdandy."

"I don't understand," Thirdburt said, staring at her ripe thighs.

"I came out here on the regular pairmate honeymoon setup," the nude girl explained. "But my pairmate was a pseudoanimal freak who ditched me for a rhino. He took this rhino back with him as his pairmate and left me here with no food or clothing."

"What happened to your Zippie?"

"He put it on the rhino so the lovetent wouldn't get wise to the switch. Out here clothes make the man—or the rhino, as the case may be." She giggled and her pink tummy, which was lightly dusted with golden hair, quivered.

"That's some tummy you have," Thirdburt remarked. "And your pubic area is nice, too."

She smiled at him. "You *like* me, don't you?"

"Sure, a lot. Your being nude and beautiful helps. If you were fully clothed and ugly, I *might* still like you—but it's doubtful."

"I appreciate directness in a man," she said, stripping the Zippie from Felix One.

"Why are you doing that?"

"I thought I'd made it clear to you," said the girl. "The tent won't accept me as your pairmate unless I'm wearing a Zippie."

"I see."

"These machines don't actually differentiate between male and female. According to an electroelephant who witnessed the whole thing, when my pairmate brought the rhino back to camp, the tent accepted the pair of them. And when he put my street dress on the rhino, the roadroller picked them up without a hitch and returned them to civilization. I couldn't get picked up because I was mateless. Now, thanks to that tree falling on the fatty, I have *you*."

"What still puzzles me," said Thirdburt, "is what your original pairmate wanted with an automated rhino."

"I told you. He's a pseudoanimal freak. The wall messed up in pairing us. I'd never honeymoon with a pseudoanimal freak if I knew he was one in advance."

"Makes sense," nodded Thirdburt.

"Well . . . how do I look?"

The girl was fully clothed in Felix One's pink Zippie.

"I liked you better nude," said Thirdburt.

It was late when they arrived back in camp. The tent greeted them cheerfully.

"Bet you're both starved."

"We'd rather cuddle first," said the girl. She smiled at Third-burt.

"Certainly. Your lovecot is all prepared."

They ducked under the flap.

"Happy cuddling," the tent said.

The girl pinched Thirdburt's left buttock. "Hope you don't mind if I take advantage of the situation?"

"Not at all," he said, and, trembling, switched off the tent.

By morning he was far from virginal.

"Well, I see you have a legally stamped, state-approved pairmate honeymoon certificate," said Bigburt to his son when Thirdburt returned to the family lifeunit.

"That's right, Dad."

"And where's your Pairmate?"

"Died on the honeymoon," said Thirdburt.

"Terrible. A terrible tragedy."

"Yes, Dad, that describes it perfectly."

"How did it happen?"

"The jungle shorted out and a nearoak tree fell over."

"Terrible."

"May I assume that I have regained your parental approval and that I am not to be disinherited?"

Bigburt patted his son on the head. "The family fortune is yours to share."

"Thanks," said Thirdburt.

All in all, mishaps considered, Thirdburt felt that he had been on a very satisfactory honeymoon.

But it was good to be home again.

✝ ✝ ✝

Lone Star Traveler

A VAST STRETCH OF TEXAS PRAIRIE, 1910. LATE summer, in the Big Bend country near the Rio Grande. Under the sun's diamond-sharp glare, through the distorting waves of rippling heat, there is movement on the plain. A crawling dust cloud caused by . . . *what?* A string of riders? A herd of wild horses? A stagecoach, perhaps, bound for the modest cowtown of Liberty-ville at the far edge of the plain?

No, none of these.

A head pokes through the dense swirl. Goggled eyes are re-vealed under a wide, black Stetson, dust-whitened at the crown, its brim curled back to reveal a tanned, heavily mustached face. Leather-gloved hands grip a massive, wood-spoked steering wheel. A long, loosely buttoned road duster flaps out to either side.

The moving vehicle is a 1909 Hupmobile, resolutely driven by its new owner, Texas John Thursday. And John is indeed resolute — grim-faced at his task of herding this cantankerous metal beast over the washboard terrain. Gullies and potholes and half-buried rocks assault the machine in its sputtering passage.

Finally, with a gasping wheeze, its engine dies and the car rolls to a stop. Texas John, plain-spoken and tall, a wide-shouldered man in his forties who still retains the rugged handsomeness of his youth, sets the brake and climbs out, swearing under his breath.

He stares at the silent machine. "Quittin' on me, are ya? Damn stubborn varmint! I shoulda knowed better than to take ya into town. Serves me right. Tryin' to impress folks with my fancy new autee-mo-beel." He kicks the side of the big, dust-yellow machine. "Damn ya to hell! Any cross-eyed, spavin-legged mule is worth *ten* of ya!"

Then, adjusting the spark, he moves to the front of the long hood, leans to grip the crank handle, and goes to work. Cranking the Hupmobile in the intense heat of the day is a hellish endeavor. Cranking . . . swearing . . . cranking. Then, a raw gout of exhaust smoke and the power plant explodes into life, allowing Texas John to resume his seat behind the wheel.

Popping and sputtering, tires biting into the loose prairie soil, the ponderous vehicle resumes its forward motion.

The Machine Age has arrived in western Texas.

The citizens of Libertyville were not fools. Thus, they stayed well clear of this new-fangled road monster as it bumped down their rutted main street. Dogs whined nervously, tails between their legs. Horses reared up with nostrils flared, neighing in alarm as the big Hupmobile sputtered past them. A wagon overturned. A woman shrieked in fear. Only the young were unafraid.

A ragged pack of children ran boldly alongside the car, hooting like banshees. At the hitching rail in front of the Greater Libertyville Bank, Texas John cut the engine, set the hand brake, and climbed down, discarding his gloves, duster, and goggles.

"Never seen me nothin' like this here critter," said a brightly freckled ten-year-old boy, staring in awe at the now-silent behemoth. "What d'ya *feed* it?"

"Cactus an' snake eggs," said Texas John, slapping a plume of dust from his Stetson. "Got real sharp teeth, it has, so you'd best stay clear. It *bites!*"

The youngster went pale, edging away from the machine. "Gee, thanks for the warning, mister."

Chuckling, Thursday entered the building.

Rufus Finley, the bank's owner, came forward to shake John's hand. He was bald and red-cheeked, with shaggy eyebrows and an expansive gut. "Good to see you, John," he said, giving the big man a gold-toothed smile. "How's Anna doing? She any better?"

"'Fraid not," said Thursday. "Sis is still doin' poorly. Doc says it's her heart. Keeps gettin' worse. She's weak as a new-born pup."

"Sorry to hear that," said Finley, knitting his shaggy brows. He peered through the front window into the street. "See you brought your new autee-mo-beel into town. Amazing invention, the autee-mo-beel. Back East, I hear tell, these things run along streets as smooth as a baby's behind."

Thursday scowled, tugging at his mustache. "Less said about the dang contraptions, the better. Next time I'll be comin' in on a horse like I shoulda done this time. Horses make sense—an' ya don't have to crank 'em, neither."

Finley realized it was time to change the subject. "Town election's next month, John. Lotta folks around here think you oughta throw your hat in the ring for sheriff."

"Yeah, an' a lotta folks are fulla hogwash," snarled Thursday. "I'm a rancher, not a fighting man."

"I wouldn't say that," argued Finley. "You're boxing champeen of the whole county."

"Well, boxin' is one thing and bein' sheriff is another. I'll stick to cattle. I come here to make my monthly deposit, not run for no office."

He removed a roll of bills from his coat and passed the money to Finley's cashier.

"I've seen you handle a six-gun," persisted Finley. "And I've seen you tame broncos that'd kill an ordinary man. We need a sheriff around here who knows how to ride and shoot."

Thursday shook his head. "Look, Rufus, I'm not gonna run fer sheriff an' that's a fact, flat and final. So quit pesterin' me about it."

"All right," sighed Finley. "Have it your way."

"I always do," grinned the rancher. And, with his deposit book duly stamped, Texas John headed for the street.

Outside, he unfolded a square of paper from his coat, checked the contents, and walked toward Robbins Mercantile: Stock Feed, Dry Goods, Fine Comestibles.

Shan was saddle-sore. His buttocks ached and his leg muscles were stiff. He was not accustomed to riding a horse, but felt that he should make his initial appearance in Libertyville on the back of such an animal. To blend in with the populace. To attract less attention. He had not come here to attract attention.

Obtaining the animal had been absurdly easy. Shan simply beamed his Disc at a bowlegged cowpuncher who'd stopped at a water hole a few miles from town to fill his canteen. The beam struck him in the back and he dropped like a stone. The horse, a deep-chested, silk-black stallion with a white mane, was really no problem. The animal didn't seem to care who was in the saddle.

Scanning the main street of Libertyville, Shan decided that the logical place to find out what he needed to know was the saloon. Cowtown bartenders could usually be counted upon as a rich source of local knowledge. Yes, the saloon would do nicely. He cantered the horse in that direction.

Dismounting gingerly in front of O'Rourke's Drinking Emporium, Shan groaned at the sudden ripple of pain that shot through both of his legs. Adding to the misery, his store-tight range boots had already raised blisters on both feet.

He hesitated at the top of the wooden porch steps and glanced back at the stallion's hanging reins. Unaccustomed to horses, he'd forgotten to tether his mount. Looking around to make sure he was alone and unobserved, he slipped the silver Disc from a leather pouch at his belt and beamed it.

Activated, the reins looped themselves securely around the hitching post.

Adjusting the angle of his new ten-gallon hat, he pushed through the batwings into O'Rourke's saloon. At this time of day the place was largely deserted. A half-dozen patrons, talking quietly among themselves, were huddled over drinks at the bar. The gaming tables were empty and a large roulette wheel in one corner stood unattended.

The saloon's most distinctive feature was hung behind the bar: a long, cut-glass mirror that had been set into an ornate, beautifully hand-carved frame. Shan stared at his reflection in the glass: staring back at him was a clean-featured, thin-shanked man of twenty-one with a thatch of red hair under his hat and guileless blue eyes that hinted of virgin innocence.

"What'll you have, stranger?" asked the bartender, a sweating, barrel-shaped fellow in a patched apron.

"Milk," said Shan softly. "With a soda cracker."

The barman grunted. "No milk. No sodee crackers. What we got is beer and bar whiskey, so what'll it be?"

"Beer," nodded Shan. As it was being drawn from the keg he said: "I'm looking for a man named John Thursday. He has a ranch near the river."

"Then you're in luck," declared the barman, trimming a spill of foam off Shan's glass. "Texas John just come inta town in that fancied-up horseless carriage of his. Likely he's over to the feed store. Where do you hail from, stranger?"

Shan sipped his beer, ignoring the question. He pushed a coin across the bar. "I'd best go find John Thursday."

A sudden thunder of hoofbeats from the street. Then an angry shout: "There's my hoss!" Two burly cowpunchers, riding double on a chestnut mare, had pulled to a dusty halt outside the saloon. Through the window, Shan recognized one of them as the bow-legged man from the water hole. Now the fellow burst in, waving a naked Colt in his right hand. His partner, a massive character with ham-sized fists, was directly behind him.

"By Jasper, here he is!" shouted Bowlegs, pointing the gun at Shan. "Here's the lowdown, piss-ass hoss thief what stole Blackie."

Shan smiled. "I'm truly sorry I had to borrow your animal," he said, "but circumstances called for it."

Bowlegs appealed to the startled bar patrons: "Ya see, gents, this here piss-ass thief *admits* to grabbin' my black."

"Which means we hang him here an' now," declared the second puncher.

And they hustled Shan out to the street.

Inside the grocery and feed store old Pete Robbins glanced outside, then paused as he filled a barrel with oats. "Happenin' again," he muttered darkly. "Smack dab outside. Bold as brass."

Texas John turned to face the old man. Around him was a week's provision of flour, sugar, coffee, and hardtack. "Somethin' bothering ya, Pete?"

"We got us another hangin'. Right on Main Street, in fronta all the kids an' wommin folk. A disgrace, if you ask me. When are people around here gonna start actin' civilized?"

"Yer right," agreed John. "Just hold onta my order. I'll be comin' back." And he headed for a group of townsfolk gathered around Libertyville's "hanging tree," a tall, black oak that towered above the livery stable.

When he arrived on the scene the two determined cow-punchers were in the act of tying a noose around Shan's neck.

"What's goin' on?" demanded Thursday.

"Any pie-eyed, half-wit kin see what's goin' on," growled the bowlegged man. "We're gonna hang a stinkin' hoss thief is what's goin' on."

"Yeah," said his surly companion. "Just you stay outa this, John Thursday. No damn concern a'yours."

"I say different," John told him. "This here kinda thing con-cerns us all, an' it's gotta stop." He glared at the bowlegged man. "Just how much is yer hoss worth—the one that got stole?"

Bowlegs narrowed his eyes. "Why . . . a *hundred* dollars wouldn't buy ole Blackie."

Thursday took out his wallet and extracted a sheaf of bills. "Here's *two* hundred, an' ya kin keep the hoss. This is just to let the boy go."

Bowlegs ran a slow tongue over his lower lip. "Two hundred is a sizable lotta jack."

"We got a deal?" asked the rancher.

"Yeah," said Bowlegs, stretching out a grimy hand for the money.

Thursday paid him, then removed the noose from Shan's neck.

Excitement over, the crowd broke up and drifted away, followed by the two cowpunchers, now gleefully slapping one another on the back over their new-found riches.

Texas John turned to the young man. "What's your moniker, son?"

"Shan is the name, first and last. And you must be John Thursday."

"That I am."

"I'm glad you arrived when you did. Otherwise, I would have been forced to deal with them."

John snorted. "*Deal* with 'em! Hell, boy, you're not even packin' a gun. You'da dealt with them right enough—by kickin' yer legs in the air while that rope choked the life outa ya."

"It was most kind of you to intervene," said Shan. "How may I reimburse you? I carry very little cash on my person."

"You kin work off the two hundred at my place. Pay's a dollar a day, sunup to sundown, with a bunk fer yerself, an' all the grub ya kin eat throwed in. Sound fair enough?"

"Yes, sir." Shan nodded. "That sounds fair enough."

"An' don't call me 'sir.' I'm just plain John to everybody this side'a Hell. And when I get down there, they can call me any damn thing they've a mind to."

"One fact you should be made aware of," Shan said. "I'm from the city, so I know nothing about ranching."

John squinted at him. "Well, then . . . I guess you'll just hafta *learn*."

Which was how, in the summer of 1910 in the Big Bend country of western Texas, a red-haired young man known as Shan became a working hand at John Thursday's Triple-Z Ranch.

Shan was impressed with the Triple-Z. Its acreage, blanketed with a multitude of grazing cattle, seemed to go on forever—while its rambling main house, two barns, corral area, and snug, newly painted bunkhouse exemplified the ideal of ranch life. Indeed, John Thursday had carved his own special empire from the prairie wilderness and could take justifiable pride in his accomplishment.

At the house, first thing, Shan was introduced to Texas John's sister, Anna Thursday—a pale, bedridden woman with bright, bird-like eyes and a strong voice that belied her frailty. At her request, the rancher left Shan alone with Anna so she could "get to know the boy."

Shan sat down on a chair next to the bed.

Her first comment was typically direct: "John tells me you're a horse thief."

Shan smiled. "I meant no harm. I simply needed proper transport."

"Mighty odd way to put it," she said. "How is it that you're a cowboy without a horse?"

"I'm not a cowboy, ma'am. I'm a city boy."

Her bright eyes searched his face. "What city?"

"I've lived in a great number of them. No one in particular." He shifted in the chair. "But, if you don't mind, I'd rather not talk about my past."

"All right, although you'll find I'm a very curious woman." She hesitated. "Do you like sagebrush tea?"

"I've never had any."

Thursday poked his head into the room. "Anna makes the best herb tea in Texas!"

Shan grinned.

He was off to a good start.

"This is home fer the next seven months—'till ya work off yer debt," said Texas John.

They were inside the Triple-Z bunkhouse and Shan was trying out an empty bunk.

"Soft enough," he said. "And clean. I'll rest well here."

"Yeah," nodded John, "so long as ya don't mind all the heavy snorin'. I bunk twenty men in here at night, an' most of 'em snore loud as a saw through timber."

"It's doubtful they'll disturb me," said Shan. "I'm a sound sleeper."

A rough-hewn cowboy entered the bunkhouse. Hooded eyes. Bearded. In dusty range gear. And strong enough to wrestle a gorilla.

"This here's my foreman, Jake Slater," said Texas John.

"I'm Shan," said the stranger, shaking hands.

"You'll need a hoss," said Slater, with a sly wink at Thursday. "An' we got jes the proper one picked out, right John?"

"Sure do," nodded Thursday, suppressing a grin. "We call him 'Hellfire' 'counta his red coat, but he's gentle as a lamb."

"As a wee woolly lamb," agreed Slater.

"I'm not much of a rider," Shan admitted.

"Oh, you'll get along fine on Hellfire," said Texas John.

"That you will," nodded Slater. "He's just the hoss fer a tenderfoot."

At first sight, Hellfire *did* seem docile as a lamb—head down, eyes glazed with afternoon boredom, his tail casually switching at flies. The copper-hued horse slowly raised its head to regard the foreman as he carried a saddle from the barn and slung it over the stallion's back. Hellfire obediently opened his mouth for the bit as Slater arranged the bridle, then tightened the cinches.

"Ya see," said John Thursday to Shan, "ain't he jes like we said?" He unlatched the corral gate for the young man. "Care to give him a try?"

"All right," said Shan, "but don't expect much."

"Oh," muttered Thursday under his breath, "I'm expecting a *lot.*"

Hellfire waited, head down, as Shan approached. Fumbling the reins, the stranger—his foot slipping twice from the stirrup—awkwardly mounted. Throughout, the big horse remained motionless . . . but the instant Shan's full weight descended on his back, Hellfire seemed to go mad.

Throwing himself skyward, he landed with a stiff-legged jolt that snapped Shan's head back, causing his new hat to go sailing into the dirt. Now the young man hung on desperately as Hellfire twisted like a dervish and rotated in frenzied circles.

At the fence, John Thursday and Jake Slater whooped in delight, tears of laughter running down their cheeks. "Stay with him, son!" they shouted. "Ride 'em, cowboy!"

Suddenly, horse and rider vanished behind the barn. As soon as they were safely out of sight, Shan activated the silver Disc in his belt pouch.

Hellfire found himself abruptly airborne, levitated to a height ten feet above the corral floor. The stallion's eyes rolled wildly as—stationary in space—he snorted in fear. A quiver of raw terror rippled the big animal's flanks.

Shan's voice was icy calm: "*Now* will you behave?"

At the corral gate, Thursday and Slater watched as Hellfire emerged from the shadowed edge of the barn, trotting gently, with Shan sitting easy in the saddle.

"You were right," the young man said to them as he neared the gate, the reins loose in his hands. "He's exactly like you said—a wee woolly lamb."

The two older men, staring in shock, did not reply.

The next day, after chores were done, Shan and Texas John stood in deep prairie grass on a flat clearing between low hills. Twelve tin cans had been lined up on a series of rocks some fifty feet away. Thursday had unholstered his heavy Colt .45 and now held it, barrel-down, by his right side.

"An' yer positive ya never fired a weapon at no kinda targets before, livin' or dead?" John asked.

"No, never," declared Shan. "In the city, I had no need of guns."

"Well, out here ya just might have a *big* need for 'em," said Thursday. "Man's gotta know how to defend hisself. This here is wild country, an' a gent without a gun is like a cat without claws."

"I'll take your word for it," Shan said.

"Ya hear a lotta talk about quick draws," said Thursday, "but it ain't how quick ya draw that counts. It's what you kin *hit* once ya clear leather."

Texas John swept the Colt up to arm's length and began firing. Six rapid shots.

Shan blinked. Half of the rocks were bare; six of the tin cans were gone.

"An' *that's* how ya do it," said Thursday, reloading the Colt. "Now try fer the other six while I go fetch us more bullets."

Thursday walked toward their horses, tethered behind a stand of tall boulders at the edge of the clearing.

With the rancher out of sight, Shan removed the Disc from his belt and beamed it at the remaining targets while, simultaneously, he fired the Colt into the air six times.

When Thursday returned with fresh ammunition, he scanned the rocks. Bare. No tin cans. Six for six.

"Kid," he said to Shan, "you sure as hell are one *fast* learner!"

And the stranger smiled modestly.

That night Texas John took his new cowhand into town, to

O'Rourke's saloon, to meet its owner, Bernadette Mariana Rebecca O'Rourke.

"He don't have no last name," Thursday told her, "or at least none he'll 'fess up to."

"Shan is name enough," she said, shaking the young man's hand with a firm grip.

"Happy to meet you, ma'am," said Shan.

"I'm no 'ma'am' around here," she told him. "Everybody in town calls me 'Becky,' and that'll do fine from you."

She was in her late thirties and dressed in a tight-waisted, red velvet dance-hall gown that displayed an ample bosom. Her smile dazzled, and her eyes were a deep lake-blue. A too-firm jawline kept her from outright beauty, but Becky O'Rourke was attractive enough to capture any man's fancy.

"How is it you don't stock milk at your bar?" Shan asked her. "I had to settle for beer."

"I take it you're not a drinking man," Becky said.

"Liquor addles the brain and destroys the body," Shan declared.

Becky laughed. "I'm mighty glad my customers don't share your view, or I'd be out of business." She clucked her tongue thoughtfully. "Tell you what . . . I just got me three cases of sarsaparilla. Parson MacDougall ordered it for the church ladies' social next week. Maybe you'd like some a'that."

"Sure would," nodded Shan.

"He likely built up a thirst breakin' Hellfire," said Texas John. "That critter near killed three of my best riders, but Shan here stuck to him like a burr on a saddle blanket."

"Well . . . I am truly impressed," said Becky. "You must be *some* bronc buster."

"No, I'm not," protested Shan. "The horse and I simply reached a mutual understanding." He hesitated. "About that sarsaparilla . . ."

"Go ask Joe, my barkeep," she told him. "Tell him I said it's on the house." She took Thursday's hand. "Me an' John here, we got some talking to do."

As Shan headed for the bar, Becky led John Thursday upstairs. Once in her sitting room, she fixed him a drink ("from my private stock"), then settled down next to him on the overstuffed rose-colored sofa.

"What's on yer mind, Becky?"

"You know damn well what's on my mind," she snapped. "Just when in tarnation are you gonna ask me to marry you?"

Texas John sighed heavily. "Ya know I rightly can't. Not with Anna the way she is. She *needs* me."

"So do I, John." Her blue eyes were moist. "We've been sparkin' for two years now. At this rate, I'll be a white-haired old lady before you get around to popping the question."

He looked pained. "I can't, darlin'. We gotta wait. Anna's likely to pass on soon, God help her, an' then it'll be different."

"There's another thing," Becky said. "You keep avoiding my questions about what your life was like before you started the Triple-Z."

"I can't get inta that," he said. "Over an' over I keep tellin' ya I can't."

"And over and over I keep on asking." Her voice was intense. "John . . . if I'm gonna be your wife, I've a *right* to know."

"In due course, Becky," said Thursday. He put down his drink and took her into his arms.

"You think you can just kiss me and that'll shut me up," she scolded.

"That's right," he said, pulling her closer. "That's what I think." And they kissed.

Downstairs, at the bar, Shan was finishing his second bottle of sarsaparilla when a callused, thick-fingered hand gripped his shirt collar and spun him around. He faced an unshaven giant of a cowpuncher whose mouth was twisted with scorn. His breath reeked of stale beer and whiskey.

"Well . . . if it ain't the skinny little runt of a hoss thief what I shoulda hung by now," growled the big man.

Shan regarded him placidly. "Even for this untutored region of the West, your grammar is remarkably poor. Given your atrocious vocabulary, you are particularly fortunate that your raw physical bulk allows you to eke out a crude living and maintain your basic lifestyle, however unsavory."

"Luke," said a fellow cowpuncher standing next to the giant. "I ain't for certain sure, but I'd say yer bein' insulted."

"Yeah? Waal, I don't hafta put up with no yella runt of a hoss thief smart-talkin' back ta me," snarled the giant, as he lifted Shan into the air with one hand. With the other, he jammed a long-barrel Colt against the boy's neck. "I figger he'll shut his yap quick enough once I've blowed his head off."

"Stow the iron, Luke!" Texas John was at the upper stair landing, his own Colt in hand. His eyes burned with anger. "That there boy works for me. Put a bullet in him, an' yer a dead man."

Luke dropped Shan and holstered the Colt. Looking up, he raised a balled fist, round as a cannon ball. "C'mon down here, Thursday . . . you an' me, we'll settle this man-to-man."

At this, Texas John jumped over the banister and landed on top of his challenger, igniting an all-out brawl that bloodied more than two dozen customers and saw most of the room's furniture destroyed.

Including Becky's prize mirror, which had been shattered by a tossed spittoon.

At this point, a shotgun blast rocked the saloon, freezing the combatants. Becky O'Rourke stood atop the bar, brandishing a sawed-off, her eyes points of enraged blue fire. "Get out of my place now—all of you—or by God I'll scatter your guts from here to Christmas!"

When the saloon was empty, Texas John told Shan to wait outside in the buckboard while he talked to Becky.

Flushed with anger, she stood in the middle of the room and surveyed the splintered tables and chairs, the smashed chandelier, the broken bottles. The roulette wheel lay on its side in one corner. Shards of glass crackled under her shoes.

"How *dare* you wreck my place!" she snapped, glaring at Thursday. She turned to regard the shattered mirror behind the bar and sadness filled her eyes. Her voice became muted. "That mirror was freighted in by wagon all the way from New Orleans," she said. "A genuine French antique. Priceless. And now look at it!"

John had his Stetson in his hand and twisted it as he spoke. "First, I didn't wreck yer place. The other boys done that. I jes jumped Luke Henry a'fore he kilt the youngster. I never meant for any a'this to happen, Becky."

She sighed. "No . . . I guess you just did what you had to. God knows that scurvy polecat would have shot poor Shan if you hadn't stopped him."

"Look, I got me more money than I need," said John Thursday. He thrust a roll of bills into her hand. "Lemme pay yer damages, especial fer yer mirror. When I saw ole Seth Johnson heave that brass spittoon, I knew yer mirror was a goner."

"No, John. But I appreciate the offer." She pushed his hand away. "This isn't the first time my saloon's been wrecked, and it won't be the last. Cost of doing business." She sighed again. "As for the mirror . . . it's one of a kind. Money isn't going to bring it back."

John shrugged in resignation. "As ya say, Becky. But if ya ever need cash, ya know where to find it."

He gave her a hug, kissed her cheek, and headed out the batwing doors for Shan and the waiting buckboard.

Three A.M. in the Triple-Z bunkhouse. The air quivered in a cacophony of snoring from the slack mouths of twenty sleeping punchers.

Shan sat up, slipped out of his blankets, and swiftly dressed. Quietly, he left the building. Walking quickly out to the barn, he saddled Hellfire, mounted the big stallion, and then began galloping into the darkness.

In Libertyville, at Becky O'Rourke's saloon, he tethered Hellfire and climbed the wooden porch steps, making certain the warped boards didn't creak. Main Street was totally deserted; only the questing howl of a distant prairie wolf disturbed the silence.

A new, rough-lettered sign had been nailed to the padlocked front door:

CLOSED FOR REPAIRS

YOU'LL HAVE TO GET DRUNK
SOMEWHERE ELSE

Walking quietly, Shan circled the porch, searching until he found a boarded-over side window. He pried one of the boards loose, then slipped into the building.

Inside, a yellow shaft of moonlight striped the floor, revealing the night's chaos. An abandoned battleground.

Shan moved to the bar, removed the silver Disc from his belt pouch, then beamed it at the shattered French mirror. Instantly, in a glittering, soundless movement, the broken pieces began smoothly refitting themselves, like pieces in a jigsaw puzzle. Once the original pattern had been reformed, the pieces began seamlessly melding together. Frame and glass were now intact. Perfectly restored.

The flawless, gleaming surface reflected Shan's satisfied smile.

Early morning at the Triple-Z.

A sound of hoofbeats.

Becky O'Rourke rode into the yard fronting the main house, calling out: "John! John Thursday!"

The rancher appeared at the doorway, a straight razor in his hand, a white froth of lather covering his lower jaw. He looked stunned to see her.

"Becky, girl. What brings ya out here this time'a mornin'?"

"I'm meeting Hank Sutter over at the Lazy-M," she said from the saddle of her roan. "He wants to buy that acreage I own in the east county. But I had to stop off to say God bless you, John, for what you did."

"I don't understand," John stammered. "I ain't done nothin' that rates no blessin'."

"You call finding me a new mirror—from God knows where—and sneaking in last night to put it up behind my bar . . . you call that *nothing*? I think it's just about the grandest thing a man could do for the woman he loves, and I'd jump off my horse this second and give you a smacking big kiss, except for all that shaving cream under your mustache."

Thursday shook his head. "But I don't fer the life a' me know what yer—"

"I have to go," she declared. "Hank Sutter's waiting. See you later, darlin'!"

She turned the roan and galloped off, leaving Texas John Thursday standing on the porch, looking totally confused.

Several years earlier Thursday had set up a full-sized boxing ring in his central barn. Although the sport had always been dear to his heart, his workouts at the ranch were generally considered, in the beginning, as evidence of his eccentricity. No one in Libertyville had taken him seriously as a boxer until, despite his age, he'd won the title of Amateur Champion of Western Texas. After that, he was well respected both for his fistic abilities and for his farsighted wisdom in setting up the boxing ring.

So each day, after the morning chores were done and before the big noon meal, Thursday made it a practice to spend two hours in his converted barn, working the light and heavy bags, skipping rope, and boxing with the other ranch hands. His most frequent sparring partner was a husky, long-armed cowman named Sid Benson.

Shan and Thursday had been repairing sections of north pasture fence since sunup when John called a break and invited the young man to come to the barn and watch him box Sid Benson.

When the first session had ended, John yelled down from the ring: "Wanta put on the gloves and have a go?"

Shan shook his head. "I'm no boxer."

Texas John grinned at Benson. "He said he was no rider, either, an' look what he done with Hellfire. An' he tole me he couldn't shoot, then knocked off six cans outa six, neat as ya please." He leaned down toward Shan. "C'mon, take Sid's gloves and step inta the ring with me."

Reluctantly, the young man removed his shirt and then climbed over the ropes. He looked frail and vulnerable next to Thursday's trained, muscled body. Benson helped Shan with the padded boxing gloves, lacing them tight. The young man looked nervous and uncertain.

"I don't know about this," said Shan. "I could get hurt."

"Naw!" scoffed Texas John. "I'll be pullin' my punches . . . jes be playin' with ya."

"All right—but only *two* rounds. Agreed?"

"Agreed," nodded Thursday. He grinned at Benson. "Sid'll keep time for us."

Shan readied himself for the bell.

The first round proved him hopelessly outmatched. Light-footed, gliding across the ring, Texas John fast-jabbed the younger man—pop-pop-pop. Shan reeled back, his gloves up in an attempt to fend off the barrage.

"C'mon kid, *hit* me!" urged Thursday. "Let's see some action!"

At the bell, Shan stumbled to his corner and dropped onto the wooden stool, gasping for breath. His lips were puffed and swollen, a small cut on his lip was bleeding, and he told Sid Benson that his right glove needed to be taken off and retied.

"Gotta watch that left jab a'his," Benson warned as he removed the glove. "John's killin' ya with his left."

"I thought he was going to pull his punches," groaned Shan.

Benson chuckled. "Oh, he *is*. Otherwise, you'd be out cold by now."

As Sid went to get him a fresh cup of water, Shan eased the Disc from his belt pouch, made a quick adjustment to the shimmering silver object, then slipped it into his right glove before Benson returned.

Round 2. Thursday, in total command of the ring, pressed Shan toward the ropes with a lightning flurry of body blows.

"Hit me!" the rancher taunted. "Let's see ya throw a real punch."

Shan ducked away from another left jab, saw his opening, and delivered a long, looping right uppercut that landed square on the point of Thursday's chin.

The champ was knocked across the length of the ring, through the ropes, and slammed to the barn floor.

Dazed, John sat up, rubbing his chin. "Now *that*," he said, "is what I call a punch."

And he stared at Shan in genuine awe.

Later that afternoon Shan took the buckboard into Libertyville to purchase several gallons of maple syrup at the mercantile. "Punchers go through maple syrup faster'n I can buy it," Texas John had complained. "Bring back whatever Pete has."

When Shan entered the store, Pete Robbins was in the back room checking out a new shipment of dry goods, with his daughter filling in behind the counter.

Molly Robbins, an engaging, slim-bodied young woman with merry brown eyes and an inviting smile, walked over to help the new customer.

"I'm Shan," he said. "From the Triple-Z."

"I'm Molly Robbins," she declared, forthrightly giving him her hand. "You're new at the Z."

"That's right," nodded Shan. "John Thursday took me on after he saved me from a hanging."

"He's a good man," she told him. Discreetly, she didn't ask about the hanging; everyone in town knew what had happened. Instead, she asked him what he needed by way of supplies.

"Maple syrup," he said. "John forgot it on his last trip into town. How much do you have in stock?"

"I think we have three gallons left," she said.

"Then I'll take all three." As he was paying her, Shan noticed that she couldn't seem to take her eyes off him. "I notice that you're obviously attracted to me," he told her, "and while I find you to be a very pretty young lady, I am obligated to tell you that there is no possibility of a romance between us."

Molly Robbins stared at him in shock. "What makes you think that I'd ever—" Flustered, she couldn't finish the sentence. "You must be insane to say such a thing to me!"

"I'm sorry if I have offended you," declared Shan. "I am simply trying to be honest."

"*Honest!*" She trembled with anger. "You're outrageous!"

Another young man—dark-haired, with sharp eyes and a wolfish cast to his features—had entered the store during their exchange. Shan noted that the newcomer wore his holstered Colt slung low along his leg in the manner of a veteran shootist.

His suspicion was verified when the youth paused at a rack of weapons, unpegged a new, pearl-handled six-gun, and spun it rapidly in his hand, testing its weight and balance.

"How much for this?" he asked Molly, who had turned her back on Shan. He flashed her a wide smile as he looked her over. "Well, now. This must be my lucky day. Ain't you somethin'."

She smiled back and named a price for the Colt. The newcomer was paying her for the weapon as Shan, carrying the gallon tins of maple syrup, left the store.

Perhaps he *had* been too direct with Molly Robbins, he reflected as he put the syrup into the buckboard. He did, in fact, find her very appealing, but a relationship with her was impossible. Scientifically impossible.

Or so he kept telling himself.

Late afternoon in the south pasture, with a depleted sun riding the tip of the hills, Shan and Texas John had been rounding up strays and now the rancher suggested a break.

Even this late in the day the summer heat was still intense, and they stretched out in the shade of a large boulder. John's back was against the rock as he fired up his pipe.

"I been meanin' ta have us a talk," he said.

"About what?" asked Shan. He was sitting cross-legged, whittling at a stick.

" 'Bout some stuff I jes don't savvy," said Texas John. "Becky's mirror fer instance. She thinks I went an' got her a new one, an' that's tommyrot. But *somebody* sure did."

The young man shrugged. "No way to figure who," he said.

Thursday looked steadily at him. "I got me a notion you had somethin' to do with it."

Shan said nothing as he continued to whittle.

"Then there's Hellfire—the way he was raisin' high hell one second, an' meek as ya please the next."

"We get along," said Shan.

"An' the way you plastered them tin cans first time out . . . an' that punch ya hit me with in the barn. John L. Sullivan hisself woulda been proud'a that one."

"I got lucky both times," said Shan. "You're the boxer, not me. And you can shoot better than I could ever hope to do. I was just lucky."

"Uh-huh," nodded John, as he puffed out a thin, blue cloud of pipe smoke. "Maybe you'd like to say jes exactly where it is ya hail from."

"It's a place you wouldn't know about," declared Shan. "You'll have to take my word on that." He put the stick aside. "What about you, John? You've never mentioned the death of your wife."

Thursday leaned forward and drew his brows together. "How d'ya know about Elly?"

"There's talk. I just know."

"She died givin' birth to our first child," said Texas John in a quiet voice. "I was right there in the room when . . . when I lost 'em both, her an' the baby." He hesitated, his tone soft, regretful, the pain alive in his eyes. "Never had me no sons nor daughters. Guess now I never will."

"There's Becky," said Shan. "She loves you. She could bear children."

"I know . . . an' Becky's a fine woman." He sighed. "But with Anna so sick an' all . . ."

Thursday stood up, knocking the ashes from his pipe against the side of the rock. "Sun's almost down. Let's get back ta work."

And their talk ended.

The pearl-handled Colt flashed against the sun, spinning in a bright arc into the waiting hand of its new owner.

"So that's the fancy piece ya bought in town?" asked Buck Haines. He was as massive as an oak, with untrimmed hair flowing under his black hat and a thick tangle of graying beard. His nose had been broken in two places, and three of his front teeth were missing. His dark eyes were cold and humorless, sunk into a face that seemed skinned in saddle leather.

His son, Bobby Haines, ran a slow finger along the glossy pearl handle of the new Colt. "Bought it in Libertyville from a right pretty little store gal. Her name's Molly, an' she's a sweet flower, jes ripe for the pickin'."

"See that ya stay outa her rose garden," warned his father. "Small town like that . . . we don't wanta create us no attention." He scowled at his son. "Didn't tell her yer name did'ja?"

"Naw," said young Haines. "I ain't no fool."

"Gun like that . . . people remember it, an' they remember the man that packs it. When we hit the stage, you keep that pearl job outa sight."

"Sure, Pop. You can count on it."

Buck turned to the others in his gang: five desperate looking characters whose hard faces and low-slung Colts revealed their trade. They sat around the ashes of the previous night's campfire that had been built in a clearing, within the shelter of scattered boulders.

"You boys ready?" Buck asked.

They nodded. Colts had been loaded and rifles primed. The horses had been fed, watered, and were ready to gallop.

"An' jes ya remember, Bobby," Buck said to his son, "we're goin' after the strongbox—not to have us no shootin' party. Don't wanna kill nobody. Stage robbery's a small thing, but murder stirs up the hornets."

"Sure, Pop."

"Jes keep that ta mind," said Buck Haines.

And they prepared to ride.

The drapes were now kept drawn in Anna Thursday's bedroom because her eyes could no longer tolerate sunlight. Thus, even in midday the room was dim.

In this gloom, Texas John stood next to her bed and held his sister's withered hand in his own. ". . . an' the doc says he can't do anythin' more, Sis. It don't look good."

Anna smiled weakly, her face like brittle parchment. "I know it's my time, John, and I'm ready to move on. I'm not afraid to die. I'm only afraid of what you'll do after I'm gone."

"There's no changin' my mind on that," he said. "I'm gonna give it all back and git that load off my shoulders."

"But what if they—"

"Hush!" he commanded. "I won't have you frettin' about me. I'm gonna be fine."

"But what about the Triple-Z?"

"I'll give up the ranch, too, if that's how the hand plays out."

"But all your work . . . your dreams . . ."

"Don't matter. There's a time ta clear the books an' start clean. When ya—" He hesitated, softening his tone. "When ya move on, I square my accounts. I can't keep pretendin' that the past never happened."

"You're a good man, John. After all these years there's no reason for you to suffer for what's long done and over."

"Nothin's over 'till I give it back," he said. "We both know that."

She sighed and settled deeper into the pillows. "I'm so tired now," she said, her words labored and weak. "I need to sleep, John." Her eyes fluttered closed.

When she was breathing evenly John Thursday stepped quietly from the dimness of the room. It would not be long now.

Not long at all.

For the Haines gang, robbing the stage to Libertyville was child's play. They were well practiced in the art of stage robbery and expected no trouble with this one.

"Here she comes," said Bobby, pulling a checkered bandanna across his face. The other men did the same.

"Now!" shouted Buck—and the seven outlaws galloped out from a narrow cut in the canyon wall to confront the rattling coach as it rounded the long curve known as Devil's Twist.

The shotgun guard threw down his weapon and thrust both arms high as Jed Perkins, the stage driver, tossed away his Colt and also raised his gloved hands.

"Don't shoot, boys," said Perkins, nervously shifting his wad of tobacco from one cheek to the other. "We don't aim ta give ya no bother."

"That's what we like to hear," said Buck Haines. "Toss us down that strongbox."

Perkins did this.

Bobby blew off the lock with a single shot. "Well, lookee here!" he said as he held up a thick sheaf of greenbacks.

Scooping up the money, Buck Haines swung his horse around. "Let's move out," he said to the others. "We got what we come fer."

"Wait up," said Bobby. "I wanna see what all's inside."

He stepped to the dust-filmed coach and pulled the door wide. He peered in at a young couple cowering back against the leather seat. The woman wore a linen travel duster and bonnet, while the man sported a derby hat, the glint of a gold watch chain peeping from under his vest.

"Git down from there," Bobby ordered. "Both a'ya!"

Hesitantly, the couple climbed from the coach and stood together in front of the open door. They looked thoroughly frightened.

"You two married?" asked Bobby.

"Yes," said the man. "And my wife is about to have our child. We need to reach the doctor in Libertyville. Every minute counts."

The girl held both hands to the swell of her stomach. Her condition was obvious.

"C'mon, Bobby! We gotta ride!" shouted one of the outlaws, a horse-faced man called Ringo.

Buck Haines turned and viciously slashed him across the face with his leather riding quirt. "Didn't I tell ya never to use none'a our names!" he snarled. "Damn ya, next time ya ferget, I'll plant a slug in yer gut!"

"Sorry," muttered Ringo, as blood seeped from his cut cheek.

Buck gestured toward the coach. "If my boy wants to talk to these here folks, then we kin wait. Let him be."

Bobby was standing close to the pregnant woman. "Gonna have you a squallin', little snot-nosed brat, huh?"

"Please," begged the derby-hatted young husband. "You've got the money. Let the stage go on. My wife *must* have a doctor!"

Bobby Haines chuckled and kept his weapon leveled. "Let's have this first." He grabbed the gold chain and jerked the watch free.

"*Now* will you let us go?" asked the sweating man.

"Jes' shut yer yap," snapped the outlaw as he moved back to the girl. She was wearing a gold and amethyst necklace.

"That too," he said. "Gimme."

She put a protective hand to her neck. Haines slapped her hard, then grabbed the necklace and pulled it free. Staggering from the blow, she fell to the ground.

"You bastard!" shouted her husband. "I'll—"

He lunged forward. Haines raked the barrel of the heavy pistol across the young husband's skull, knocking him senseless.

"Enough!" his father ordered. "Git mounted an' let's ride."

Bobby stuffed the necklace and watch into his shirt pocket, then vaulted into the saddle of his pinto as the others spurred their horses into a quick gallop.

Soon they were gone, leaving a cloud of rapidly thinning dust to mark their passage.

From the high ridge overlooking Devil's Twist, Shan saw the coach below, motionless, the team horses fretting and stomping their hoofs in the day's heat. Three men were huddled over a woman lying in the roadway.

He'd been riding fenceline for John Thursday and had decided to allow Hellfire to have a free run; the horse had taken them to the high lip of Devil's Canyon. Now Shan jockeyed the big, red stallion down a steeply angled rock flume to the valley floor.

When he reached the stagecoach, Shan hailed the three men. They looked drawn and on the edge of desperation.

"This here lady's about ready to bust loose with a kid any second," Jed Perkins told him. "You ain't a doc by any chance, are ya?"

"No," said Shan, "but maybe I can help."

He quickly dismounted and knelt beside the young woman. She was clutching her distended stomach; her face muscles were stretched in pain. Closely spaced spasms racked her body, causing animal sounds to come from her throat.

"This is my wife, Mae, and I'm Bill Thomas," said a young man about Shan's age. A bloodstained bandanna was tied around his head. "We were robbed, and one of the thieves struck Mae. She fell and that put her into labor. None of us knows anything about delivering a baby."

"That's the God's truth!" muttered the shotgun guard. "What we need is a doc, only there ain't time to fetch one."

Shan waved them back and instructed Mae Thomas to breathe "deep and slow," telling her that she and her baby were going to be fine. He removed the Disc from his belt pouch and made an adjustment. The silver began to glow a shimmering blue.

"What are you doing?" she gasped.

"Trust me," said Shan. He rearranged her skirt and then removed her petticoats, leaving her legs free. He began moving the Disc over her midsection in a slow, circular pattern while his other hand stroked her head in a soothing rhythm that visibly relaxed her.

Mae groaned softly. A final spasm—and an infant's pink head emerged from between her legs. Shan lifted the newborn male free of her body as easily as a cake is lifted from the oven. Shan asked the guard for his bolo tie, which he used to tie off the umbilical cord before severing this last physical connection between mother and child. The baby was now free, a separate human being.

"Lord a'mighty, she done it!" marveled Jed Perkins. "She done give birth!"

Shan checked the infant's mouth for obstructions, then gently slapped the child's buttocks until it began to cry. He carefully wrapped Mae's son in a discarded petticoat, then placed the child in her arms. Overcome with joy, she began crying.

"You have a healthy son, Mr. Thomas," he said to the stunned father. "And your wife will be fine."

The baby continued wailing as the adults around him smiled in relief.

At the Triple-Z, on the long wooden veranda, Texas John paced back and forth, scowling. He stopped to face Shan.

"An' yer dead sure the driver said the name was 'Bobby'?"

"That's what he told me," said Shan. "And the gang's leader also called him 'son.' The driver was clear on what he heard."

"It's them, by hell!" exclaimed Thursday. "The Haines bunch. I never figgered they'd range this far south."

"You know them?" asked Shan.

Thursday's face tightened. "I know Buck Haines—an' he's as mean as a stepped-on rattler."

Shan stared at him. "Then you and Haines—"

"We tangled once," nodded Texas John. "Long time ago. It don't matter now. The thing is, he's back. An' there's no tellin' what he's upta."

"You're worried."

"Wouldn't anybody be, with the Haines gang in these parts? I jes hope they keep movin' is all."

Thursday's eyes were troubled, clouded with dark thoughts.

That night, at the square dance in town, Shan was startled to see Molly Robbins approaching him from across the plank floor. He was sitting on the sidelines with Texas John and Rebecca, watching the action as Molly came up to them.

"Howdy," said John. "Ya here with yer Pa?"

"No, Daddy's back at the store," she said. "I came with Tug Hollister, but he ran off to spark some widow lady visiting from Sweetwater." As she answered Thursday, her eyes remained on Shan.

"You're sure lookin' mighty nice tonight with your hair up like that," said Becky. "That a new party dress?"

Molly ran her fingers along the seam of her nipped-in bodice. "Yes. Came in from St. Louis last week on the stage. Ordered special."

"Well, you're pretty as a picture in it," nodded Becky. Then, to Shan: "Isn't she?"

"Yes, she is. I mean, you are." He met Molly's direct gaze.

"Ask her to dance," John urged. "You'd like to, wouldn't you, girl?"

"Yes, I would."

"I've never square danced," said Shan.

"C'mon," said Molly, taking his hand. "I'll teach you."

On the floor, Shan discovered that square dancing was most enjoyable. A quaint Western folkway that had much to recommend it. As they whirled through the steps, following the lively fiddle music and the directions of the caller, Molly told him she had forgiven him his "rudeness" at the store. Would he like to go riding with her tomorrow?

He nodded, "It's my day off at the ranch. I'd be honored to ride with you, but please keep in mind what I said at the store. I know you don't understand right now, but please believe that I'm trying to avoid your being hurt later."

"I've decided to trust your good intentions. You're not like the other boys I know," she told him. "The way you talk is so . . . so different." She smiled. "And I never met anyone who couldn't square dance."

"I'm from the city, remember?"

"Don't they dance in the city?"

"Not like this . . . not in the city I'm from."

Later, at the punch bowl, as Shan filled Molly's glass, she nodded toward Texas John and Becky who were sitting across the room. Their heads were close together and they were smiling into one another's eyes.

"They make a beautiful couple," Molly said.

"They do," said Shan. "And they're going to have five beautiful children together."

Molly blinked at him. "You say the strangest things!"

"It's a strange world," he said. "I suppose you could call me a fish out of water."

She didn't even *try* to understand what he meant by that.

Molly had packed a full picnic basket for their ride and it was now strapped to the saddle of her beloved "Whiskers," a spotted gelding she'd raised from a colt. Beside her, Shan was mounted on Hellfire.

When they reached a cluster of cottonwoods on the banks of a sunlit stream Molly suggested that they stop. "This is a lovely spot," she said. "Let's have our picnic here."

Shan readily agreed. "I've been thinking about your picnic lunch since we passed the road to Pecos," he confessed. "I'm ready to eat."

"You *do* have picnics where you come from?" she asked him as she spread a blanket over the grass.

"We have a large park," he said. "People go there to conduct what I suppose would correspond to a picnic."

She unpacked the wicker basket, which was filled with fried chicken, potato salad, fresh-baked bread, and chocolate cake. As each new dish was brought forth, Shan's eyes gleamed. "Everything looks so good," he said.

"What was your life like before you came to Libertyville?" she asked.

"Quite ordinary," he replied. "There's nothing very unusual about me."

"On the contrary," she said, "*everything* about you is unusual. I don't think you're being quite honest with me."

Shan smiled. "I thought that was what got me into trouble with you in the first place—my honesty."

"I didn't mean it that way. I mean honest about who you really are."

"I'm Shan," he said. "And I work for John Thursday at the Triple-Z. There's little more."

Molly stared at him for a long moment. "I think there's a *lot* more."

"Maybe," he said. "But what there is, I can't tell you. Instead, I want to hear about you. For instance, where did you grow up? Here? In Libertyville?"

"No. In Philadelphia. My father sent me to boarding school there. He was a drummer before he came West to open the store, so he couldn't take care of me."

"You mean he was a musician?"

She laughed. "No, although that's a funny thought. A drummer is a salesman. That's what he did, and he had to travel most of the year when he was doing it."

"And your mother?"

"She died before I was old enough to remember her," Molly replied.

"How did you like boarding school?"

"*I hated* it! I wanted to be with Daddy, but he said it was no life for a child." She sighed. "The only subject I really liked was French. Someday I hope to travel to Montreal so I can study the language. Eventually, I'd like to teach it."

"A worthy ambition," said Shan.

"My father wouldn't agree with you. He expects me to marry some cowpuncher here in Libertyville, raise a flock of kids, and then—with my husband—take over his store after he retires. But that's not the kind of life I want."

"Then keep your goal in mind," Shan told her. "Live your own life, not your father's. That's the wisest thing you can do, for everyone's sake."

The sky suddenly darkened and a gusting wind began to shake the trees.

Molly stood up, pointing. "Out on the plain," she said. "A *twister!* Really big one. And it's headed straight for town."

On the distant edge of the flat plain a long, quivering black ribbon had unfurled from sky to earth.

"You stay here," said Shan. "We're only two miles from Liberty-ville. I'll ride in and warn them."

"Can you make it in time?"

"Hellfire is fast," declared the young man. "I can make it."

"Then hurry!" she urged him. "I can't ride that fast. I'll wait here."

Shan was already mounted on the red stallion. Bending low over Hellfire's neck he urged the horse into a furious gallop in the direction of Libertyville.

Once he had cleared the woods and was beyond Molly's sight, however, Shan abruptly changed course, riding Hellfire straight into the tornado's path.

When he was close enough to feel the storm's savage force surging around him he raised the silver Disc and beamed it full at the howling funnel of primal energy.

The twister seemed to hesitate, as if considering its next move. Then—success!—it began to whirl away in a reverse direction toward the empty plains.

Shan returned the Disc to his belt, swung Hellfire around, and then headed back for the cottonwood grove by the stream.

Two grizzled hunters who had witnessed this amazing event from the porch of their cabin were awestruck.

"That there twister . . . it jes up an' turned tail like a whupped bobcat!" declared one.

"End'a the world's at hand fer sure, jes like the Good Book says," moaned the other. "We was saved by the grace a'God this time, but mebbe next time the Good Lord will see it different. We best do some prayin' now, Jeb."

The tornado continued on its new route. Now it was only a dim streak of black, fading to gray along the far horizon.

In Anna Thursday's bedroom the doctor murmured soothing words to his patient, repacked his medical bag, and met John Thursday in the outer hallway.

"Is she any better?" asked the rancher.

The doctor's face was grave as he shook his head. "You're going to lose her, John."

"How much longer?"

"Her heart is getting weaker. It'll give out, probably before next week."

"Is she in pain?"

"No, not now. Perhaps . . . in a couple of days."

"Thanks, doc. I know ya done what ya could."

"I have indeed. Anna's a good woman. I just wish I could've saved her."

They shook hands and the doctor left the house.

Thursday entered Anna's room, saw that she was still awake, and sat down on the chair beside the bed.

In a quiet voice she asked him: "Have you changed your mind?"

"About what?"

"Don't play with me, John," she said, frowning at him. "About what you said you would do after I'm gone."

"I have to tell the truth," he said.

The finality of his statement silenced her. Anna knew that further argument would be futile. But there was one last thing she could do.

She asked her brother to bring the writing board to the bed, along with her stationery, pen, and ink.

"Who you goin' to write to?" he asked, not caring if he was trespassing on her personal business.

"Never you mind. Let me do what I have to do, John. It's going to be my last request."

Abashed and somewhat ashamed, he brought her the stationery and writing board, then left the room without another word.

Anna dipped a long pen into the ink pot and began to write . . .

Dear Aunt Hattie,

　　The Good Lord is about to call me home, but before I depart this Earth I must beg you to help my dear brother — your only nephew, John. He is on the verge of a very rash act that will surely result in terrible consequences . . .

Breathing with difficulty, she continued on with the last letter she would ever write.

Afternoon along the sun-swept expanse of the Rio Grande.

Shan and Texas John were watering their horses after the day's roundup. Shan was kneeling at the bank, filling his canteen when John nudged his shoulder, pointing.

A flimsy wooden raft, bearing three young children, emerged from a bend of the river.

"Them's the Albernathy kids," exclaimed Thursday. "Little Timmy an' his two sisters. They oughta be in school!"

Shan grinned. "Didn't you ever play hookey?"

"Well, now that ya mention it . . ."

Timmy was handling the crude wooden oar, homemade like the raft. He paddled while his two giggling sisters urged him to go faster.

"They seem to be having a fine time," said Shan. He took an apple from his pocket and held it out to Hellfire. The horse snorted, snatched the apple from his master's hand, and began chomping contentedly.

"Good boy," said Shan, rubbing the big stallion's satiny muzzle.

"They'll be into white water a'fore they know it," said John. "This here is a dangerous part of the river."

"How dangerous?"

"Waterfall's ahead. With sharp rocks. Big drop over them falls. The raft'll break up fer sure."

The children were now out of sight around the next bend.

"We'd better do something," said Shan, mounting Hellfire. "Get them off the river before they reach the falls."

"I'll toss 'em a rope an' we can pull 'em ashore," said Thursday, who had also mounted.

"Then let's go!"

By the time they caught up with the raft it was into a section of white-water rapids. A glancing blow against a boulder in mid-river knocked the oar from Timmy's hand. The three children were suddenly helpless in the surging grip of the river, with the raft twisting and spinning in the foaming current.

"They'll never be able ta grab no rope now," declared Thursday. "Takes all they got jes ta hang on."

"The falls," said Shan tensely. "How far?"

"Jus 'round the bend," said the rancher. "They'll be smashed to bits. I'm goin' in after 'em."

Texas John was stripping off his shirt when Shan stopped him. "Stay here! You can't fight that current. I'll handle this."

"Handle it *how*?"

"Watch me," he told the older man. Shan slipped the Disc from his belt pouch and made a quick adjustment. He swung around, facing the river.

Too late. The raft had vanished around the final bend that led to the falls.

With Thursday following, Shan rushed along the bank to a high point of ground just above the raging waters. Below, the raft had almost reached the lip of the falls, poised for the long drop onto the rocks. All three of the children were screaming when Shan beamed the Disc.

The raft quivered, then lifted itself clear of the water, rising like a magic carpet with the children huddled in its center.

As Shan directed the Disc's beam the raft slowly descended, landing gently on the ground directly in front of Shan and a totally astonished John Thursday.

Back at the ranch Texas John took Shan into his private study, firmly closed the door, and told the young man to make himself comfortable because they had some serious talking to do.

Thursday sat down behind his desk while Shan took the chair facing it.

"All right, boy," said John, "jes how did ya pull off that stunt at the river? Are ya some kind'a miracle man?"

"No more than you are, John — but I have this."

And he placed the silver Disc on the desktop.

Thursday picked it up and turned it over in his hand.

"Got kinda like little buttons on the side," he said.

"Don't touch any of those," warned Shan. He reached out: "I'll take it back if you please."

The rancher handed over the Disc. "I saw ya use this thing at the river. Is this what moved the raft?"

"Yes," said Shan. "It allows me to suspend or reverse gravity, so I can control objects in space. Also, it can fire a laser beam that has immense power because it's so concentrated."

"Lay-sir?" John lowered his brows. "What in tarnation is a lay-sir?"

"I don't think you would be able to understand my explanation," Shan said.

"Try me, son."

"This device contains a crystal in which atoms, when stimulated by focused light waves, amplify and concentrate those waves, emitting them in a narrow, extremely intense power beam."

"Yer right," nodded John. "I don't understand a damn word."

"I used the Disc to restore Becky's mirror, tame Hellfire, knock off those tin cans, and deliver that punch in the barn when we were boxing. And then, of course, I used it to save the children."

"This . . . this silver doohickey . . . it done all that?"

"Yes," replied Shan. "And there's more."

"More?"

"I can focus body energy through my hands. We all have the

power of touch, it's just a matter of knowing how to release it. Most people use only ten percent of their brain. Where I come from, we use over fifty percent."

"Hell, boy, where *do* you come from?"

"I can't reveal my place of origin at the moment—but I can tell you that I came here with a mission to perform."

"What kinda mission?"

"You'll find out at the proper time. And then I'll be able to tell you everything. For now, you'll simply have to trust me and know that I came here to help you."

"An' ya won't say what ya come here *fer?*"

"Not now. Not today. But soon."

"Well . . ." Thursday sighed, flattening his hands on the desk. "I been keepin' some secrets a'my own, so I kin see how a gent can't 'fess up ta everthin'. An' ya *did* save them Albernathy kids an' that's a fact. They woulda been dead by now, 'cept fer you. So I guess I'll jes hafta wait out the full truth."

"Thanks, John. I appreciate your trust."

The rancher chuckled. "Them Albernathys . . . they ain't gonna believe how ya saved their young'uns. They'll figger the kids made up the whole wild yarn. Can't blame 'em none. I know I'd never of believed it unless I seen it."

"There's one other thing," said Shan. "What you witnessed today . . . everything we talked about . . . you tell no one. Not Anna . . . not Becky . . . *no* one. Understood?"

"Understood," nodded John. "But I feel like I'm livin' some kinda dream an' I can't wake up."

Shan smiled. "No dream, John. It's all as real as the sun in the sky."

At the town post office in Hannibal, Missouri, all incoming letters and packages were sorted in a small room just behind the front service counter.

Postal clerk Arly Willows, a balding scarecrow of a fellow whose watery eyes blinked constantly behind bottle-thick glasses, emptied a canvas sack onto a wooden table and began sorting the day's mail.

A particular letter caught his attention. He plucked it from the stack, squinting to make out the wavery, hand-scrawled words on the envelope:

Miss Hattie Grover
3337 Forest Avenue
Hannibal, Missouri

"I'll be damned!" muttered Arly. Looking over his shoulder to make certain he was unobserved, he stuffed the letter into his vest. Then he walked to the front of the office.

Portly Earl Gates, Hannibal's postmaster, had just finished waiting on a customer. He turned to his thin-faced employee.

"You look a bit odd, Arly," he said. "Something wrong?"

Willows took off his glasses and scrubbed at his eyes. "I think I've got the gripe coming on," he said. "Feeling kind of dizzy. I need to get home to bed."

"Well then, you trot right on," said Gates. "Got sick time coming as it is. I'll handle things here."

"Thank you, Mr. Gates. I'll do that," said Willows. "I'll just head on home."

But Arly Willows didn't head for his home. Instead, he walked briskly to the rail depot and boarded the next westbound train.

The letter to Miss Hattie Grover was still in his vest.

Becky O'Rourke ran a slow hand along the frame of her restored bar mirror and smiled fondly at Texas John.

"I'm so grateful to you for this," she said. "It's almost as nice as a marriage proposal."

"C'mon over here," he said, nodding toward a table at the rear of the saloon. It was early afternoon and the room was deserted. Even the barkeep dozed on his stool in the languorous heat of the day. A fly circled lazily in the air near the batwing doors.

Becky and John sat down at the table. He looked solemn and depressed.

"After Anna's gone," he said, "a lotta things are gonna change in my life."

"How do you mean, John?"

"All of yer questions about me are gonna be answered," he declared darkly. "But ya won't like what ya find out."

She reached over to take his hand. "Nothing I find out could affect the way I feel about you. I *love* you, John."

He bowed his head. "An' I love ya too, Becky—but sometimes love ain't enough."

"It's all we need," she said, pressing his hand. "You'll see."

He said nothing. The pain of what lay ahead caused him to close his eyes. There was a storm gathering in his life and it would likely destroy him.

And everything they had together.

*   *   *

"I *knew* it'd come," smiled Buck Haines, holding the letter in his hand. "I figgered she *had* to contact ole Hattie sometime, an' you were right there, waitin' for it. Good work, Arl."

"Thanks, Buck." Willows was transformed; he had discarded his thick glasses and store-bought suit. Now he wore range gear, and a Colt was strapped to his thigh. "I aim ta put on some weight. Workin' as a skinny-ass postal clerk ain't my idea of the good life."

Buck gave him a gap-toothed smile. "Well, you're back with us now, me an' the boys, an' we're soon due fer a *real* good life, with enough money to buy all the women and whiskey in Texas."

He turned to the others, who were sprawled about the camp. "Arl here is what ya might call 'Fate's Messenger.' He brung this letter all the way from Missoura, an' by God, it tells me jes where to find Jack Oliver, damn his black soul!"

"What ya got agin' this Oliver fella?" asked Ringo.

Buck Haines drew his lips back in a bitter snarl. "We got us an ole score to settle, me an' Jack," he said. "He took somethin' away from me that I'm gonna git back. This letter tells me all I need to know, includin' what name he's been usin' all this time."

"Which is?" asked Cheyenne, a ferret-eyed half-breed with a knife scar running the length of his left cheek.

"Thursday," said the outlaw. "Texas John Thursday. An' as the Good Lord would have it, he's not more'n ten mile from this here camp. Got a spread outside Libertyville."

"Are we headin' there?" asked Little Charlie, a slope-jawed gun-man with a patch over one eye.

"Not quite yet," said Haines. He nodded to his son. "Bobby, I got a job for ya."

Young Haines raised his head . . . waiting for orders.

Shan was with Molly Robbins at the mercantile, helping her move some heavy grain sacks, when Bobby Haines dismounted outside and staggered through the door.

He banged a fist against the counter. "Service!" he shouted. "Where's that cute 'lil gal that sold me a shootin' iron?"

"I'm here," said Molly, wiping her hands on her apron as she approached the cash register. "How may I be of service?"

Haines leered at her, swaying back against the counter. He seemed to be very drunk. "Ya kin gimme a kiss ta start with!" And he reached for her.

The girl twisted away as Shan stepped between them. "Leave her alone."

"Stay outa this," warned Haines, drawing his Colt, "or I'll blow ya to hell!"

"Put up the gun," commanded a voice from the doorway.

Thursday was there, his rifle leveled at Bobby Haines.

Clumsily, Haines holstered the Colt, his face twisted with rage. "You talk big, mister—with a rifle in yer hands! Maybe you'd like to settle things another way."

"How?" asked Texas John.

"With *these!*" Haines raised his two fists.

"My pleasure," said Thursday. He put the rifle aside, walked up to Haines, and knocked him senseless with a single blow.

"Help me get this piece'a rotten dogmeat outa here," he said to Shan, who was grinning ear-to-ear.

"You sure settled things," the young man said as he helped John pick up the outlaw. Together, they dragged him to the door and tossed him into the street. Haines landed face down in the wagon-rutted dirt. Coughing, with blood running from his nose, he sat up groggily.

"Here!" Molly threw his hat after him. "Don't forget this," she said. "Wouldn't want you to get sunstroke."

Haines stood up, glaring. A small crowd had gathered at the front of the store, staying well clear of the enraged gunman.

"You, old man!" Haines pointed at John Thursday. "I'll be back, come sunup, but I won't be alone. I'll be with my Pa, Buck Haines, an' the rest of the boys. We're gonna burn this stinkin' town to the ground an' you along with it. That is, if ya got enough guts to face us!"

"So you're young Haines," said Thursday. "I shoulda guessed, what with ya bein' a bully an' a cheap braggart jes like yer Pa. You go tell him ta come on in. We'll deal with him an' his mangy crew the same way we dealt with you!"

"Oh, I'll tell him," said Haines as he mounted his horse. "Ya kin damn well be sure'a that."

And he rode off at a fast gallop.

Silently, the crowd watched him go.

"You stay here, Molly," said Texas John. "Me an Shan hafta see the sheriff."

The office of Harrison Dobbs, sheriff of Libertyville, was six doors up from the mercantile store. When Shan and Thursday walked in they found the lawman hurriedly cleaning out his desk.

Dobbs was a small, stoop-shouldered man who affected a thick mustache that was carefully curled at each end. He attempted to compensate for his lack of height by wearing high-heeled boots. Now he was stuffing personal items into a green carpetbag.

"What's goin' on, Harry?" asked John Thursday.

"*Hell* is what's goin' on," he replied without looking up. "Come sunup, when the Haines gang gets here, this town is finished."

The rancher stared at him. "Ya mean ya ain't gonna be here ta face 'em?"

"Dang right I ain't," declared the little man. "An' anybody who does is gonna be fit for buryin'. Ya heard what young Haines said . . . they're gonna burn down the place."

"Not if we stand up to them," said Thursday.

Dobbs finished cleaning out his desk and closed the bag. "Lotta folks around here seem to think you oughta be sheriff—so *you* stand up to 'em. Me, I'm no fool. I'm ridin' out fer good."

And he left the office, moving quickly to his tethered mustang. Dobbs tied the carpetbag to the saddle, then mounted, turning to face them, reins in hand.

"My advice to ya both," said Harry Dobbs, "is to skedaddle outa town a'fore them Haines boys show up in the mornin'. By this time tomorrow, there won't *be* no Libertyville."

And, in a drumming cloud of dust, he was gone.

At the outlaw camp Buck Haines greeted his son. "How'd it go, Bobby?"

Young Haines was grinning. "Jes like you said it would, Pa. Whole town knows we're comin' in. They'll scatter like chickens."

"Well, I jes bet ole Jack ain't one of 'em," said the elder Haines. "He knows we got a personal score to settle and he'll stick around to settle it. Meanin' he's gonna die."

"That old man's got no chance," agreed Bobby. "Ain't nobody faster with a six-gun than you. But why d'ya think he won't cut an' run?"

"Pride," said Buck. "His pride'll hold him there. In a way, he's gonna be killin' hisself."

"I wanta see it," said Bobby, excitement in his voice. "I wanna see you gun him down."

"You will," said his father. He turned to the others. "Git ready. We ride at sunup."

That night at the ranch, in Anna Thursday's candle-lit bedroom, the dying woman pleaded with her brother.

"Please don't do what you're planning, John. They'll put you in jail and claim the ranch. Everything you've built up . . . it'll all be lost. Promise me you won't do it."

"That's a promise I can't make," said John softly. "After all these years, I gotta do what's right."

She nodded, knowing he was committed. Thursday leaned down to kiss her cheek.

"You been more than a sister ta me," he said. "Ya been a light ta guide me in this world. It's gonna be mighty dark without ya." Tears were rolling down his cheeks. "I'm gonna miss ya somethin' fierce, Sis. God, how I'm gonna miss ya!"

She smiled weakly. "I've had a good life, all told, and I'm ready to move on. But I want you to know . . . that no woman could have a finer brother." She drew in a long, shuddering breath. "Now send in Shan. I want to say something to the boy."

Her voice was barely above a whisper. As John walked from the room, he knew he was leaving her forever.

Within moments Shan was sitting in the chair by Anna's bed. His hand held hers; its warmth felt strong and calming to the dying woman.

"John won't talk to me about you," whispered Anna. "But I know you're real special. And I know you're going to be able to help my brother after I'm gone."

"You're right," said the young man. "I can help him."

"He's going to need you, son. Don't fail him . . . Just please don't fail him . . ."

Her voice caught, then she exhaled very slowly, and Anna Thursday closed her eyes for the last time.

Later, in his study with Shan, John talked about the good years with his sister at the ranch.

"She always backed me up, an' never laid no guilt on me fer what I was a'fore I bought this ranch," he said. "Anna was a rare one."

"She was indeed," agreed Shan.

"I done me some bad things in my young days," said Texas John.

Shan nodded. "Back when your name was Jack Oliver," he said. "Twenty years ago, when you robbed a government gold train with Buck Haines."

The rancher stared at him. "But how could ya—" Then he smiled. "I see. Anna told ya."

"No, she told me nothing about your past," Shan declared. "Not a word. Yet I know all about you. I can't reveal *how* I know—quite yet—but I know."

"By this time I oughta be usta to yer big surprises," said Thursday. "Jes when willya be ready to quit bein' so all-fired mysterious?"

"Soon now," Shan said. "*Very* soon."

It was almost dawn. The eastern sky at the edge of the plains beyond Libertyville was no longer black; a pale, gray luminescence had replaced the night's darkness.

Despite this very early hour the town's main street swarmed with activity. Store owners and private citizens were frantically loading wagons, carts, and carriages with supplies and personal goods. In front of the Greater Libertyville Bank the massive iron safe was dragged into the street by a team of horses where it was lifted, via a crude rope-pulley, into the bed of a heavy supply wagon.

The townspeople were desperate to clear out of Libertyville before the Haines gang arrived.

Inside the saloon, in the quiet of her upper living quarters, Becky O'Rourke was listening to John Thursday as he told her the full story of his past, when his name had been Jack Oliver and he'd ridden the outlaw trail.

"I was still crazy wild in them days," John admitted. "After me an' Buck pulled off the government train job, we had a fallin' out. He threatened to kill me—so I shot him an' rode off with the gold."

"What happened to it?" she asked. "Where's the gold now?"

"Where it's been hid all these years since I first come here," said Thursday. "It's buried next to the back wall of the old Spanish mission just outside town. Part of it went to buy my ranch an' the stock I needed. The rest is still buried out there.

"Reason I kept quiet fer so long was fer Anna's sake," he said. "I didn't want Sis thrown out homeless once I lost the ranch." He looked down. "An' I never told *you* none'a this, cuz I was ashamed'a what I'd been and done."

"I would have understood," she said. "I *do* understand. You're no outlaw, John."

"I was once, but I've lived with my guilt long enough. Now that Anna's gone, I'm turnin' myself in along with the gold. But first, I gotta *defend* it."

"What do you mean?"

"The ruckus with Bobby Haines was set up by Buck. He sent Bobby in ta act like he was drunk an' start a fight—all so's he could scare folks outa town by word'a the gang comin' in. An' it worked." Thursday pointed to the window. "Look out there on the street. Everybody's leavin'—just like Buck wanted."

"What about Sheriff Dobbs? Won't the sheriff be able to—"

"He was the first ta run!" declared Thursday. "An' now all the geese is followin' after him."

"Does Buck Haines know about the gold . . . about where it's hidden?"

"He knows *now*. Somehow, he found out. But he'll hafta kill me ta git it!"

"You can't face the whole Haines gang single-handed!"

"I'll have Shan with me." Thursday chuckled. "An' that boy knows a trick or two."

"I'll stay here and fight them with you," she declared. "I've got my sawed-off and I know how to use it."

"The *hell* you will!" John Thursday said, glaring at her.

Farther down the street, at the mercantile, Molly Robbins was saying goodbye to Shan as her father finished loading their supply wagon. They were heading East. Permanently.

"I've had me enough Wild West," Pete Robbins had declared. "I'll open me a store where things are civilized and outlaws don't go around burnin' down whole towns!"

"I'm proud to have known you," Shan told Molly. "Now it's time for you to go and live your life. I'm sorry, but there's no way that I can be a part of it."

"But I'll come back to you," she said, tears in her eyes.

"That's not possible," he told her. "I must go to a place you can never reach."

"But Shan—"

"When you get back East, go to Montreal, just like you planned. Perfect your French there. Become a teacher. Find a good man and get married. Have a family. Believe me, Molly, the good life you seek is waiting for you back East. And you *will* be happy, I promise."

He kissed her, then waved farewell as her father whipped up the horses. The heavy supply wagon rolled down the street, diminishing with distance.

Shan did not move until it was out of sight.

Then he headed for O'Rourke's.

Becky and the bartender had taken down her antique mirror and it was now wrapped carefully in blankets. Along with Texas John, the three were loading it into a wagon in front of the saloon when Shan walked up to them.

"Becky refuses to go," Thursday told Shan. "If she stays, they'll kill her."

"I'll take care of it," Shan said quietly. "Just leave her to me."

Sunup.

Buck Haines spun the cylinder of his long-barrel Colt, making sure the weapon was fully loaded. Slipping the gun back into its holster, he let his eyes range over the other seven outlaws who were standing near their saddled horses. Bobby, Ringo, Little Charlie, Arly Willows, Dex Givens, Cheyenne, and Laredo Slim.

"Sun's up," said Bobby.

Buck Haines smiled. "Gonna be a real treat, meetin' up with ole Jack Oliver again." His voice rose to a shout: "Let's ride!"

And the Haines gang swept away from their camp in a sudden thunder of hoofs.

Toward Libertyville.

Shan and Becky sat inside the deserted saloon at a corner table. No, she is *not* going to run. She's not going to leave the man she loves. Since John is staying, so will she—and there's nothing Shan can do or say that will change her mind.

"You could die here," declared Shan.

"I can take care of myself. If I can run a saloon, I can handle a few scurvy outlaws."

Shan moved his chair close to hers and leaned in to look her right in the eyes. Then he reached out and touched her arm.

"You understand that you really should go," he said softly, stroking her arm. Gently, he moved his hand to the top of her head. Becky didn't flinch or resist; she looked deeply relaxed, curiously focused on hearing each of his words. His touch vibrated through her body with a pleasant sensation she had never felt before.

"You need to go," Shan said. "It's the right thing to do."

Becky thought carefully, then slowly nodded. "Yes," she repeated softly, ". . . the right thing to do."

Thursday walked up to their table.

"She's decided to leave," Shan told him.

"Yes." Becky stood up. "I'm ready."

She exited the saloon without another word and climbed into

the high seat of the wagon. The bartender, holding the reins, looked surprised to see her.

"I'm leaving town," she told him. "It's the right thing to do."

The wagon pulled away. Shan and Texas John Thursday stood alone in the middle of Main Street in the pale light of a new day.

Buck Haines eased forward in the saddle, shading his eyes against the early morning sun. His horse shifted restlessly as Haines scanned the dusty length of Main Street.

"Bare as a bone," he said to his son, who had reined up his horse next to Buck's. "You done real good, Bobby. Ain't nary a soul left in town."

"What about Jack Oliver?" Bobby asked. "I thought you said he'd stay on."

"He'll show his face eventual," said Haines. "I'll have my chance to kill him."

"What now, Buck?" asked Laredo Slim, whose vast bulk belied his name. The horse he'd ridden into Libertyville was badly winded.

"You boys stay here an' burn this one-hoss cowtown flat to the ground. Teach folks not to mess with the Haines gang." He nodded toward his son. "Me an' Bobby, we got some business out at the mission. Meet us there when yer done with this place."

"We're gonna have us one high ole time," declared Ringo, grinning broadly. "I purely enjoy seein' things burn!"

"Won't be nothin' left but a pile'a ashes when we're done," said Dex Givens.

Buck smiled at Bobby. "Ready to be rich, boy?"

"Ain't never seen me no gold bars," said the young outlaw. "How many of 'em do you reckon is buried out there, Pa?"

"Lots," said Buck, gold hunger in his eyes.

And they spurred their horses into a gallop.

The remaining six members of the gang dismounted in front of O'Rourke's saloon.

"Let's wet our whistles a'fore we set fire to the place," said Little Charlie. "A shame to waste free whiskey."

The others roared agreement, filing into the deserted saloon. Their boots rang like gunshots in the long room.

Cheyenne hopped over to the bar and brought forth a quart of bourbon. He pulled the cork and took a healthy swig, then passed the bottle along to the others.

"I could use me one'a them fancy women right about now," said Ringo. "Drinkin' an' whorin' is what makes this ole world go round."

"Shut yer hole," snapped Cheyenne. "We're here to do a job. Let's git to it."

When the six men left the saloon, their bellies glowing from a generous intake of bourbon, they encountered a slim-bodied young man standing in the middle of the street.

He stared at them, silent and unmoving.

From the high porch, the outlaws hesitated, grinning at one another.

"Looks like one'a the chickens forgot to run," said Laredo Slim.

"He must be loco," said Little Charlie. "How's he figger to stand up to us?"

"An' he ain't even packin' a gun," scoffed Ringo.

"You'd better climb on those horses and ride out," said Shan.

Ringo spat a thick wad of tobacco juice from the side of his mouth and glared at the youth. "An' what if we stay right here an' burn down this piss-ass town a'yours?"

"Then I'll be forced to stop you."

Ringo walked down the porch steps to his tethered mustang, removed a wooden torch tipped in black pitch, and struck a match to it. Instantly, the pitch ignited.

He raised the flaming torch in the air as the others joined him at the bottom of the porch. "An' jes how do ya aim to stop us, sonny?"

"I'll show you," said Shan.

He whipped up the Disc and beamed it at Ringo's right hand. The torch leaped from Ringo's fingers and landed on the outlaw's head.

Slapping wildly at his burning hair, Ringo yelled: "*Kill* him! Shoot the bastard!"

Shan felt a bullet from Little Charlie's Colt fan his cheek as he levitated the outlaw off the ground, then dumped him—sputtering and swearing—into a water-filled horse trough.

The youth whirled, then beamed the six-gun out of Laredo Slim's hand, caused the Colt to reverse itself in mid-air, then club its owner across the forehead, knocking him back onto the porch steps.

Cheyenne was next. He was deposited, head first, into a pile of horse dung, while Shan sent Dex Givens and Arly Willows sailing through the saloon window in a shower of broken glass.

All six outlaws ended up bundled together by a rope that seemed alive as it looped itself around them, tying its own knots.

Smiling, Shan replaced the Disc in his belt pouch.

"I'd like to know how ya done what ya done to us," said Little Charlie, still dripping from his dip in the trough.

"That's a bit complicated," said Shan. "I'd like to stay and have an enlightening chat with you boys, but right now I have another job to do."

He whistled sharply. Hellfire appeared from the rear of the saloon and trotted up to him.

"Yer the Devil hisself come to Earth, ain't ya?" murmured Ringo, staring up at Shan as the youth mounted Hellfire.

"I'm no devil," said Shan. "I'm just an ordinary fellow who happens to believe that rabid curs like the lot of you belong behind bars."

They glared at him and began twisting against their bonds.

"I ought to warn you: the more you struggle, the tighter that rope's going to get. So it's best to just settle down and wait. You'll be taken care of eventually."

Shan rode away, leaving the six frustrated outlaws writhing in the dust of the street.

An ear-splitting roar, and the back wall of the old Spanish mission exploded into fragments of rock and clay. As the smoke cleared, Buck Haines crouched down to peer into the hole created by the blast of dynamite.

"D'ya see it, Pa?" asked Bobby, who was just behind him.

"Yeah . . . I *see* it, by God!" He stood up, smiling broadly. "Come here and look fer yerself."

Young Haines leaned in to savor the dull gleam of exposed gold, then let out a whoop. "We're *rich*, Pa! Jes like ya said we'd be!"

"Not quite," said a voice from the mission doorway. Texas John stepped out, a gun in each hand. "This gold belongs to the government, not to you. And that's where I'll be takin' it."

"The hell you will, old man!" shouted Bobby Haines, sweeping up his gun to fire at Thursday. His shot struck the tall rancher in the shoulder, causing him to drop his right Colt, but—triggering his left—he slammed Bobby into the dirt with a bullet through his head.

A death shot.

"Just you an' me now, Buck," he said tightly.

"I been waitin' twenty years ta kill ya," said Buck Haines. "An' by Christ, now I'm gonna do it!"

Twisting sideways, he fired directly at Thursday.

Texas John staggered under the bullet's impact. A sudden rush of blood darkened his chest. Willing strength into his left hand, he fired back twice at Haines, both of his bullets striking the outlaw.

Haines pitched forward with a startled grunt, rolling over onto his back. His eyes popped wide as he stopped breathing.

Shan skidded Hellfire to a stop and leaped from the saddle to kneel beside Texas John. The older man was very close to death.

"Don't . . . let them take . . . the gold," he whispered, blood bubbling at his lips.

"I won't," Shan promised.

"And . . . tell Becky . . . that I . . ." The rancher's voice failed; his fingers clenched spastically, then totally relaxed.

Texas John Thursday was dead.

In the shocked silence of the moment Shan stood up. A soft wind blew the scents of sage and prairie grass into his nostrils and the morning sun lay hot on his shoulders.

He removed the Disc from his belt pouch, adjusted it, then beamed John Thursday's lifeless corpse.

A pulsing multi-colored mist settled over the body. The bullet wounds began to close and the rancher's skin soon began to glow with an inner luminescence. Currents, like miniature bolts of lightning, crackled and sparked around him.

Shan put away the Disc and waited until John's eyes opened. The multi-colored fire mist faded from his skin.

"Welcome back," said Shan.

Thursday sat up, puzzled. His fingers probed the wet spot on his clothes where his wound had been. He shook his head in confusion. "Can't figger it. I thought sure he got me."

"He did," nodded the youth. "Buck Haines killed you. He put a bullet in your chest and your heart stopped." Shan smiled. "I started it again."

John Thursday nodded, accepting the miracle. "I know now where ya come from, with all'a your powers. It's in the Bible, in Ezekiel . . . what it says in there about comin' to Earth in a chariot'a fire. Ole Zeke, he was talkin' about folks like you." He drew in a breath. "Yessir, I know where ya hail from. From Mars mebbe, or one'a them other planets in the sky at night."

"No," said Shan. "I'm from the same planet you are—this one. And the same state. I'm from Texas, John . . . *future* Texas, a hundred and fifty years from now."

With a helping hand from Shan, Thursday stood up, then sat down heavily on a section of ruined wall. He pulled out his kerchief and mopped his forehead. "Ya lost me, boy. How kin ya be from a place that ain't happened yet?"

Shan picked up a stick and drew two separate lines in the dust. "Think of time as a road," he said. "You are *here* on the road now, in 1910,"—and he poked the stick into the ground. "I'm farther along up *here*, in 2060." Again, he used the stick to indicate his position. "I traveled back, down the road, to where *you* are."

"But *how*? How'd ya git here?"

"In a ship. A Timeship. It carried me back to the Old West . . . *here*, to Texas, in the year 1910."

"I don't savvy any'a this, but supposin' it's a fact. Then I ask ya, why? What brung ya here?"

"*You* did," said Shan. "Where I came from, in 2060, our history has recorded that a reformed outlaw named Jack Oliver, generally known as Texas John Thursday, was shot to death by his former partner, Buck Haines, at the old Spanish mission outside Libertyville. The Haines gang escaped with a stolen government gold shipment after they burned the town.

"Since you didn't have any children, the family line ended with your death. Therefore, no one was able to stop the plague."

"What plague?"

"The one that killed my wife and my parents," said Shan. "A deadly supervirus that ravaged my world. I'm one of only a few survivors."

"But if all this is fact, what good can ya do comin' back to me?"

"By saving your life, I've been able to change the future," declared the youth. "Like switching a train to another track. Now you can marry Becky and have children. And *they* will have children.

"Your great-great-great grandson, Bennett Oliver, will become a brilliant scientist. He will develop a process that will annihilate the plague virus, and because of his work, millions of lives will be saved."

Texas John shook his head. "I can't marry Becky. When I turn in the gold, they'll take away my ranch and put me in prison fer the rest of my life."

"No. For saving Libertyville and returning the gold, the governor will grant you a full pardon. And you'll be able to keep your ranch."

"How do ya know that if it ain't happened yet?"

Shan smiled. "It's a matter of mathematics—the physics of

action and reaction. There are many alternate futures. I simply activated another alternative."

John looked at Shan through narrowed eyes. "Sounds like a lotta hogwash to me."

Shan shrugged his shoulders. "You've seen what I've been able to do. You don't have to understand how it works."

"Ya saved my life, an' that's fer sure. So what can I do fer you by way'a thanks?"

Shan laughed. "I was hoping you'd ask something like that. I'd like to take a souvenir back with me. Your Hupmobile, if that's all right with you."

"You're welcome to it!" Thursday said enthusiastically. "Ya talk about the future. I kin tellya *one* thing fer damn sure—there ain't no future in these autee-mo-beels."

Shan smiled, but he didn't reply.

Back at the ranch they entered the stable where John kept the Hupmobile. John cranked away, but the car wouldn't start.

"We have a problem," Shan announced. "The Timeship can't enter the past—your present, right now—unless the mathematical coordinates match precisely."

"Meanin' what?" asked Texas John.

"I'm supposed to meet the ship just beyond Libertyville, but we're running late. I could miss it."

"Then *you* crank!" Thursday said.

"Let's try this instead," said Shan, beaming the Disc at the car's hood.

Success! The engine burst into rumbling life.

"Hop in," said John, "an' we'll git this pesky critter on the road."

Tying Hellfire's reins to the back of the ponderous vehicle, Shan climbed into the high passenger seat next to Thursday.

"We're off!" declared John, and the big car began to roll.

As the Hupmobile bounced and rattled over the broken surface of the prairie Shan became apprehensive.

"Can't you get this car to move any faster?" he asked Thursday.

Texas John lowered his driving goggles to glare at his passenger. "Hell, no! We're doin' almost ten miles an hour as is, an' over this kinda ground, that's as fast as she can go."

"We're almost there," said Shan. He pointed ahead. "Turn right, just past that stand of rocks. There's a clearing on the far side. That's my pickup point."

Once the big machine had passed the rocks, Shan told Thursday to stop.

"This is the contact area," he said, stepping to the ground. He began checking the terrain, then groaned and slumped to his knees.

"What's wrong?" asked John from the driver's seat.

"It's too late," murmured Shan. "The ship has come and gone."

John got out to stand beside the younger man. There was a deep depression in the ground that was surrounded by charred sagebrush.

"Yep. Sure looks like *somethin'* landed here!"

"It's my fault," Shan said. "I should never have stopped for the car. If we'd come here straight from the mission, I would have met the ship."

"Mebbe it'll come back fer ya."

"Impossible," said Shan. "The space-time elements must match exactly to create a passageway for the ship to appear at this spot. It can't return again. Now, I'll have to die here."

"Die?" John stared at him. "Why can't ya stay on, go East, marry that sweet Molly Robbins, an' start a new life?"

"Because my body isn't vibrationally attuned to this century. My genetic structure will disintegrate. By your standards, I'm 175 years old. If I stay here, within another month my cells will begin to break down. Within weeks, I'll be dead."

He slumped to the ground now and sat cross-legged, his head bowed in a posture of defeat.

"I'm right sorry," said Thursday.

"At least I accomplished my mission," declared Shan in a subdued tone. "I saved your life, and the lives of all the people who would have been struck down by the plague. If I have to die here, it's been worth it."

Texas John looked skyward, shading his eyes against the sunglare.

"Somethin's *up* there," he said.

Shan raised his head as a vast humming surrounded them. A shimmering wheel of silver and gold was descending from the sky.

The Timeship!

"... so when you altered the future by saving Jack Oliver's life, you created a new set of time-space coordinates," Captain Edwards was explaining to Shan. "I was able to reprogram the ship for a second entry." He shook hands with Shan. "Congratulations! Your mission has been a complete success."

The proud young man introduced him to the rancher whose life had been saved. The captain's grip was firm and resolute as he shook Thursday's hand.

John grinned. "Glad ta know ya. Never met me no space man a'fore."

"That machine you arrived in," said Captain Edwards to Shan. "What, exactly, *is* it?"

"A gas-powered 1909 Hupmobile, with an internal combustion engine," Shan told him. "And it's a gift from John. I'm taking it back with me."

"How very generous of you," Edwards said to the rancher. "Giving it up must be quite a sacrifice."

"A sacrifice it ain't!" muttered Thursday. "Be damn glad to git rid'a the thing. Never give me nothin' but grief."

The captain chuckled and turned back to Shan. "Ready to go?"

"In a minute. I still have something to tell John," he replied.

"Signal when you're ready," said Edwards. He shook the rancher's hand again. "I don't need to wish you luck, Mr. Thursday, because I know you're going to have a marvelous life. Been a pleasure meeting you."

"Obliged," nodded Thursday.

The sun-dazzled, silver-and-gold Timeship hovered silently in the sky just above them as the captain beamed himself aboard.

For the first time since Anna's death, tears filled John Thursday's eyes.

"You have a long, productive life ahead of you," said Shan. "You and Becky and your five children . . ."

The rancher found it hard to speak. "I dunno what to say . . . all ya done fer me . . . fer Libertyville . . . fer Becky . . . an' savin' all them folks in the future . . ."

"*You'll* be saving them," smiled Shan. "Your blood will flow into future generations. Because of you, Bennett Oliver will live to stop the plague."

Shan climbed into the high seat of the Hupmobile. He raised a hand to signal the hovering craft.

A glowing, red beam speared down from the underside of the Timeship to envelop car and driver.

The big Hupmobile wavered, then lifted from the ground and was smoothly beamed into the hovering ship.

Shan waved a final goodbye.

From the prairie, Texas John waved back. The ship's hold closed.

A rising hum. A flash of glowing metal.

The Timeship was gone.

John Thursday mounted Hellfire and began riding toward his future life under the vast Texas sky.

Three thousand copies of this book have been printed by the Maple-Vail Book Manufacturing Group, Binghamton, NY, for Golden Gryphon Press, Urbana, IL. The typeset is Electra with Becka Script display, printed on 55# Sebago. Typesetting by The Composing Room, Inc., Kimberly, WI.

The Colonial Silversmith

The research for this book was partially supported
by a grant from the American Philosophical Society

The Colonial Silversmith

His Techniques & His Products

Henry J. Kauffman

Professor, Industrial Arts Education
Millersville State College
Millersville, Pa.

Drawings by
Dorothy Briggs
Staff Artist
Smithsonian Institution
Washington, D.C.

Thomas Nelson

The Colonial Silversmith

His Techniques & His Products

Henry J. Kauffman

Professor, Industrial Arts Education
Millersville State College
Millersville, Pa.

Drawings by
Dorothy Briggs
Staff Artist
Smithsonian Institution
Washington, D.C.

Thomas Nelson

© 1969 by Henry J. Kauffman

All rights reserved under International and Pan-American Conventions.
Published in Camden, New Jersey, by Thomas Nelson Inc.
and simultaneously in Toronto, Canada, by Thomas Nelson & Sons (Canada) Limited.

Design by Harold Leach

Library of Congress Catalog Card Number: 71-101526

Printed in the United States of America

Acknowledgments

Writing this part of the book is doubtless the most pleasant part of such a survey. Pleasant, not only because it is evidence that long hours of research and writing have been completed, but also because it gives the author an opportunity to thank the various people and organizations for their help in assembling the contents of the book.

Work that has been done over a long period of time does not permit the author to keep a perfect record of all who have made numerous contributions. I do want to especially thank Samuel Kirk & Son, Inc., Colonial Williamsburg, and The Henry Francis du Pont Winterthur Museum for the invaluable suggestions they have given the author and for making their facilities for research available to him. In addition, the following people have rendered unstinting help on many occasions: Mrs. Louise Belden, Miss Helen Belknap, Howard T. Brenner, Alfred Clegg, Paul Day, Philip Hammerslough, Frank Horton, Charles Hummel, Joe Kindig, Jr., Ian Quimby, Kenneth Roberts, and John Rouse.

Finally, I would like to emphasize that the unique contents of the book are the attractive drawings made by Dorothy Briggs. Her knowledge of technical drafting, her aesthetic sensitivity, and her tireless patience in dealing with the minutia of the drawings, are fully appreciated by the author.

The inevitable errors in a survey of this type are the responsibility of the author who will be grateful for corrections and constructive criticisms.

Contents

The Colonial Silversmith

mo 14 21	William Plumsted is Dr to a pepper Caster wt 5:8 fashn	1: 0 —
	Recd of Francis Richardson 46:4 oz dwt of Silver to be made into Buckels	
23	William Logan is Dr to a pr of Garter Buckels wt 12:21 dwt	0 — 10 — 6
	Recd of Samuel Shoe Maker 9:9 oz dwt of Silver to be made into a pr of Casters	
	Recd of Ozwel Peal 20 oz dwt of Silver to Be made into a Tankard & 16:1:17 oz dwt of Do to be made into a Poringer	
	Ozwel Peal is Dr to a Gold Stay hook wt 4:21 dwt gr	0: 19 — 6
th 25	Jeremiah Warder is Dr to 6 Spoons wt 11:3:16 oz dwt gr	5 — 18 — 6
	Anthony Duche is Dr to 4 Silver Spoons wt 7:6 oz dwt ar 9/0 to makeing the above Spoons	3: 5 — 8 0 — 12 —
st 31	Rebecca Coleman is Dr to two Poringers — wt 12:14:12 oz dwt gr fashn	1 — 4 —
st	Ozwel Peal is Dr to two Poringers wt 15:6:19 oz dwt gr fashion	

Introduction

Every book has its *raison d'être,* in some cases evident and easily recognized, in others subtle and difficult to discern. One author wishes to bring a new discovery into sharper focus, another to preserve knowledge of the past which will probably be important to posterity.

The purpose of the present volume is to record and thereby to preserve information about the tools, materials, techniques, and products of the silver trade in America in the eighteenth century. During that period, goods were made almost entirely by hand methods, although the lathe was probably present in the shops of a few silversmiths. *The Colonial Silversmith* is an account of the production of useful objects from silver.

In the past, research has followed traditional patterns, emphasizing historic style, regional differences, and the names and genealogy of craftsmen, and owners, but making only limited comment regarding such matters as materials, tools, and techniques. As a result, most experts know that John Coney was one of the first important silversmiths working in America, but their knowledge of the metallurgy of silver is very meager. Unfortunately, there has been not only a dearth of knowledge about such matters, but even misinformation.

Today, of course, new importance is being attached to metals and their fabrication. The tremendous utilization of metals in contemporary life has increased people's interest, which, in turn, has aroused curiosity about the metal technology of the past. Scholars, researchers, and antiquarians now are beginning to realize that a knowledge of materials and modes of manufacture can aid in determining when, where, how, and why an object was made; this insight can also help them to integrate the relation-

Page from a day book (1744-1748) of Joseph Richardson of Philadelphia. Some entries document the fact that patrons provided the silver to be wrought into specific objects for them. *Courtesy Historical Society of Pennsylvania.*

ships of such data with other facets of life in the past. In addition, the possession of this heretofore obscure information will assist many craftsmen in creating objects of metal by hand methods, and in experiencing the satisfaction which comes from producing an object personally—an experience all too rare in the mid-twentieth century.

The perceptive reader of this book will doubtless make comparisons between the old methods and contemporary ones, a practice that could

Entries in the day book of Joseph Richardson, Jr., of Philadelphia in 1797 indicate that he was in the wholesale business by today's standards. Apparently it was very fashionable to have eagles engraved on arm bands at that time. *Courtesy Historical Society of Pennsylvania.*

Death notice of Peter Getz, famous silversmith of Lancaster, Pennsylvania, which appeared in the *Lancaster Journal*, January 6, 1810. *See page 36.*

𝕯𝖎𝖊𝖉,

In this borough, on Friday evening, the 29th ult after an illness of two days, in the 47th year of his age, Mr. PETER GETZ, the original improver of the new printing-press, constructed with rollers in lieu of a screw.

He was famous for his ingenuity.

---

arouse in the injudicious a feeling of contempt for old methods which were followed longer in America than in Europe because the so-called "scientific era" was slow in coming here. While Savery, Newcomen, and Watt could give their full time to battling the technological problems of the steam engine, Americans were busy fighting Indians, building relatively primitive shelters, and wresting the fare for their tables from a rich but elusive store on land and sea. In addition, our craftsmen were restricted by the system of English mercantilism, which discouraged the manufacturing of badly needed objects of metal.

Nevertheless, it must be realized that however unfavorable conditions were here for manufacturing ("making by hand"), many craftsmen were busy at their benches throughout the eighteenth century. Their newspaper advertisements attest to the fact that a competitive economy was slowly arising and producing such outstanding results that even experts often have difficulty in determining whether certain objects were made here or in Europe. However, although a distinctive style slowly emerged in the eighteenth century, the problem of identification was compounded by the fact that metals, regardless of where they were mined and refined, rarely have unique or distinctive characteristics.

Whatever may be the state of the reading public's knowledge of such historical matters, its information about metallurgy and technology is perhaps scantier. It may be assumed, however, that most readers know that, although the properties of various metals frequently differ, they often have certain common properties. For example, most metals are heavy and hard, some are inert, others deteriorate rapidly, and still others can be combined to form "alloys."

To be Sold, by Public Vendue,

On Wednesday, the 8th August next,

AT the late residence of Peter Getz, deceased, in South Queen-street, the following articles, viz : —

A COMPLETE

TURNER'S LATH,

with all the necessary apparatus, in the best of order ; a *smith's vice*, nearly new ; files of every description, with a variety of other articles, superfluous to mention in an advertisement.

The sale will commence at 10 o'clock in the forenoon. Attendance will be given by

CHARLES REISINGER, *Adm'r.*

July 23, 1810.   10–2oq.

Notice of the Public Vendue of a complete turner's lathe in the *Lancaster Journal*, July 23, 1810. Getz was a very versatile craftsman and used the lathe for his work in silver as well as the many other pursuits he followed.

The alloys were created to obtain qualities not found in a single element. Thus, pure silver is relatively soft and has few commercial uses, but when a small percentage of copper is added a reasonably tough and useful alloy is created.

In many ways man has adapted and formed metals for his use and welfare. He has learned that metals can be softened into liquid by heating, a quality called "fusibility." Man has further discovered that, when hot metals are cooled, they can be solidified in the shape he chooses, a process known as casting.

Another of man's discoveries is that metals can be changed into various shapes by hammering (extended in length or width and proportionally reduced in thickness) when they are either hot or cold. This quality is called "malleability." Since silver is quite malleable, most objects of this metal are products of the hammer.

Man has also bent or drawn metals into desired shapes when hot or cold. This quality is called "ductility." Metals with a high degree of ductility can be drawn into thin wires, gold being the highest and silver second in this property.

In addition to these methods of altering the shape of a single piece of metal, pieces can be joined together in many ways with or without the application of heat. Two pieces of iron, heated to a "pasty" condition, can be welded together with a hammer without the use of a flux (cleaning agent) or solder. This procedure was used extensively by colonial craftsmen and is known as "welding."

Objects consisting of more than one part were frequently joined by solder, which has a lower melting point than that of the metals to be joined. Thus, by applying heat with a soldering iron or a forge fire, the various parts of an assemblage could be more or less permanently joined. All soldering operations require a flux to keep the metal clean and to allow the solder to flow throughout the joint.

Another device, the rivet, was often used to join parts made of copper, brass, tin, and iron, but rarely employed on objects of silver. Handles of wood were attached to objects of metal by inserting a tennon into a ferrule and securing the two parts by inserting a pin.

A brief summation of data such as this, of course, makes no pretense of being complete, but it can supply the reader with an insight into some of the mysteries of the world of metals. Additional data will be supplied as the need appears throughout the book.

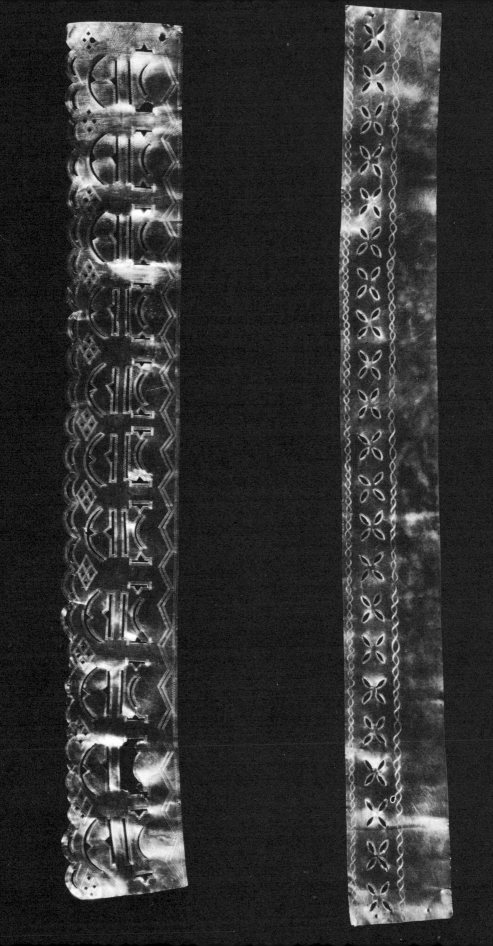

The Metal

Silver has played an unusual role in the civilization of many lands for centuries. Because silver is a precious metal, its role in the eighteenth century was significantly different from that of other metals.

Throughout the sixteenth, seventeenth, and eighteenth centuries all mines of gold and silver in Europe were royal mines—the property of the king. In areas as small as England and France it was comparatively easy for the royal eye to watch mining activity and for the royal hand to collect his just return. The remote location of prospective mines in the New World encouraged entrepreneurs to try to find deposits of precious metal ore in order to work them for their own interests. There would doubtless be enough customers here to patronize the poacher and the potential for great wealth seemed very sure, if rich deposits were found. Unfortunately, they found little silver or gold here, and were, therefore, forced to turn their energies toward finding and refining less exotic metals such as copper, lead, and iron.

The prestigious position of silver among the other metals doubtless exists because it is considered a precious metal. The uses made of it create an image of wealth and luxury. The lowly American Indian shared this concept, for he made only objects of adornment from it when he was able to find it in a state sufficiently pure for him to work. The affluent colonist had his silver plate, consisting of objects with associations of luxury—porringers, tankards, chalices, spoons, candlesticks, and bowls. The prestige of the church was also enhanced with the possession of chalices, flagons, and patens of silver. But more significant than such uses is the fact that silver was used as a medium of exchange. Coins were

Headbands made by American Indians in the early nineteenth century. Examples of such work are extremely rare. *Courtesy Philadelphia Museum of Art.*

made of it in Greek and Roman times, and its use for money has increased from then until now. As a matter of fact, it is now regarded as so precious that substitutes, such as bronze and nickel, are being used for coins, and silver has gained a higher status than it ever had before.

In reading the history of early North America one is not particularly impressed with the importance of the European search for silver and gold. The zeal for the metal has been lost or hidden behind a façade which emphasizes the desire for owning property, the search for personal and religious freedom, as well as the expedient action of clearing English jails. The zeal also lost its fever pitch early in Virginia, where it was probably the most intense, because a "green gold" called tobacco provided the wealth which the ambitious planter sought in America.

The royal family of England and the prosperous merchants must have had mixed emotions, however, concerning the settling of America, as they witnessed the greatest population migration of all time to the New World. They did know their natural resources were rapidly being depleted; they were importing wood and metals from Scandinavia and Russia. If approval for migration needed any stimulus, certainly it was nurtured with the knowledge of the great wealth Spain was acquiring from her colonies in the Western Hemisphere.

A short résumé of some of the important facts will focus attention on the eventful activities of the time. It is reported that on April 12, 1519, Cortes, under the aegis of Spain, landed at what is now Veracruz, Mexico. Fascinated by stories of the great wealth of the inland cities, he destroyed his ships and pressed onward with a band of about 400 men. He professed only friendliness for Montezuma and his subjects, and he was rewarded with gifts, such as a Spanish helmet filled to its brim with gold dust and a disk of silver as large as a cart wheel. Cortes reciprocated by capturing the emperor and slaughtering his subjects.

The wealth of Mexico at the time of Cortes' invasion staggers the imagination. It is said by Benjamin White in his book, *Silver, Its History and Romance*, that:

> During the reign of King Montezuma the cities [of Mexico] abounded in products of the loom, featherwork, drinking vessels of gold and silver, collars, bracelets, and earrings of the precious metals, as well as grain, fruits, cacao, and articles for literary use such as paper manufactured from the ungainly but useful cactus. The writ-

The battery process of forming a sheet of silver from an ingot. Plate I from *Dictionaire des Sciences*. Diderot, Paris, 1763.

ing then current was in the form of Hieroglyphic painting. Montezuma maintained a large army, whose dress consisted of quilted cotton, a useful defense against the arrows of Indian tribes. The great chiefs wore cuirasses overlaid with thin plates of silver or gold. Their heads were protected with silver or wooden helmets surmounted with plumes of waving feathers, producing an effect martial and picturesque.

The palace of the kings comprised a vast pile of buildings. The decorations were gorgeous, the walls were draped with rich hangings and the roof inlaid with cedar and scented woods. A quarter assigned to workers in precious metals was to be found in the market-place, where articles could be purchased for use or ornament. Here were to be found on sale many curious silver toys, fashioned ingeniously in the form of birds, or fishes with movable scales.

Much of this wealth came from the great central plateau of Mexico, which was overlaid with a mass of igneous rocks containing such metals as silver, gold, and copper.

Mexico was ruled by Spain from 1521 until 1821. It was autocratically ruled by five governors, Cortes being the first, and sixty-two viceroys. The agents of the rulers were very adept with divining rods, and in extracting secrets from natives concerning the location of rich deposits of silver. From 1542 until 1832 one region produced silver bullion worth more than 667 million pesos. It is estimated that from 1521 until 1891 the silver produced in Mexico was worth more than 4 billion dollars and, if modern mining methods had been used, the figure might have been doubled.

The preceding figures might lead one to assume that Spain's success in securing wealth from the New World in the sixteenth century was the prologue to England's attempts at colonization, the first successful one occurring at Jamestown in 1607. It should be noted that this project was

Anvils, stakes, swages, hammers, and dies used by the silversmith. Plates X and XIII from *Dictionaire des Sciences*. Diderot, Paris, 1763.

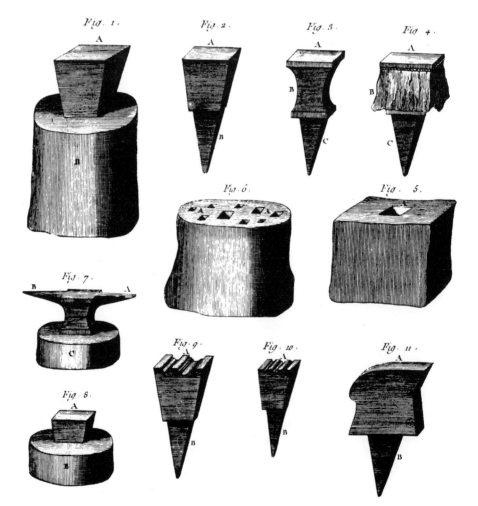

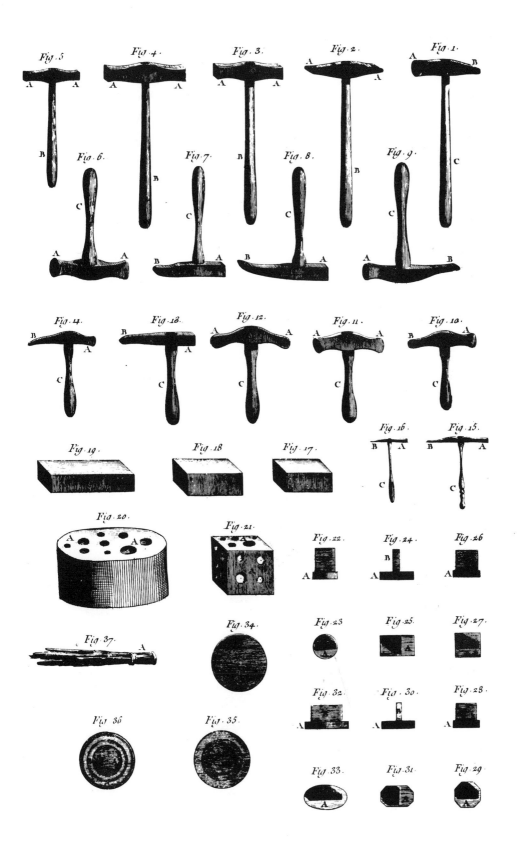

a cooperative venture between the royalty and others who volunteered either their money or their services. And, most significantly, the reasons for colonization enumerated in the charter of the Virginia Company of London were to expand the kingdom, to find a passage to the Orient, and to prospect for precious metals. The only direct feudal relationship with the king was the fact that he was to receive a percentage of the precious metals found.

There is no evidence that provision was made for the mining and refining of precious metals by the first contingent of settlers sent to America; however, the "first supply" which arrived included two goldsmiths, named William Johnson and Richard Belfield. At that time a goldsmith also worked with silver and was equally familiar with both metals. In a letter written to his cousin, John Revoire of Guernsey, Paul Revere, Jr., states that after leaving military service in 1782 he returned to his trade of "Goldsmith" and manufactured fine articles of silverware. Later, a refiner named William Callicut convinced the settlers he had found small deposits of silver and that more could be had for the digging.

Disenchantment concerning the existence of precious metals must have come early in the wake of Virginia colonization, for in 1608 Captain Newport in his report emphasized the richness of the soil and the great quantities of fish, of timber, and of clay for making brick. The possible exports he mentioned included sturgeon, clapboard, wainscot, saxafrage, tobacco, dyes, furs, pitch, resin, turpentine, oils, wine, soap ashes, iron, copper, and pearls, but details regarding the resources of silver and gold were very vague.

Comment by Captain John Smith corroborates Newport's findings, for he says the following about the situation:

> But the worst [of our difficulties] was our guilded refiners with their golden promises made all men their slaves in hope of recompenses: there was no talk, no worke, but to dig gold, wash gold, such a bruit of gold, that one fellow desired to be buried in the sands lest they should by their art make gold of his bones.

The scarcity of gold and silver ores in Virginia is confirmed by the fact that no notices regarding the mining of silver are reported in the *Virginia Gazette* in the eighteenth century. Although foreign intelligence probably had a higher priority as news than local happenings, it is very likely that any activity related to local resources of gold and silver would have been broadcast to the citizens through their important news media.

It is very evident that little silver was found in what is now continental United States in the seventeenth and eighteenth centuries. It should also be noted that the problem of scarcity was compounded by the lack of the metallurgical knowledge required to find and refine silver, a skill which few men must have had at that time.

Silver is obtained by a number of methods. For centuries man knew it existed in nature in a pure form and little knowledge was needed to fashion such metal into small objects of utility and beauty. It has been noted the American Indian made limited use of the metal. Deposits of silver ore usually occur in dry barren areas, such as the southwestern United States, Mexico, Peru, and the arid tablelands of Chile. The ores are known as red silver ore, horn ore, and argentite. Silver is also a by-product of other major mining enterprises, the Anaconda Copper Company being one of the largest producers of silver in America today.

Argentite, a combination of silver and sulphur, is the ore from which silver is most frequently obtained. It is black in color and is often present in areas where native pure silver has been found. It was such black residue from gold workings which led to the discovery of the Comstock lode in Nevada in the late 1850s. The gold workers, being unaware of the value of the substances they were discarding, sold the fringe interest of the mine for a bottle of whiskey, some blankets, a horse, and $2,500 dollars. In the year 1863 silver worth $5 million was dug from the lode, and four years after the deal was made, the mine was valued at $7.6 million.

The appearance of red silver ore also conceals the identity of the valuable metal; a piece containing as much as 60 per cent silver looks to be rusty and worthless. Horn silver is combined with chlorine and is virtually colorless; deposits of this ore have been found in South America.

Silver is also frequently found to be combined with copper or lead. In such cases the major product frequently is not silver, but as a by-product silver is terribly important. One of the unique combinations of silver with other ores is evidenced in the modern discovery of silver at Cobalt, Ontario, Canada. The deposits were first discovered in the late nineteenth century, when the Temiskaming and Northern Ontario Railway was built. As a matter of fact, excavations for the railroad revealed the bed, which has since become one of the most productive silver sources in the world. Deposits vary from native ores in chunks the size of a man to dentritic ore, where veins resemble the trunk and limbs of a tree. Although the major product is silver, the ores contain valuable portions of cobalt, nickel, and arsenic. The Nipissing mine of the region produced from 1904 to 1915 silver valued at $22.1 million.

Despite the fact that prospecting for precious metals in America in the eighteenth century offered little encouragement, the hope for success seems never to have been abandoned. Men experienced in the mining and refining of metals were sent here, many of Germanic origin, because central Europe was the most advanced area in the working of metals. This condition accounts for the presence of so many Germans working in the mines and furnaces of the English colonies.

Only scattered reports are extant about the finding of deposits in America. In 1648 Governor Winthrop, of Massachusetts, reported that the iron works (probably at Saugus, Massachusetts) was going well, and that some silver had been detected in the iron. Thus, at this early date it is evident that men knew silver might become a valuable by-product of other mining operations.

There were rumors of the mining of precious metals in Pennsylvania in the time of the Dutch and Swedish settlements; however, ancient mine holes seem to be the only surviving evidence of such activity there. In 1740 a group of Germans was reputedly operating a copper mine in Duchess County, New York, which also yielded a profitable amount of silver. This facility was abandoned and resumed a number of times, but no deposits were found to warrant continuous operation. About 1750 a shaft 125 feet deep was sunk near New Milford, Connecticut, for the extraction of ore with a content of silver and gold. A German goldsmith is thought to have secretly carried on some silver smelting operations there, but the search for silver was abandoned in favor of the development of ores producing native steel.

It is evident that the only area on the eastern seaboard where sizeable amounts of precious metals were produced was in North Carolina. The so-called "Appalachian Gold Field" crosses the western part of that state. More comment is made about the gold found in the region than silver; however, since both metals are frequently found together, it is likely that some silver was found there. Thomas Jefferson knew about the deposits, and in 1799 a lump of gold was found which is said to have yielded twenty-five pounds of gold twenty-three carats fine (pure gold is 24 carats fine). The Gold Hill Mines of Rowan County (North Carolina) produced a quantity of gold and the Washington Silver mine in the same state produced not only gold and silver, but also iron and lead. Despite all this fragmentary activity, it must be unfortunately concluded that virtually no silver bullion from native ore was available to American silversmiths in the seventeenth and eighteenth centuries. No substantial sources of silver were available until the important discoveries were made in Nevada in the 1850s.

Writers about American silver are unanimous in their opinion that the metal of the silversmith was obtained by melting down coins or remelting earlier objects which were outdated in style. The ruthless destruction of early masterpieces by American silversmiths is an unfortunate event to record, but the advertisements of the craftsmen prove they were willing partners in this catastrophe. Their need for metal was acute and they had little stake in preserving the pieces made by their predecessors, or by English silversmiths. The pressure to keep pace in America with the latest London fashions was persistent, even after the Revolution.

The remelting of coins can be considered the lesser of the two evils. In most cases they were not American coins, so the loss can be accepted with less discomfort. It can hardly be claimed that the aesthetic importance of coins was comparable to that of such vessels as bowls, tankards, and porringers. It was not their unimportance aesthetically, however, that got them into the melting pot, but the absence of banks to protect a man's wealth in coins. It was very difficult to identify one's coins if they were luckily recovered from a thief, so they were turned into identifiable objects often bearing the imprint of the maker, and sometimes the monogram or cypher of the owner. Of course, both of these marks could be removed; however, the wrought object was easier to identify than coins.

It must be noted here that the melting of coins in the eighteenth century did not give rise to the stamping of words such as "COIN SILVER," "COIN," or "PURE COIN" on objects made in the second quarter of the nineteenth century. Objects bearing such imprints are usually less than .900 fine silver, while the standard for sterling has been .925 fine

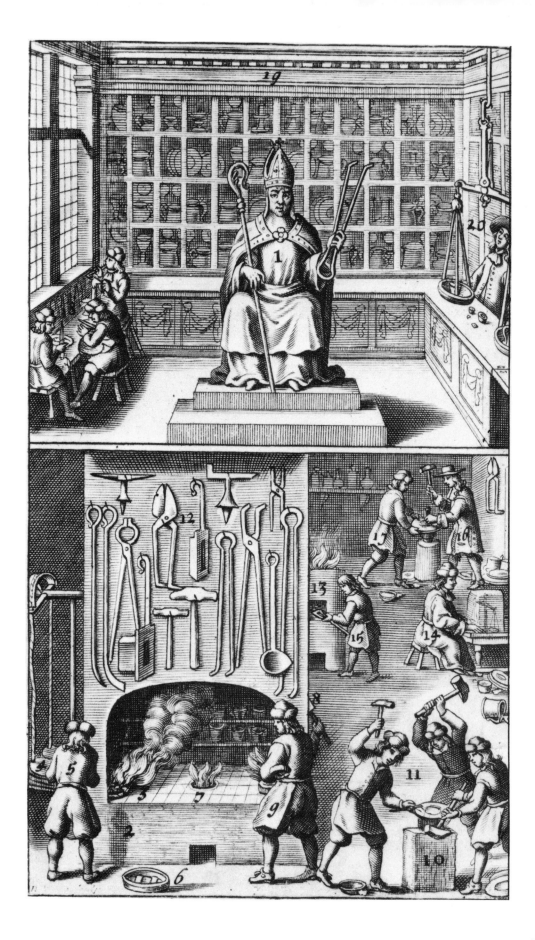

for many centuries. The balance of the sterling alloy has been universally copper. The addition of copper improves the quality of silver by giving it a richer color, and improves its durability and workability.

The origin of the word "sterling" is explained in a publication of Handy and Harman, called *The Handy Book for Manufacturers*. Their explanation follows:

The Name "Sterling" Is a Contraction
of the Word "Easterling"

In the 12th century five free towns were banded together in the eastern part of Germany under the name of the Hanseatic League. These towns were free not only to make their own laws, but also to issue their currency. When trading with English merchants they gave their coins in payment for British cattle, sheep, grain, and other products. The British soon learned that these coins, which they referred to as the coins of the Easterlings, were always dependable. It is said that Henry II employed some of these Easterlings to improve and

The Intent of the Frontiſpiece:

1 *St.* Dunſtan, *The Patron of the* Goldſmiths *Company.*
2 *The Refining Furnace.*
3 *The* Teſt *with Silver refining on it.*
4 *The Fineing Bellows.*
5 *The Man blowing or working them.*
6 *The* Teſt *Mould.*
7 *A Wind-hole to melt Silver in without Bellows.*
8 *A pair of Organ Bellows.*
9 *A Man melting or boyling, or nealing Silver at them.*
10 *A Block, with a large Anvil placed thereon.*
11 *Three Men Forging Plate.*
12 *The Fineing and other* Goldſmiths *Tools.*
13 *The* Aſſay *Furnice.*
14 *The* Aſſay-Maſter making Aſſays.
15 *His Man putting the Aſſays into the Fire.*
16 *The Warden marking the Plate on the Anvil.*
17 *His Officer holding the Plate for the Marks.*
18 *Three* Goldſmiths, ſmall-Workers, at work.
19 *A* Goldſmiths *Shop furniſhed with Plate.*
20 *A* Goldſmith *weighing Plate.*

A 2   I Do

Frontispiece and explanation. From *A Touchstone for Gold and Silver Wares.* London, 1677.

standardize the English coinage which had become debased. The standard adopted is probably accounted for by the system of weights used.
It was based on 11 troy ounces, 2 pennyweights of fine silver and 18
pennyweights of alloy. The word "alloy" was used to designate the
base metal (silver). The original designation Easterling Silver was
later abbreviated to "Sterling Silver" and the term has come down
through the centuries as representing a mark of high quality.

The same publication confirms the composition of sterling silver by saying that:

> The standard sterling alloy contains 925 parts of silver and 75 parts
> of copper per thousand when cooled. At a normal rate of casting,
> the microscope shows both of these constitutents to be present. The
> alloy is entirely liquid at 1640 degrees F. and solid at 1435 degrees F.

Thus from a strictly technological point of view the metal used by
silversmiths to fabricate objects should be called "sterling," for the metal
is not pure silver. Because the term "silver" has been used to describe this
metal for so long a time, it will continue to be used in its traditional concept in this survey.

After the silversmith had obtained his precious commodity from which
his product was to be wrought, he was faced with many problems. The
first one was to get the metal into a form from which objects could be
made. Most authorities on silversmithing simply say that molten metal
was cast into ingots and then hammered into a sheet by a process called
"battery." These procedures are succinctly illustrated in Plate I from the
Diderot Encyclopedia. The same illustration also shows men forming objects of silver on stakes and anvils. Plates X and XIII from the *Diderot
Encyclopedia* show various tools used by the silversmith. *See pages 19, 20,
and 21.*

An earlier illustration, the frontispiece of *A Touchstone for Gold and
Silver Wares* (1677 ed.) shows men assaying the metal; over the furnace
is mounted a number of the tools used by the silversmith at that time.
On the right edge men are shown beating a plate on an anvil. On the
upper part of the illustration is an engraving of St. Dunstan, the Patron
of the goldsmiths.

An English authority on silversmithing points out that these procedures
were used long after other metals were rolled thin on a rolling mill. Possibly the use of the hammer was continued because it was thought that
hammering compacted the molecular structure of the metal better than

Coffee pot by Philip Syng, Jr. This unusually graceful, highly ornamented vessel is an outstanding product of one of America's great silversmiths. *Courtesy Philadelphia Museum of Art. Photograph by A. J. Wyatt, Staff Photographer.*

rolling; furthermore, it was a much cheaper procedure as long as labor costs were low, as they were in England in the eighteenth century.

Obtaining the sheet of metal from which to form his object must have been a tedious task for the silversmith in America; however, this was just one of the technological problems he had to resolve. The polyglot sources of his metals suggest that its fineness was a matter demanding his constant attention.

This problem was held to a minimum if he remelted objects of silver wrought in England, for the English government operated assay offices throughout the country and their control of quality was very good. In addition, the appropriate officers of the guild kept a watchful eye on the products of the members there, and objects made of substandard metal went back into the melting pot or were confiscated. In America there were no guilds to discipline the actions of the silversmiths, and only one assay office was briefly operated in Baltimore—from 1814 until 1820.

There are conflicting opinions concerning the fineness of silver used by American silversmiths. Tests made by one party made it very evident that the sterling standard was maintained in the quality of metal used. On the other hand, tests for the alloy have been made as a part of the Andelot-Copeland Museum Science Project, a cooperative program between the Henry Francis du Pont Winterthur Museum and the University of Delaware. Samples from five American spoons were sent to Ledoux & Company at Teaneck, New Jersey, for spectrographic analysis. The results showed that the lowest copper percentage was 10.50 and the highest 14.50 per cent. The copper results were obtained by semiquantitative X-ray fluorescence. Other similar analyses were made of a larger number of spoons, and the results invariably showed a higher copper content to be present than the sterling standard.

The fact that the sterling standard was not adhered to by all silversmiths is attested by the following advertisement which appeared in *The South Carolina Gazette,* May 2, 1743:

> William Wright is removed into the House where Mr. James Matthews liv'd before the Fire, near Col. Brewton's where he has to sell by retail Barbadoes Rum, Sugar, Molasses, Maderia Wine and Sundry other Goods, at very reasonable rates especially for Ready Money. And whereas 'tis complained that the Silver which is worked up here is not true Sterling Standard, this is to acquaint all Gentlemen and

others, that the said Wright will warrant it to be true Sterling Standard, he will finish his work with the utmost Dispatch. William Wright.

In addition to the problems related to the fineness of his metal, the
silversmith was also plagued with its high cost and the subsequent frugality required in working it. It seems certain that each batch was weighed
when he received his supply, the weight of the object being of such importance that it was frequently recorded on it and, of course, the unused
portion had also to be accounted for. The filings were so valuable that a
leather apron was stretched from the craftsman to the workbench to
prevent their falling to the floor and to easily effect their recovery in a [7]
jar or other container.

But the most demanding facet of silversmithing was the craftsman's
need for an understanding of design and the various ways available to
achieve a desired result. He constantly had to compete with the latest
mode from London, not to mention the fastidious personal tastes of his
patrons. His patronage lay almost completely between rich people and
the church, both of whom were not likely to accept a second-class product and had the discrimination to know when they were getting it.

If any craftsman required the full seven years of apprenticeship to
learn the required techniques of working a medium, as well as sundry
other abilities such as skillful designing, business acumen, and finding
a market for his product, it was the silversmith.

Before embarking on an explanation of the various technological techniques of his work, it should be understood that all products made of
silver (and gold) were called plate. This term applied equally to hollow
ware and flatware. A research into the etymology of the word "plate"
has not brought to light any definite logic in the application of the term
to the objects involved. It is intimated by some writers that the word
evolved very early when only flat objects were made, particularly plates,
and thus the word was indiscriminately used by later generations in
describing all objects made of silver and gold. Dictionaries of the eighteenth century do not include the word in this context. One of the few
definitions found appears in *Zell's Popular Encyclopedia,* 1871, which
is as follows:

> Plate, n [Fr. *plat;* Ger. *platte;* from the Greek, *platys,* broad, flat].
> A flat or extended piece of metal.—Armor, composed of flat, broad
> pieces of metal.—Gold and silver wrought into various articles of

household furniture.—A shallow, flattish dish or vessel from which provisions are eaten at table.

This term must not be confused with the procedure of plating metal, which means that an outer layer of metal is applied to change the appearance and character of certain base metals. Although electricity is used in this process today, objects were "silvered" long before the use of electricity, particularly surfaces on the faces of surveyors' compasses.

The Workshop

There is no doubt that the nature and location of the workshop of the silversmith changed over the years from the time the first craftsman worked here until 1800. The early economy of limited resources doubtless often resulted in the workshop being located within the dwelling of the craftsman as had been done in Europe in earlier times. Possibly the next step was to build the shop near the house, as James Geddy did in Williamsburg, Virginia. That his residence was the more important of the two is attested by the fact that it was built on the corner of Duke of Gloucester Street and the Palace Green, with his shop located next to the house on Duke of Gloucester Street.

By the end of the century embryonic zoning practices were appearing; for example, a silversmith in Philadelphia might have had his shop located on Market Street, while his home was in Germantown. The concentration of shops in a particular area of the city made it convenient for the shopper; he could make his purchases in one area, rather than scurry around to different parts of the city.

Reconstructed and restored shops in Williamsburg carry out the plan that the front portion was devoted to exhibition and sales. A prospective buyer could easily view the ware through a large mullioned window, or easily step in off the street after he decided to make a purchase. Shops were not as efficiently arranged then as factories are today; however, forges when present were placed behind partitions, thus confining the smoke and dirt to one area so that the workers could polish or engrave in well-lighted and pleasant surroundings.

Possibly the most interesting surviving artifacts from the shops of early craftsmen are the attractive signs which hung on a bracket, or were otherwise supported, in the front of the shops. These signs were usually in the form of one of the products of the craftsmen: cordwainers were

View of the residence of James Geddy, a silversmith working in Williamsburg, Virginia, in the third quarter of the eighteenth century. Geddy is thought to have practiced his craft in his home and rented the east shop to merchants or other craftsmen. The floor plan of the house, as well as the exterior appearance, indicates that Geddy was a successful businessman. A costumed hostess stands in the doorway of the Geddy residence.

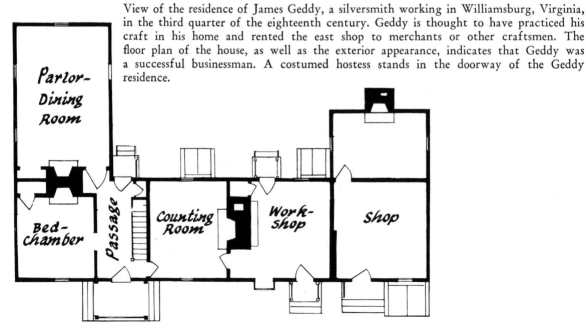

identified by shoes, tailors by scissors, and silversmiths by objects pertinent to their trade. For example, Isaiah Wagster, a goldsmith and jeweler in Baltimore, Maryland, identified his business as being "At the Sign of the Crown and Pearl." Such signs are highly prized today because of their decorative value; however, it should be noted that the major reason for depicting the craftsman's product in his sign was to accommodate prospective buyers who were unable to read.

It is also very significant to know that many silversmiths practiced allied trades along with their major one of fabricating objects of silver. These sidelines were influenced somewhat by the locality in which the business was operated. Craftsmen doing business in a large city were apt also to be merchants, often selling imported goods along with their own products. The advertisement of Thomas Yon in *The South Carolina Gazette*, August 27, 1763, points out that:

> THOMAS YON, At the sign of the Golden Cup in Beef Market Square, has just imported in the Friendship, Capt. Ball, from London: A neat assortment of jewellry, an eight day clock, and a silver mounted gun: which he will sell for ready cash on a small advance The silversmith's business is carried on by him as usual, and he con-

The sign of James Geddy with the initials "I.G." inscribed on a two-handled loving cup. The crisp lines of the architectural details are evidence of a substantial building and a successful craftsman. Unfortunately, the cup does not photograph well because it is the color of silver, so it does not stand out sharply as it does when viewed from the street.

tinues cleaning and polishing old plate, the same as new. Ladies and
gentlemen that employ him, may depend on his utmost diligence in
executing their commands, and he hopes for a continuance of their
favors.

Less logical pursuits are found among the business activities of other
silversmiths, particularly if they worked in rural areas which were not
populous enough to keep a craftsman busy making tankards, mugs, or
mourning rings. An interesting advertisement of Peter Getz, a silversmith
working in Lancaster, Pennsylvania, appeared in *The Pennsylvania Herald
and York General Advertiser,* Wednesday, April 28, 1790, telling that,
"He also furnishes artificial Teeth, perfectly resembling the real, without
inconvenience to the party." His death notice in the *Lancaster Journal,*
January 6, 1810, reads as follows: "Died, In this borough, on Friday
evening the 29th ult. after an illness of two days, in the 47th year of
his age, Mr. Peter Getz, the original improver of the new printing-
press, constructed with rollers in lieu of a screw. He was famous for his
ingenuity." *See page 13.*

Drawings illustrating observations about the architectural details found in American
silver. A knowledge of such details was essential to the success of any silversmith. *See
page 44. Courtesy Metropolitan Museum of Art, New York.*

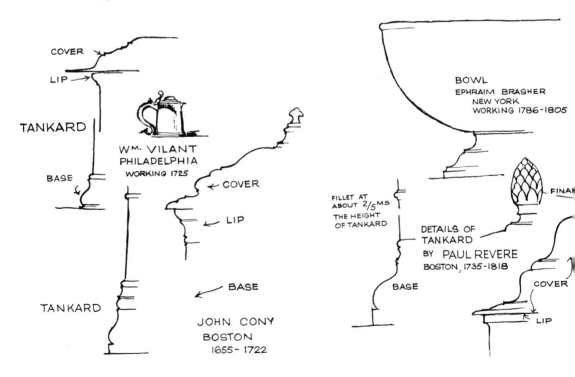

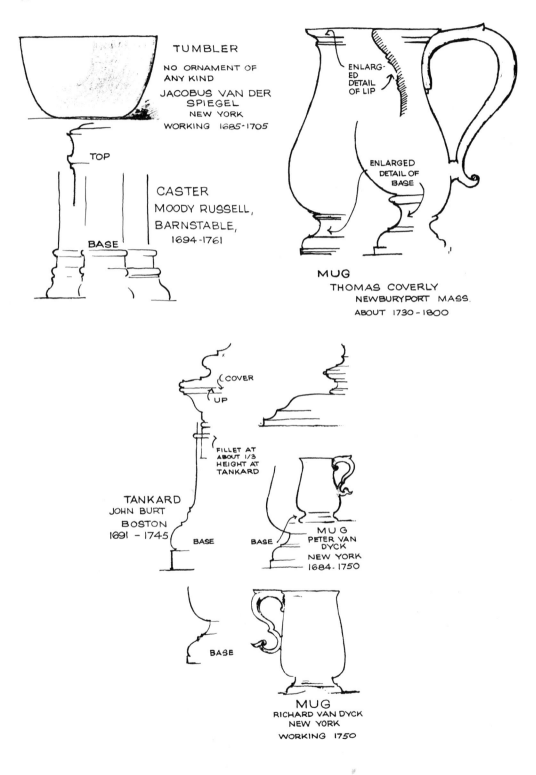

TUMBLER

NO ORNAMENT OF
ANY KIND

JACOBUS VAN DER
SPIEGEL
NEW YORK
WORKING 1685-1705

TOP

CASTER
MOODY RUSSELL,
BARNSTABLE,
1694-1761

BASE

ENLARG-
ED
DETAIL
OF LIP

ENLARGED
DETAIL OF
BASE

MUG
THOMAS COVERLY
NEWBURYPORT MASS.
ABOUT 1730-1800

COVER

UP

FILLET AT
ABOUT 1/3
HEIGHT AT
TANKARD

TANKARD
JOHN BURT
BOSTON
1691 - 1745

BASE

BASE

MUG
PETER VAN
DYCK
NEW YORK
1684-1750

BASE

MUG
RICHARD VAN DYCK
NEW YORK
WORKING 1750

From *The Pennsylvania Herald and York General Advertiser*, April 28, 1790.

Although Mr. Getz was inventive and a fine craftsman to boot, his trades were outnumbered by those of John Inch, who advertised as follows in the *Maryland Gazette*, March 11, 1762.

JOHN INCH, SILVERSMITH

Hereby gives notice, That he still carries on his Silversmith's and jeweller's Business, buys gold and silver, and keeps Tavern as formerly, and has provided himself with a good house painter and glazier lately from London who shall work for any person very reasonably. He also keeps good passage-boats, and has not of his own and others, Vessels fit to carry grain etc. to and from any part of Chesapeake-Bay; he has also for sale a convict-servant Woman's Time. Lately imported, who is a good Stay-maker; a great quantity of Oakum, ship breadth, Delph and Stone ware of divers sorts, too tedious to mention.

The products of all craftsmen reflect various social or economic practices of the era in which they worked. Some of the most curious products of silversmiths and goldsmiths of the eighteenth century were objects related to mourning. One would naturally expect a silversmith to make mourning rings, but one of the unique products was "works in hair." Hair was manipulated into a variety of designs and was often seen mounted in silver, which, of course, explains why the silversmith worked in this unusual medium. An advertisement of G. Smithson in *The South Carolina Gazette*, April 3, 1775, includes a number of unusual items, but particularly focuses attention on his work with hair.

SMITHSON, G.   (Goldsmith)
G. Smithson,
   Returns his most grateful Thanks to his friends for their encouragement, and begs to inform them that he has removed from King-street, to the house late Greenwood and Walker's opposite Mr. Beale's warf, on the Bay; where he humbly solicits the continuance of their Favors. He makes all kinds of Jewellers and Goldsmiths Work, Swords, Cutteaux, Spoons, Buckles, etc. as reasonable as can be imported. Likewise works Hair in Platts, or other curious Forms, such as Landscapes, Flowers, Figures of all kinds, Mottos, Posies, or emblematical Devices, without any assistance from Coulers; engraves Coats of Arms, Crests or Cyphers on Seals or Plates; also Copperplates for Shop-bills, etc. Mourning and Wedding rings on the shortest notice.

Another important facet of the work of the silversmith was repair work. It is very evident that metal was in short supply in America, and a twisted spoon or a broken fork could be more easily repaired than made anew. Furthermore, the frugality of most of the colonists induced them to try repairing before an order for a new object was placed. An advertisement of James Rutherford supports the hypothesis that repair work constituted an important part of the trade. The following advertisement appeared in *The South Carolina Gazette*, November 18, 1751.

   James Rutherford, a regular bred gold and silversmith, just arrived from Edinburg, makes and mends all kinds of plate, and other work in his business, after the best and newest fashions, on reasonable terms. He likewise works in Jewelry, and clasps broken China in the neatest manner, which is work never done here before. His shop is at Mr. William Bisset's, Tayler, in Church-street, next door to Mr. Manigault's.

The wide range of work done by these craftsmen suggests that their shops must have been interesting places, and the number and type of their tools limitless. Inventories of the tools used by several craftsmen are preserved, one of the most extensive being that of Richard Conyers, a London-trained gold and silversmith, who migrated to Boston in the late seventeenth century. The inventory was made by two silversmiths, Jeremiah Dummer and Edward Webb, on April 4, 1709. It might be safely assumed that most craftsmen of the eighteenth century used similar tools, for the technology of the craft changed very little throughout the eighteenth century in America. The value of the tools was attached to each item in the inventory, but because there is little relevance today between the nature of the tool and its value, this information will be omitted from the listing.

1 Large forging anvil
9 Raising anvils
1 Large planishing Teast
1 Spoon Teast
4 Spoon Punches
7 Stakes
1 Skillet & Ingott
Old files 4 lb
2 Gravers
1 Cutting chisel
1 Nurling iron
3 Old brass pans
2 Copper pans
Old Brass patterns
1 Large Vise
3 Forging hammers
25 Small hammers
1 Ring swage
1 Clasp stamp
1 Tankard swage
12 Cutting punches
6 Dapping punches
1 pr Flasks
3 pr Sheers
4 pr Handvises
5 pr Plyers
2 pr Nealing tongs
1 pr Casting tongs
1 Drawing bench
1 pr Large bellows
1 pr Hand bellows

5 Anvils
2 Ditto
4 Small Teasts and Swages
6 Spoon punches & 4 weights
17 Cutting punches
27 Dapping punches
1 pr Large stock sheers
3 pr hand sheers
12 Forging hammers
25 Small hammers
10 Cornellions 1 Chrystall
10 Glass necklaces
5 Ivory boxes
Enamell
A parcel Small pearl
Large pearle
1 pr Large holding tongs
1 Iron
1 pr Flasks
1 Glew pott
1 pr Hand Bellows
2 Boxes chassing punches
15 Canes
15 Sword blades
1 Glass case
1 Large raising anvil
1 Large skillett
9 Rings with Stones and pearls
3 Ditto with large stones
1 pr Gold earrings
Pearl drops

1 pr screw plates
2 Engines for swages
3 pr Compasses
2 Iron Triblits
3 Drawing irons
1 Nurling iron
1 Pestle 1 Ingot 1 Ladle
1 pr Small screw plates
1 Small ingott
1 pr Board Vise
3 pr scales
3 pr Brass weights
1 pile Weights
1 Sett of Small weights
1 Button stamp
9 training Weights
Glass case
2 Burnishing stones
Old cast brass
3 Bell weights
1 Pile old weights

1 Large stone ring
1 pr Stone earrings Sett in silver
1 Gold ring with Six Small stones
2 pr Stone buckles
2 Stone girdle buckles
1 Olde hatt buckle
6 pr Stone buttons
3 pr Ditto
—pearle
1 Lead Stone
2 Bone heads for canes
4 Ditto
1 Knife handle
1 Watch
1 Silver tankard and Tobacco box
Seventy-seven Ounces of Silver in
     Sundry old & New things in the
     hands of Thomas Milner at /8
     per oz.
4 Chrystalls for Watches

The function of all the tools mentioned in the inventory cannot be definitely established today; however, some reasonably sound conclusions can be drawn from the terminology used. The "skillet and ingott" entry suggests that molten metal was poured into a skillet of cast iron, which subsequently shaped the metal into a disk suitable for the forming of round objects, after it was beaten to the desired thickness. The bellows were used to fan the fire in a forge filled with charcoal.

A variety of shears were available for cutting metal, the largest pair being mounted in a tree stump or on a bench top, where great pressure could be exerted on them with both hands and, if necessary, the weight of the body. Tongs were obviously used to handle hot metal, particularly in the "nealing," or annealing process. The flasks indicate that objects were cast in sand; as for the other tools, such as swages, stamps, chisels, files, plyers, and a glue pot, their function has not changed through the years.

A close scrutiny of the foregoing list inevitably leads to the conclusion that the basic tools of the silversmith were hammers, punches, anvils, and shears. Although the blacksmith has been regarded as king of the hammer-men, the fact that Conyers owned sixty-five of these tools would confirm that he also was in the running. An inventory of the tools of John Burt (1693-1745/46), another Boston silversmith, taken March 20, 1745/46 contains forty hammers. Most of the hammers look very much alike to the untrained eye, but subtle nuances between many of them were quite significant to trained craftsmen. Each silversmith had his favorite tools for doing specific jobs and the loss of one was regarded as a catastrophe. Some of the tools, of course, were made by the silversmith and these would naturally be among his favorites. It is also likely that apprentices were taught to make tools in order to increase their regard for them and to teach them the processes involved, in case they ever needed to make their own. The large number of tools in inventories might be explained by the fact that many of the journeymen employed apprentices who had no tools of their own and, therefore, the tools had to be supplied by their masters.

The large number and variety of hammers is a fascinating aspect of the craft, but, more importantly, one must be aware of the care taken of these tools. All the stakes and hammers had to be kept at a mirror-bright finish for the craftsman to work efficiently. The slightest flaw on the surface of a hammer would be transferred to the surface of the metal with each hammer-blow, and thus the surface of the precious metal would be impaired. Perfection was particularly important on the face of the planishing hammer, for it was the last one to touch the surface of the metal. When hammers and stakes were not in daily use, they were covered with tallow to prevent deterioration. If rusting or flaws did occur on the surface, they had to be eradicated and the tools refinished before being used again.

Despite the fact that fastidious care was taken of the tools, they had to be repaired then as they must be now. An advertisement of Samuel Bissel in the *Boston Gazette*, March 4, 1717, indicates that he "was lately come from England." He also mentions that he was making "all sorts of Blacksmith's and Goldsmith's anvils, Brick irons and stakes," as well as putting "new faces" on old ones at his shop at Newport, Rhode Island. Thus, the painstaking thriftiness of the craftsman is apparent in the way he used his tools, just as it is in his salvaging scraps of silver.

Despite the importance of the heat of the forge, the polish of the hammers and anvils, and the quality of the metal, the most essential factor in silversmithing was the training of the apprentice. It should be noted at the very beginning of this facet of the discussion that, although all the master craftsmen wanted "smart" apprentices, the silversmith emphasized this quality more than other craftsmen. There certainly must have been a hierarchy among tradesmen and the silver and goldsmith must have been at the very top.

Registered for Mr. Charles LeRoux the 23rd day of July Anno Dom. 1719. This Indenture Wittnesseth that Jacob TenEyck aged about fifteen years hath put himself and by these Presents doth Voluntarily and of his own free Will and Accord by and with the Concent of Coenraet TenEyck his father put himself apprentice to Charles LeRoux of the City of New York Goldsmith with him to live and (after the Manner of an Apprentice) to serve from the fifteenth day of July Anno Dom. One thousand seven hundred and Nineteen till the full Term of seven years be Compleat and Ended. During all which Term the said Apprentice his said Master Charles LeRoux faithfully shall serve his Secretts keep his lawfull Commands gladly Every where Obey: he shall do no damage to his said Master nor see to be done by Others without letting or giving Notice to his Master, he shall not waste his Masters Goods nor lend them unlawfully to any, he shall not Commit Fornication nor Contract Matrimony within the said Term, at Cards Dice or any Other unlawfull Game he shall not play whereby his Master may have damage, with his own Goods nor the Goods of others during the said Term without Lycense from his said Master he shall neither buy not sell, he shall not absent himself day nor night from his Masters Service without his leave nor haunt Alehouses Taverns or Playhouses but in all things as a faithful Apprentice he shall behave himself toward his Master and all his during the said Term. and the said Master during the said Term shall by the best Means or Method that he can Teach or Cause the said Apprentice to be taught the Art or Mystery of a Goldsmith. shall find or provide unto the said Apprentice sufficient Meat Drink and Washing in winter time fitting for an Apprentice and his said father to find him Apparell Lodging and washing in summer time and his said Master to suffer his said Apprentice to go to the winter Evening School at the Charge of his father. for the true performance of all and Every the said Covenants and Agreements Either of the said parties bind themselves unto the Other by these presents. In Wittness whereof . . ."

Typical indenture of the eighteenth century. *Courtesy The Museum of Fine Arts, Boston.*

The reasons for this situation are readily apparent. In the first place, the boy had to be scrupulously honest, for he had access to metal of great value, and no master wanted to wake up in the morning and discover that he had been robbed. Since it would have been impossible to identify an ingot of silver in those days, a thief would not have had much difficulty in disposing of such an item. Of equal importance is the fact that the apprentice was working with a metal of great value, and spoilage was certainly frowned upon by the master craftsman. It was possible that an apprentice would work long hours and many days on an object; to discard it and start anew would have been a disastrous procedure.

It might logically be pointed out here that it is almost impossible to find among the products of craftsmen working in the eighteenth century a counterpart of what the twentieth century calls "seconds." Considerable experience by the writer in restoring objects of metal to their original appearance and function has led him to the conclusion that his work was necessary because the utensil had been subjected to ill usage or indiscreet restoration by an incompetent craftsman in the nineteenth century. Thus, the demands on the workmanship of the apprentice were pressing and it is not unlikely that a sizeable number of them were "washed out" before they served their stint and became master craftsmen.

But more importantly, the most demanding facet of the boy's training was an aesthetic insight into the design of the objects he was creating. It is true that many of them were apprenticed to craftsmen who had been trained in England, and thus the taste and sophistication of English products were reproduced in America. But by the end of the eighteenth century the trade was pretty well Americanized, yet a high standard of craftsmanship and design continued to exist in the products of the American silversmith. A quotation from *American Silver of the XVII & XVIII Centuries,* written and illustrated by Cass Gilbert, focuses attention on this very important matter. *See page 36.*

> It was, to me at least, a real discovery to find that in practically all old American and much of the English silver, of what we call the "Colonial Period," the mouldings were replicas or refinements of architectural mouldings of the classic Roman or Renaissance periods.
>
> The Graeco-Roman echinus frequently forms the cup; the fillet and cavetto follow below in classic sequence, as in the tankard by William Vilant of Philadelphia, in the Clearwater Collection, or in the upper moulding of the shaft of the caster by Stephen Emery (1752-1818).

Sometimes the Attic base appears complete with the conge of the column and its fillet, then half-round moulding, fillet, scotia, taurus, and plinth in perfect sequence and proportion as though copied from the base of a Corinthian column. In other pieces there are various combinations of mouldings forming base, cap and cover, all of them of exquisite shape; the cyma recta and the cyma reversa, fillet, bead, ovolo, and cavetto are wrought together with the knowledge and skill of masters of architecture.

These were no uncommon craftsmen . . . nor were they lacking in erudition. They knew their precedent and their proportions and yet knowing worked with free hands, controlled only by the knowledge of their art and impeccable taste.

Because the silversmith made such outstanding products, it becomes evident that he naturally transacted business with a clientele which was an important sector in the society of the period. It might also logically follow that the silversmiths, therefore, became engaged in important matters outside of their daily tasks of hammering, soldering, and polishing.

One example of a craftsman's reaching a position of prestige in his community is that of Joseph Richardson, Sr., of Philadelphia. The following résumé appeared in the *Pennsylvania Journal* after his death on November 22, 1770.

On Saturday morning last died Joseph Richardson, Esq. an eminent Merchant of this city, in the 64th year of his age; a Gentleman whose private virtues, and public spirit justly claimed the friendship, esteem, and confidence of his fellow citizens and others. He served for several years as a representative in the Assembly of this province, with steadyness, integrity and advantage to his country. He filled several other offices of public trust with assiduity and reputation, and devoted a great deal of time to settling disputes and controversies among his neighbors and others; a conduct truly praiseworthy, and for which he deserves the highest encomium. His unexpected death is deeply mourned and lamented by his family and friends, and his loss, as a very useful member of society, regreted by his countrymen, who demonstrated this respect to his memory, by attending his funeral in great numbers to the Quaker's burying ground in this city, where he was interred on Monday.

Thus, esteem for a man's products and for his character seem to coincide, and posterity, sharing this approbation, will be eager to examine the products of such outstanding craftsmen.

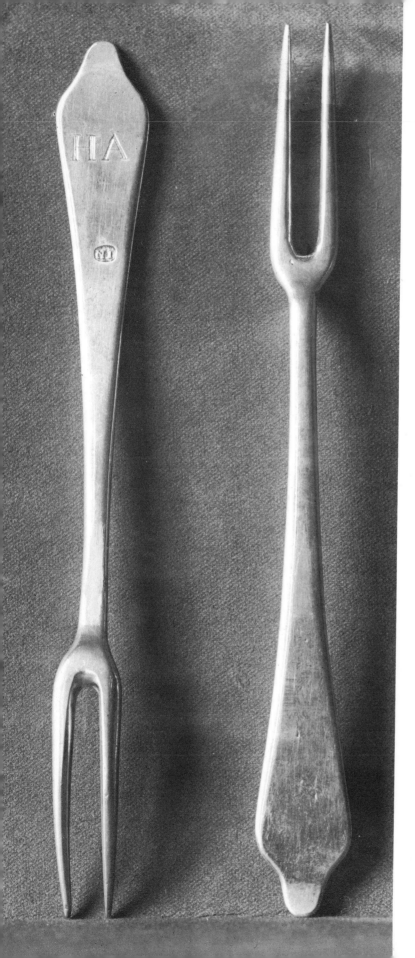

Silver forks made by John Noyes (1674-1749) of Boston. Forks of the type are exceedingly rare. *Courtesy The Museum of Fine Arts, Boston.*

Forks and Spoons

The making of a fork will be the first of the processes used by the silversmith to be scrutinized. Such a procedure might logically be questioned by perceptive readers who know that forks made entirely of silver were very scarce in the eighteenth century. It is reported that forks were invented in Italy and brought to England in the seventeenth century. Despite the fact that they were regarded as objects of luxury in England and America, it is interesting to note that the inventory of silver items owned by Abram de Peyster, who died in New York in 1728, included thirty-seven silver forks. The fact that they were not described as "silver-handled" suggests that they were made completely of silver and were not the silver-handled type which became popular later in the century. The tines of the silver-handled fork were made of steel.

The reason for choosing the fork as the first example of silversmithing lies principally in the fact that silver's most important quality, malleability, was particularly important in the making of this object. Another, and more easily understood, word for malleability is "stretchability." A second reason for its choice lies in the fact that relatively little skill was required to make it.

First, a blank of metal had to be obtained before the stretching procedure could be started. It is not probable that a small piece of silver of the approximate size needed to make a fork was prepared, for the processing of many small pieces would have been wasteful of time and more difficult than the pounding out of a larger piece. When a piece of the desired thickness became available, a small rectangle was removed by sawing, shearing, or cutting with a cold chisel. This blank was undersize for the finished fork, because allowance had to be made for stretching the metal at the desired points. Next, the metal had to be annealed (softened) to relieve the strains incurred in the battery process, commonly known

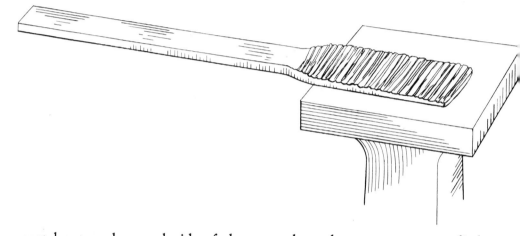

as work-hardening, which inevitably occurs when most metals are hammered.

The actual production of the fork started by placing the broadside of the blank on a silversmith's anvil, known as a stake, and striking it cross-wise with the straight end of a cross-peen hammer. This rounded-wedge-shaped hammer, falling with some pressure upon the silver, spread the

metal outward on each side of the spot where the pressure was applied. Repeated blows of the hammer increased the length of the blank and re-duced its thickness, at the same time slightly increasing its width.

Next, the handle end of the blank was placed on the stake, and blows applied lengthwise with the wedge end of the hammer. This procedure increased the width to the dimension desired for the handle and also di-minished the thickness of the blank.

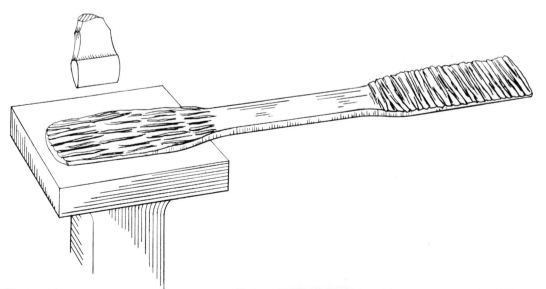

The center portion of the blank was then laid edgewise on a stake and struck with the cross-peen hammer until the desired width and thickness were produced. This operation not only reduced the width of the blank, but also increased the thickness where the handle would otherwise have been very weak. The metal had to be annealed several times during the forming process.

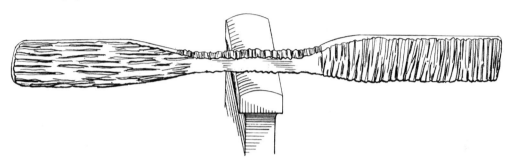

The blank was then thick and thin, wide and narrow at the proper places, but the entire surface was badly distorted from such vigorous pounding. To make the entire blank reasonably smooth, the craftsman used the slightly convex face of a planishing hammer. Each blow partially overlapped another until the entire surface was covered.

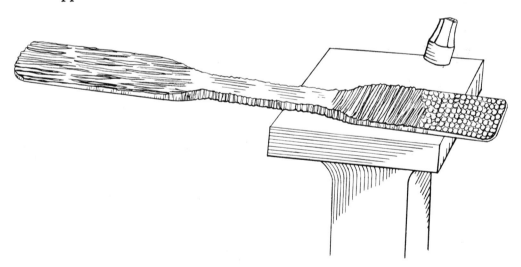

A meticulous craftsman planished his products several times, each time easing the pressure of the blow and more nearly producing an even surface. The shallow facets produced by this technique are often barely visible on old objects of silver, for they were partially removed by the craftsman in the finishing process, as well as by the housewife who polished them hundreds of times throughout a lifetime of use. The marks produced by the planishing process were not the sharp pock marks found on pseudo-reproductions made in the twentieth century.

The final layout of the shape followed. The tines (either two or three) were marked with an awl as was the design on the end of the handle. An effort was made to achieve the final form as nearly as possible with the hammer to avoid wasting any of the precious metal by cutting it away. The final design was achieved by sawing details of the shape which could not be achieved by any other method. Later, edges were made smooth and

contours refined by using such abrasives as pumice or rottenstone. At this point the blank was smooth, straight, and flat. The desired relationship of the tines with the handle was obtained by a few deft blows with a mallet while the silver was supported on an appropriately shaped stake.

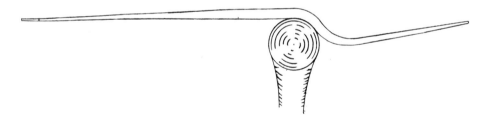

Finally, it should be noted that repeated heating and cooling of the silver created an oxidation of the surface of the metal called fire-scale. The areas of the fork which were filed and polished were bright, so the surface was divided into bright and dark areas. It is likely that the silversmith removed most of the fire-scale before he declared the product ready for the customer.

It has been pointed out that some forks were made entirely of silver and used in the eighteenth century; there is, however, a preponderance of evidence that spoons were much more plentiful. As a matter of fact, historians and antiquarians suggest that they were not only more numerous, but that they were the first objects of importance made by silversmiths in America.

The great number of spoons arises from a variety of circumstances. In the first place, they were small objects and required little metal for their manufacture. They were a major eating utensil, particularly if only one utensil was available. Although not completely satisfactory, they could substitute for either a fork or a knife. It is also evident that it was a symbol of wealth, and the saying that a child was born with a silver spoon in its mouth was probably almost a matter of fact in many cases.

Like the fork, the blank for the spoon was obtained from a larger sheet which had been reduced to the approximate thickness desired. The form, however, was not a perfect rectangle, for the bowl of the spoon required more width than the tines of the fork. Therefore, the blank was a little wider at one end than at the other.

Work could start at either end. To form the blank for the bowl, the metal was placed broadside on a stake and struck lengthwise with the cross-peen end of a hammer until sufficient width was provided. The dotted line on the drawing indicates the shape of the finished bowl. It must be noted, however, that at the narrow portion in the center toward the rear of the projected form of the bowl, the metal was not stretched, but left its full thickness to provide adequate metal for forming the rat-tail on many spoons of the period.

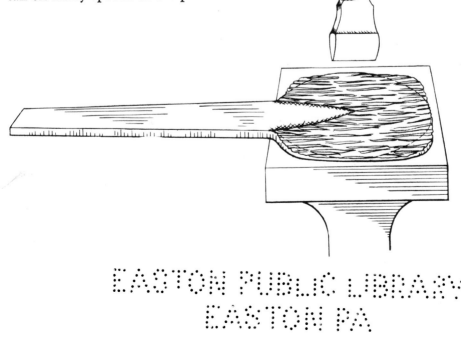

Next, the handle end of the blank was placed on a stake and struck lengthwise, until the desired width was obtained.

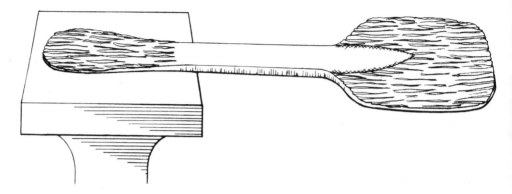

Finally, the center portion of the handle was placed edgewise on a stake and pounded until the desired thickness and width were obtained. Throughout these forming processes the blank had to be annealed several times.

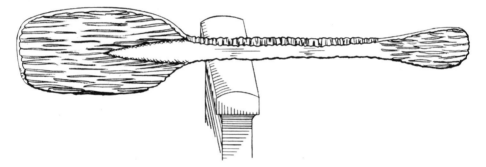

Because the cross-peen end of the hammer distorted the surface of the metal, it was necessary to make the surface reasonably smooth by planishing it, as was done with the fork. The ridge in the center, however,

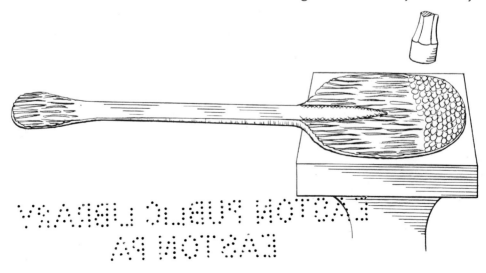

was untouched in this procedure for its full thickness had to be maintained. This heavy part not only made the spoon rigid, but also added to its attractiveness.

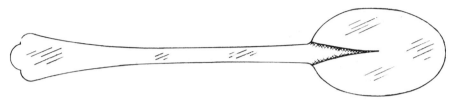

After the layout for the finished shape and size of the spoon was completed, hammering and filing brought it to its final form. Then the flat surface of the bowl was rested on a lump of lead and the bowl made the proper depth with a hollowing hammer. The radius on the face of the hammer coincided as nearly as possible with the finished shape of the bowl, so that no unusual depressions were created which had to be removed. The soft lead allowed the ridge, or rat-tail, on the bottom of the bowl to "seat itself" without distortion while the bowl was hammered into the desired contour.

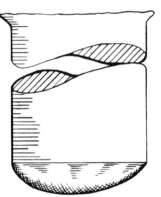

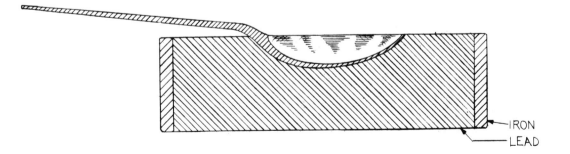

Swage of iron with an eagle engraved in the surface. Has a small terminal tab which overlapped the bowl of the spoon. By laying the blank of silver on the swage, with excess provided for the tab or in some cases the rat-tail, the desired shape could be hammered into the bottom surface of the spoon. *Courtesy Old Salem, Inc., Winston-Salem, North Carolina.*

Some silversmiths had a swage for shaping the rat-tail, before the bowl was shaped. A flat piece of iron had a tapering groove filed into it into which the ridge was pounded to form the rat-tail. Such a device was used in the eighteenth and nineteenth centuries to create a rat-tail, an impression of a shell, or an eagle on the bottom of the bowl. After the desired impressions were made the spoon was then hollowed on the lead.

In the *Diderot Encyclopedia* a swage with male and female parts is shown. With such a tool the rat-tail was simultaneously shaped with the bowl of the spoon. In any of the three methods described irregularities were created on the inner surface of the bowl, which had to be removed by scraping.

The final filing and smoothing were given to the spoon, and the handle bent to its proper relationship with the bowl. The elliptical shape of the

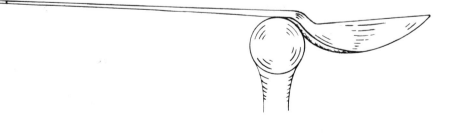

bowl illustrated was widely used in the first half of the eighteenth century. Toward the end of the century the shape of the spoon became narrow at the end opposite the handle, resembling the shape used throughout the nineteenth and into the twentieth century.

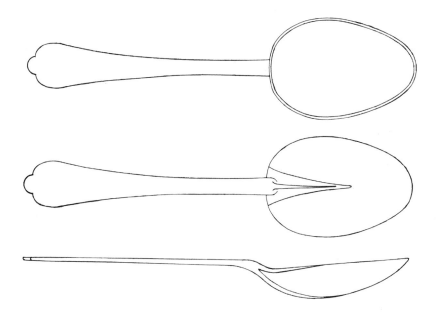

Two spoons by John Burger, New York, late eighteenth century. The shape of these spoons is typical of the period. The handles were quite slender near the bowl, the rat-tail was usually omitted, and the end of the bowl became more pointed. This bowl shape was widely used with the later "fiddle pattern" handle and is much the same shape as a bowl in modern times. *Kauffman collection.*

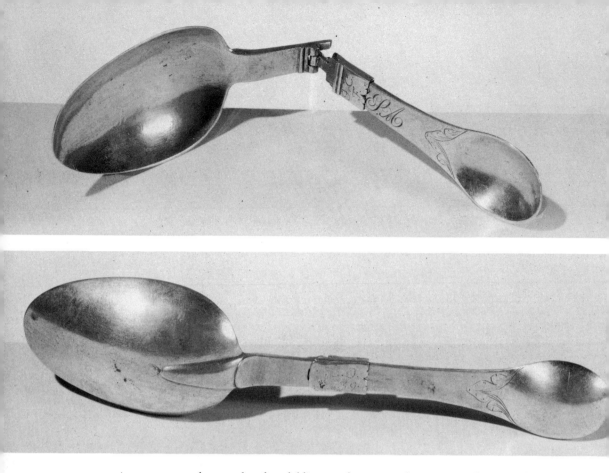

A most unusual example of a folding pocket spoon by Caesar Ghiselin, Philadelphia (1670-1734). The trifid arrangement of initials can be faintly seen on the top of the handle near the hinge. They are probably the initials of the owners. The large initials could be those of a later owner. It is possible that the rat-tail form on this spoon, as on some others, was filed instead of swaged. *Courtesy Philadelphia Museum of Art; photograph by A. J. Wyatt, Staff photographer.*

A description of the production of a spoon, and possibly a fork, would not be complete without some explanation about the name and/or the initials usually found on the handle, rarely on the bowl. The name of the maker was imprinted on the bottom side of the handle with a steel die, which created an intaglio impression on the silver. ("Intaglio" indicates that a depressed cartouche was made with raised letters.) The die was made of steel; however, the shaping and making of the letters was executed while the steel was soft, and the steel later hardened to withstand the frequent pressure applied by striking the top end with a hammer. An imperfect impression of the maker's name can be attributed to the fact that the die was not held evenly when the name was imprinted, or that it could have been obscured at a later time by injudicious polishing.

In the earliest times the silversmith, because of frugality or precedent, used only the initials of his given name and surname in his die. In the eighteenth century he usually used the initial of his given name and his complete surname, and on some occasions used his full name. In the nineteenth century the place of manufacture was often added, particularly

The frugality or, possible better, the ingenuity of the colonial silversmith and his patron is exemplified in these objects combining forks and spoons, called "sucket forks." The word "sucket" is derived from "succade" which, in the fifteenth century, referred to fruit preserved in sugar, either candied or in syrup. The term was also used in describing vegetables which had been similarly treated. *Courtesy The Heritage Collection, Old Deerfield, Massachusetts.*

This style of spoon was made in America at the beginning of the eighteenth century. The ovoid shape of the bowl, slightly flattened at each end, was accompanied by a "rat-tail" under the bowl. The width of the stem slowly widening into three lobes at the end was known as a "trifid" end. The sharp indentations at the end of the handle soon were changed into three rounded notches. These are called "wavy-end" handles. *Courtesy Henry Francis du Pont Winterthur Museum.*

if he worked at a prestigious place such as Philadelphia, New York, Boston, or Newport.

Needless to say, the absence of a maker's mark usually deflates the value of an object, unless it can be identified through family ownership, or by recognizing in it the unique style of a particular maker. It might also be noted that some early unmarked pieces have been imprinted in modern times with the names of famous craftsmen. The authenticity of marks can usually be confirmed or denied by experts who have made a comprehensive study of the subject.

L
S ✝ H

Near the end of the handle one often finds initials engraved on the top or bottom. Sometimes three initials appear in a triangular arrangement, the upper one standing for the family name of the groom, while

Intaglio die for marking objects made of silver by J. Vogeler, a silversmith working in early nineteenth century in Salem, North Carolina. *Courtesy Old Salem, Inc. Winston-Salem, North Carolina.*

the bottom two stand for the given names of the bride and groom. A similar arrangement of initials is often found inlaid on pieces of furniture such as clocks or cases of drawers. If the object were a wedding or birth gift, a date was sometimes included.

Although it cannot be said that engraving was absolutely a part of silversmithing, some silversmiths were very competent engravers. They not only engraved a few initials on a spoon, fork, or tankard, but also executed intricate designs, such as coats of arms, on important objects of silver. Advertisements in newspapers often enumerate these various skills of the silversmith, such as the one of Dan Carrel, who advertised in the *Charleston City Gazette and Advertiser,* on April 20, 1790, as follows:

DAN CARREL
Silversmith and Jeweller
At the sign of the Silver Coffee Pot—No. 129 Broad Street, Makes, Sells, and Repairs anything in the above branches. Counting—house-watch seals, coats of arms, and all manner of Engraving on gold, silver, steel, etc., executed in the best manner, and on reasonable terms. . . .

Among some of the well-known silversmiths who were competent engravers was John Coney, who engraved the plates for the first paper money printed in America, and the illustrious Paul Revere, better known as a sentryman than as an engraver. An advertisement in the *Boston Gazette,* February 4, 1765, focuses attention on the fact that Revere not only engraved his silver products, but also copper plates for printing.

Spoon by John Vogeler. The imprint of an eagle was made from the swage block with two eagle impressions on it. *See page 54. Courtesy Old Salem, Inc., Winston-Salem, North Carolina.*

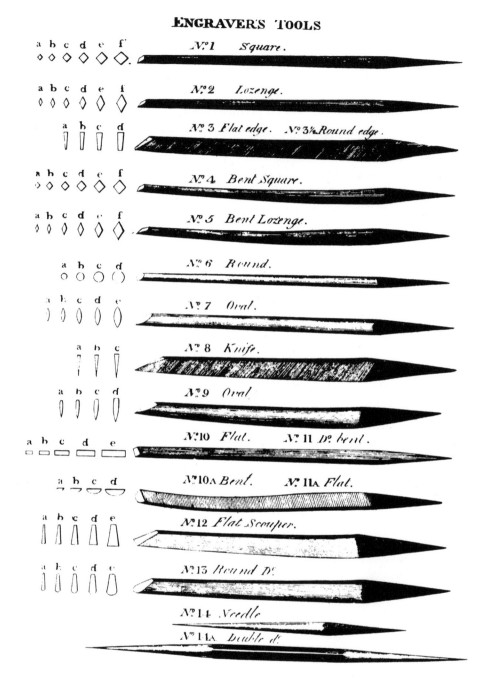

ENGRAVERS TOOLS

Typical shapes of engraving tools used by a silversmith in the eighteenth century (and in the twentieth). When new, they were two to three inches long, excluding the handle; however, they were frequently made shorter by deliberately breaking them or because of frequent sharpenings. From *Key to the Manufactories of Sheffield* by Jos. Smith, 1816. *Courtesy Sheffield City Libraries.*

SCRAPERS &c

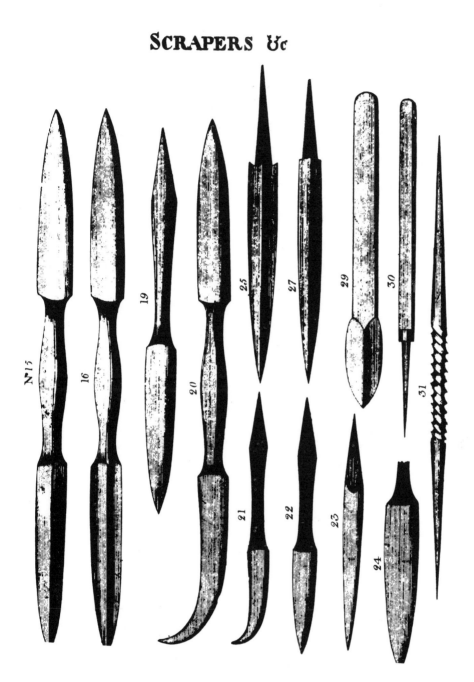

Scrapers used by engravers to remove unwanted irregularities from the surface of the metal being engraved. From *Key to Manufactories of Sheffield* by Jos. Smith, 1816. *Courtesy Sheffield City Libraries.*

The advertisement is an unusual one for the eighteenth century, for, in fact, it describes a product of the combined efforts of two men, an incident which did not occur very often at that time.

> Just published. And to be Sold by Josiah Flagg, and Paul Revere, in Fifth Street, at the north end of Boston, a collection of the best Psalm-tunes, in two, three, and four Parts, from the most celebrated Authors; fitted to all Measures, and approved by the best Masters in Boston, New England. To which are added, Some Hymns and Anthems; the greater part of them never before Printed in America.
>
> Set in Score by   Josiah Flagg
> Engraved by   Paul Revere

The art (or craft) of engraving was executed by holding a short V-shaped tool (called a graver) with a small stubby handle between the thumb and the forefinger, the other fingers steadying the position of the tool as it removed small slivers of metal from the surface. A steady and controlled application of pressure was essential, for if the tool slipped from its intended course, the surface of the metal was marred with a deep scratch. Such scratches had to be repaired by a scraper, which removed metal adjoining the scratch, or by a burnisher, which smoothed the surface by rubbing adjoining metal back into the scratch.

Finally, for the silversmiths who never became competent engravers, there were craftsmen who were exclusively engravers. Such a man was John Sacheverell, who advertised in the *Pennsylvania Gazette,* March 22, 1732, as follows:

JOHN SACHEVERELL
GOLDSMITH
Who performs all sorts of Engraving or Carving in Gold, Silver, Brass, Copper, Steel, after the newest and neatest manner.

It seems evident from a survey of two of the smallest and simplest objects made by the silversmith that his craft was a very demanding one. The best of them were skilled in many facets of their trade, and their surviving products are among the most sought of any product of the eighteenth century.

Plates and Basins

After discussing the making of a fork and spoon of silver, one's attention might logically turn toward the making of another eating utensil, a plate. It is a well-established fact that many early plates were made of wood and of pewter; however, it is somewhat puzzling to discover that few plates were made of silver. As a matter of fact, only one plate is mentioned in *Historic Silver of the Colonies and Its Makers*, by Francis Bigelow, and none is listed in the index of *American Silver of the XVII & XVIII Centuries*, by C. Louise Avery. One plate is illustrated in *American Silver* by John Marshall Phillips, who curiously emphasizes the richly engraved rim of the plate made by John Coney, but neglects to comment about the rarity of plates. The plentiful supply of drinking vessels, ranging from those used for communion to those used in taverns suggests that owners of silver vessels were more interested in drinking than in eating, albeit some of the drinking occurred in the church, not only at communion, but also at funerals.

It is interesting to note that even outside the context of silver objects, the word "plate" is an elusive one. For example, the term does not appear in the Fourteenth Edition of *The Encyclopedia Britannica*, nor can it be found in other common sources of such information. The first definition, however, under the word plate in the *Encyclopedia: or a Dictionary of Arts and Sciences, and Miscellaneous Literature*, printed by T. Dobson, in Philadelphia, 1798, gives the following information:

> PLATE, a term which denotes a piece of wrought silver, such as a shallow vessel off which meat is eaten.

It has been previously pointed out that the word "plate" was widely used in the seventeenth and eighteenth centuries to describe all objects made of silver or gold. In this context most references define the word "plate," but far fewer mention it as a utensil used when eating.

63

If there were few large ones, there certainly were many small ones called patens. Patens were small plates, usually five to seven inches in diameter, used to serve bread in communion services in England and America. It might be logically concluded that, although the poverty of the colonists did not permit silver plates to be made for eating in the home, the combined resources of a congregation might have permitted such a one to be used in their church. It might also be pointed out that other communion vessels, such as flagons and chalices, were also made of silver.

Because of an erroneous idea developed in modern craft classes about the technique used to form shallow vessels, it seems logical to first dispel the idea that shallow plates were beaten down into a preshaped mold of hard wood, the depression having the desired shape and depth of the product. Although this procedure does enable an embryonic craftsman to produce an object, this technique restricts the depth and diameter of the product unless a very large number of molds is available, and this was not the procedure followed by the silversmiths of the eighteenth century.

The process used in making a plate or a paten was called "sinking." Sinking invariably infers stretching (ductility) but by tension rather than by compression, as was used in the making of the fork and the spoon.

To make a shallow plate the sheet metal was first uniformly reduced to the optimum thickness for the object to be produced. A plate twelve inches in diameter required a thicker piece of metal than a plate six inches in diameter. It will be evident that the metal was slightly thinned in the sinking operation; the reduction of thickness, however, in such a shallow vessel was a negligible consideration.

The work was started by cutting an annealed disk slightly oversize to allow for final trimming. The diameter of the depressed portion was struck from the center with a compass, if round; a template was used for other shapes.

The end-grain of a hard piece of wood, such as maple or birch, was then set upright in a vise. The arc of the outside diameter of the plate was then inscribed on the flat top surface of the block, so that the sinking line coincided with the edge of the block. Two nails were driven into the top surface of the block and, as the disk was rotated against the nails,

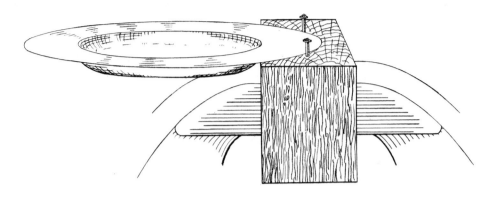

blows at the sinking line created a slight depth, which was increased by repeating the operation until the desired depth was obtained.

After each rotation of the disk the edge, or intersection of the flat rim with the dished part, became rounded a bit. The rim was made flat by

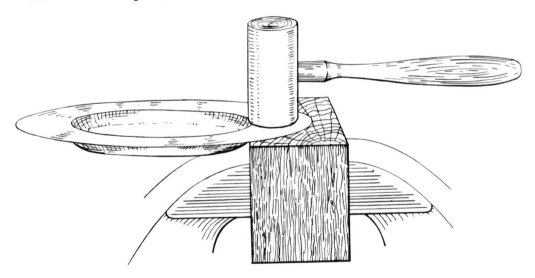

striking it with a hammer or a mallet. This procedure usually created a wavy contour in the edge, which was removed by placing the plate upside down on a flat surface and applying pressure with a block of hard wood and a hammer. After the desired depth was obtained, the bottom had also to be made flat by using a flat-faced mallet or a small block of wood with a hammer. After the shaping was completed and the rim and the bottom of the paten made flat, the uneven booge or bulge had to be

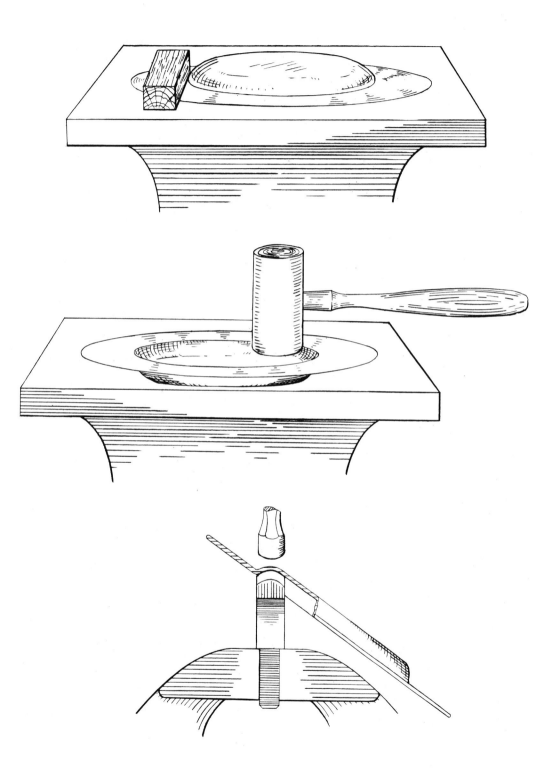

planished to make the metal hard and bring the shape into perfect roundness. This was a difficult operation to perform on such a small area, with
a depth of possibly only a half inch.

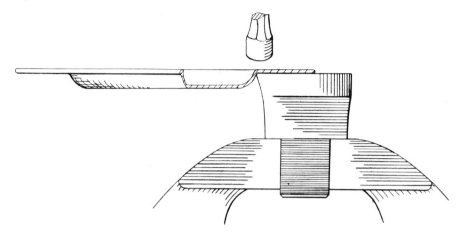

Finally, the flat rim was lightly planished to make it rigid and provide
an even-textured finish found on objects of silver made by hand methods.
The usual trimming and polishing with pumice made it ready for the
customer.

Although the word "basin" and the various uses of the object are not
completely obsolete, it must be admitted that confusion could easily arise
concerning the form and function of the two objects, bowls and basins.
Such confusion is not completely a matter of semantics today for the
Oxford English Dictionary, Oxford, 1933, comments as follows about the
two objects:

> Historically, a *bowl* is distinguished from a *basin* by its more hemi-
> spherical shape; a 'basin' being proportionally shallower and wider, or
> with the margin curved outward, as in the ordinary wash-hand basin;
> but the actual use of the word is capricious, and varies from place to
> place; in particular, the ordinary small earthenware vessels, used for
> porridge, soup, milk, sugar, etc., which are historically bowls are so
> called in Scotland and in U.S., are always called in the south-east of
> England, *Basins*.

The significant point of difference seems to relate to their shape, and
tradition supports the statement that a basin is "shallower and wider"
than a bowl. This difference, combined with the fact that basins often

have a wider brim than a bowl, suggests that a basin is closely related to a plate; at least there were a number of similarities in their making. As a matter of fact, one might almost say that a basin was a hybrid between a plate and a bowl.

The wide brim seems to have been an essential part of the basin made for domestic or baptismal use, for most of them have such a brim. However, one made by Philip Syng as a gift to Christ Church in Philadelphia from Robert Quary has a very narrow brim and really resembles a bowl, as do a few others. They generally range in diameter from ten to fourteen inches, but John Coney made one with a diameter of seventeen inches which is owned by the Second Congregational Church of Marblehead, Massachusetts.

One must assume that there was a logical reason for wide brims because so many had them. They certainly were an aesthetically pleasing feature; they provided an adequate hand-grip when in use, and on many, significant inscriptions were engraved. The Reverend Brattle, who apparently owned one for domestic use, bequeathed it to his church for baptismal use with directions that an appropriate inscription be placed on it. The inscription is, "A Baptismal Basin consecrated, bequeathed, & presented to the Church of Christ in Cambridge, his Dearly beloved Flock, By Revd. Mr. Wm. Brattle Pastr of the Sd Church: Who was translated from his Charge to his Crown, Febr 15: 1716/17."

It was a general rule that, regardless of the technique used to manufacture a vessel, one of great depth required a thicker piece of silver than one that was shallow. If a basin had a flat horizontal brim, the first stage of production was similar to the making of a plate. The diameter of the depressed part was inscribed on the disk, nails were properly placed in a block of wood so that the inscribed line coincided with the edge of the block. By holding the metal firmly against the nails and the flat top of the block, the bulge or booge was started with a sinking hammer. By rotating the disk and striking it with the hammer, a depression similar to that of a plate was soon created. The usual precaution had to be taken to keep the transitional edge sharp and the brim flat.

After the object looked like a plate, the silversmith could obtain the desired depth for his vessel by using one of two methods, or possibly both. He could transfer his object to the tree trunk and by tensional stretch-

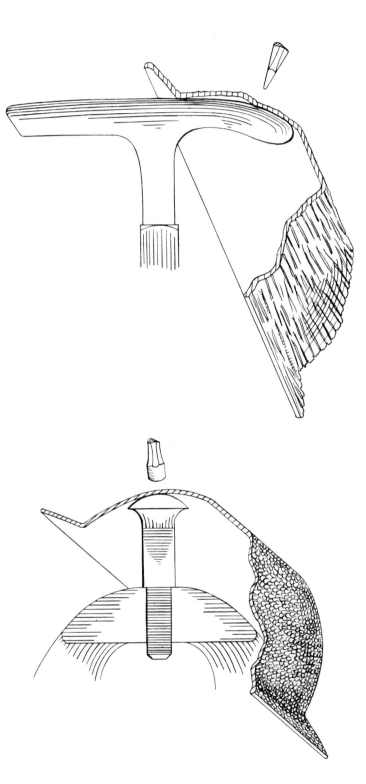

ing make the piece considerably deeper. There were, however, distinct dangers in using this method exclusively, for continued stretching made the metal paper-thin or possibly made a break in it.

The better procedure was to place the basin upside down on a round stake and really raise the metal, as was done in making cups and beakers. This method of stretching by compression permitted an even stretching of the metal, and minimized the hazards of thinness and breakage.

After the desired shape and size were obtained, the distorted surface of the metal had to be made smooth by planishing it. This procedure could be done on the same stake used to stretch and shape the metal. Some basins have a domed center, which is difficult to avoid in the planishing process, and also provides a solid footing on which the basin rests. The usual filing and polishing were the final steps in the making of a basin.

Cups and Beakers

Other objects made by the silversmith, which appear to fit into the "simple" category, are cups and beakers. Dictionary definitions are very imprecise in distinguishing the characteristics of the two objects; however, it is generally agreed that a cup is a short vessel used for drinking and a beaker is a tall one employed for the same purpose. It might also be noted that while American cups have handles, beakers usually do not.

The earliest method for making these vessels, and the most desirable from the connoisseur's point of view, was to fashion them of one piece of metal, a process called raising. This fundamental and important procedure will subsequently be explained in full detail, for it was by this method that most of the important hollow ware of the eighteenth century was made.

A method used late in the century was to make separate patterns for an object, one for the sides and another for the bottom of the vessel. After these patterns were placed on sheets of silver, the craftsman traced around them, cut the metal to size, shaped the parts, and assembled them by soldering. Objects formed by this method have one vertical joint in the side and a circular one around the perimeter of the bottom. Although the obvious joinery in most pieces fabricated by this method was expertly done, sometimes the joint at the bottom is quite indifferently finished.

To make a cup of one piece of metal the craftsman first had to cut a disk the desired size. This size varied among craftsmen, for each used personally developed techniques, but the differences were slight. Great care was exercised in cutting the metal, since waste had to be held to a minimum.

The raising procedure was begun by laying the disk of metal on the end section of a large tree trunk, which was standard equipment in most

shops. The end grain of the wood had the combined qualities of hardness and resiliency, which permitted the metal to bend or stretch in direct relation to the pressure applied to it with a hammer or a mallet. After many years of use, hollows of different diameters and depths developed in the wood, and the silversmith could choose the one best suited for his immediate need. Because of their great weight, the sections of wood were not attached to the floor, and they were probably lower than bench height, so that the craftsman could sit on a low stool while he worked.

By using a hollowing hammer, one with a radius larger than that of a sinking hammer, the craftsman struck the disk in a series of concentric circles, starting at the outer edge and working inward toward the edge of the bottom, or vice versa. This procedure is known as tensional stretching. In this way a form was created with a flat bottom and flaring sides. Although considerable depth could be obtained by this method, it had only limited use for to obtain great depth the metal would be stretched too thin, and the large diameter of the disk could *not* be reduced to the small diameter of the top of the cup. Thus, to make the sides perpendicular to the bottom another technique had to be employed. Hammer blows were applied to the outside of the disk instead of to the inside, as was originally done. This was *raising*.

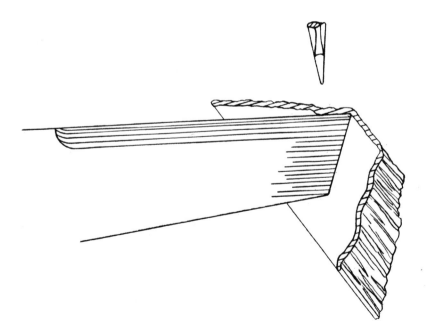

It must be quite evident that to create a shallow bowl from a disk of metal was a relatively easy task, for little shaping had to be done and, therefore, a modicum of skill was required to execute such work. As the contour of the piece changed from the horizontal to vertical, the degree of skill required increased in direct ratio to the work involved. If the diameter of the neck of an object were smaller in diameter than the sides, the problem of raising increased proportionately. A cup appears to be a simple object to make, and by comparison to many others it was; however, it is likely that apprentices practiced the raising technique with a piece of copper many times before they were allowed to work with silver. The working properties of copper are similar to those of silver, and in case of failure in initial trials, the loss of copper would be much less costly than that of silver.

To start the raising process the partially shaped disk was supported on a stake in an inverted position so that it could be struck on the outside. The very slightly rounded end of the stake supported the disk at the point where the raising procedure was to begin. By striking the metal with a raising hammer slightly in advance of the point on which it was supported, the metal was slowly contracted, the diameter reduced, and the sides raised. A skillful craftsman could raise the sides from a horizontal to a vertical position in about three or four "passes" over the outer surface of the metal.

Certain problems were encountered in the raising process. The object had to be kept perfectly round, an even thickness had to be maintained at all points and, when finished, the top had to be level.

The top edge could be kept reasonably level by careful workmanship and by striking any high point which developed with the hammer. This process was called "upsetting" in blacksmithing, but in silversmithing it was called "caulking." Sometimes caulking was deliberately done to increase the thickness of the metal at the top edge, thus making it more rigid and attractive. A certain amount of filing could also be done; however, this was a wasteful procedure and frowned upon by good craftsmen. The ridges created in the sides of the cup could be kept to a minimum by careful workmanship, thereby reducing the time required for planishing to make the surface smooth.

Regardless of the skill of the silversmith in the raising process, the sides had to be completely planished, and the bottom made smooth and flat on a bottoming stake. The angle between the sides and the bottom had to be carefully squared, but not hammered to force a slit in the metal or make it unusually thin at the point of intersection.

The bottom edge of the cup was often decorated by attaching an ornamented band of silver. This procedure also slightly increased the diameter of the base and made the object appear more stable. The band of silver

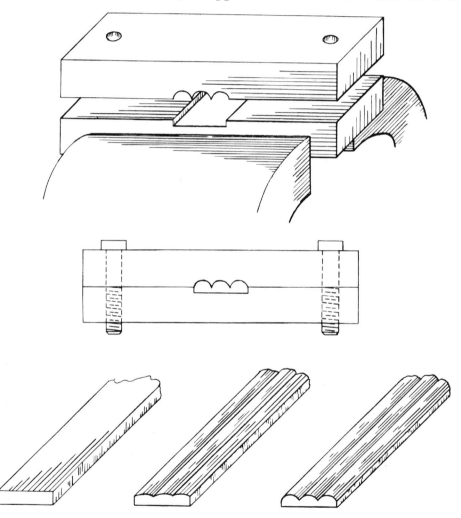

was ornamented by drawing it a number of times between two bars of steel, which were either bolted to the bench-top or pinched between the jaws of the vise. The bars were bolted together with a space between

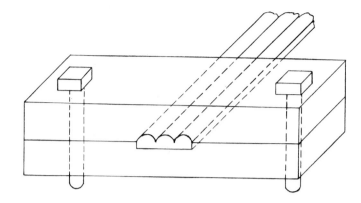

them of the size of the full band of silver. One bar was flat and the planned design was filled into the edge of the other. After each pass of the silver between the bars, they were drawn closer together until the full design was scraped into one side of the band.

Many cups had handles made of strips of silver, cut from reasonably thick slabs of metal. In cross-section they would have been square or rectangular. These strips were formed over suitably shaped stakes and soldered in place when the bottom band was applied to the cup.

Because considerable soldering was involved in the making of such articles as cups, mugs, and tankards, some consideration might be given to the procedure of soldering the various parts together. It is a general rule that solder should be easier to fuse than the metal intended to be soldered.

Simple and charming cup made by Benjamin Hiller of Boston late in the seventeenth century. The ornamented band on the bottom is not identical to the design in the directions, but was probably made by the same method. Height, $2\frac{15}{16}$ in.; diameter of top, $3\frac{1}{16}$ in.; diameter at base, $2\frac{5}{8}$ in. *Courtesy Henry Francis du Pont Winterthur Museum.*

This statement simply means that solder must have a lower melting point than the metals to be soldered. Solders preferably should have the same color as that of the metals to be joined, but this condition is rarely possible.

The most common solders are divided into two classes, hard and soft. The hard solders (used to solder silver), are ductile, will bear hammering without breaking, and are prepared partially of the metal which is to be soldered, with the addition of other metal by which a greater degree of fusibility is obtained. The hard solder for silver was composed of silver, copper, and zinc. It was sold to silversmiths in a granulated form, by the name of "spelter solder." Some silversmiths are thought to have made their own solder.

For successful soldering procedures the surface of the metals to be joined had to be clean and perfectly fitted together. The various parts were held together by soft iron binding wire. The cleaned surfaces were kept clean by applying a mixture of borax and water, borax being one of the items found in the inventories of silversmiths.

After all the preparations had been made, the object was held over a small, but very hot, forge fire until the solder flowed into the desired areas. Only minute amounts of solder were used, so that excesses did not have to be removed from conspicuous places; however, on obscure joints excessive quantities were often used and are still found.

If a beaker were really a large cup, it is very evident that the major difference in the production of the two objects was that a larger disk was needed to make the beaker. It might also be noted that, although some

cups flared noticeably outward at the top, this characteristic is almost universal in regard to beakers. The flaring shape made them attractive because of their increased height and increased the rigidity of the top edge.

A great number of beakers were made in a variety of styles over a long span of years. Over five hundred, identified as products of American

Pair of beakers of the early eighteenth century with reeded bands applied at their bases. Made by Moody Russel (1694-1761), working at Barnstable, Massachusetts. *Courtesy Metropolitan Museum of Art, The Sylmaris Collection, Gift of George Coe Graves, 1928.*

craftsmen, are found in New England churches. The largest group of Colonial beakers has a plain cylindrical body with a flaring lip, and a molded band applied to the base. Such a style was popular in the sixteenth and seventeenth centuries in Holland and England, and probably accounts for the wide use in America in the eighteenth century.

Possibly the next form to evolve in America was the inverted bell shape, which flared at the top but receded to a smaller diameter at the bottom, to which a variety of bases were attached. One made by John Coney, inscribed with the date 1715, is owned by the Old South Church, Boston. A similarly shaped one with two handles is owned by the Church of Christ at Norwich, Connecticut. An example of the inverted bell shape by John Dixwell (1680-1725) of Boston, is fluted about one third of its height from the bottom and is mounted on an attractive molded band, which serves as a base. Jeremiah Dummer made a similar one; however, his is a bit more decorative, for he chose to spiral his fluting.

Throughout the century a continuous array of forms and ornamentation was presented by the craftsmen of the country. The tall Dutch style,

Pair of beakers made by Myer Myers. The strips of silver on the bottom edge of the beakers was drawn in a manner similar to the process used in making the like part for the cup. Myers made many other attractive objects of silver, but photographs of them are not available. *Courtesy Henry Francis du Pont Winterthur Museum*

An example of an attractive beaker made
by Samuel Kirk about 1825. The Samuel
Kirk Company is the oldest manufacturer
of silver objects in America. *Courtesy Henry
Francis du Pont Winterthur Museum.*

often called trumpet shaped, remained popular; some of these were pro-
fusely engraved. Myer Myers (1723-1795) of New York made a pair
late in the century in a classical form with straight sides similar to the
form of contemporary teapots. The straight-sided form was produced
in the nineteenth century, one bearing the mark of Samuel Kirk (1793-
1872), of Baltimore. The flaring sides of his product are straight and
both the top and bottom are ornamented by applied moldings in the
style of the late eighteenth century.

The interrelationship between form and function in an object is often
evident, as it is in a caudle cup. This vessel was really a hybrid form between a cup and a bowl, and although it was used for drinking, the contents might have been logically served from a bowl.

Most definitions of "caudle" explain it as a gruel, mixed with ale,
sweetened and spiced. Although this combination of ingredients sounds
rather palatable to the taste of the mid-twentieth-century man, it seems
less attractive when he learns that gruel is defined as "a drink made of
grain broths, often consisting of oatmeal, or malt drinks not hopped." It
is reported to have relaxed the drinker and was popular at occasions such
as weddings, feasts, baptisms, and funerals.

An extremely simple but charming caudle cup made by John Dixwell about 1698. The handles were cast or cut from strips of heavy silver and soldered to the body. The facets left by the planishing hammer can be faintly seen. Dixwell's mark is tastefully stamped near the top of the left handle. *Courtesy Henry Francis du Pont Winterthur Museum.*

Caudle cups are low vessels possibly three to four inches deep with about the same diameter. Their contour resembles the shape of a gourd with a bulbous body and the top third portion cut away to provide an opening for the vessel. The ones with lids closely resemble the shape of a complete gourd.

The method of constructing a caudle cup was very similar to the techniques used in making cups and beakers, except that the raising was done on a stake with a rounded, rather than a sharp, end. The sides were raised and planished, and some examples are known which have no ornamentation; however, if a repoussé design such as fluting was desired, the metal had to be annealed and the contour expanded from the inside by using a tool called a "snarling iron."

This procedure was done by using a "nurling iron," so-called in the inventory of Richard Conyers, but now termed a "snarling iron." This tool was made of a tapered piece of steel about eighteen inches long, square at the large end (possibly ¾ in. x ¾ in.) and tapering to a diameter of about one-fourth inch at the small end. The round small end was given a slight radius and bent, projecting upward about three inches.

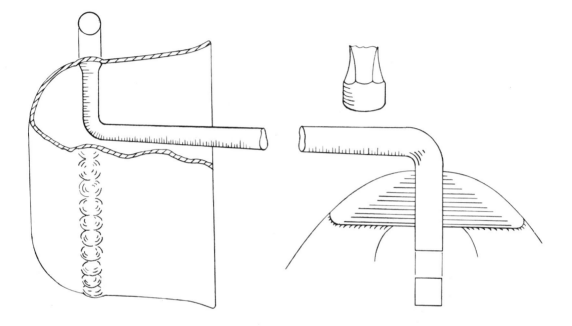

The square end was placed in a vise and the hollow vessel slipped over the opposite end, with only a very light pressure bearing it on the rounded end. By striking the bar in the top near the vise with a hammer, vibrations were created which simulated the effect of hammering the inner surface outward with a hammer but, of course, this area was so small it could not be reached with such a tool. A bulge of any desired shape and depth above the surface of the metal could be created by this procedure. The snarling iron was also used to increase the total diameter of such larger objects as teapots, when it could be more conveniently used than a hammer for such a purpose. The raised or repoussé area created by using the snarling iron was imprecise and, after sufficient height was obtained, the vessel was filled with pitch to give the surface of the metal some support, but also to permit a certain amount of resiliency. The repoussé design was then precisely defined on the outside of the vessel by using hammers, punches, and gravers; however, the total depth (similar

Caudle cup made by Jeremiah Dummer (1645-1718), Boston, Massachusetts. The cast handles were used also by two contemporaries of Dummer. The gadrooned pattern around the base was also popular at the time. *Courtesy Henry Francis du Pont Winterthur Museum.*

to bas-relief) was created from the inside. On some objects repoussé was sparingly used, while on others the entire surface seems to have been "worked." Repoussé work is usually associated with highly ornamented pieces, such as a Monteith bowl by John Coney, which John Marshall Phillips describes as "the most ambitious surviving piece by an American silversmith." *See page 97.*

Porringers and Bowls

Insofar as the function of an object, such as a teapot or a strainer, is evident from its shape and size, it is interesting to note that the identification of the role of one object of silver, namely, the porringer, has defied the ingenuity and imagination of historians for a long time.

The name, shape, and size of the vessel immediately suggests that it was used for serving porridge, or any other soft food appropriate for a child or an invalid. The use the child made of the porringer is still a matter of conjecture. The handle suggests he used it for drinking, but this hypothesis adds only another facet to be resolved in the mystery surrounding the object. The giving of porringers as gifts for children in modern times has perpetuated the idea that they are for the child's use. There does not seem to be any documented historical evidence for such a fact; at least, none has been found in this research into objects made of silver in the eighteenth century.

The flat bottom of the vessel suggests that it could be heated, possibly by a spirit lamp, but food was rarely cooked in silver vessels and drinks were heated by thrusting into them a hot poker of iron. It has been suggested that they might have been used for sugar before the advent of the covered sugar bowl, as were caudle cups and other low bowls.

The most bizarre theory is that surgeons carried a porringer in one pocket, and a lancet in another, both of which were used in the bleeding of patients. The lancet was used to puncture the blood vessel of the patient, and the porringer, pressed tightly against the body beneath the incision, caught the escaping blood. Bleeding was a common practice in Europe and America and, if a porringer were not used, some other vessel in general use was needed.

Regardless of their role, they are attractive objects, and few collectors

Silver porringer made by Jacobus van der Spiegel (1668-1708), of New York. This porringer has what might almost be called a standard bowl, for the shape of that portion changed very little throughout the time porringers were made. The delicate fret-work terminating in a heart-form is an attractive feature. *Courtesy Philadelphia Museum of Arts; photograph by A. J. Wyatt, staff photographer.*

of silver would regard their acquisitions complete without a few examples. As a matter of fact, they are so attractive that some collectors make a specialty of collecting them. They range in size from about four to six-and-a-half inches in diameter, with a corresponding variation in their depths. One of the largest extant is attributed to the great silversmith, John Coney, and many small ones can be seen in museums throughout the country. Very few have covers, although it is possible that many covers have been lost by owners who were indifferent to the value and importance of the treasures they possessed. Despite their size, shape, or function, they must have been useful vessels; one family inventory of the seventeenth century reported nine among their possessions.

The general shape of a porringer was that of a shallow open bowl with a flat base, slightly domed in the center. The sides closely approximated a half-circle with a narrow band flaring outward at the top. This band was an attractive feature; it could have served as a pouring lip, but its major purpose was probably to make the rim rigid for otherwise the edge would have been easy to bend. Although the shape of the porringer was pleasing, its greatest charm lay in the variety of handle forms. They will be discussed after the making of the bowl is detailed.

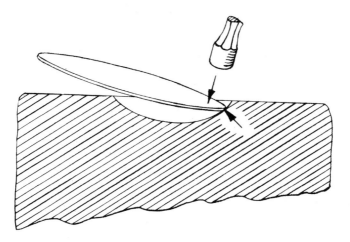

The porringer was made by the raising and/or stretching procedure, and thus the first step was to cut a disk of metal to the desired size. The band from the edge of the bottom to the edge of the disk was placed on the end grain of the tree trunk and slightly deepened by striking it with a hollowing hammer. When this process was finished, the object looked like a modern saucer.

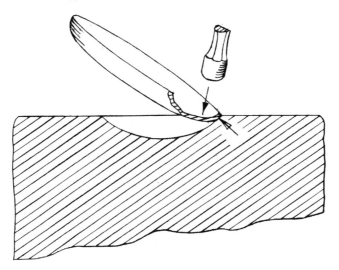

The problem of further deepening the bowl and reducing the diameter of the top was pursued as in the raising of a caudle cup, which the porringer closely resembled. The partially domed disk was then placed upside down on a stake and the sides raised, while the diameter of the top was simultaneously reduced.

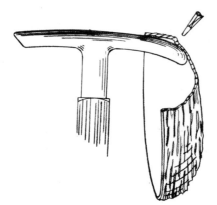

After the desired shape of the sides was obtained, the semicircular form was planished and made smooth.

Next, the narrow edge of the top of the rim was bent outward on the edge of a stake with a sharp corner, and the inner portion of the bottom was domed on the end grain of a block of wood or a piece of lead. All of this work slightly distorted the levelness of the remaining part of the bottom, and this was made flat by applying pressure from the top.

The handles of porringers, most of them having only one, are by all odds their most exciting feature. They vary in size according to the size of the porringer, and are usually made of one piece of silver, possibly one-sixteenth to one-eighth inch in thickness. They are soldered to the bowl near the top edge. Some are horizontal while others bend upwards slightly; however, the position of those which angle upward might be the result of long use.

Bottom view of a silver porringer showing the common shape of the bowl and the way the handle was "butted" against the bowl for soldering. The design of this handle could have been formed by the casting process; however, the very small openings in other handles were probably punched or sawed. *Courtesy Henry Francis du Pont Winterthur Museum.*

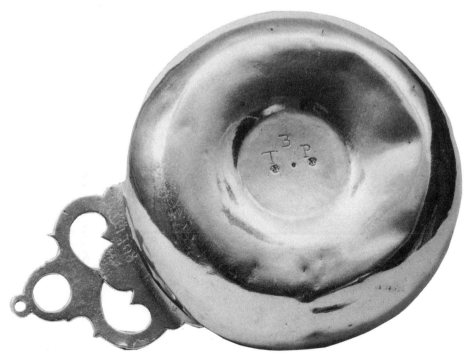

There is a great variety in the designs, the quality of which gives them their charm. In the center of the handle was usually left a solid panel, on which the initials of the owner were often engraved. Around the panel were placed designs of endless variety, consisting of circles, hearts, quatrefoils, half-hearts, half-moons, and the like, and a confusion of scrolls which defy description. In later porringers a feature known as a "keyhole" came into extensive use by a number of silversmiths. This opening was placed at the end of the handle away from the bowl, and resembled the opening in an escutcheon used to decorate key holes in furniture.

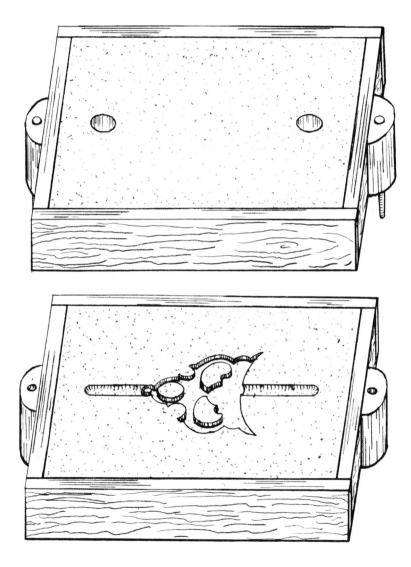

The designs in the handles were produced by a number of tools. The standard method for making holes, or openings, in sheet metal was with a punch, and this was doubtless a very popular one because, in addition to an opening, some form could be given to it by using a punch with an appropriate shape. It is evident that much filing and engraving was done after the openings were made, for punching was not a precision process and there was probably no more noticeable evidence of a slovenly silversmith than a poorly wrought handle on a porringer. It is also known that some were cast with the openings in them.

In casting a handle for a silver porringer a "pattern" of wood was first made which was a replica of the intended handle. This pattern was then placed in the middle between two boxes, called a "flask," which had neither tops nor bottoms. Sand was rammed tightly into them, enclosing the pattern, so the parts of the flask could be handled without the sand falling out.

Vertical openings were cut through the sand to the center of the flask, the two halves were separated, the pattern removed, and the flask reassembled. The thinness of the handle required that the sand be dried so the molten metal would not be unduly chilled as it flowed through its intended course. Molten metal was then poured into one of the vertical openings. It dropped to the center of the flask, filled the cavity created by the pattern, and rose in the second vertical opening.

After the handle cooled it was removed from the sand, the excess metal was removed, and the handle finished by filing and polishing.

The widest part of the handle was usually set against the bowl for aesthetic and practical reasons. A long stretch of metal joining the bowl

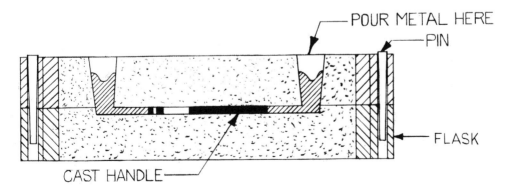

SECTION

made the juncture strong and rigid, which was important then, for planned obsolesence was not a common practice in those times. After the proper fit was achieved, the usual flux and hard solder was applied, followed by heating until the solder flowed throughout the joint. Finally, unwanted tool marks, such as those left by a file, were removed, the object was properly polished, and it was ready for a wealthy patron to step inside the door of the silversmith's shop.

Porringers with "key-hole" handles reached the zenith of their popularity about the middle of the eighteenth century; however, they continued to be made to the end of the century. The earlier examples had openings in the now solid center portion of the handle. These openings were a vestige of an earlier style made in America and England. This example was made by Richard Humphreys (c. 1722-1791) of Philadelphia. *Courtesy Philadelphia Museum of Art.*

Although the word "bowl" is in common usage today, a search into the references of the eighteenth century reveals that the word was not as generally applied to vessels then as it is now. The only definition found in a publication of the eighteenth century is in the *Encyclopedia: or, a Dictionary of Arts, Science and Miscellaneous Literature,* published by Thomas Dobson, Philadelphia, 1798. Curiously the definition there refers to the word first in its relation to a game by saying that, "BOWL, denotes either a ball of wood, for the use of bowling; or a vessel of capacity, wherein to hold liquors."

The definition in the *Oxford English Dictionary,* 1933, not only continues the confusion of the use of the sphere or spherically shaped object, but also the spelling of the word. It points out that as early as A.D. 1000 a Saxon word "bollan" was used to describe a vessel for holding water, and specifically points out that:

> The normal modern spelling would be BOLL which came down to the 17 c. in the sense of 'round vessel', and is still used in the sense of 'round seed-vessel'; but the early ME. pronounciation of -oll as owl (cf., roll, poll, toll, etc.) has left its effects in the modern sense of 'vessel' which is thus at once separated in form from other senses of its own (see BOLL sb^1), and confounded with BOWL sb^2 a ball, from the Fr. boulee.
>
> A (round) vessel to hold liquids, rather wide than deep; distinguished from a cup, which is rather deep than wide. Usually hemispherical or nearly so.

It is, of course, evident that a porringer is a bowl and thus might not have been given any singular consideration; however, its unique shape and mysterious uses suggested that such matters be emphasized. Other uses for bowls were for holding punch, sugar, sauces, posset, or for serving berries.

A discussion regarding the making of a low bowl might logically start with the techniques used to produce a vessel called a "shallow drinking bowl" in the collection of silver objects at the Henry Francis du Pont Winterthur Museum.

Because this bowl is round, the silversmith chose a disk of silver and started pounding it over the well-beaten trunk of a tree, heretofore frequently mentioned. Because the sides do not turn inward, and the object

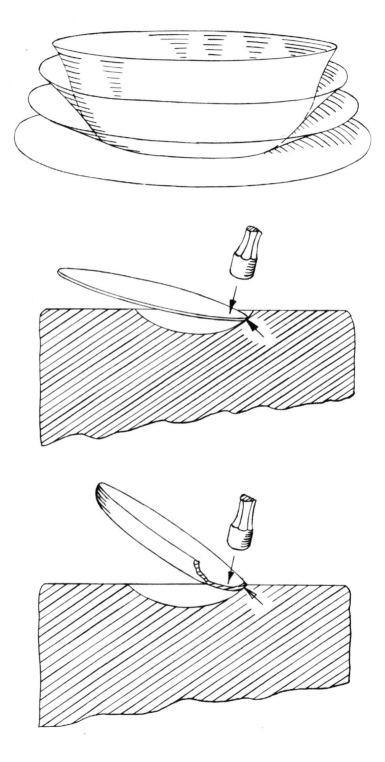

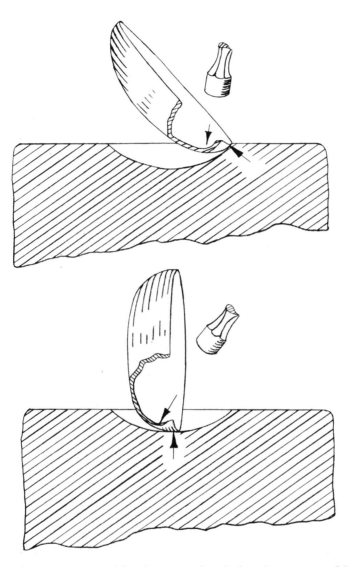

is not very deep, it is possible that much of the shaping could be done with a hollowing hammer on the tree trunk. The disk was struck with a hammer in concentric circles, starting at the outside and working inward to the edge of the bottom, which remained flat. After each complete "pass" of hammer blows from the outer edge inward, the disk was slightly changed so that the form was actually depressed through tensional stretching until the desired depth was obtained. This work distorted the surface of the metal; to restore it a planishing hammer was used.

Shallow drinking bowl believed to have been made by Henricus Boelen about 1690, in New York. The modest style of the decoration seems very well suited to the vessel to which it was applied. Height, $1\frac{9}{16}$ in.; diameter at top, $4\frac{5}{8}$ in. *Courtesy Henry Francis du Pont Winterthur Museum.*

The decoration of this particular bowl was done by a technique called chasing. The bowl was filled with pitch, and the desired design drawn on the outer surface of the metal. Then, with a chasing hammer and a wide variety of special chisels and punches, the design was slowly pounded below the surface of the bowl, but no metal was removed in this decorative process, and no areas were raised from the inside as was done in repoussé. One of the most common uses of this technique was in the decorating of lids for warming pans made of copper or brass. The design is almost as equally evident on the bottom as on the top of the lid; however, the detail is not as precise on the bottom. Generally speaking, this technique required less skill than other modes of decorating, such as engraving or repoussé.

The production of this bowl by John Coney probably required all the knowledge and techniques at the command of this very skilled silversmith. John Marshall Phillips, one of the outstanding connoisseurs of American silver in modern times, described this bowl as "the most ambitious surviving piece by an American silversmith." Coney was a master-craftsman and it is not surprising that he should have produced such a *chef-d'oeuvre. Courtesy Yale University Art Gallery, Mabel Brady Garvan Collection*

It is likely that most silversmiths chased their own products, but the following advertisement from the *Pennsylvania* (Philadelphia) *Packet*, July 13, 1772, indicates that at least one man was a professional chaser.

JOHN ANTHONY BEAU

A celebrated Chaser, in Fourth street, opposite the new Lutheran Church, being lately arrived in this city from Geneva, Takes this method to recommend himself to the favour of all the Public, and acquaints them that he performs all sorts of chasing work in gold, silver, and other metals, such as watch cases, coffee and tea pots, sugar boxes, cream pots, tea., in the gentlest and newest taste. All persons who will honour him with their employment in any such work, may be assured that he will use his utmost endeavours to give them universal satisfaction. He likewise offers his services to teach ladies drawing, and to give them the best principles to learn very soon, let it be figures, ornaments, flowers, or designs for embroidering, etc., all at reasonable prices, and such hours as best suits the scholars.

Most low bowls have two handles mounted opposite each other. Some were made of several strands of wire twisted together, others were made of strips or squares of silver, and some craftsmen twisted the squares to give an effect of roundness, which was decorative and comfortable to hold. A few examples have handles that were cast. They were shaped in a variety of forms and attached by using the customary "silver solder."

There were, of course, an endless variety of bowls made of silver, for many uses. Many of them are usually referred to as punch bowls, particularly the larger ones which might have been logically used for such a purpose. Some were simply hemispherical in shape with a molded top edge and a heavy molded foot such as one made by Myer Myers. Others, such as the famous Sons of Liberty bowl by Paul Revere, Jr., have a very subtle reverse curve in their side contour without a molded edge at the top, but a very substantial molded base. The zenith of American silversmithing in the eyes of John Marshall Phillips was reached in a Monteith bowl by John Coney.

These bowls were designed with concave scallops around the top edge presumably named for a fanatical Scot, Monsieur Monteith, who wore a cloak with similar notches in the bottom edge. The notches reputedly served to hold the bases of wine glasses which dipped inward into cold

E.R.A.

Silver "slop bowl" of the Federal period made by Samuel Williamson who worked in Philadelphia from 1794 until 1813. The mirror-like finish indicates that he was an expert planisher, and the beaded edges are a Philadelphia "bench-mark." *Courtesy Philadelphia Museum of Art; photograph by A. J. Wyatt, staff photographer*

water or ice, preliminary to using them for drinking. The highly ornamented top edge was often constructed so that it could be removed and thus a plain-topped bowl for other purposes became available.

Mugs and Tankards

Of all the terms applied to vessels used for drinking, the word "tankard" is probably more loosely used than any other. This situation arises from the fact that a tankard is a vessel with prestige; the common and unwarranted use of the word in the market place suggests that the merchant is attempting to assign qualities to vessels which in reality they do not possess. The license for such indiscriminate use arises from the fact that references of the eighteenth century rarely define the words "mug" and "tankard," and those which do are imprecise about significant and distinguishing details. The distinction is clearly pointed out in *Zell's Popular Encyclopedia*, Philadelphia, 1871, which states that a tankard is "a large vessel for the reception of liquors; also a drinking mug with a cover, as a tankard of London porter." The clue to the difference is that the tankard has a *cover*. This definition does not imply that no other similar vessels have covers, for flagons do, but they are not regarded as being vessels for drinking and they usually have a larger capacity than that of a tankard.

The difference between a mug and a tankard seems unimportant to the uninitiated, for they both were used for drinking, and, it is important to note, similar techniques were used to make the bodies of the two.

To make a mug with straight flaring sides, the silversmith started with a disk of annealed silver and hollowed the form over a tree trunk, as previously explained. He then turned the disk upside down and began raising the sides, simultaneously reducing the diameter of the disk toward the top. Thus far the analogy parallels the making of a cup or beaker.

One would expect that the craftsman continued to reduce the diameter of the mug toward the top until the final desired diameter of the mug was achieved. If this procedure were followed, the mug, like the cup,

100

would have been made of one solid piece of metal. However, in none of the mugs examined by the writer was such a procedure followed.

The sides were raised until the diameter of the top of the workpiece was the intended diameter of the base of the mug. The shape flared outward toward the top. At this point the bottom of the piece was removed and, because it retained its original thickness, it was thick enough to be stretched and provide a bottom for the large end. In the meantime, the

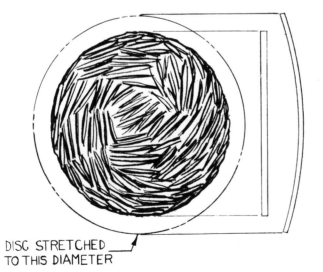

DISC STRETCHED
TO THIS DIAMETER

shell was inverted so that the small end was at the top and the large diameter at the bottom. After the disk was stretched, it was bowed inward and soldered into the bottom of the mug. The bottom was raised a bit from the very bottom of the shell so that it did not touch the table top when it rested in its natural position.

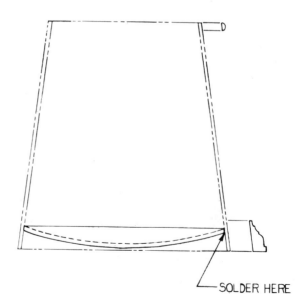

SOLDER HERE

The top edge of the mug could be made thicker and more rigid by
caulking, or it could be reinforced by applying a molding, produced in
a manner similar to the one used to create the band for the bottom of
the cup or by a swage. A heavier molding was made and applied to the
bottom edge of the mug. Both moldings were attached by the use of
hard solder, which provided virtually a permanent joint between all parts.

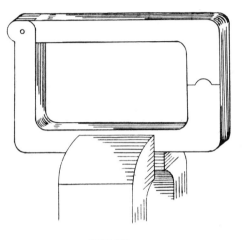

SWAGE

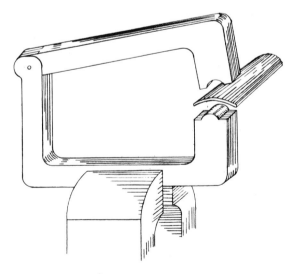

SWAGE

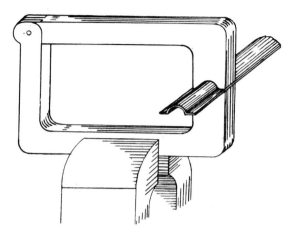

The handles of mugs throughout the seventeenth and early eighteenth centuries were strips (or straps) of silver, similar to those used on cups, except that they were wider and thicker because a mug was a bigger vessel. They were cut from heavy pieces of silver and shaped for a comfortable grip.

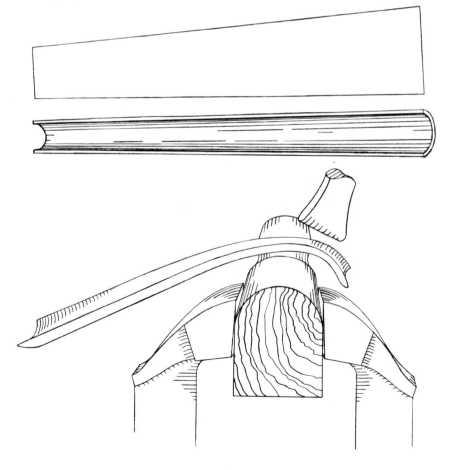

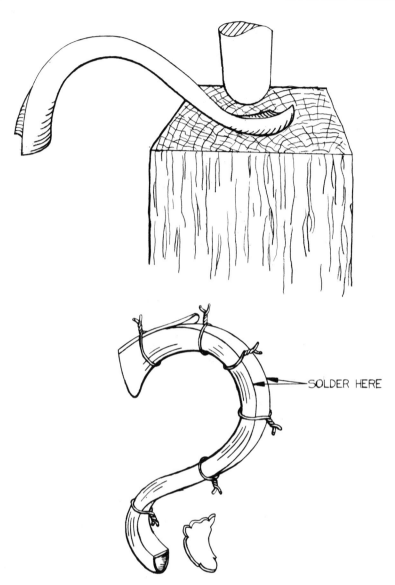

SOLDER HERE

As the amenities of life improved in the eighteenth century, changes were reflected in the objects made, particularly those of silver, for their status reflected that of the affluent society. The flat band continued to be used, but underneath it a half-round band was attached to increase the cross-sectional size of the handle and make it more comfortable to hold. This procedure more than doubled the quantity of silver needed, and greatly increased the cost, for the fabrication of such a handle re-

Silver straight-sided mug made by Francis Richardson, working in Philadelphia in the first half of the eighteenth century. The style of this mug is typical of the period and doubtless pleased the Quaker taste for simplicity. *Courtesy Henry Francis du Pont Winterthur Museum.*

quired much time. The top end of the handle lay flush against the side of the mug, but the bottom flared away and terminated in a fancy form created by the addition of a small plate, attractively shaped. Later, a band encircled the mug, dividing the side into two sections, the bottom a bit shorter than the top. Cyphers and other decorative motifs were engraved on the sides.

The image of silver tankards is unique among objects made of this metal, for, as a group, they are probably the most desirable to own. It must be pointed out, however, that several other single pieces surpass any tankard in prestige. Among these objects, well known today, is the bowl made by Paul Revere for his fifteen fellow members of the Sons of Liberty. This bowl was made on the eve of the Revolution and is inscribed (engraved) with appropriate sentiments, as well as the names of the members. Another object rich in its historical association is the inkstand made by Philip Syng, Jr., in 1752 for the assembly of Pennsylvania. Its significance arises from the fact that it was used by the signers of the Declaration of Independence and of the Constitution. Although it is not an extravagant masterpiece of workmanship, it is difficult for the imagination to conceive a more important use for an object of any metal by any American craftsman.

A fitting introduction to the tankard of the late seventeenth and early eighteenth century might be an excerpt from *American Silver* by John Marshall Phillips:

> The most popular drinking vessel, judging from inventories in an age "potent in potting," was the cider or ale tankard, with its straight tapering body reenforced by a moulded base and rim, a low flat cover, raised by a horizontal ram's horn, or cupped thumbpiece, and a massive scroll handle terminating in a shield. . . .
>
> The usual capacity was a quart but two larger examples are known, one by Jeremiah Dummer, the other by his master, Robert Sanderson, fashioned for Isaac and Mary Vergoose. [One is known to have been made by Benjamin Hiller of full gallon capacity.]

Close attention to details of shape and construction reveals that the body portions of tankards and mugs with straight sides were very similar in the early eighteenth century. Both were similarly raised from a disk of metal with the sides flaring outward, after which the bottom was removed. Because it retained its original thickness, the bottom could be stretched until it was large enough to cover the wide end of the flaring cylinder, it having been inverted in both cases. Both had reinforcing bands applied at the top and bottom edges, but the tankard was supplied with a lid and a thumbpiece, while the mug was not.

Throughout most of the first half of the century, the lids of tankards were low with flat tops. They were formed by using a disk of silver with the same diameter as that of the intended final dimension of the lid. The

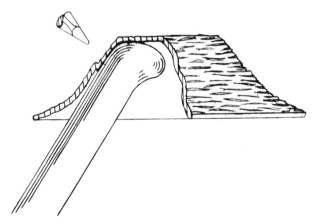

inner portion of the lid was deepened over the edge of a piece of hard wood with a sinking or hollowing hammer, in a manner similar to that employed in the making of a plate. A reasonably wide, flat edge was retained, as in the plate, and the bulge, or booge, was planished to make it smooth and uniform in roundness. Usually, a small offset was created at the bottom of the bulge, which gave the lid a finished appearance. The embryonic lid was then turned upside down when placed on the tankard, with a portion of the flat edge overhanging the sides of the vessel. A crenelated design was sometimes cut into the edge of the lid at the front, to further enhance its elegance.

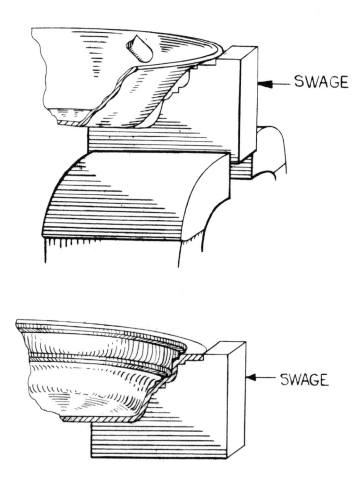

Swage used in making a dome-shaped lid for a tulip-shaped tankard. *See page 112.*

After the lid was formed, it was placed over the opening in the top of the vessel, and preparations were made for attaching the two together. A thumbpiece was made by casting a design in sand or cuttlebone, and a hinge strap was formed by casting or hammering a piece of heavy silver into the desired shape. It should be noted that although both these parts served an important function as parts of the tankard, they were equally important for the decorative touch they added to the vessel. Knuckles forming a hinge were fashioned in one end of each of these parts, with a pin running through them, so that the various parts could be disengaged, if necessary. The joints in the hinge had to be meticulously filed and fitted, so that smooth and unrestricted action between the lid and the body was possible. (There should be no reason to create frustrated drinkers.) If a presumably old piece does not show normal wear on the hinge knuckles, certain doubts could arise concerning its authenticity or its age. (It seems rather evident that our ancestors were frequent drinkers.) A long, tapering body drop was often attached to the bottom of the handle, to enrich the design and make attachment to the body more secure.

Possibly one of the final operations in the making of the handle assembly was to file the bottom end of the handle to accept the desired fitting. The designs of these finials varied with each maker; however, such shapes as shields and cherubs' heads were popular with many craftsmen. Obviously, some finials were very simply made, while others were masterpieces of the craftsman's art. The last act before soldering was to cut or file a hole in the very bottom of the scroll end of the handle, to allow the heated and expanding air to escape; otherwise, it was virtually impossible to make a perfect soldered joint between the handle and the body of the tankard.

Soldering the handle and the thumbpiece to the tankard was done in separate operations. The thumbpiece was attached to the lid, and the handle was secured to the body at two points. If every procedure went according to plan, a pin was then forced through the knuckles of the hinge, and the tankard was ready for final polishing and the market place.

The description of this straight-sided, flat-topped, low tankard should not lead the reader to conclude that only such types were made in the eighteenth century. Although the techniques of the silversmith permitted a very quick response to changes in style, unlike the pewterer who had invested in expensive molds which he was loathe to discard, it is very evident that traditional styles in silver lingered on, usually with several transitional changes, until a clearly new design evolved. For example, in 1768 Paul Revere continued to make straight-sided tankards, although they were taller and thinner than those of the early style, and had a domed lid usually associated with a later style in tankards. A flame-like finial was mounted on top of the lid and a molding encircled the body, a feature rarely found on the early tankard.

Nor must one suppose that all those of the early type were plain and unornamented. In the collection of the Henry Francis du Pont Winterthur Museum is a tankard with a hinge strap in the design of a lion's head; a cherub's head graces the bottom end of the handle, and a cut-leaf border surrounds its base. This example was made by Jacob Boelen (1657-1729) of New York for Everett and Engeletie Wendell of Albany, who were married in 1710. Their initials are engraved in block letters on the handle in the traditional pattern of a triangle, with the W at the

Straight-sided tankard made by Jacob Boelen of New York, probably early in the eighteenth century. The cocoon-shaped thumbpiece, the cast decorations, and the cut-leaf border design are typical features of early tankards made in New York. Height, 7 1/8 in; diameter at base, 5 3/8 in.; diameter at top, 4 3/4 in. *Courtesy Henry Francis du Pont Winterthur Museum.*

Tankards showing a variety in body shape and size, as well as in the appendages, such as handles, lids, thumbpieces, bases, and handle endings. The largest tankard was made by Benjamin Hiller of Boston late in the seventeenth century, and is a full gallon capacity; height, 10⅜ in. The smallest example was made by Elias Pelletreau (1726-1810) of New York. The pear-shaped (tulip-shaped) one was made by Phillip Syng, Jr., of Philadelphia, (1703-1789). *Courtesy Henry Francis du Pont Winterthur Museum*

Tulip-shaped tankard made by Philip Syng, Jr., of Philadelphia about 1750. Although this piece might be described as elegant, there is evidence of the Quaker taste for simplicity to be found in it. *Courtesy Philadelphia Museum of Art*

top, under which are placed the two E's. In addition to engraving, the techniques of chasing and repoussé were sparingly used to decorate tankards throughout the eighteenth century in America.

Possibly the most extravagant form of ornamentation used on tankards in the early part of the century was a technique previously called "cut-leaf," but usually referred to as "cut-card." The presence of such work

The Gift of Mary Bartlett Widow of Eph.ᵐ Bartlt. to the third Church in Brookfield. 1768

Tankards made by Paul Revere for the Brookfield Church. The inscription confirms the donor and the date. This is the only entry for six tankards recorded in the existing account books of Paul Revere. *Courtesy Henry Francis du Pont Winterthur Museum*

on tankards made in New York can be easily explained by the fact that it was a very popular form of decoration in Holland in earlier times. It could have come to America directly from Holland, or possibly via England, where it was also favored among silversmiths in the second half of the seventeenth century.

The term "cut-card" arises from the fact that the decoration appears to be a series of cutouts, like small cards, which were usually applied above the band encircling the bottoms of tankards and beakers. Later, the designs were cut into the edge of a strip of metal, instead of on separate pieces.

The strip was easier to manage in the soldering operation, particularly because interstices had to be clean and uncluttered with excess solder. If surplus solder did manage to fill joints inadvertently, of course, the deft hand of the silversmith could remove it with a graver.

Additions, such as veins and linear designs, could be added to the outside contour to enrich the effect, and, if the whole work were cleverly done, it sometimes appeared as if another technique were used, such as repoussé. The tolerant attitude of the British toward the fine Dutch craftsmanship in New York permitted the craftsmen to continue their traditional techniques after the British took over the city in 1665.

Although the straight-sided, flat-topped tankard is highly prized by collectors today, the fastidious and affluent patrons of the mid-eighteenth century probably learned of a new style of tankard. This new style is discussed in *Historic Silver of the Colonies and Its Makers*, by Francis Bigelow, who describes it as it was about to invade America:

> In the middle of the eighteenth century the tankard with a "bellied" or bulbous body, a domed cover, and a high moulded foot, with and without a moulding encircling the body, came into vogue in England, and its popularity was the greatest in the third quarter of the century. Today this form is frequently described as pear or tulip-shaped.

Any observer who has given serious consideration to the evolution of styles in any media would know that the bulbous-bodied tankard did not appear "overnight." Nor was the transition in style confined to tankards, or to any field of the decorative arts. The early flat-topped tankard was compatible with the furnishings of medieval times, which lingered long with the aristocracy of England, and subsequently were popular in America when the country was first settled. Although the image of the colonist is usually one of poverty, inventories of estates of the seventeenth century reveal substantial accumulations of silverplate. Naturally, the first tankards made here were replicas of those the silversmiths saw about them, sides flared outward, in the style to which the patron was accustomed. Unlike today, the potential buyer of a tankard probably did not urge the silversmith to create a form which was new and different from the status quo. The evolution was slow, but the flat top was eventually discarded for a domed one, bands of molding encircled the bodies, and decorative motifs were more widely used. Finally, a style was evolved that was light in appearance, graceful in line, and completely compatible with the walnut and mahogany furnishings in the style of Queen Anne and the Georges.

Despite the grace and beauty of the tankard with a bulbous-shaped body, not many were made in America. This curious situation could not be attributed to the inadequacy of the silversmith, for most of them were very highly skilled men. Few new tools or processes were involved in their making, and the prestige of the latest English styles seems to have been evident at that time in all the furnishings of the house.

Craftsmen had been making straight-sided tankards with domed lids, there was no drastic change in the style of the handle, and the body was not greatly different from those being made for caudle cups. The technique for making the base was essentially the same as the one used for the lid; however, some adaptation had to be made to fit the part to the flat bottom of the body.

Shaping the body was started by placing the disk of metal over the well-beaten tree stump, where hammer blows were applied concentrically from the outer edge to the edge of the bottom, which remained flat. It has been pointed out that this type of tensional stretching had limitations, although considerable depth could be achieved before the craftsman had to move his work to the outside of the vessel. With a raising hammer and appropriate stakes, he simultaneously reduced the diameter of the disk and raised the side to the desired depth. This work is done by compressional stretching, which is a very versatile technique by which the shaping of the metal can be minutely controlled. Finally, the whole body had to be planished to remove the distortions created by the raising

process, and the top edge was caulked (made thicker than the body by beating it with a hammer). The increased thickness made the edge more rigid, and gave the craftsman an opportunity to create a design there which merged the body and the lid into one attractive design unit.

To make the base, the craftsman again laid the disk of metal on the tree trunk and created a dish-shaped object with a flat bottom. Then he inverted the piece and brought it as close as possible to the desired shape and size by raising it over a round stake with a radius on the end.

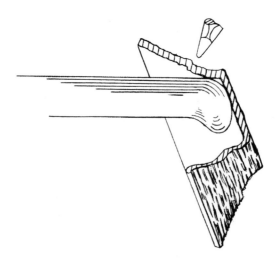

It is obvious that now the base was roughly shaped but lacked the ogee design which is the major design element in such bases. To produce this feature, the silversmith used a tool called a swage. This implement

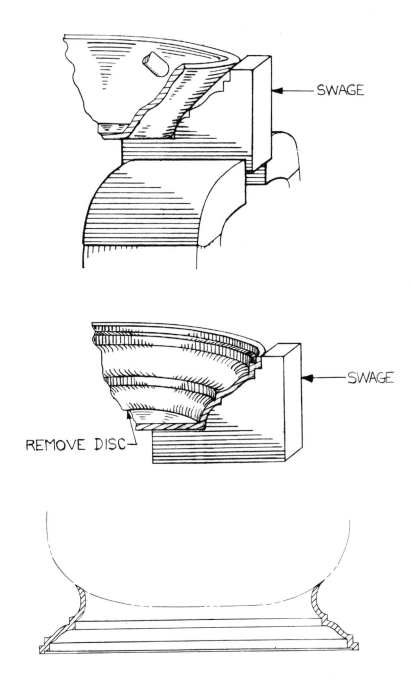

was made of iron or steel plate, possibly three eighths of an inch thick, into which the profile of the desired shape was filed. It was pinched tightly in a vise and, as the disk was rotated over its edge, the silver was slowly beaten with hammers and punches until the finished product was formed. Swages were very common tools in the eighteenth century, being used by craftsmen in other metal trades as well. Finally, the flat bottom was removed, the upper portion of the form turned outward, and fitted to the bottom of the tankard and soldered in place.

Teapots and Coffeepots

The evolution in the style and the size of the teapot was greatly influenced by the social customs prevailing in the various countries in which hot tea was consumed. Because the social conventions and technological processes in most areas of early America came almost exclusively from England, one must explore the early use of tea in that country. It is known that the English custom of tea-drinking began in the second quarter of the seventeenth century. At that time its price was exorbitant, being six to ten pounds for sixteen ounces, and it was used mostly for medicinal purposes. As it became cheaper, its magic influence on the health of the drinker probably diminished, in spite of which the great English custom of drinking tea became widespread. Samuel Pepys records in his diary of 1660 that he sent out for a cup of tea, "a China drink of which I had never drunk before."

It is easy to understand that in the beginning, because of its limited use, no special vessel existed for dispensing it, and those extant at that time were interchangeably used, as reported by Francis Bigelow in *Historic Silver of the Colonies and Its Makers*:

> At first apparently no difference in size was made in the English teapot, coffee pot, and chocolate pot; but after several years the teapot was made lower than the coffee pot and chocolate pot and in later years broader. In the late nineteenth century teapots were made in many different shapes.

The earliest form to become popular in America was influenced by a contemporary style in England, a pear-shaped vessel in the style of Queen Anne. At least one such pot, which was made by John Coney of Boston (1655-1722), has survived.

American silver teapot, early eighteenth century, by John Coney. Engraved with arms of Jean Paul Mascarine. Height, 7⅛ in. *Courtesy Metropolitan Museum of Art. Bequest of A. T. Clearwater, 1933.*

Although this pear-shaped style became a very sophisticated form later in the eighteenth century, the one made by Coney was obviously an embryonic type, well wrought but not particularly pleasing from an aesthetic point of view. There is a crude relationship between the different parts of the body, which had no ornamentation except for the coat-of-arms of one of the owners engraved on the side. The spout is small and tight against the body, the handle is large with only a thumbpiece protruding from its semicircular contour, the base is small and barely evident, and the knob on the lid does no more than conform to the over-all simple pattern of the piece. The hinge is very small and close to the lip of the pot, and was designed only for function without adding to the intended design of the pot. The only part that seems to have been specifically ornamented is the spout, which is in the form of a gooseneck. In spite of these deficiencies, this style of pot is compatible with that of contemporary tankards and is very attractive in the eyes of many connoisseurs.

The shape of the body is very similar to that of some caudle cups and both were probably made in a similar manner. A disk of metal was placed on the end of a tree stump and struck with a hollowing hammer until a saucerlike contour was obtained. It was then inverted and placed on a

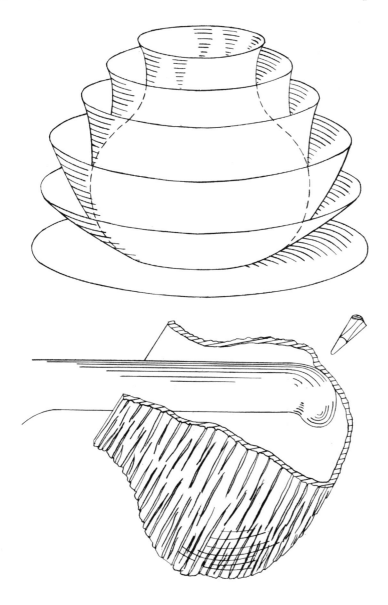

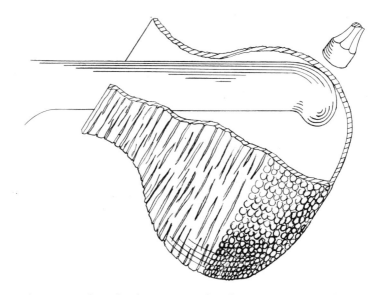

stake with a round end, the outer edge being contracted with a raising (cross-peen) hammer until the desired depth was achieved, as well as the desired diameter of the opening of the vessel. The edge was caulked to increase its thickness and provide adequate metal for forming the lip of the pot. The lid was made in a similar way; however, the knob was shaped by "turning" it on a lathe. It is probable that a man as experienced and well equipped as Coney owned a lathe; however, because it was a facility little needed by a silversmith, most other craftsmen had their turnings made by a professional "turner." One of these was Thomas Gregory, who placed the following advertisement in the *Pennsylvania* (Philadelphia) *Gazette,* on May 3, 1753.

THOMAS GREGORY

In Third-street, Philadelphia, opposite Church-alley and near Market-street, Makes and sells all sorts of brass work suitable for mills, heads for dogs, brass dogs, shovels and tongs, candlesticks of all sorts, chaise and chair furniture, gun furniture of all sorts, spoon moulds, shoe buckles, bell metal skillets and kettles, house and horse bells, and a variety of other, things too tedious to mention, at the most reasonable rates.

N.B. The said Gregory turns all sorts of iron, brass, pewter and silver; likewise gives the best price for old brass, and mends all sorts of brass work.

The handle was made of wood because of its low conductivity of heat; then, too, its rich dark texture made a pleasing contrast with the bright luster of the silver. It was almost semicircular in shape, and was attached to the pot by tenons which were inserted into two flaring cylinders. Pins, crosswise in each cylinder, held the handle of wood firmly in place. The outer ends of the cylinders were banded to make them attractive, to make them rigid, and to create a pleasing transition from the metal to the wood.

The technique used in making the spout is somewhat shrouded in mystery; however, it could have been made by one of three methods. It could have been cast in halves, and this was entirely possible, for andirons and candlesticks of brass were made by this method throughout the

Globular teapot made by Jacob Hurd of Boston about 1750. Wood is used in the knob and for the handle because of its nonconductivity of heat. The spout is mounted very high on the pot, but as a whole this example is attractive. This style has a great deal of prestige, for a portrait of Paul Revere by John Copley shows the craftsman holding such a pot. *Courtesy Henry Francis du Pont Winterthur Museum*

eighteenth century. Or each half could have been pounded in a swage of iron, thus requiring two swages to make the two halves of the spout. Or it could have been made from a sheet of silver, cut to a prescribed flat pattern and shaped into a cylinder with bends at the top and bottom.

To make a swage a pattern of the spout first had to be made of wood, with provision to separate it into halves through the middle. By using each half separately, a cavity was formed in iron in the reverse of the exterior of the pattern. A piece of silver, larger than the cavity, was laid over it and beat down until the general outline of the form was achieved. Next, a heavy sheet of lead was laid over the silver and struck with a hammer until the silver was forced into the small contours without cracking the metal on the high ridges. This method gave an almost finished surface to the exterior of the spout; however, the outer interstices had to be made sharp and clean with files and gravers after the silver was removed from the swage. The edges of the joint between the halves were fitted perfectly, and the two halves were then soldered together. The solder used for this operation had a reasonably high melting point, so that the joint did not "open" when the spout was soldered to the pot.

A flat circular band of silver, possibly three eighths of an inch wide, was fitted to the bottom and soldered in place to keep the pot in an upright position. This very simple base was compatible with the design of the pot and enhanced its aesthetic quality. After all the parts were attached, the pot was polished with pumice to remove scratches and evidences of fabrication, and finally rottenstone was used to give the metal its maximum luster.

Although the teapot by Coney has unmistakable charm, it is very evident that its lack of ornamentation and stubby form were somewhat incompatible with the light and elegant house furnishings of the later portion of the eighteenth century. There is evidence in a similar pot made by I. Ten Eyck, of New York, that an inevitable progression in style was occurring. His domed cover had a molded band, while the body had an incised band at the point where the exterior form changed from convex to concave. The gooseneck spout extended farther from the body and terminated at the top in a form described as a "snake's head." The hinge connecting the lid with the body was placed a greater distance from the body than on the Coney pot, with the result that it now became a prominent decorative and functional part of the pot. Wood was used, not only for the handle, but also in the knob of the lid, where its quality

Teapot in the Queen Anne style made by Daniel Christian Fueter, New York, about 1760. The body was shaped from a disk, starting on the end grain of a tree stump and then raising it over a stake. It was brought to its final shape by careful planishing, the marks often being more evident on the inside surface than on the outside. The case and the lid were both started on a tree stump but the final detailed finish and form was achieved by hammering, using a swage. Height, 7¾ in. *Courtesy Henry Francis du Pont Winterthur Museum*

of not conducting heat must have been appreciated by all who used the vessel. Ten Eyck did retain the simple base used by Coney, but it, too, finally lost status, and a molded base similar to the one used on tankards with a bulbous-shaped body came into popular fashion.

It is interesting to note that globular-shaped teapots were also made in America. These really needed molded bases to enhance what was otherwise an unattractive form. Little imagination was required to envision the molded base of the globular teapot on the pear-shaped one, and a number of silversmiths produced such vessels with what might be called a "stunning" result.

The form of the pear-shaped teapot, like most of the other forms of the period, became quite refined and made by the same methods of other objects about the middle of the eighteenth century. There was a marked difference in the diameter of various parts of the body of the pot, the molding around the lid was made more pronounced, the cross-section shape of the spout was sometimes paneled instead of being elliptical or round, and the molded base was added. The spout continued to be mounted low, as it should have been but was not always on the globular form, and the entire pot could be described as an harmonious and attractive creation in silver. It might be pointed out that the form rarely was ornamented in the rococo style so widely used on other vessels in the third quarter of the eighteenth century.

There was virtually no change in the techniques used to produce such pots from the making of the tulip-shaped tankard. An old exercise was adapted for the making of the molded base, which is explained in the survey relating to the manufacturing ("making by hand") of tankards.

By mid-century some containers were being made for sugar and cream, but the tea set *per se* did not appear on a grand scale until the final quarter of the period, which was dominated by the making of objects from sheet silver, and is generally called the "Classical Period." This was the era when the Revere star neared its zenith, but to many critics the craft of silversmithing began to lose the luster it had achieved at mid-century.

At this point in the discussion of the materials, tools, techniques, and products of the silversmith, it must be recognized that there were constants and variables in the trade throughout the eighteenth century. For example, there was no change in the metal and very little in the tools, but there certainly were innovations in the style of the product and in methods of production. Before proceeding with some of the fundamental changes, most of which occurred in the second half of the century, it should be noted that, as a whole, the eighteenth century might be regarded as the "Golden Era" of silversmithing in America. In most cases the workmanship was superior, the objects were exquisitely wrought, and the designs were modest and aesthetically pleasing.

There were, however, inevitable forces that changed many facets of the trade. An expanding and more affluent population created a demand for more products of all kinds. Improved means of transportation and technological advances provided facilities for increasing production, but in the eyes of most connoisseurs the quality of the product was not improved. This diminishing quality can be attributed to a number of circumstances, but the fact that the product more rarely became the work of one man, laboring at his bench from sunrise to sunset, seems to have been responsible for some of the deterioration.

Although the pounding of a tankard or a teapot from one piece of metal was a procedure demanding skill and patience, the demand for these products seems to have been met and a reasonably adequate supply of objects was available for those who could afford to buy them in earlier times. It might be pointed out that the rewards for competent craftsmanship were rather high, and many craftsmen became fairly wealthy, holding positions of importance in their respective communities, as well as in the nation.

The most significant factor that brought basic changes to the trade was the introduction of rolled sheet silver, and the developments which arose from this innovation. The silversmiths no longer had to cast and pound his coins into sheets of suitable shape and thickness for the object he proposed to make; he could buy his sheet metal from a merchant, or a fellow craftsman who had the facilities for rolling sheet. (The high cost and infrequent use of rolling equipment did not warrant such a purchase by every silversmith.)

The following advertisement from the *Pennsylvania* (Philadelphia) *Packet*, October 23, 1789, focuses attention on the movement of events mentioned above. The contents of the advertisement indicate that, although some of the older tools continued to be in demand, a new era had arrived.

> The American Bullion and Refining Office, No. 1, Carter's alley, Second street,
>
> Is just opened for the purchase of old gold, silver, copper, brass, pewter and lead: the utmost value will be given for each of these articles; and as soon as a sufficient quantity can be collected, the refining will commence; also, the button, buckle, and plate manufactory when artists bred to any of these branches will receive liberal encouragement, and may be supplied with fine gold, silver, and flat-

ted metals. Wanted, the following tools and utensils; forging and raising hammers, triblets and beck irons; polishing wheels, collars and mandrels; ingots and skillets; a piercing press, a small anvil and spoon taste; moulds and screws; large and small weights, scales and vises; draw bench and plates; a large iron mortar and pestle. Persons having such articles, new or old, will receive a fair price, by applying as above.

Philadelphia, October 12.

To an observer of current and past events, it must be evident that the problems created by the easy availability of sheet silver were numerous and difficult to resolve. Silversmiths who were trained in the traditional way of making a silver vessel by raising it from a disk must have been very loathe to accept a procedure which looked like a "short cut," namely, the creation of a form with a joint from top to bottom. It is probable that the change was very welcome to those with more liberal views and a keener eye for favorable bank balances. One certainty of the situation is that on October 23, 1789, a refining office in Philadelphia advertised that craftsmen could "be supplied with fine gold, silver and flatted metals."

It is difficult for a person inexperienced in the making of metal objects to appreciate the catastrophic change this new method of fabricating brought to the trade. The workman no longer hammered and annealed for endless hours to obtain a flaring cylinder, for now by a method of drafting he could draw the shape, cut out the pattern, form the metal, and solder the joint in a small fraction of the time consumed to obtain the same result by the raising method.

A paragraph from *American Silver of the XVII & XVIII Centuries* by C. Louise Avery accurately describes the course of events and styles at that time. She tells that:

> The teapots by Revere and Schanck illustrate a style popular in England in the last quarter of the eighteenth century and much copied by contemporary American silversmiths. Sheet silver was rolled thin and shaped into oval, octagonal, or waved outline. The sides, of course, were vertical and the base flat. In the eighteenth century examples the spout is usually straight, the lid low and slightly domed. The contemporary scheme of decoration by bright-cut engraving was eminently suited to these formal but dainty shapes. The teapot was often accompanied by a stand on four feet.

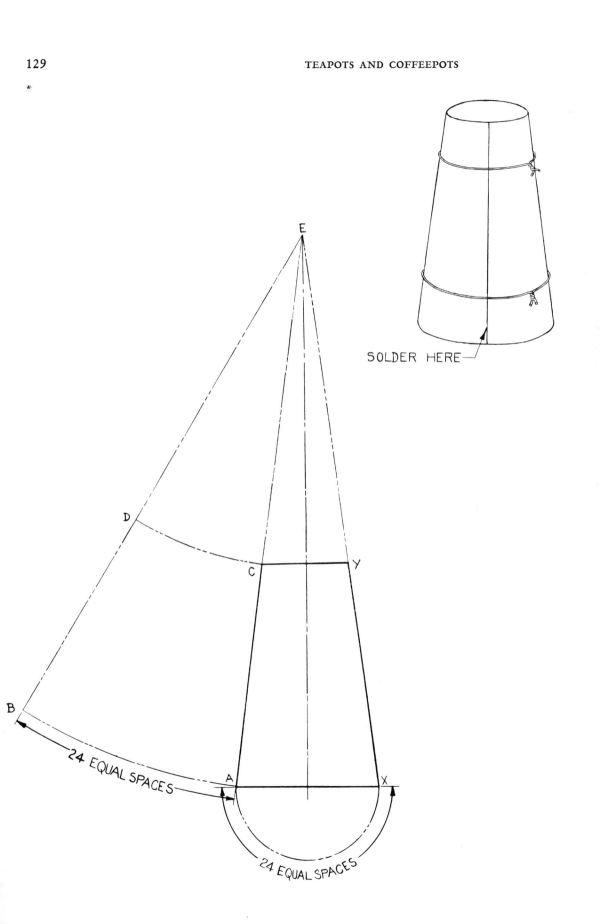

SOLDER HERE

24 EQUAL SPACES

24 EQUAL SPACES

A very elegant coffeepot made by Jacob Hurd, Boston, in the second half of the eighteenth century. This form could have been raised from a disk or made from a sheet with a joint under the spout or the handle. The latter method was used over a long span of time, but was most widely followed after rolled sheet became available. The lid was probably shaped in a swage. Height, 10¼ in. *Courtesy Henry Francis du Pont Winterthur Museum*

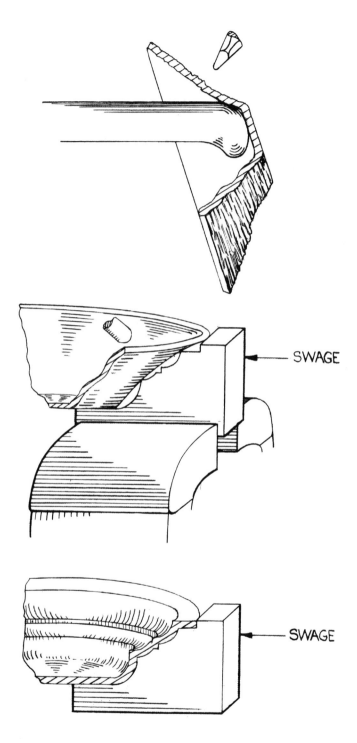

This description of a new style and its accompanying techniques must not lead the reader to think that all silversmiths immediately discarded the method of making hollow ware by raising, for some, particularly if they worked in areas less sensitive to change than the big cities on the seacoast, continued to remain competitive in the business and made attractive pieces. As a matter of fact, it is very evident that there was some hybridization in the trade, for the stretching and contracting techniques used for centuries on disks of silver were now used on some of the cylinders of metal created from thinner sheets of silver. It might also be noted that at least one form used a century earlier was revived and adapted to the classical pattern. The handles of wood used on such teapots and coffeepots closely resemble the one used by Coney on his pear-shaped teapot. Thus, it is very evident that silversmiths retained the practices which seemed best for hand methods of production, and discarded others when better ones came into general use.

It has been stated that at the beginning of the century silver was an expensive commodity; this situation caused objects made from it to be expensive and production was on a "piece-by-piece" basis for very evident reasons. Conditions changed slowly; in 1762 Mary Bartlett left two thirds of her estate to the third precinct of the Brookfield Church to be spent for silver vessels for the communion table on which both her name and that of her husband were to be engraved. This bequest resulted in the making of six silver tankards by Paul Revere, engraved as directed, and dated 1768.

Although the act of Mary Bartlett was evidence of some affluence, it hardly matches the elegance and grandeur seen in a tea and coffee service made by Joseph Richardson, Jr., in Philadelphia about 1790. Totaling nineteen pieces, the set includes a coffeepot (now distinctly differing from the teapots by its height and great over-all size), two teapots, a sugar urn, milk pot, waste bowl, tea tongs, and twelve spoons. With such evidence one can hardly dispute the fact that silversmithing and its prod-

Coffee and tea service made by Joseph Richardson, Jr., Philadelphia, about 1790. These objects are evidence of Philadelphia's rise to a position of leadership in the arts despite its late start in comparison with earlier settlements in New England and Virginia. Richardson obviously used both old and new techniques in making these vessels. *Courtesy Henry Francis du Pont Winterthur Museum*

1798

12th N° 27

Samuel Richards . . . . . . is . . . . . C̄ʳ   75

By Cash . . . .   66..19. 5.

Rachel Richards . . . . . is . . . Dʳ

To a fluted Silver Tea Pott wᵗ 26.17
To a ditto . . . Slop Bowl . . 16.14
To a . . . ditto . . . Sugar Dish . 18.12
To 6 . ditto 6 Table spoons 13.12   62-3 a 10/ 55.18.7
To 12 . ditto 12 Tea spoons . . 6.14 . carv'd hands . 8..3..
To 2 ditto Sauce ladles . . 3.12.12 ditto ditto . . 4.16.2
To 1 Soup ladle . . . . . . 6.13.12 ditto y fluted . . 2.15 —
To 1 Silver Sugar tongs . . . 1.6.12 ditto . ditto . . 4.12.6
To 2 ditto Salt ladles . . . . 11.12 . . . . 1 .11..
To 1 Meat carv'd Handle for Tea Pott 12-6
To 6 plain Tea Spoons . . . 3.12.0 . . . . 2..2..6
To 1 ditto Table spoon . 4.13.12 . . . . . . 1 . 1 - 3
To engraving 3 Cyphers a 7/6 . . £1..2-6
To ditto . . . an 6 Table spoons . . . . -7.6
To ditto . . . 18 Tea spoons 11.3
To ditto . . . 1 Soup ladle . . . .2..
To ditto . . . 2 Sauce ladles . . .2.6
To ditto . . . Sugar tongs, & Salts . .2.9
To ditto . . . Cream Pott . . . 5..   2..13-6 £ 84..9..7

Entries in the day book of Joseph Richardson, Jr., of Philadelphia in 1798 indicate that one order included most of the silver items for a dinner service. There are plenty of spoons and ladles, but no knives and forks. The cream pot (mentioned last) may have been intended as part of the tea service with a fluted pattern. *Courtesy Historical Society of Pennsylvania.*

ucts had reached its grandest era. Few products of the nineteenth century deserve the high commendation given to their predecessors.

Little need be said about the modes of fabrication in the "Classical Era." A logical variety was given to the shapes of vessels by making some with straight parallel sides, which were easy to form; while majestic coffeepots, along with holders for sugar and cream, were given vaselike forms, produced by the old method of raising a disk. A knowledge of coring might have permitted the smith to cast a spout for the coffeepot in one shell-like piece, the gallery was just another exercise in punching or drilling with subsequent filing, and the pineapple finials on the lids of the pots were cast and finished with files and gravers. The flaring base with its square bottom was fabricated from two pieces of metal and joined with solder and the entire base unit was attached to the body by the same method.

The tops and bottoms of the teapots with straight sides were cut out of a larger sheet with snips, the sides shaped over a round stake and fitted perfectly before the vertical joint was soldered. This joint was usually placed under the handle or the spout, as these were the most inconspicuous places to put it. The pattern for the spout was shaped by conical projection, and it also had a joint from end to end. The domed lid was shaped on the traditional tree trunk and made smooth with a planishing hammer on an appropriately shaped stake. After the object was assembled, it was polished and ready for the market place.

One facet of silversmithing in the Avery quotation, however, needs special attention, namely, the term "bright-cut." Authorities are usually vague in defining bright-cut, although the following description from *Three Centuries of English Domestic Silver,* seems to adequately describe how the glittering effect was achieved.

> Bright-cutting was at its most popular in the 1790's. It seldom appeared on spoons after 1800 but on tea services might be introduced as late as 1815, sometimes combined with other decoration. In this form of engraving the tool employed, in various sizes, was a gouge, sharpened chisel-wise, beveled from corner to adjacent corner and having two cutting points. Edge and point were used as required to produce what was really a kind of chip carving, outlining patterns of flowers, ribbons and so on by cutting narrow channels with variously slanting sides to produce the delicate faceted effect.

The final manner of creating hollow ware from rolled sheets of silver is succinctly described in *Old English Silver* by Judith Banister. She calls it "turning up from a cone."

> A less onerous method of making hollow-wares such as tankards and coffeepots, and one used at least since the seventeenth century, is to turn up the body from a cone of silver [sheet]. A suitably sized piece of silver is seamed to form a cylinder or cone, and then it is hammered to shape over a stake. The faint marks of the seam can often be detected inside the pot, usually along the line of the handle joints. In turning up from a cone, the process of corking [caulking] cannot be used, and a mouth wire and the base or foot must be soldered in.

It is unfortunate that the story about silversmiths of the eighteenth century does not end with a completely happy note; however, they were unquestionably the greatest artisans of America and their products attest to their achievements.

Other Objects

It was pointed out in the introduction that the major part of this survey would be devoted to the tools, techniques, materials, and products of the silversmith in America in the eighteenth century. As one proceeds with such an examination, the fact becomes evident that some objects of silver do not fit the matrix which has been planned, and that a larger scope must be created to give the reader as comprehensive an over-view of the subject as possible. Thus, the author is confronted with the problem of breaking down the subject matter into sections. Such a procedure is fraught with many pitfalls, for any division of the subject tends to make one section appear to be more important than another. In this case, the objects chosen for the previous sections were selected on the basis that they are important examples, and that their making involved many of the fundamental processes in the fabrication of objects of silver. There is no implication that they are the most important nor the most valuable.

Most of the objects included in this last section of the survey are found in well-known collections; however, no claim is made for this survey as being a complete coverage of the subject. Many unrecorded objects are located in small collections, and have received no public notice, but most of the well-known articles are described and often some comment is made about how they were fabricated, the latter facet being the major reason for this entire survey.

APPLE CORER

Only one example of this diminutive object has been found; it is in the Heritage Collection at Old Deerfield, Massachusetts. It consists of two principal parts, each of which are about the same length, the over-all

Apple corer of the early eighteenth century with the mark "T.H.," an unidentified maker. Some children were born with a silver spoon in their mouths, maybe some were born with a silver apple corer in their hands. *Courtesy The Heritage Collection, Old Deerfield, Massachusetts*

size being 5¾ inches. The handle appears to be turned from a solid piece of silver, to which is attached a number of knifelike blades to remove the core without the usual halving of the apple.

BASKETS

English baskets of the eighteenth century are usually round or elliptical, with or without a base, and have a semicircular handle attached by riveted joints which permit the handle to be raised or lowered. The bodies were created by the sinking and raising processes and usually are evidence of fine workmanship in shaping and piercing. The bodies have a lacelike quality due to the extensive piercings over most of the holding area.

At least two American baskets are known, both being in the Winterthur Collection. Both have rectangular shapes with rounded corners and no piercings. Both have applied bases made of strips of silver, one with

Basket by John McMullin, Philadelphia, about 1800. Insofar as many utensils for the table were made of silver, one would naturally think that such an object would have been very attractive for serving cake. Length, 12½ in.; width, 8⅜ in.; height, 3⅛ in. *Courtesy Henry Francis du Pont Winterthur Museum*

a three-ribbed molded edge at the bottom, while the other has a ga-drooned border. Both are described as *cake baskets*.

BOXES

Boxes were usually small and used for carrying or storing such commodities as nutmeg, snuff, tobacco, sugar, and the like. They were made in many shapes, the most common being square, round, rectangular, and elliptical, with some being in the shape of a heart. Their small size suggests that they were designed to be carried in a pocket or a purse, and their ownership was usually indicated by initials, which were beautifully engraved on the lid.

The frugality of the silversmith in using small pieces of silver, left over from the making of larger objects, created a perfect opportunity for him to make a small box. This engraved snuffbox was made by Benjamin Brenton (1695-1749) in Newport, Rhode Island, about 1725. The delicate motif engraved on the lid suggests that he was a good engraver or had a good one do the work for him. Length, 2⅝ in.; width, 2 in. *Courtesy Henry Francis du Pont Winterthur Museum*

There were, of course, exceptions to the usual sizes and shapes, one of them being a sugar-box by John Coney. His product is elaborately embossed and is mounted on a set of four legs with scrolled feet. The lid is attached with a hinge, and a heavy ring of silver wire mounted on the very top of the lid provides a satisfactory handle with which to open the box.

Braziers are among the most decorative and useful objects made of silver for use on the table. Various ways have been devised to keep food warm while on the table and, obviously, a silver brazier was one of the most attractive means for this purpose. *Collection Philip Hammerslough*

BRAZIERS

The term "brazier" is interchangeably used with "chafing dish" when the object is made of silver for table use. It might be pointed out, however, that some large braziers made of brass are used in Spain and other countries in the Mediterranean area to provide a modicum of heat for an entire room.

The ones of concern here are made of silver, and resemble a bowl that is pierced to provide a draft for burning charcoal or a spirit lamp within, and are mounted on legs which also project beyond the top of the brazier. At the bottom the legs keep excessive heat from marring the top of the table. The extension above keeps the container in a horizontal position, and supports a vessel containing food. The earliest types were made completely of metal, but in the eighteenth century pads of wood were used on the bottoms of the legs to more fully protect the top of the table from the heat. Attractive handles of wood were also attached, so that they could be more easily managed at the table.

A piece with a similar function, called a dish ring, was made by Myer Myers, of New York, although his product lacked the spirit lamp, legs, and handle. The flaring circular band is pierced with interlacing cyma recta and cyma reversa curves, which provide a very interesting and rich decorative design and assist in dispersing the heat of the dish placed upon it, before much of it is conducted to the top of the table. In the middle of the delicate design motifs, a cartouche in the shape of a heart provides an attractive area for the engraving of three initials, possibly those of the owner.

BUCKLES

Knee-breeches buckles (at the knee) and shoe buckles were common products of the silversmiths. Often they were not made completely of silver, but were backed by other metals such as brass or bronze. The front surface of some were decorated with medallions of Washington.

BUTTONS

One would hardly look for such prosaic objects as buttons to be made of silver, but the elegant dress of the period doubtless warranted their use. Because of indifference, or their small size, few have survived.

Social customs always seem to have been subject to whims and fancies beyond the "call of duty." A silver buckle with medallions of Washington seem to fit such a category. *Courtesy Henry Francis du Pont Winterthur Museum*

Buttons by Peter Getz, who worked in Lancaster, Pennsylvania, toward the end of the eighteenth century. Although these objects seem very humble products for a silversmith, it should also be noted that Getz made some very elegant pieces also. *Courtesy Philip Hammerslough*

CANDLESTICKS

It is very evident from the scarcity of candlesticks in exhibitions and collections, that either very few of them were made, or very few have survived. This observation is confirmed in *American Silver of the XVII & XVIII Centuries* by C. Louise Avery, who says that:

> Candlesticks are comparatively rare in the Colonies, one of the very few examples of the earliest type being made by Dummer, now in a private collection. It follows the contemporary English style and has a square shaft representing clustered columns, square nozzle, and similar flange at the base of the shaft, and square moulded base.

This medieval style was used by other American silversmiths, one pair by Cornelius Kierstede being in the collection of the Metropolitan Museum, New York. The columns were formed by hammering sheets of silver into parts of a column and then soldering them together. They

Pair of candlesticks made by Samual Williamson, working in Philadelphia in 1794. The shaped baluster stems have reeding reminiscent of a similar procedure used on pewter objects made in Philadelphia at the same time. Height, 5¼ in. *Collection Philip Hammerslough*

were simply decorated by arranging the parts in an interesting manner, or by fluting and reeding. The bases are square or octagonal, and slightly raised to give a minimal decorative quality. Their molded edge was simply executed, however; an example made by Coney had its base ornamented by the gadrooning technique.

By the middle of the seventeenth century a baluster type stick, cast of silver, became popular in England. About a half century later this

Candlesticks were a very necessary household item in the nineteenth century, and are probably more prized now than they were then. They could be used on tables, stands, mantels, and window sills, for example, and all households had some, of one material or another. The faceted candlesticks by John Coney were presented to Tutor Henry Flynt by his students at Harvard University. They are very attractive, but not unique, for an English example is made in the same style. *Courtesy The Heritage Collection, Old Deerfield, Massachusetts*

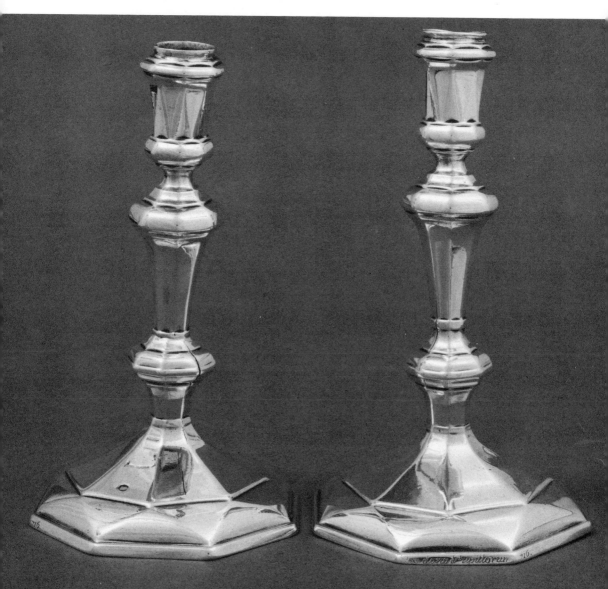

style became popular in America, because it could be quickly cast of silver and, of course, they were fashionably compatible with other fittings of the household. Most of the baluster type are round; however, John Burt made an octagonal pair.

One of the most exciting pairs of baluster sticks is the pair made by John Coney, now in the Heritage Collection at Old Deerfield, Massachusetts. These are cast in a faceted design, which was much more difficult to execute than a round or octagonal one; however, the work seems warranted for the refracted light from its facets suggests a similar action from precious stones cut in this manner. The status of these candlesticks in the eyes of the owner is evident, for a photograph of them serves as a frontispiece in *The Heritage Collection of Silver* by Martha Gandy Fales and Henry Flynt.

Snuffers and trays of silver were also made by the craftsmen to serve with the sticks which they seem to have infrequently made.

CASTERS

The term "caster" seems to have been derived from the function of an object used to cast various substances through holes onto food. Despite the fact that salt was usually served from an open dish, it was also shaken

Casters were a pleasing adjunct to table accessories and a pair such as these were both attractive and useful. This pair was made by Benjamin Burt, Boston, about 1765. Height, 5⅛ in.; diameter of base, 1¼ in. *Courtesy Henry Francis du Pont Winterthur Museum*

Cruet stands, which contained casters among their assembly, are very elegant and doubtless were a scarce commodity in the eighteenth century. This stand was made by Daniel Christian Fueter, New York, about 1760. The casters bear the mark of a London silversmith for 1752. Height of stand, 9 1/16 in. *Courtesy The Heritage Collection, Old Deerfield, Massachusetts*

through a caster, as were other commodities such as pepper, sugar, and flour. Small casters were called "muffineers"; however, the word "muffineer" was often used to describe a dish for holding muffins.

Many of the early casters were straight-sided and round, although some were octagonal. They were usually fabricated from sheet silver and have a vertical joint which is soldered with hard solder. More elaborate shapes appear in the eighteenth century in such shapes as vases, balusters, and pears. The openings in the top were often highly ornamented, and some have turned finials.

Some casters were integrated parts of cruet sets, which were very ornamental in table settings, not to mention their usefulness. Oil and vinegar were usually added to the other condiments; however, the containers in cruet sets were usually made of glass with silver tops and fitted into a base made of silver. One cruet stand made by John David (1736-1798), of Philadelphia, held glass containers with silver tops bearing the touchmark of a London silversmith.

CHALICES

Chalices are reported to have been the only ecclesiastical vessels of silver never used for domestic purposes. Their function was to hold wine in the communion service of the church. The chalice was passed to the parishioners to take a sip as they sat in the pews or knelt at the altar. This practice continues to be followed today, particularly by some of the religious sects in Lancaster County, Pennsylvania, as well as many others.

The top portion of most chalices was raised like a small bowl into the shape of an inverted bell or vase and mounted on a thin stem with a flaring base. An enlarged portion, called a knop, was often placed near the center of the stem as a decorative device and to provide a firm grip while using the object.

The narrow stem and base were fabricated from sheet silver, for it would have been very difficult to raise such a slender form. The flaring base was probably stretched from the metal used for the stem with a cross-peen hammer over a stake. It was then planished and possibly a small decorative edge was added by using a swage.

Some European examples have lids, which add to their decorative and sanitary qualities.

CUPS (two-handled)

A number of two-handled cups have survived, but documented evidence about their use is rather confused and fragmentary. They were an important object, however, for a photograph of one is used on the dust jacket of *An Introduction to Old English Silver* by Judith Banister, and one is prominently illustrated in *American Silver* by John Marshall Phillips with the following caption:

> The richness of the metal and beauty of form in the Queen style is enhanced by the finely cast handles and engraved ornamental inscription of this monumental two-handled cup by Jacob Hurd, a presentation piece of 1744, honoring an early naval victory in King George's War.

One in the Heritage Collection is low, resembling the traditional form of a caudle cup, with a molded base, two handles, and a lid with three projecting studs, which served as feet when the lid was inverted and used as a tray to hold the cup. It is highly ornamented with embossed designs around the lower portion reaching almost halfway up the side of the cup; the lid is ornamented in a similar manner. This one was a gift to Judith Bayard, when she was christened on December 13, 1698.

The term "grace cups" is used by Kathryn C. Buhler in her book entitled *American Silver,* although the implication of her terminology is not explained. It seems that their major purpose, and one which has survived until today, seems to have been to reward a person or organization for an outstanding act or achievement. In his book *Old Silver of Europe and America,* E. Alfred Jones supports the idea that the cup was used as a reward for an act of merit. He tells that:

> The two-handled cup and cover, 12⅜ in. high, now in the Essex Institute at Salem, was presented by the province of Massachusetts to Colonel Benjamin Pickman, a man of consequence in that old Massachusetts town, for his great services in promoting the famous expedition to Louisburg, also commemorated by some English caddies given to William Peperell, illustrated later. It was made by William Swan (1715-1754) of Worcester, Massachusetts, after some English cup as that by George Wickes of London, about 1730, once the property of the celebrated John Hancock and Illustrated in Mr. Bigelow's book (No. 117).

It seems to be abundantly obvious that these objects were of great importance, and, therefore, the quality of workmanship found in their construction indicates that they were skillfully produced. There was cer-

This handsome two-handled cup with cover is an extravagant display of the technique of the silversmith. Made by John Coney, it was presented to Harvard University by Governor William Stoughton, who died in 1701. The Stoughton arms are engraved on it. *Courtesy Fogg Art Museum, Harvard University.*

tainly some variation in the procedures used to make them, but the large upper portion was "raised" in the traditional manner of making hollow ware, as were the handles and bases. The example by Jacob Hurd is sparcely ornamented, the craftsman using the traditional combinations of curves and flat areas to produce the molded parts of the lid and the base. The natural S curve of the handles complements the simple charm of the body, and over-all it is one of the most charming pieces of American silver extant.

FISH SERVERS

Fish servers are in a different category from cutlery because they do not have a cutting edge. Many are in the shape of a fish (a very logical design), and most of them were ornamented by piercing and/or engraving. The handle is offset above the level of the table so that it could be easily grasped for use.

Fish servers frequently have the shape of a fish, but the silversmith who made this one seems to have been imaginative and created a different form. This one shows a number of the techniques of the silversmith such as piercing, engraving, and embossing. The handle of ivory is also a very attractive feature. *Collection Phillip Hammerslough*

GUNS

One of the most interesting and elusive areas of craftsmanship in silver is the work done on guns. The conclusions are different than with the workmanship on swords, for many of the men who did the silverwork on swords signed their products. The frustration in not being able to identify the craftsman who executed work in silver on guns is particu-

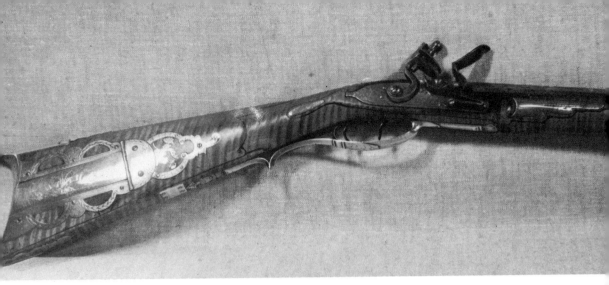

The reverse side (cheek side) of the Kentucky rifle with a patch box made of silver. The high quality of workmanship is not only evident in the inlaying of silver, but also in the carved designs in bas-relief and the design engraved on the large piece of silver in the center of the butt-end of the gun. *Alfred Clegg Collection.*

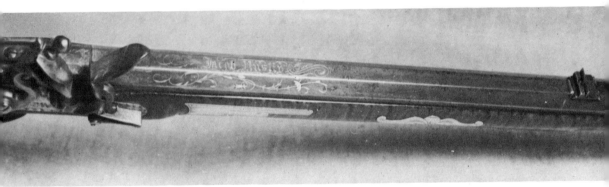

A Kentucky rifle with stock of curly maple and mounts of silver. The style of the various parts, such as the patch box and the trigger guard, suggests that the gun was made in the early years of the nineteenth century. The maker's name, Jacob Ruhlig, is inlaid with strips of gold in the top facet of the barrel. *Alfred Clegg Collection.*

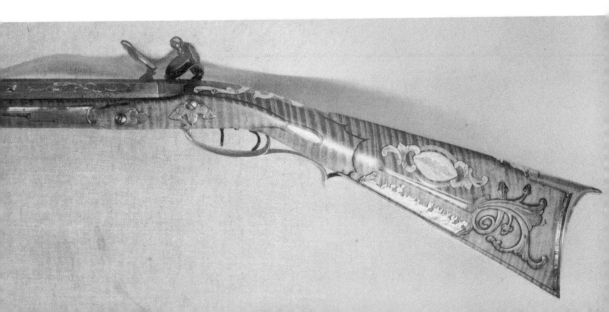

larly vexing because relatively few such guns exist, and their most attractive feature remains a matter of mystery.

There are a number of reasons for the uncertainty about the identity
of the worker who produced the mountings of silver. It is generally
agreed that in the early portion of the eighteenth century most of the
work done on a gun was by one man, the gunsmith. He welded the barrel,

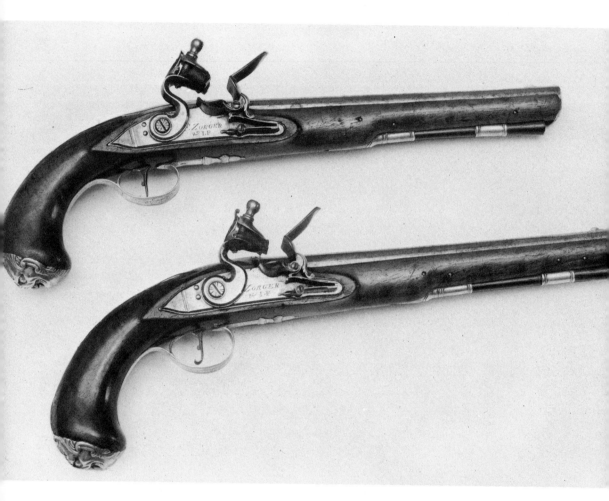

Pair of pistols made by Frederick Zorger (1734-1815), York County, Pennsylvania.
It is thought that these pistols were made between 1765 and 1780, possibly for a
member of the Continental Congress when it met in York. The stocks are of curly
maple with silver mounts; i.e., stock butt plate with mask, trigger guard, and ramrod
pipes. On the lock is inscribed "F. Zorger/& I.F.," and on the top of the barrel near
the breech, "York Town," *Courtesy Henry Francis du Pont Winterthur Museum.*

cast the brass, carved the wood, and fitted the barrel. They were bleak days, however, and little, if any, silver is found on guns of this era, with perhaps the exception of a few silver inlays.

During the greater part of the eighteenth century the gun is thought to have been principally the product of the gunsmith, so if any silver-work is found on the gun, it is highly likely that he did it. There were, however, two alternatives to such an hypothesis. The gunsmith could have salvaged silver parts from a gun made in Europe and used them on one of his products without any commitment concerning the maker of the silver parts. He also could have "sub-contracted" the work in silver to an American silversmith who did not identify his product with his usual mark. Such a procedure could have been followed because the gun-smith did not wish to disclose the maker of the silver parts of the gun.

Near the end of the eighteenth century the situation regarding the making of metal parts for a gun changed, particularly in urban centers where large hardware stores were located. Advertisements appear in news-papers indicating that such stores sold gun mountings, and brass founders are known to have followed the same procedure. Specialization was also occurring among gunsmiths and some are known to have particular in-terest in making barrels, locks, and other parts.

This situation, combined with the rising affluence of the populace, created a demand for guns with silver mountings and many more inlays. The Winterthur Collection includes a pair of pistols with silver mount-ings made by Zorger, a gunsmith working in York, Pennsylvania, in the late eighteenth century. There are other examples of similar work; how-ever, the identities of the silver craftsmen remain anonymous.

One Kentucky rifle with a flintlock (of the nineteenth century) in the Clegg Collection in Birchrunville, Pennsylvania, is completely mounted with silver parts. This is probably one of the earliest and fin-est examples of such work in America, and the craftsman added the final flourish of using gold to inlay his name in the top facet of the octagonal barrel. Unfortunately, the identity of the silversmith is un-known; however, it is the writer's guess that the parts were made by the gunsmith.

In the percussion era of gunmaking the use of silver mountings be-came more common, particularly, when "presentation" pieces were made.

INDIAN MEDALS

It is a well-established fact in the history of United States that some questionable business transactions were conducted with the Indians when land was bought from them. There is also a suspicion that some transactions with the red men were influenced by the presentation of such gifts to them as guns and silver medals. The guns had an obvious function in the survival of the Indian, but the silver medals which were suspended around their necks by a chain had only a decorative value. These highly polished objects must have had a great appeal to the Indians and they were made over a long period of time. Although they did not constitute "hard money" in business transactions, it can readily be recognized that a few such medals judiciously distributed could create a favorable relationship between the two parties involved. They were usually the gift of a Governor or a President to persons who held prestigious positions among the Indian tribes.

The relationship between the white man and the Indian was a capricious one. The few surviving medals are evidence of one means the white man used to influence his neighbor. *Courtesy Henry Francis du Pont Winterthur Museum*

One is known showing an Indian dropping his tomahawk, and accepting a peace pipe from a white man. It cannot be said that the implied contract of peace was always binding on both parties; however, the medals are very romantic survival of colonial affairs in America.

Many of the earliest types were a simple form of sheet silver with appropriate subjects engraved on the surfaces of the silver. Some were made by Joseph Richardson, Jr., of Philadelphia, and Dan Carrel of Charleston, South Carolina, inserted the following advertisement in the *Charleston Gazette,* on July 25, 1791.

DAN CARREL

No. 129 Broad-street

Manufactures all kinds of silver, gold, and jewelry work. viz: silver Indian work, plate work, all kinds of spoons, buckles, small work, gold lockets, buttons, rings, etc. paintings, hair work, engraving, gilding, etc. The workmen he employs and his experience in the business, enables him to do most of the above work equal in every respect and cheaper than those imported. Cash or goods for old gold and silver.

The simplicity of these objects combined with the great demand for them has caused some unscrupulous craftsmen to make modern reproductions of them which have drifted into the market place and have been sold as genuine originals.

INKSTANDS

An early inkstand was called a "standish," the latter term being used until the middle of the nineteenth century. Only a few made by American silversmiths have survived, the most famous one, previously mentioned, being in Independence Hall, Philadelphia. It was made in 1752, by Philip Syng, Jr., in Philadelphia, and was used by the signers of the Declaration of Independence and of the Constitution. In recent years it has been on display where it was originally used.

The flat traylike portion of the object was probably made like a salver, although the flat surface in this case has been indented to hold the three containers on its top. The fit of these containers is so precise that even today considerable pressure is required to remove them from their shallow indentation. The three containers consist of one for ink, one for sand used to "dry" the ink, and one for the quills. There are holes in the

Inkstand made in 1752 by Philip Syng, Jr., of Philadelphia. Its importance was recognized early in the twentieth century for it was illustrated on a postcard, probably sold as a souvenir at Independence Hall. *Independence Hall Park Collection*

top of the quill holder into which quills were inserted when not in use, and its handle supported the holder when the quills were distributed to the signers.

Another example was made by John Coney (1655-1722), Boston, Massachusetts. This one has a triangular shape and the handle is attached to the tray instead of to the quill holder. The tray is mounted on three animals lying in a prone position, their raised heads seemingly holding the tray in its proper place.

LADLES

Ladles obviously have a close kinship with spoons. They were made in a similar manner, but in a variety of shapes and sizes. The bowls ranged from round to elliptical, and some were fluted like the one made by Samuel Edwards, now in the Winterthur Collection. Many of the fine examples have ferruled handles into which wood or ivory is attractively fitted.

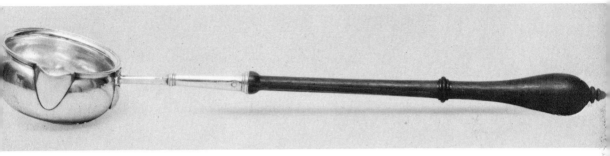

Ladles are among the most charming products of the American silversmith in the eighteenth century. Many are made entirely of silver. The handle of this one is particularly attractive because part of it is made of wood. It was made by Simeon Soumain (1685-1750) of New York, about 1725. *Courtesy Henry Francis du Pont Winterthur Museum*

NAILS

The role of a nail has been a very humble one in all civilizations which used them, and they are of more ancient origin than most men would suspect. There was a great variety in size and function of nails in the eighteenth century; however, little attention has been focused on those made of silver. There was probably a reasonably good demand for nails made of silver for they were not only functional, but highly decorative as well. Peter Getz, a silversmith working in Lancaster, Pennsylvania, obviously made some of silver for F. Stineman who was a local hardware merchant. The invoice includes a number of other items which were common commodities and procedures for a silversmith.

In the nineteenth century a Lancaster gunsmith named Melchior Fordney used silver tacks to ornament his rifles of the highest quality. Few men used silver tacks as imaginatively as Fordney, and the result was a very fortunate one. It should be noted that he used them entirely for decorative purposes.

Pitchers were made in many shapes and sizes for a variety of purposes. There were small, pear-shaped ones for cream; late in the eighteenth century some larger examples simulated the shape of ceramic style commonly known as "Liverpool." This one was made by Paul Revere; the inscription indicates for whom made. *Courtesy Henry Francis du Pont Winterthur Museum*

PITCHERS

There was considerable variety in the size and shape of pitchers made of silver. Possibly the most attractive small form was made about the middle of the century in the inverted-pear shape, mounted on three legs, with a strap handle of silver. These were used principally for cream and, although none seems to match the design of contemporary teapots of the period, they are compatible and are often exhibited together.

The bodies were raised from a disk of silver, like most of the hollow ware of the period, and are usually fine examples of craftsmanship. Their small size confronted the silversmith with a challenge in the raising procedure, much more than a larger teapot or bowl. The cabriole legs were cast and attached by soldering them to the body. The handle was attached by a similar method.

Larger pitchers made in the late eighteenth century sometimes had covers and were possibly used for cider or other drinks. A form very much copied in silver and pewter was made by Paul Revere in 1804 and was inspired by the ceramic pitchers made in Liverpool. The bulbous center recedes in diameter almost equally toward the top and the bottom. The lip is attached and the handle appears to be made of a piece of tubing not very attractively shaped, but quite functional in its relationship to the vessel.

SALTS

Containers for salt fall principally into two categories. One is a closed caster as has been previously described, the other being a circular open dish from which salt was removed with a small spoon. The common salt dish was really a small bowl mounted on three legs, somewhat in a cabriole form with a hoof pattern at the base.

Another dish type was mounted in a circular shell which has a noticeable flare outward toward the base. This type is regarded as the earliest and usually is very modestly decorated.

Open salt made by A. Carman, working at Kingston, New York, in 1770. *Courtesy Henry Francis du Pont Winterthur Museum*

SALVERS

The terms "salver" and "tray" are interchangeably used today to describe the same object, and in reality they serve the same function, namely, the serving of food or drinks. In style they range from a circle with a simply molded edge to a slightly more elaborate form with a cast edge soldered to a flat sheet of silver, and finally, to trays with very elaborately scalloped edges resembling the form of the piecrust edge of a tilt-top table. One of the latter type was made by Paul Revere and would be regarded as an extravagant design by any standards. Revere also made an oval example with a molded edge which included two handles. Such appendages are rarely found on salvers made of silver.

There were many designs of salvers by many makers. This one was made by Jeremiah Elfreth, Jr. (1723-1765), about the middle of the eighteenth century. *Courtesy Philadelphia Museum of Art*

One of the most attractive examples, made by Thomas Edwards of Boston (1701-1755), is virtually a square form with a concave cutout in each corner. The simply molded edge is enhanced by a design engraved next to it on the bottom surface of the tray.

SAUCEBOATS

Although sauceboats were used in Europe long before they became fashionable in America, it is interesting to note that the American examples are regarded as the most attractive by some connoisseurs. They usually have oval bodies with a shaped edge and a long lip or spout. The open, double-scrolled handles resemble similar handles on other objects, but on sauceboats they are fastened only at the bottom, instead of at

One of a pair of sauceboats by Christopher Hughes, working in Baltimore 1771-1790. The initials "D E G" stand for their owner, Daniel E. Grant, who owned the Indian Queen Tavern and later the Mountain Inn of that city. The lack of silver articles in the Federal style suggests that Hughes was not very productive in his later life. He died in 1824. *Courtesy Old Salem, Inc., Winston-Salem, North Carolina*

Sauce pan with lip, cover, and turned handle of wood, made by J. Richardson, Jr., Philadelphia (1793-1815). This style shows a new trend from the earlier raised bulbous pattern. The cover is an attractive feature not usually found in earlier examples. *Courtesy Philadelphia Museum of Art.*

the top and the bottom, as they usually are. The sauceboats are mounted on four legs with designs peculiar to the craftsman who made them. One by John David has a shell motif on the foot as well as at the top of the leg where it is attached to the body of the sauceboat.

The bodies were probably started by the tensional stretching technique because it is easily used on objects that are not circular. After some depth was obtained by this method, additional depth could be obtained by inverting the form and placing it over a stake and striking the outside with a cross-peen hammer. The entire piece had to be planished to regain a smooth, slightly faceted surface. The legs were cast and attached with hard solder, as was the handle.

They were made widely in America by silversmiths working along the seaboard from Boston to New York, Philadelphia, and Baltimore.

SAUCEPANS

Saucepans were relatively small, in comparison with sauceboats, and served a different function. They are usually round with a bellied form reaching its greatest diameter near the bottom. They have short lips or spouts, and long handles mounted at a right angle to the spout. The handle consists of a metal ferrule attached to the body of the pan, into which a turned piece of wood is fitted. It is thought they were used to heat and serve a brandied sauce.

SKEWERS

Old skewers of any metal are scarce items today and, because relatively few were made, those of silver are among the scarcest. They look like long, flat nails with an opening in the larger end to assist in inserting and removing them from the meat. Their function was to attach the meat to a spit, as the spit rotated before the open fire on the hearth.

SPOUT CUPS

Spout cups are usually small, bulbous-bodied objects with slender handles and a small, curved spout, seemingly pressed tightly against the body of the vessel. Their principal use is thought to have been for feeding children, but they might also have been used for serving such drinks as tea or coffee.

Spout cups are possibly one of the less attractive products of the silversmith; however, their number indicates they had a very useful function. This one was made by John Dixwell of Boston late in the seventeenth or early in the eighteenth century. *Courtesy Henry Francis du Pont Winterthur Museum*

STRAINERS

Strainers are charming small objects designed to be placed over the top of vessels to remove any unwanted substance from liquids poured through them. They were usually circular and simply shaped small bowls with many holes providing the straining function. They were kept in position by two handles, mounted near the top on opposite sides of the bowl.

SWORDS

Although other objects of silver, or partially of silver, were produced through the combined efforts of a silversmith and a craftsman in another media, the division of work between them was in no case more precise than in the making of silver hilts (handles) for swords. The rea-

A silver-hilted sword was obviously evidence of luxury and stature in the eighteenth century. Few complete scabbards have survived. This one is stamped " J. Bailey, Fecit." *Courtesy Philadelphia Museum of Art; photograph by A. J. Wyatt staff photographer*

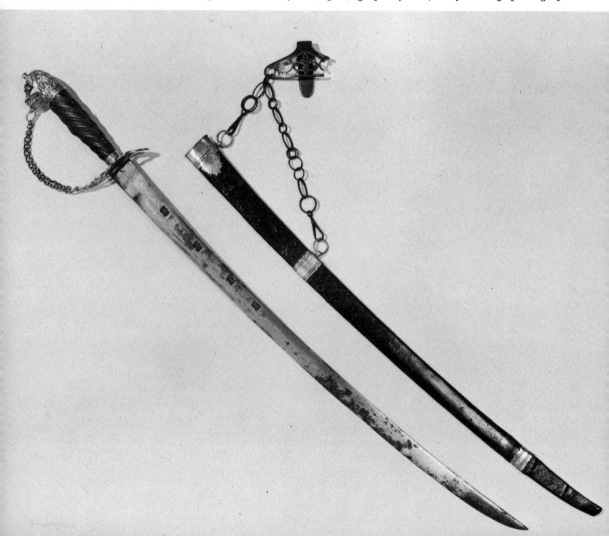

son for the division is easily evident. The making of the hilt involved the casting of silver from a pattern of the appropriate design and for ease in handling. The making of the blade required the skill of a cutler, or blademaker, for it was forged of steel. Forging iron was an everyday experience for a blacksmith, but the forging of steel required a keen sensitivity to the problems involved lest all the carbon be burned out of the steel and the blade lose its elasticity.

Tea caddy made by Joseph and Nathaniel Richardson, working in Philadelphia, 1771-1791. This caddy is of great interest to the technologist because the metal used to make the body was salvaged from an earlier object made of silver. An old and muchworn monograph remains on the inside surface. *Courtesy Philadelphia Museum of Art; photograph by A. J. Wyatt, staff photographer*

TEA CADDIES

A tea caddy of this period might logically be expected to be a part of a complete tea service, and this one could have been. However, it is also possible that a family could afford only a caddy and thus used it with objects of china, or regarded it most highly for its ornamental quality. It is interesting to note that this precious commodity of tea was secured by a lock. It should also be noted that the lock was fastened with rivets rather than soldered to the inside surface of the body of the caddy.

TEAKETTLES

The design of teakettles usually followed that of the contemporary teapot, or vice versa; however, there were some differences in the location of the spout and the handle. In the eighteenth century they were globular, pear-shaped, or in the shape of an inverted pear. The lids were attached by a hinge and one made by Jacob Hurd has a knob made of ivory, which is both attractive and very functional because of its non-conduction of heat.

They were supported on a band of silver which was raised from the level of the table by three or four legs, providing space for a spirit lamp to boil the water in the kettle. Tea was not brewed in the kettle (quite a misnomer) but water was heated and poured into the teapot.

Teakettles are rare items, possibly because they were very difficult to make, and the resulting cost so high that only a few affluent families could afford one.

TEA URNS

Late in the eighteenth century when the classical urn shape became very popular, tea urns replaced teakettles. The urn was mounted on a flaring round base, which in turn was soldered to a square form with feet at each corner. A small faucet was attached at the bottom of the urn for dispensing hot water. It it thought that at times tea instead of hot water was placed in the urn.

THIMBLES

A thimble is defined in *A Dictionary of Arts, Manufactures, and Mines* by Andrew Ure, New York, 1865, as:

A small truncated metallic cone, deviating a little from a cylinder, smooth within, and symetrically pitted on the outside with numerous rows of indentations, which is put upon the tip of the middle finger of the right hand [how about left-handers?], to enable it to push the needle readily and safely through cloth or leather, in the act of sewing. This little instrument is fashioned in two ways; either with a pitted end, or without one; the latter, called the open thimble, being employed by tailors, upholsterers, and generally speaking, by *needle-men.*

Thimbles were made by cutting silver into strips the desired size of the flat portion and formed into a band; this was joined with hard solder. A dome was stamped by using a concave and convex tool, between which

Thimble, decorated with foliated borders and two cupids holding a cartouche for a monogram (which has worn off or was never engraved). The name "I. BVRT" is placed above the border of the thimble Height, ¾ in.; diameter, $\frac{11}{16}$ in. *Courtesy The Historical Society of York County (Pennsylvania)*

a small disk of metal was placed and the convex one struck with a hammer. The two parts were joined with silver solder. The pits were created with a tool bearing protrusions, the inside of the thimble being previously fitted tightly to a mandrel to prevent the indentations from creating uncomfortable projections there.

TONGS

Two types of tongs were used to handle lumps of sugar in the eighteenth century. One was a simple strip of metal bent into the shape of a U with shaped finials on each end to grasp the sugar. The form of the ends was often similar to a small teaspoon which was obviously very functional and added a decorative quality to the object. The spring-like quality of these tongs was created by hammering the silver on a steel stake.

Another type of tong had an action like that of blacksmith's tongs,

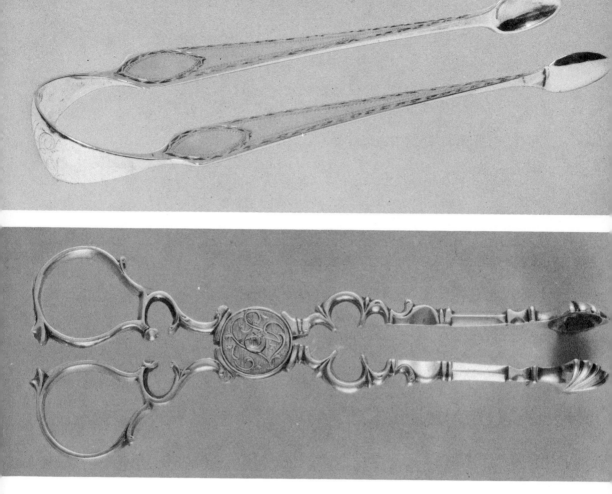

The tea tongs are part of the nineteen-piece tea and coffee service made by Joseph Richardson, Jr. They are an extremely clever example of craftsmanship in silver The scissors-like tongs are also beautifully executed but in an extremely different manner. They were made by Charles Oliver Bruff of New York. Length, 5 in. *Courtesy Henry Francis du Pont Winterthur Museum*

but more nearly resembled the shape of a small scissors. The two members were elaborately contoured from the handles to the ends of the tongs. A circular portion at the hinge was beautifully engraved on one example made by Charles Oliver Bruff (1735-1785), who worked in New York and advertised that he made "tea tongs" (sugar tongs).

TUREENS

A tureen is usually described as a large vessel used on the table for serving soup. They are, of course, very common in porcelain and pottery, but quite rare in silver. Some were made by raising a disk in a process similar to the making of a bowl (which they really are) and were pro-

vided with handles and a lid. Some were probably equipped with a tray
and a ladle, appendages which were useful for the serving of soup.

One of the outstanding tureens is in the Hammerslough collection and
was made by Peter Getz, of Lancaster, Pennsylvania. The lid is highly
domed and richly ornamented, terminating in a finial which served as a
knob for removing and replacing the lid.

This soup tureen was made by Peter Getz of Lancaster, Pennsylvania, about 1780 for
Aaron Levy, of Philadelphia and Lancaster, whose ownership is indicated by the script
capital L in the octagonal medallion underneath the engraved bowknot. It has a round
convex body on a spreading molded foot. The loose, domed, overhanging cover has
original repoussé work decoration. Poppy-bud handle surmounts poppy-leaf base; two
ring handles have shell motif and are hinged on body below rim. Height, 8¾ in.;
diameter, 7 in. *Courtesy Philip Hammerslough*

MISCELLANEOUS

The cross-section sampling which this survey has made of many collections in America focuses attention on the fact that none is really complete. This condition exists because no collector or museum could have access to all types of objects over the short span of years they have been collecting, and also because examples of all the work done by silversmiths have not survived. A scrutiny of the day books of Joseph Richardson, Jr., and Joseph Richardson, Sr., of Philadelphia shows that in addition to many of the enumerated objects in this survey they made the following items:

Baking dishes	Pap boats
Bells	Pap spoons
Bodkins	Pincushion loops
Breast pins	Scales
Chains	Sconces
Cloak hooks and eyes	Seals
Double-jointed tea tongs	Shoe clasps
Drinking tubes	Silver ferrols (ferrules)
Earrings	Spectacle frames
Girdle buckles	Spring boxes
Hairpins	Stock buckles
Hooks and eyes	Tweezers
Locket chains	Whip heads
Milk pots	Whistles
Pannikins	Wine cocks

They also repaired hundreds of objects. Many of them they doubtless made; however, one might suspect that many were imported and some were made by other craftsmen who no longer lived in the city of Philadelphia, or possibly had died; for, contrary to procedures today, the obsolescence of these objects was unlimited. They were designed to serve for generations, and obviously many of them did.

One can assume that silversmiths living in New York, Boston, Newport, or Charleston did a similar range of work, with some variations, and thus the total output of the American silversmith in the eighteenth century staggers the imagination of anyone who understands the tedious and slow processes involved in the daily work of this important artisan.

Summary

M any facets are involved in making a survey of a culture at any particular time. Such an observation is particularly true of this survey of techniques used by the eighteenth-century silversmith in America when objects were produced by hand methods. Such elements as time, style, economic conditions, and foreign influences are only a few of those which plague the author and complicate the hypotheses.

For example, no one knows when the first object was made, by whom it was made, or where. The culture of the seventeenth century was not blessed with initials such as I.B.M. and records are meager even for the most thickly populated areas such as Boston, New York, Philadelphia, and Charleston. Fortunately, some personal diaries, ledgers, and church and civil accounts survive from the eighteenth century which are very beneficial in some facets of the survey, but of little help in technology which is its major purpose. As a matter of fact, items such as style and place of origin were very vaguely regarded here until the twentieth century, and today uncertainty exists about when and where some objects of silver were made.

The normal procedure for the technologist is to look to European sources, which are very valid in evaluating American technology for all of the first craftsmen came from Europe. The system of apprenticeship perpetuated European practices for at least one generation in America and because they were so refined and highly developed they were not easily discarded. European influences are not only evident in silversmithing, but also in other trades such as gunsmithing, papermaking, and so on.

One of the most difficult problems to resolve in a technological survey is to determine when one practice was dropped and another substituted. As a matter of fact, one can virtually say that some were never discontinued for, at the moment, they seem to be beyond improvement. In one room of a big present-day manufacturer of silverware not one machine is to be found and, curiously, the work which was at one time done almost entirely by men is now done by women. Admittedly, the light for working is a little brighter than it was in the eighteenth century. In another room of the same manufacturer are tools once operated by hand power, but virtually identical tools are now motivated by tireless electric motors. The factory continues to produce unique objects and one can truthfully say that the virtues of production by hand methods are still very evident. Fortunately, or unfortunately, depending on the economy and the whims of the buyer, most objects of silver today are produced rapidly in identical patterns and it is for this reason that this effort has been made to preserve a knowledge of the techniques of the past.

Although no precision in dating can be made in such a survey, it has been the intent of the author to give some chronological sequence to the contents of the book. Comment has been made that the earliest pieces made in America were medieval in character and were compatible with the architecture and furnishings of the church and the house. Although some of these objects were ornamented, the forms were relatively simple, and could be made with a few tools. The sophisticated styles of mid-eighteenth-century England soon came to American shores, and American craftsmen were competing with "imports" in style and workmanship. In addition, they had a rapidly rising sense of national patriotism on their side, and eventually a craft of silversmithing was flourishing in America.

Many of their products are handsome, some are elegant, and few people know how they were made. The reader of this book will get some insight into this fascinating aspect of the craft, and thus become a more perceptive student of some of America's finest products of the eighteenth century.

Selected Readings

Avery, C. Louise, *American Silver of the XVII & XVIII Centuries*. New York, Metropolitan Museum, 1920.

Banister, Judith, *English Silver*. New York, Hawthorne Books, Inc., 1965.

———— *Old English Silver*. London, Evans Brothers, Ltd., 1965.

Bigelow, Francis Hull, *Historic Silver of the Colonies and its Makers*. New York, Macmillan, 1917.

Buhler, Kathryn, *American Silver in the Museum of Fine Arts, Boston*. Boston, Boston Arts Museum.

Clarke, Hermann Fredrick, *John Coney, Silversmith*. Boston, Houghton, Mifflin, 1932.

Colange, L., *Zell's Popular Encyclopedia*. Philadelphia, T. Ellwood Zell, 1871.

Diderot, Denis, et al., *Encyclopédie, Dictionaire des Sciences, Recueil des Planches, sur les Sciences, les Artes Liberaux, et les Artes Méchaniques*, 12 vols. Paris, Briasson et al., 1763.

Fabroni, Giovanna Valentine Mattia, *Diary of a Visit to England, with sketches of Machinery, Locks, Manufacturing Processes, etc.*, 1778-1779.

Fales, Martha Gandy, *American Silver in the Henry Francis du Pont Winterthur Museum*. Winterthur, Delaware, 1958.

———— and Flint, Henry N., *The Heritage Collection of Silver*. Old Deerfield, Mass., The Heritage Foundation, 1968.

Forbes, Esther, *Paul Revere and The World He Lived In*. Boston, Houghton Mifflin, 1942.

The Handy Book for Manufacturers. New York, Handy & Harman, 1955.

Hughes, Bernard and Therle, *Three Centuries of English Domestic Silver 1500-1820*. New York, Praeger, 1968.

Jones, E. Alfred, *Old Silver of Europe and America*. Philadelphia, J. B. Lippincott, 1928.

McLanathan, Richard B. K., ed., *Colonial Silversmiths, Masters and Apprentices*. Boston, Museum of Fine Arts, 1956.

Phillips, John Marsgall, *American Silver*. New York, Chanticleer Press, 1949.

Pleasants, J. Hall, and Sill, Howard, *Maryland Silversmiths*. Baltimore, Lord Baltimore Press, 1930.

Prime, Mrs. Alfred Coxe, *Three Centuries of Historic Silver*. Philadelphia, Pennsylvania Society of the Colonial Dames of America, 1938.

Schwahn, Christian, *Workshop Methods for Gold- and Silversmiths*. New York, Chemical Publishing Company, Inc., 1960.

Wenham, Edward, *The Practical Book of American Silver*. Philadelphia, J. B. Lippincott, 1949.

White, Benjamin, *Silver, Its History and Romance*. London, Hodder and Stoughton, 1917.

Index

(Italics refer to pages of illustrations)

Yeow! I'm in Charge of a Human Being!

by Mary Ellis

Perfection Learning®

About the Author

Mary Ellis began baby-sitting when she was 12 years old. That was a long time ago, but kids really haven't changed that much. She can still remember her first nighttime job. The young parents left her with a new baby for several hours. The baby slept most of the time. Mary sat and watched the baby sleep. She listened to the wind howl through the trees outside. When the parents finally came home, they began fighting. Mary sneaked out the door and ran one block home. She never did get paid for the job. And she never went back to that house. After that, things improved. Mary had a long career of baby-sitting that lasted through her college years. In fact, her last job in college was as a nanny to a two-year-old. Today Mary lives in Texas and works with children. Her own children are grown.

Use this book as general information or as a resource to help you deal with a child of a certain age.

Note: Throughout this book, I have used the word *parents* when talking about the adults that children live with. Remember that in this book, the parents are the adults who have the job of caring for and raising the children. They may be single parents, couples, relatives, or friends.

6 7 8 9 10 11 PP 18 17 16 15 14 13

49476

PB ISBN: 978-0-7891-1964-3
RLB ISBN: 978-0-7807-6103-2
eISBN: 978-1-6138-4851-7
Printed in the United States of America

Table of Contents

Chapter 1

First Things First

Are you "cut out" to baby-sit?

So you're thinking that baby-sitting is a good way to earn money. Well, it can be fun too. And baby-sitting can be rewarding. You're working with children *and* making money.

But first, you must ask yourself some questions. If you can answer yes to these questions, then you will probably make a very good baby-sitter.

Do you like young children?

Young children are cute. But they can be trying too. You must be able to handle their nonsense.

Little children don't have a very good sense of humor yet. What they think is funny, you might not.

They don't have much control over their feelings. They don't always know right from wrong. And they can get hurt easily.

This is all normal. They have a lot of growing to do before they are grown-up.

So, keeping this in mind, do you really like children?

Can you allow children to be themselves?

Young children like to do the same things many times. They might want one kind of cereal over and over again. They might want you to play the same game many times. Or they may always tell you the same corny joke.

Children need to do this. They are learning about the world. Doing things over and over again helps them. Part of growing up is knowing that you aren't the center of everything. Little kids just don't know this yet. They'll want what they want, not what you want.

So, keeping this in mind, can you allow children to be themselves?

Can you keep your temper?

Young children can be very hard to handle. They can cry for a long time. They can also get so angry that they are out of control. Older children may try to play tricks on you or ignore you.

No matter what, you must be able to keep your temper. You must know that you can never hit a child in your care.

Also, you should never talk in a mean way to children. You should never try to hurt their feelings. If you have a short temper, you shouldn't baby-sit.

So, keeping this in mind, can you keep your temper?

Are you able to be in control?

Sometimes children won't do what you ask. They may not go to bed or stay in the yard. They may ignore you if you tell them not to do something.

Rules are for children's health and safety. When you're in charge, you must be firm about the rules.

Sometimes there won't be a rule. Then you must make up the rule. You know what's right and what's safe.

So, keeping this in mind, can you take control?

Can you keep your cool?

You should keep your cool when baby-sitting. Some things make you feel like losing your cool. Things like dirty diapers or babies who won't stop crying may frustrate you. Also children and pets making messes or someone getting cut or hurt may upset you. If you lose your cool, the children might become scared.

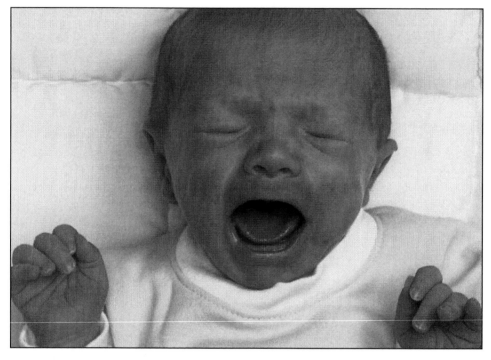

 So, if something bad happens, can you keep your cool?

If you answered yes to the questions above, read on. If you answered no to any of the questions, read on anyway. Maybe you just need more time to grow up. Next year, you may make the best baby-sitter ever.

Chapter 2

Before You Baby-Sit

How many children can you handle?

The parents of two small children call. They ask you to baby-sit for them. At the last minute, the parents call back. They ask you to baby-sit more young children. What do you do?

To see if you can handle this many young children, ask yourself these questions.

- Have I baby-sat young children before?
- Do I know all the children well?
- Have I baby-sat in this house before?
- Will my family be home if I need help?

If you answer no to any of these questions, then you shouldn't baby-sit these small children. You may want to ask a friend to come and help you. You can work together. You can also share the money you earn.

How late and how much can you baby-sit?

You should check with your parents before taking a baby-sitting job. Your family may have plans. You may have homework to get done. The job may end at a late hour. Your parents will help you decide if you can baby-sit.

You should ask your parents *how much* you should baby-sit. They will help make sure you have time for homework.

You shouldn't do homework while watching the children. You are there to baby-sit.

How much should you charge?

Before you take a baby-sitting job, you should talk with the parents. Ask them how much they will pay you.

They will probably want to know what you charge. To find out what to charge, ask your friends who baby-sit what they charge.

You can charge by the hour, by the number of children, or by the job. Your parents can also help you decide what to charge.

Sometimes parents will pay extra for baby-sitting late. You might also make extra money by doing things around the house.

What are the house rules?

Before the parents leave you in charge, ask what rules the children should follow. Here are some things you need to know.

- Where are the important phone numbers?
- Can the children have friends over or talk on the phone?
- When will the children go to bed?
- What do they need to do at bedtime?
- Can the children have snacks? If so, what kind of snack is okay?
- Can the children play outside?
- Is there a family pet to take care of?

11

Sometimes the children can help you with the rules. Sometimes they may tell you something is a rule, but they may be making it up.

When the parents return, you can ask them about the rule. Then you'll know the next time you baby-sit.

Baby-sitting for a family gets easier the more you are there. You get to know the rules better. And you get to know the children better.

Other things to know

Once you have a baby-sitting job, you must show up. If you can't be there, call the parents right away. You should give them time to find another baby-sitter. If you do this a lot, they may quit calling you to baby-sit. Make sure you back out only when it's necessary.

Find out who will be picking you up and taking you home. Sometimes your parents may need to give you rides.

Don't ride with parents who have been drinking. Call your parents and make plans with them. Sometimes your parents aren't home. Then call your grandparents or someone else you know. Don't ride with someone who has been drinking. Even if it means they won't call you again.

When you leave, the house should be clean. If you make a mess, clean it up. The children can help clean up too.

Some people want you to do housework. They may want you to wash dishes or fold clothes. Ask parents how they want the jobs done. Also ask if they'll pay you extra.

When working for a new family, ask to come early. Tell the parents you'll come free of charge. This will help you get to know the children and the house rules. The parents can answer any questions you have.

Coming early will also help the parents and children get to know you. The parents will feel better about leaving their children with you. And you will feel better about your job.

Chapter 3

Safety First

Chapter 3 helps you know what to do in case of trouble.

For baby-sitting, you should know first-aid. Call the American Red Cross. They have first-aid training for children. Also check with your school or library.

Don't forget 911. Sometimes, bad things happen while you're baby-sitting.

What if you need help?

Sometimes, small things happen that you can't handle by yourself. You may not need to call the parents, but you still need help. There may be a stopped-up sink, a runaway pet, or a skinned knee.

Always ask the parents to leave the number of a nearby adult to call for help. You can also call your own parents. Knowing that there's someone to call will make you feel better about being in charge.

Sometimes, you may need to call the parents for help. They will want to know if their child is hurt badly or sick. They will also want to know if you are unable to handle their child.

Always ask the parents you are baby-sitting for to leave a number where they'll be. They may be able to help you over the phone. Or they may need to come home.

What if you get scared?

Sometimes, you hear noises. Houses make noises most of the time. You just don't always hear them.

Don't lose your cool if you hear noises. See if you can tell what the noise is. It may be a window rattling. It may be the heat coming on. When you know what the noise is, you'll feel better.

You can hear noises outside the house too. Again, listen and see if you can tell what the noise is. If you think someone is trying to get in, call 911. Tell them what you hear. They will help you know what to do.

You may find that the noise wasn't someone trying to get in. Don't feel bad about calling 911. It's always better to be safe than sorry.

Important things to know

Try to learn as much about the children as you can. Make your own form like the one shown on the next page to write this information down. Give the form to the parents a few days before you baby-sit. They can fill it out for you.

Use the back of your form to jot down other important things you learn as you baby-sit. This may be helpful for you the next time.

Make many copies of your form. Keep them in a folder. Take the folder with you when you baby-sit. The form will help you keep track of everything, and the parents will know you are trying to be a good baby-sitter.

Here are some things you will want to know before you baby-sit.

Family name _____

Address _____

Phone number _____

Phone number where parents will be _____

Emergency phone numbers _____
_____
_____

Children's names and ages _____
_____
_____
_____

Medical and health information _____
_____
_____
_____

Bedtime _____

Snacks _____

Special rules _____
_____
_____

Notes and special information _____
_____
_____

17

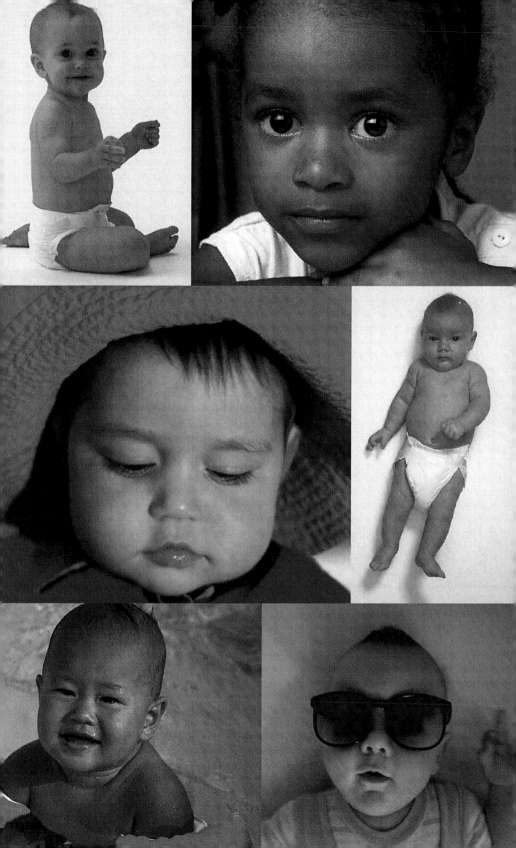

Chapter 4

Babies
(newborn–18 months)

Babies are small and helpless. They need a lot of attention. It can be hard to know why a baby is crying. You should check for these things.

- Is she hungry?
- Is she upset?
- Is she tired?
- Does she need a diaper change?

Is the baby hungry?

The parents should tell you how to feed the baby. You need to know when and what to feed him and how to feed him.

You should hold a tiny baby while you feed him. You can also set him in an infant seat. Hold the bottle up. Make sure the baby isn't getting air. This can make him feel bad.

You may feed the baby cereal or baby food with a spoon. Use a small spoon. Get just a little bit of food in each bite.

Make sure the food or milk is about the same temperature as the baby. You may need to warm it up. Ask the parents to show you how to do this.

Make sure the food or the bottle isn't too hot. The parents should show you how to test them.

Here is one way to test food or milk. Put a little on the inside of your arm. If it feels hot, let it cool before giving it to the baby.

You should burp babies after they have eaten. There are different ways you can burp a baby.

- Put him up against your chest. Rest his head against you. Gently rub or pat his back.
- Sit the baby up on your lap. Cup his chin in your hand. Then, gently rub or pat his back.

Sometimes babies burp right away. Other times, it may take a while. Don't get rough or in a hurry.

Once the baby has burped, he may want to eat more. You can feed him until he doesn't want to eat anymore. Then you may need to burp him again.

Is the baby upset?

Sometimes babies cry because they hurt. Sometimes their tummies hurt. It may take a while before the baby feels better. Here are some things you can try to help the baby feel better.

- Rub her back.
- Lay her against your chest and hold her against you.
- Hold her on your lap in a sitting position.
- Hold her against your chest while you walk around.
- Sit or stand, and rock her.
- Talk or sing to her.

Sometimes none of these things helps a baby feel better. Then you must stay calm. Remember that every baby is different. What works for one baby may not work for another. Also, what works one time may not work the next time. Keep your cool if she won't stop crying.

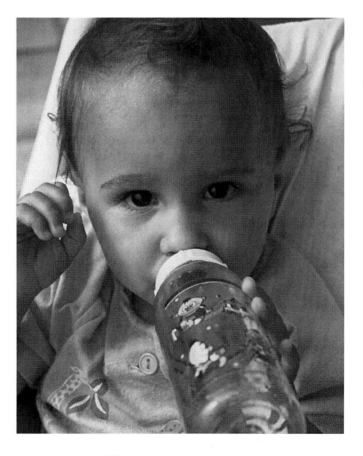

If you have tried everything and are losing your cool, put the baby in her bed. Step away from the bed for a few minutes. Get better control of yourself. Then try to help the baby again.

Is the baby tired?

Some babies will go right to sleep when they've been fed and changed. You lay them down in their beds. They smile sweetly at you. They close their eyes and go to sleep. You are a lucky baby-sitter if this happens.

Most other babies want more attention at bedtime. Make sure your attention is quiet and peaceful. This helps the baby stay calm so he can fall asleep.

Little babies like to hear a story before bed. They like to hear your voice. Babies like to be rocked. Sing a quiet song as you rock the baby.

The next trick is putting him to bed. Remember to move slowly and gently. Good luck!

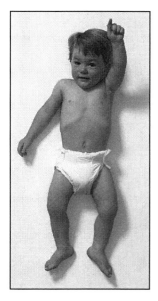

Does the baby need a diaper change?

Changing a diaper is hard. It's something you have to practice before you're good at it. Not many people like doing it.

It's hard to tell someone how to change a diaper. You should learn by watching. Ask the parents to show you how. Then try it yourself. Always wash your hands with soap after changing a diaper.

Check the diaper often. Babies don't like to wear dirty diapers. Dirty diapers can cause a rash that hurts.

You should ask before putting anything on the baby's bottom. Parents should also tell you where you should put dirty diapers.

Most parents won't want you to bathe a baby. If you need to, you can gently rub him with a warm, wet cloth.

Keeping a baby happy

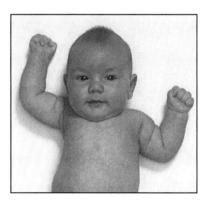

Babies love attention. They are learning a great deal at this age. They love to watch what's going on around them.

Set the baby where she can see you. She will enjoy following you with her eyes. If you're watching another child, the baby may be happy just looking at the two of you.

Babies like it when you talk to them. Look the baby in the eyes and talk away. If you smile, she might smile back. She may even start "talking" to you.

If you are caring for an older baby that moves around, be sure to keep her safe. Play with the baby with her own toys. Don't let her play with small things. Babies will put small things in their mouths. They can choke on small things.

Never swing a baby around or play rough. Playing with babies in this way is not safe.

Play with their toys instead. Talk and sing to the baby. Play games like Pat-a-Cake and Peek-a-Boo. These games help babies grow up.

Toddlers
(18 months–3 years)

A toddler is still a baby in many ways. He may still wear diapers and talk baby talk.

But toddlers get around more because they are walking. Most toddlers also run and climb. They do things that can be unsafe.

Toddlers don't think about being safe. You should think about this for them.

Almost everything you learned about babies goes for toddlers. Except the burping part. (Toddlers can burp on their own. They don't always say "excuse me.")

Baby-sitting toddlers is a lot of work. They move around fast and need your attention. You should probably baby-sit only one toddler at a time.

Feeding a toddler

Some toddlers still drink from a bottle. They can do this by themselves. But most toddlers drink from a cup.

Toddlers love to feed themselves. They may think it's funny to put food where it doesn't belong. They may put the food in their hair, ears, or nose. They may try to put the food in your hair too. Toddlers also like to throw food.

These things are messy and unsafe. You have to be firm and tell them "no." You can say no without being mean.

Ask the parents what the toddler can eat. It is normal if a toddler doesn't want to eat. Don't force him. Just let him play. He'll let you know when he's hungry.

Playing with a toddler

Toddlers love to play with simple puzzles, blocks, and games. They also like playing with stacking rings and large balls. Pans and boxes are fun too.

 **26**

Toddlers love to explore. Take them for a walk inside the house. Let them show you things. Look out windows or look in mirrors.

If it's okay to go outside, take a walk around the house. Try to find bugs to watch. Listen for special noises.

Toddlers are very busy learning to talk. If you talk a lot to them, they will probably talk back to you. You may not understand what they're saying. If you don't understand, just nod your head and keep talking. Talking to toddlers helps them learn to talk.

If the toddler gets upset, try to change the subject or start singing a song. You can also put on some music and get her to dance with you. You can talk again later, when she is not upset.

Toddlers like to know how things work. They like to put things away and then get them out again. This can become a fun game. You'll get tired of it before the toddler will.

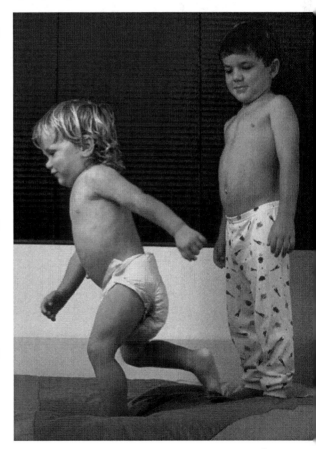

Toddlers like to move around a lot. They like to dance, roll around, cuddle, and jump on the floor.

Some things are too wild to do indoors. Outdoor things that can be fun for toddlers are running, jumping around, and riding a tricycle. They may like pushing a stroller or spinning around.

 **28**

A toddler's temper

Toddlers are just finding out about their world. They are beginning to feel some power. They want to do things by themselves. But they aren't big enough to do many things on their own.

Adults might not let them try to do things. This can make toddlers mad. When toddlers get mad, they might cry. They might feel better with a hug from you. It might also help if you can find something they can do.

Some toddlers have temper tantrums when they get mad. It's hard to handle a toddler having a temper tantrum. He may scream, cry, bite, kick, or throw things. He may do all of those things.

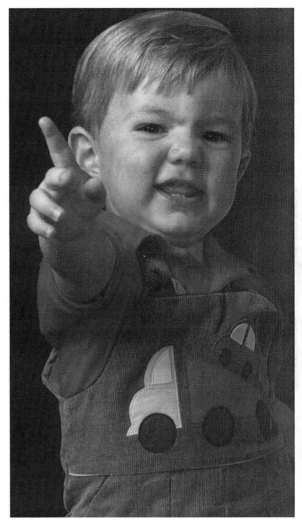

Sometimes temper tantrums can stop quickly. If the toddler doesn't stop, here are some things to try.

- Stay in the same room with him to make sure he is safe. But leave him alone.

29

- Do something that you know the toddler will want to do.
- Take the toddler to another room or outdoors if possible.

After a while, the temper tantrum will stop. The toddler will become interested in something else.

When the temper tantrum is over, act like nothing happened. Chances are the toddler will do the same.

How to get a toddler to mind you

This is a mystery. Sometimes you can get a toddler to do something by asking her. At other times, nothing works.

Offer a reward to a toddler who doesn't want to mind. Tell her she can be the fairy princess first, choose the snack, or pick a story to read. If the reward sounds good to the toddler, she may mind you.

Show the toddler what you want her to do. If it's time to pick up toys, you begin. Put a toy away. Then tell her that you get the prize. Most toddlers want what you have. So she may pick up a toy too.

Make cleanup time into a game. You can race to see who can finish first. You can see who can pick up the most toys. You might set a timer and see if you can get done before it buzzes. Toddlers love to play games!

Sometimes a toddler still won't mind you. In this case, stay calm. Yelling and being mean won't make the toddler mind. Find something else to do for a while.

How to get a toddler to go to bed

Most toddlers are very busy when they're awake. So they're ready for bed at night.

If a toddler won't go to bed, don't get mad. He may just need more time to settle down. Try reading a book aloud while he sits on your lap. Singing a quiet song will also help make him tired.

When he begins to get tired, move him to the bed. You can still read the story or sing. Yawn a few times and rub your eyes. All of this will help him get sleepy.

The only trouble is, you may get sleepy too!

Chapter 6

Preschoolers
(3–5 years)

Preschoolers are fun to baby-sit. They can talk to you. They can do many things for themselves.

Preschoolers are easier to handle than toddlers. But some preschoolers still have temper tantrums. Handle them just as you would with a toddler. Chances are, he'll feel silly and stop. He'll see that having a temper tantrum won't help him.

Playing with a preschooler

Most preschoolers like to move around. They like to play games. They have a lot of energy. They learn by doing things.

Preschoolers love puzzles and simple board games. They like to build things with blocks. They like to crawl inside and under things.

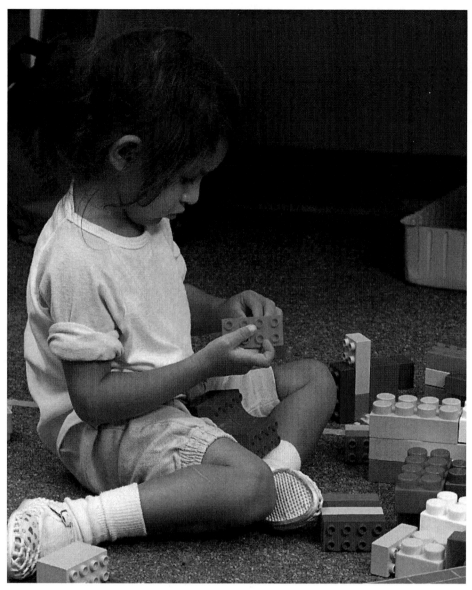

Build a tent by throwing a blanket over a table or between chairs. Take an old toy or game of your own to their house. Kids love to play with other people's toys. It's like having a new toy for a few hours.

34

How to get a preschooler to mind you

Preschoolers will mind better than toddlers. They like to please other people. But some preschoolers won't mind. They will try to explain why they shouldn't have to do something. Just tell them again nicely. Try not to argue.

If the preschooler won't mind, try offering her a reward. Preschoolers like special things too.

Sometimes a preschooler will try to hide from you. He will want you to look for him. This may not be safe. Try to find something else to play.

Images © 1996 PhotoDisc, Inc.

How to get a preschooler to go to bed

Most preschoolers will mind about going to bed. They want to please you.

Sometimes you will baby-sit a preschooler who won't go to sleep. All you can do is keep smiling and tucking in. Keep saying that it's bedtime. Don't get upset.

Most preschoolers like being read to. Some have a story they like to hear over and over. Many will be able to "read" you the story. They know it by heart because they've heard it so many times.

Let your preschooler choose the bedtime story. She may want you to read it more than once. You are helping her learn to read by reading to her. Don't try to teach her to read each word. Just read. She's learning by watching you.

If you have a favorite book at home, take it along with you. Chances are, the preschooler will enjoy it too.

Some preschoolers are afraid of the dark. Some have nightmares. If the child asks you to leave a light on, go ahead. Night-lights, hall lights, and closet lights work best. This will help her feel better.

If you read a book before bedtime, don't make it a scary one! The preschooler will be too afraid to be left alone. You might also scare yourself!

Images © 1996 PhotoDisc, Inc.

7
Chapter

School-Age Kids
(6 years and up)

By the time children are in school, they can talk well. They'll let you know what they need and how they feel. They may also tell you what you're doing wrong.

Every child is different. Some are shy. Some are outgoing. Some want to please you. Some don't. Some are bossy. Some are tricky. You will need to handle them in different ways. Always use common sense and treat children kindly.

With school-age children, the baby-sitting job may seem easy. You may think that you don't have to pay as much attention to children this age.

Just remember that baby-sitting is a job. Your job is to care for the children. You still need to play with school-age children. You need to give them your attention.

You may not know it, but you are a role model for school-age children. They may want to be just like you. Always be a good role model.

Playing with school-age children

Some children may find one quiet thing to do for a long time. Or they may move from one thing to another. Whatever they are doing, you must keep track of them.

Most school-age kids love to have an older child to play with. This is how they learn.

Keep a list of games. You can play Slap Jack or Crazy Eights with a deck of cards. With some string, you can play Cat's Cradle. You can play Connect-the-Dots or Hangman with pencil and paper.

Chapter 9 tells you how to play these games and others.

You can also help children with their homework or draw with them. You can walk around the block or just sit and talk. You can bake cookies or play computer games.

41

Images © 1996 PhotoDisc, Inc.

How to get school-age children to mind you

Sometimes the children may be as big as you are. But you are still in charge. You know the rules. You must make sure the children follow them.

Some school-age children want to be in charge themselves. Let them know that their parents are paying you to be in charge. Let them know in a firm but nice way that they have to follow the rules.

Most school-age children listen to older children. They will like it when you give them your attention.

Some families may not have a special bedtime. As it begins to get late, find quiet things for the kids to do.

If it's okay to have a snack, have something that won't keep them awake. Have milk and cookies, fruit, or crackers.

42

Children this age may still like it when you read to them. They may even want to read a book to you.

Handling school-age children can be tricky. If you let them know you're in charge and treat them with respect, they will mind you. They'll want you to come back the next time.

Baby-sitting older children

Sometimes you may baby-sit children almost your age! They may just need your help watching younger children.

Also, even older children can get scared when they're alone. Your job might be to keep them company.

Sometimes older children don't like having a baby-sitter. Let them know that you are there to be a friend and to help them.

 43

Chapter 8

Other Stuff

This chapter will help you handle special times.

Children who fight

When you are baby-sitting more than one child, they may fight. Children fight for many reasons. If you have brothers or sisters, you may have done the same thing.

Sometimes children fight by yelling at each other. But sometimes they hit each other.

Always try to stop a fight before it gets out of hand. Tell the children to go to different rooms. Give them time to cool off.

When everyone has settled down, get together to talk about the problem. See if you can find and fix the problem together.

If children won't listen to you, stay calm. Call the parents at the phone number they left. Tell them what is

happening. Maybe they can help you over the phone. Or they may need to come home and take care of the problem.

Don't feel bad about calling the parents if you have tried everything to keep control.

Children who are scared

Small children can get scared when their parents leave them. They may get upset and cry. Hold their hands and let them know that you will take care of them. Try to get them interested in a toy or game. After a while, they won't be upset anymore.

Children sometimes get scared after going to bed. Sit with them and talk softly. Pat or rub their backs. Read a short story to them. This will help settle them down so they can go back to sleep. It is not a good idea to let them get up.

Children who are handicapped

Someday, you might baby-sit a child who's handicapped. The parents will help you know how to care for their child.

Don't be afraid to ask questions before the parents leave. Also, don't be afraid to ask the child questions.

There's an old saying that goes like this: "Knowledge is power." The more questions you ask, the more you know. The more you know, the better you'll feel about baby-sitting a handicapped child.

Children who are just plain rotten

You might baby-sit a child who won't do anything you say. She may act nasty and treat you mean.

If you have tried to handle the problem, call the parents or another adult. Don't be afraid to ask for help.

Kids you want to baby-sit again and again

Baby-sitting is good for you and the families you work for. The children get to learn from you. They get to make a "big-kid" friend. They have another good role model. And the parents get a break.

You get to earn your own money. You're also learning when you baby-sit. You're learning how to get along with people of all ages. You're learning how to be a parent someday.

Chapter

Fun and Games

Kids love to learn new games. This chapter tells you how to play many games. You may have played these games when you were younger. You don't need many things to play them.

Copy these games into your baby-sitting notebook. Then you'll always have good ideas about what to play.

Card games

Go Fish (age 4 and up)

Needed: one deck of playing cards
Number of players: 2
The object of the game is to get the most pairs of cards. (A pair of cards is two cards with the same number on them.)

- Shuffle and deal seven cards to each player.
- Put the rest of the cards face down in a pile. This is the pickup pile.
- The dealer begins play by asking for a card.
- If the other player has the card, she has to give it to him.

- He continues asking until the other player doesn't have the card and says "go fish." This means the dealer draws a card from the pickup pile.
- Now it's the other player's turn to ask for a card.
- As players make pairs, they should lay them face down on the table.
- Play continues until one player lays down all of her cards in pairs. She is the winner.

Concentration (age 4 and up)

Needed: one deck of playing cards
Number of players: 2
The object of the game is to find the most pairs of cards.

- Shuffle and spread out all cards face down on a table.
- Each player takes turns turning two cards face up.
- If the cards match, that player keeps the pair and takes another turn.
- If the cards don't match, the player turns them face down again and the other person takes a turn.
- When all cards have been paired, the game is over. The player with the most pairs is the winner.

Slapjack (age 4 and up)

Needed: one deck of playing cards
Number of players: 2 to 6
The object of the game is to win all the cards in the deck.

- Shuffle and deal all cards face down to players.

- The dealer takes his top card and turns it up in the middle of the table.
- If it's a Jack, all players try to slap their hand on it first. The person who slaps the Jack first takes it and all cards underneath.
- If it isn't a Jack, the next person takes a turn.
- If a person slaps a card that isn't a Jack, he puts all of his cards in the pile in the center of the table. He can continue to play by trying to slap the Jack and get some cards again.
- When one person has all the cards, the game is over and that person is the winner.

Crazy Eights (age 4 and up)

Needed: one deck of playing cards
Number of players: 2 to 4
The object of the game is to get rid of all your cards.

- Shuffle and deal 7 cards to each player.
- Stack the rest of the cards on the table. This is the pickup pile. Turn the top card face up.
- Beginning with the dealer, each player tries to match the card next to the pickup pile. He can match it by playing a card with the same number or the same suit. If he is unable to match the card, he may play an 8. Then he can say what number or suit the next player has to match.
- If a player is unable to match, he must take cards from the pickup pile until he can match.
- The first player to get rid of all of her cards is the winner.

Games with strings

Cat's Cradle (age 7 and up)

Needed: a long string or yarn, tied in a loop

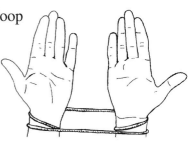

- Loop the string around both wrists, and then wrap the string around wrists one time.

- Pick up string from right wrist with left pointer finger. Let string loop behind your finger.

- Pick up string from left wrist with right pointer finger. Let string loop behind your finger.

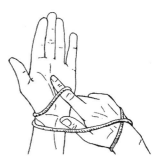

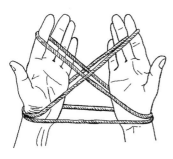

- Pull the string tight. You have made the Cat's Cradle.

You can work with a partner and make more string pictures. Use the book *Cat's Cradle and Other String Figures* by Bab Westerveld (Penguin, 1979) for lots of ideas.

Games with paper and pencil

Connect-the-Dots (age 5 and up)

Needed: Paper and pencils
Number of players: any number can play this game
The object is to complete as many squares as you can.

- Evenly space dots in rows and columns on a sheet of paper.
- Players take turns drawing lines across or down to connect 2 dots.
- Each time a player completes a box, she writes her initials inside the box.
- Play continues until all squares are made. The player with her initials in the most squares is the winner.

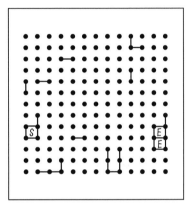

Hangman (age 7 and up)

Needed: Paper and pencils
Number of players: 2 to 4
The winner is the first person to guess what the word is.

- One player thinks of a word and makes as many dashes on a sheet of paper as there are letters in the word. He also makes a gallows for the hangman. (see picture)

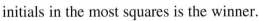

- The other player begins guessing letters.
- If the letter is in the word, it is written in the correct dash.
- If the letter is not in the word, a body part is drawn on the gallows.
- A player wins by guessing the word before the entire hangman is drawn.

Games with your hands

Paper-Scissors-Rock (age 4 and up)

Number of players: 2
The object is to try to get the most points.

- Players count to three and position their hands in one of the following signs.
  - Hand in a fist = rock
  - Hand laid open = paper
  - Two fingers in a V-shape = scissors

- Rock wins over scissors, paper wins over rock, and scissors wins over paper.

- Each winner gets a point. Play until you reach 10 or more points.

Double Thumb Wrestling (age 4 and up)

Number of players: 2 or any even number
The object is to try to pin down another person's thumb with your thumb.

- Two players stand across from each other. Four or more players form a circle.
- Grab hands by hooking fingers together and pointing thumbs up.
- At the count of 3, each player tries to pin the other's thumb down using his own thumb.
- The winner is the person who pins the other player's thumb down first.

Bedtime Stories

 Bedtime Mouse by Sandol Stoddard. At bedtime, a child finds all sorts of wonderful things, not only around the house, but also in his very own head. Houghton, 1993.

Can't You Sleep, Little Bear? by Martin Waddell. Little Bear is afraid of "the darkness all around" him until Big Bear helps him face his fear and realize the beauty of the night. Candlewick, 1994.

Dark Night, Sleepy Night by Harriet Ziefert. Illustrations and a simple text show animals asleep in their natural surroundings. Puffin, 1993.

The Goodnight Circle by Carolyn Lesser. As the turtle pulls in his head and the bullfrog settles into his squishy mud bed, the night animals wake up. The peepers, owls, beavers, and water snakes learn, eat, play, and then sleep, completing the cycle of the Goodnight Circle. Harcourt, 1991.

Goodnight Moon by Margaret Wise Brown. A little rabbit says goodnight to each thing in his room. Scholastic, 1993.

Grandfather Twilight by Barbara Helen Berger. This myth describes the beauty and wonder of the coming of twilight and the rising of the moon. Putnam, 1992.

The Moonglow Roll-a-Rama by Dav Pilkey. This story tells what animals really do when the rest of the world is asleep. Orchard, 1995.

Once: A Lullaby by B. P. Nichol. Young animals and children are shown in the moments just before they fall asleep. Morrow, 1992.

Sleep Song by Karen Ray. Rhymes copy the sounds a child hears while preparing for bedtime. Orchard, 1995.

Sleep Tight, Pete by Ellen Schecter. Pete loves bedtime stories—especially when they are all about him! Bantam, 1995.

Sleepy Dog by Harriet Ziefert. A cuddly little dog and his pet cat share goodnight kisses and playful dreams in this magical bedtime story. Random, 1984.

Ten, Nine, Eight by Molly Bang. Numbers from 10 to 1 are part of this lullaby about the room of a little girl going to bed. Scholastic, 1993.

When Sheep Cannot Sleep: The Counting Book by Satoshi Kitamura. In this counting book, a sheep finds things to count to order to go to sleep. Farrar, 1988.

Where Does the Brown Bear Go? by Nicki Weiss. Follow the animals as they head to the safety of a child's bed for the night. Puffin, 1990.

Wynken, Blynken, and Nod by Eugene Field. This is the tale of a magical moonlight sail in a wooden shoe. This is one of the most beloved bedtime poems of childhood in full-color paintings. Scholastic, 1993.